ICE CREAM AND SWEET DREAMS

ICE CREAM AND
SWEET DREAMS

Coco Simon

Simon Spotlight
New York   London   Toronto   Sydney   New Delhi

SIMON SPOTLIGHT
An imprint of Simon & Schuster Children's Publishing Division
1230 Avenue of the Americas, New York, New York 10020
This Simon Spotlight edition December 2020
Copyright © 2020 by Simon & Schuster, Inc.
All rights reserved, including the right of reproduction in whole or in part in any form.
SIMON SPOTLIGHT and colophon are registered trademarks of Simon & Schuster, Inc.
For information about special discounts for bulk purchases, please contact
Simon & Schuster Special Sales at 1-866-506-1949 or business@simonandschuster.com.
Text by Caroline Smith Hickey
Jacket illustrations by Alisa Coburn
Jacket design by Alisa Coburn and Hannah Frece
Interior design by Hannah Frece
The text of this book was set in Bembo Std.
Manufactured in the United States of America 1020 FFG
10 9 8 7 6 5 4 3 2 1
ISBN 978-1-5344-8081-0 (hc)
ISBN 978-1-5344-8080-3 (pbk)
ISBN 978-1-5344-8082-7 (eBook)
Library of Congress Catalog Card Number 2020943564

CHAPTER ONE
BRAIN FREEZE

It was one of those surprisingly cold days in spring that made you realize winter still wasn't completely over yet. I stared out the window of Molly's Ice Cream shop, where I was working my regular Sunday shift with my two best friends, Allie Shear and Tamiko Sato. I pictured pulling my favorite sunny yellow sweater out of storage and putting on fuzzy socks when I got home later.

The town of Bayville was a beachside town, which meant that we usually had a steady stream of ice cream lovers coming through the shop. But on days like today, when the thermometer dipped below 50 degrees and the wind was blowing, people had their minds on other things.

"Earth to Sierra. Are you in there?" Allie teased, waving a hand in front of my face.

"She's probably writing song lyrics in her head," said Tamiko, who was holding chalk and an eraser, and staring up at the shop's two giant chalkboards. One was for the daily special—something our social marketing and flavor genius, Tamiko, was excellent at dreaming up—and one was for Allie's ice cream and book pairings, where our bookworm, Allie, appealed to the book lovers in town by matching a classic read with just the right treat.

But today both boards had been wiped bare, and Tamiko stood staring at the wall, as if she didn't have a single idea.

"No lyrics in this head!" I replied. "At least not today. Anyway, Tessa writes most of our song lyrics. She's the one with all the inspiration."

Tessa was one of my bandmates in my rock band, the Wildflowers. And while we did write and perform our own music, I was the lead singer and left most of the songwriting up to everyone else.

"Maybe you should call her," Tamiko suggested. "Because, girl, we need some inspiration *here*. *Now*.

This place is dead! We need an amazing, fresh spring flavor to bring people in."

"You're right, Tamiko," Sierra said. "We have a reputation for more than just delicious homemade ice cream. It's our originality that keeps people coming back."

"Agreed," said Allie. "My mom can make anything work! Look how well all of the new dairy-free flavors have done."

Thanks to some "inspiration" from Tamiko's brother, Kai, Molly's had recently started carrying one or two dairy-free flavors. I couldn't believe how good they were—and made entirely with coconut milk!

"So then, *where* can we go for inspiration around here?" Tamiko wondered aloud.

"We went to the boardwalk a few times," Allie replied. "It was fun, but I don't think we'll find any new inspiration there."

"Maybe you should call Colin and ask him for some ideas," I said, nudging Allie with my shoulder.

Allie had recently been spending a lot of time studying at the library with Colin, her longtime crush and her closest friend at Vista Green.

"Why would I ask Colin?" Allie asked, blushing furiously and wiping at an imaginary spot on the clean countertops. "I doubt he knows anything about ice cream flavors."

Just then Allie's mother appeared from the little office at the back of the shop, which we all called "backstage."

"It's awfully quiet out here, girls. What's going on? No crazy new flavor ideas, Tamiko? No book pairings, Allie? Sierra can't pour on her charm if there are no customers in here!"

I loved when Mrs. Shear said I was charming. Being charming wasn't something I did consciously. I just happened to have a very outgoing personality and really liked people. When I was around a crowd, I lit up and felt naturally cheerful. What can I say? I'm a people person!

"No new pairings or specials yet," Allie said. "It's cold outside, and our brains are tired from all of our homework and eighth-grade responsibilities. We need something exciting to get our creative juices flowing!"

Mrs. Shear pulled something from her back pocket and laid it down on the counter in front of us. It was a brochure for Peg and Mary's Ice Cream Museum and Factory.

"An ice cream *museum*?" Tamiko squealed. "How have I never heard of this before?"

"It sounds amazing!" I said. "Can you imagine the toppings they must have? And different types of cones?"

"And all the old equipment and hand cranks?" Allie added.

Mrs. Shear beamed. "I thought you girls would be interested. What do you think about the Sprinkle Sundays sisters going on a little 'research' field trip with me next week? Maybe on Tuesday? I can check with your parents and make sure it's okay."

We didn't waste a second. All three of us screamed at once, "Yes!"

The only thing more fun than a field trip with your two best friends was a field trip to *an ice cream factory* with your two best friends.

"Do they have samples?" Allie asked. "They must have *samples*, right?"

Mrs. Shear nodded. "Oh yes, indeed. They have a movie about the old days of making ice cream, a production room, and even a 'Flavoroom.' I think this is just the thing we need to gear up for spring! When you have a year-round business based on a summer staple, you need to always be prepared to think big. Now, girls, put some music on, brainstorm, and see what you can come up with for today!"

Mrs. Shear left the brochure for us to look at and went backstage again to deal with whatever office work had piled up.

Tamiko browsed the brochure, while I put on an upbeat song from my current favorite playlist on my phone.

Allie stared and stared at the chalkboard before finally saying, "What do you guys think of pairing *Alice's Adventures in Wonderland* by Lewis Carroll with our Tea and Crumpets flavor? After all, the Mad Hatter tea party scene is pretty famous, and tea is a good drink for a cool spring day. . . ."

"I love it!" I said, clapping my hands. Allie always came up with the best ideas for book pairings.

Tamiko shook her head sadly. "You're doing your job, Alley Cat. If only I could do mine. My mind has just been blank lately! I promise—I'm going to do better, or my name isn't 'Tamiko Sato'!"

I wrapped my arm around Tamiko's shoulder and

gave her a squeeze. "Knowing you, you'll have five fabulous new ideas before tomorrow. Don't worry. We're a team! And we've got our factory tour to look forward to. We'll get tons of new ideas!"

Tamiko nodded, but I could tell she still felt bad. Recently Tamiko had gone through a bit of a braggy phase, thinking she was the queen of just about everything—art, schoolwork, our jobs at Molly's. She'd ended up hurting her brother in the process, and since then she had been more subdued than usual. I was ready for the old outrageous and out-landish (but not braggy!) Tamiko to make her return.

"We're going to come up with something new and fabulous, or we're not the Sprinkle Sundays sisters," I said. I wrapped my other arm around Allie and pulled them both to me. "Get ready for greatness!"

CHAPTER TWO
WHO'S A STAR?

After work I walked home, enjoying the chill in the air and wondering what delicious food my father might be making for dinner. My parents were both veterinarians and ran their own veterinary clinic. They often worked long hours during the week, so they always made sure to have a big family dinner on Sunday evenings, and usually my father was the chef. Both of my parents had been born in Cuba, and my father liked nothing better than to spend an afternoon cooking up one of his grandmother's favorite recipes for the family.

I was feeling so excited about the beautiful spring day and the ice cream museum field trip with my friends that I practically skipped up the steps to my front door. When I burst inside, I dropped my bag in the hallway and yelled out that I was home.

"*Hola! Ya llegué!*"

From upstairs my mother replied, "*Hola*, Sierra!" but from the kitchen I heard only a "Whoops! That was more than a pinch."

A *pinch*? A pinch of what?

I smelled something rich and slightly smoky cooking. I couldn't quite place it, which was unusual because my nose knew most of my father's signature dishes by heart. I headed toward the kitchen, but paused to pet my cat, Marshmallow, as she twined between my legs.

"What is that yummy smell, Papi?" I asked as I stepped into the kitchen. But to my surprise, my father wasn't there. It was my twin, Isa, standing in front of the big gas range, stirring an enormous pot of something. "Oh, hey. What are you doing?"

Isa flipped her bangs out of her face and rolled her eyes. She was practically an expert at both gestures. "I'm making *cocido de garbanzos*—chickpea stew."

I thought hard for a moment. I didn't remember ever having *cocido de garbanzos* before. "Is that one of Papi's dishes?"

Isa shook her head. "No. He got called in for an emergency—a schnauzer ate some raisins and needed his stomach pumped. And Mami is catching up on paperwork, so Papi told me I could be in charge of dinner. I went online, found a recipe, and went for it. I think I just overdid it on the paprika, though."

Isa shrugged, as if it didn't matter too much one way or the other. I had *not* inherited the cooking bug from our father, and my idea of making a snack was to grab a granola bar on my way from one activity to another. But Isa, who was my identical twin and yet pretty much my opposite in every single way, had begun to cook recently and was trying increasingly harder dishes.

I couldn't help being impressed. I had almost zero confidence in my kitchen skills (I didn't even scoop the ice cream at Molly's—I ran the cash register and handled most of the customer service issues!) and never would have tried to make a completely new recipe by myself without my father there to help me.

Isa was always willing to try something hard and risk failing. That was why she was the only girl on an all-boys travel soccer team. She'd had the guts to show up and try out for it. And once the coaches had seen how good she was, they'd had to take her. It was something I'd always admired about her.

"Will Papi be home in time to eat with us?" I asked.

Isa shook her head. "I don't think so. The food is ready now, and he said not to wait for him in case they have to keep the schnauzer for observation for a few hours."

"How did the owners not know that raisins are poisonous to dogs?" I wondered aloud. "We've never even *had* a dog, and we know that. Raisins, grapes, avocados, gum with xylitol, chocolate. They're all bad for dogs."

Isa laughed. "I know, right? But I guess everyone can't be the daughters of two veterinarians. We've grown up listening to all the things our parents have had to fix for other people's pets, so it makes sense that we'd know it."

Something about the way Isa had grouped us together, as "the daughters of two veterinarians," made me feel strangely warm inside. Normally Isa tried to pretend that we *weren't* identical twins. She wore black almost exclusively, while I wore bright colors, textured tights, and fun leggings. She'd had her hair cut into a fauxhawk a year ago and dyed the tips purple, while I left mine long and curly and naturally brown. It was nice to hear her mention us being the same in some ways.

"Your stew smells great," I told her. "It's the perfect thing to eat on this chilly spring day!"

Isa beamed, clearly pleased by my compliment. "That's exactly why I picked it," she said. "Cold weather means soup!"

"I'll set the table," I offered, "since you did all the cooking. And I'll tell Mami to come and eat with us."

The stew turned out to be delicious, and while our Sunday dinner wasn't as festive as it usually was, because my dad was gone, the meal was still pretty nice. For a moment I felt a pang for my friend Allie, whose parents had divorced more than a year before. She now split her time between her mom's house and her dad's apartment. She'd even had to transfer schools at the start of seventh grade, which meant that she no longer was at school with me and Tamiko. Her parents did a great job of keeping things friendly, and they even had dinner together, all four of them— Allie, her mom, her dad, and sometimes her brother, Tanner. But I wondered what it would be like in my house to not have our regular Sunday family dinners.

I unexpectedly volunteered to do all the dishes myself, even though I absolutely hated cleaning up. My parents did too, which was why our house was usually a bit, well, untidy. But I did the dishes anyway, so that Mami could get back to her paperwork and because Isa had obviously worked hard to make our dinner. She cheered when I offered and practically ran to escape up to her room.

By the time I'd finished the dishes and wiped all the counters, I was enjoying the lingering warmth and smell of the kitchen so much that I decided to do my homework there, even though I normally preferred the privacy of my bedroom.

I wanted to make sure I saw Papi went he got home, and I wanted to also remind myself how lucky I was to have my family together, all in one house. Maybe we weren't perfect all the time, but we were there for one another.

I gathered my books and spread out at the kitchen table. I started on my geometry homework first. Even though I was usually a whiz at math, geometry was taking some time for me to get used to. Rays, planes, complementary and supplementary angles . . . it was like a new language. I loved computing numbers in my head. In fact, I did it all the time working the register at Molly's. But geometry was a totally different kind of math.

To my surprise, after I'd been working for about a half hour, Isa came back downstairs and plopped down in the chair across from me.

She was nibbling on a dark chocolate bar. It must have been stashed up in her room. If Isa had a weakness, it was dark chocolate.

She sat quietly for a minute or two, just watching me work on problem number fifteen. This was not how things normally went in our house. Isa did not *linger* around any of us—she liked to be alone. Something had to be up.

"What's up?" I said finally.

She shrugged innocently. "Why should something be up?" she asked.

I gave her the I-know-my-twin-sister face and raised an eyebrow. "Since when do you enjoy watching me try to figure out the degree of an angle?"

"It's thirty-seven degrees," she said. "You've got to subtract fifty-three from ninety, because *that* one is a right angle. You can tell by the little square mark there, and that's how you know they total ninety."

I looked back down at my paper and saw that she was right. I hurriedly did the equation on my homework sheet so that my teacher could see how I'd gotten the answer.

"Thanks," I said.

"No big deal." Another minute or two passed, and then Isa said, "So, what's new with you, rock star? Do the Wildflowers have any gigs coming up? I haven't heard you practicing as much."

This conversation was almost unprecedented. Isa cared about my *band*? She had come to a few of our performances, but she almost never asked me— randomly—how things were going with the group.

"Um, well, we've been practicing, but I guess not quite as much lately. Everyone's had so much schoolwork. Plus, we don't have a gig coming up right now. But I'm sure we'll get back into our groove soon."

"Would you say your voice is in good shape?" she prodded.

I put my pencil down. "Excuse me, *what*? Why are you asking me all this stuff?"

Isa opened her eyes wide, playing innocent. "Can't I take an interest in my dear, sweet twin sister?"

I narrowed my own eyes. Something was up. Something was *definitely* up. "Spill it, Isa. You're acting weird, maybe even more weird than when you snuck a *snake* into the house last year and told me that your grand plan to hide it from Mami and Papi was to keep it in your closet forever."

Isa laughed. "Not one of my best ideas."

I laughed too, in spite of myself. I couldn't help it. Seeing Isa happy made me happy. "Just tell me whatever is going on with you, so I can finish my homework."

"Okay, okay." She pulled a folded piece of paper from the front pocket of her hoodie and handed it to me. The paper felt soft, and the creases were slightly worn, as if it had been folded and unfolded many times.

I opened it. It was an ad.

It's time to find the
NEXT YOUNG SINGING
SENSATION!
Could it be YOU?
Come and audition for the
WHO'S A STAR? singing contest!

If you're selected as a finalist, you will
appear on our local TV station,
where fans will decide our big winner!

I read over the flyer twice, soaking in the information. I had heard of Who's a Star? They traveled around to different cities, holding local singing contests for teenagers. The judges were real music producers, and the winner of the contest got a free, exclusive tour of the music recording studios in Los Angeles and would sing a song on an upcoming holiday special on national TV.

"What do you think?" asked Isa. "I saw the flyer posted on the bulletin board outside the grocery store earlier, and I thought you should do it."

I felt a series of tingles all over my body. I was nervous, excited, scared, hopeful, and anxious. A singing contest? It was like a dream come true!

"When is it?" I asked, my eyes scanning the tiny type at the bottom of the page.

"It's the end of next week."

"Next *week*? Isa, I can't be ready by then. What will I sing? Am I even good enough to try out?" I blubbered.

Isa raised her eyebrows. "There's only one way to find out, right?"

I nodded, trying to take deep breaths. I could feel something like hope blooming in my stomach. I knew I couldn't get ready for the audition by myself, though—I'd need my band to help prepare me. And of course I needed Allie and Tamiko to tell me if I could even do it!

I wanted to call them all immediately. But I also wanted to tell them in person. And maybe think about it overnight . . . just in case. Just in case I wasn't sure I was brave enough to audition in front of real talent professionals and other kids who'd surely been singing much longer than I had. After all, I'd just started with my band last year. I hadn't had any formal training or anything!

I was sunny Sierra. I was charming and outgoing. I was good at juggling lots of things, and I tried to be a good friend to my Sprinkle Sundays sisters. But was I a star? I didn't know. But it seemed like there was a way to find out.

CHAPTER THREE
THE REAL DEAL

When I walked into school Monday morning, I immediately set out to find Tamiko and MacKenzie, one of my other close friends at school. I was bursting at the seams to tell them my news. I wished for the millionth time that Allie was still at MLK Middle School with us, and not living it up over at Vista Green, which was a recently renovated school with amazing cafeteria food and new, functioning lockers. Who needed good food when you had your besties with you?

I finally found Tamiko outside the science lab wing, asking for notes for a lab she'd missed. She was wearing her favorite purple-and-red minidress and a pair of black high-top sneakers, with her hair pulled into three skinny braids. She was always coming up with something new and different to wear to school.

"TAMIKO!" I yelled as I skidded to a stop in front of her. I'd been using my speed-walk, something I'd perfected after years of rushing from classes to student council meetings to soccer practices to band practices, etc. My speed-walk was almost a run, but more in control, and kept the teachers off my back about running in the halls.

Tamiko whirled around, looking alarmed, as if she were expecting me to yell "Fire!" or something. Whoops. Maybe I needed to tone it down.

"WHAT?" she yelled back.

I stood in front of her, bouncing on my toes. "I have to tell you something, but I want to tell Allie at the same time, and probably MacKenzie, too. How can I do that?"

I realized as I was talking that I was maybe, *possibly* making this whole audition thing a much bigger deal than it really was. Anyone up to eighteen years old could try out. There would be tons of talented, older, more experienced singers there at Who's a Star? Why did I think this was worth getting so amped about? Did I really think I had a shot?

Either Tamiko was able to read my face or she just knows me really well, because she said, "There *is* a way for you to tell us all at the same time—at lunch! I'll text Allie and let her know we're going to video-chat with her while we eat. Okay?"

I bounced a few more times. "Okay. I realllllllly want to tell you now, though."

Tamiko grinned and leaned in closer. "Go ahead, then. . . . Tell me."

"No! I'm going to wait. I think. Yes! At lunch! I've got to run to social studies because Mrs. Saunders hinted on Friday that we might have a pop quiz this morning."

"Oh, fine. Go study." Tamiko whipped out her phone and texted Allie. "I'll be ready for your news at lunch! I can't wait!"

To my surprise, the morning flew by. I was actually grateful for the fact that I had some of my harder classes on Monday mornings, because it kept my mind busy, when all I wanted to do was space out and think about the Who's a Star? contest.

At lunch I found Tamiko and MacKenzie already waiting for me at our usual table. MacKenzie looked up and waved as I made my way over to the table, and it was obvious Tamiko had filled her in.

"That was the longest morning of my *life*," Tamiko said dramatically. "Don't ever do this to me again, Sierra Perez."

"I won't," I promised. "Anyway, I feel silly making a huge deal about this. I should have just called you all last night!"

MacKenzie nodded. She was wearing a wide green headband that contrasted beautifully with her long red hair, and she looked almost as anxious as Tamiko to hear my news.

"I'm getting Allie up for a video chat now.... Hang on." Tamiko propped her phone up against a math textbook, and MacKenzie scooted around beside us so she could see the screen too. Allie's face popped up a minute later, surrounded by bookshelves.

"Allie, are you in the *library*?" asked Tamiko.

"Yes!" she whispered. "We're not allowed on our phones in the cafeteria anymore. I'm in the stacks. Shhh! Now tell me the news! Sierra, do the Wildflowers have a new gig somewhere?"

"Or did one of your songs get picked up on the radio?" guessed MacKenzie.

"Are you guys making a music video? I could help style you!" Tamiko offered. "Please let me style you."

At this point it was abundantly clear that I had oversold my news. But there was no choice but to plunge ahead.

"Nothing has happened . . . *yet*," I said. "But Isa saw this flyer yesterday for a contest over in Hamilton, and it's for teen singers, ages thirteen to eighteen. It's the Who's a Star? singing contest. If you make it past the first round of auditions and become a finalist, you can appear on TV!"

Even as I said it, I started to get more and more excited. I wanted to win. I really, really wanted to win.

Allie gasped, then immediately clapped her hand over her mouth. "Sierra!" she whispered loudly. "That is amazing! That contest sounds like it was *made* for you!"

Tamiko started applauding, and MacKenzie squealed and gave me a huge hug.

"This is awesome! It'll be so much fun! And now I can style you for your *audition*!" Tamiko shrieked.

I waved my hand at her, urging her to keep her

voice down. I didn't think I wanted everyone to know about it. What if I didn't do well? And everyone knew? They would all ask me about it the next day. It seemed like something I might want to keep just between me and my besties. And my band. And my family.

"You're such a great singer, Sierra," MacKenzie gushed. "And you have a lot of presence on stage when you sing. It's your charisma!"

"And her natural beauty and charm," Allie chimed in.

"And her natural sunshine," said Tamiko.

I could feel myself blushing. I knew I could count on my friends for some confidence-boosting and compliments! Normally I didn't need them so much. I usually felt very good about my schoolwork and activities and even myself. But this was different. It was the real deal. Singing in front of *judges.*

"Okay. Let's keep a lid on it for now, because I'm not sure I want everyone in the whole school to know, all right?"

All three of my friends nodded in agreement. "Totes," said Tamiko.

"On the down low," agreed MacKenzie.

Allie suddenly looked up, alarmed. "Guys," she whispered. "I'm about to get busted. But I'll talk to you all later tonight! Congrats, Sierra!"

"Don't congratulate me!" I said. "I haven't done anything yet."

Tamiko put her arm around me. "Greatness just follows some people around, Sierra. You can't help that you're naturally awesome."

The Wildflowers almost always practiced on Mondays, which gave me a great opportunity to tell them my news too. But I wanted to be a little more chill about this announcement. After all, my bandmates were musicians. They would understand immediately how stiff the competition would be at this contest. They'd know that I would be up against some very, very good singers.

Our band practiced at Reagan's house in her garage, which was all set up with a large space for the instruments, as well as an old couch, a rug, some lamps, and a mini-fridge. Reagan had red hair, and she was always wearing it in unusual ways. Today she had it slicked back into a high bun, and then had pulled and sculpted the bun itself to look like a shiny hair bow. It was really impressive.

Tessa sat tuning her guitar, while Reagan poured some pretzels and peanuts into bowls for everyone, and Kasey flipped through some sheet music. It was just like the start of every other practice, and it was so nice to NOT be thinking, worrying, or talking about the contest for a moment that I decided to wait until the end of our practice to tell them. That way I wouldn't be a distraction either.

We warmed up with a few of our favorites, including a song Tessa had written specifically for me a few months before, called "Stand Up, Speak Up." It was a reminder that being nice wasn't more important than remembering to stand up for yourself and your friends. I sang it at home all the time in the shower. It had become one of my personal anthems.

Practice went well, but not great. I was distracted, so I forgot the lyrics to a few songs that I knew really well, and Reagan seemed a bit off beat here and there. But overall it was fun, and we brainstormed some new ideas for songs.

When we'd finished, we all plopped down onto the couch and passed around the pretzel bowl. I had to go home for dinner shortly, but I was always starving after school, and singing made me hungry too.

I decided this would be a good time to make my announcement.

"So I think I'm going to try out for a local singing contest next week," I said casually. "It's in Hamilton. I have to prepare a song, and if the judges choose me as one of the ten finalists, I get to appear on TV."

Immediately Tessa, Reagan, and Kasey all jumped up and started talking at once.

"A contest?"

"Ten finalists?"

"You'll be on TV?"

Reagan grabbed my hand and held on, jumping up and down while holding it. "This is so great! You'll be the best. I know it!"

"And you'll look beautiful on TV," added Tessa. "You have such great curly hair."

I was quiet for a moment. Then I asked, "Do you guys really think I can do it?"

They all screamed at once, "YES!"

"We'll *make* you do it," said Kasey. "Just remember when you win to mention that you're in a band!"

"And that it's called 'the Wildflowers,'" said Reagan.

"I can't believe I know a celebrity," added Tessa teasingly. "You're going to do *great*."

I nodded, pleased that they were all excited for me. I hadn't quite expected them to react so optimistically. But my band knew what it meant to do something like this. It took a lot of guts!

"I just wish you'd told us at the start of practice today so we could have helped you rehearse!" said Reagan. "I've got a study group tonight for a project, so I can't practice any longer."

"And I have three tests tomorrow," said Kasey glumly.

"How about an extra practice this Wednesday?" Tessa asked. "To help Sierra get ready? We can have her perform different songs for us, pick which one works best, critique her performance . . ."

Critique. I wasn't sure I liked the sound of that. It was probably a smart idea, though.

"You just wait," said Reagan. "You're going to be so prepared, the judges won't believe it. You'll have talent agents and managers calling you."

Suddenly the small amount of nerves I'd had flapping around in my stomach started to creep up the back of my neck. This contest wasn't like band

28

practice in Reagan's garage, or singing in someone's backyard for a group of kids hanging out together. Or recording songs and playing them for our friends.

This was real. It was PUBLIC. And it was going to be a little scary.

CHAPTER FOUR
SUNSHINE AND SECRETS

Normally my mom picked me up from band practice at Reagan's on Mondays, but today it was my dad who came.

I slid into the front seat beside him and gave him a kiss on the cheek. "*Hola*, Papi."

"*Hola*, Sierra," he replied. "How was practice?"

"Good! We're working on some new songs, which is fun because it means we're trying new things. It can be hard, though, because it takes us a while to get them to sound good!"

My dad nodded. "It is a beautiful thing to create music, Sierra."

I knew this was a good opportunity to tell him about the contest, but I wanted to tell him and my mom together. So I purposely changed the subject.

"How was everything at the clinic today?" I asked.

My dad shook his head. "Very busy. Some days it's *too* busy. Your mother and I wouldn't mind a quiet day now and then. But I guess it's good that so many people are taking care of their pets."

Not long ago my parents wouldn't even have thought of letting me and Isa have any pets at home, because they were so busy taking care of them at work all day! But then, luckily, a litter of kittens came our way, and my parents let us each keep one. Marshmallow and Cinnamon were like members of our family now.

"Wait, Papi! Stop. Pull over!" I pointed to the right. "There's Isa, walking home."

My dad pulled the car over. Isa was walking just ahead of us down the sidewalk, her back to us. She had her enormous headphones on, and she must have been listening to something she liked, because her head was bobbing back and forth as she walked.

"Isa!" I called out. *"Isa!"*

My dad honked the horn, and finally she turned around, scowling. When she recognized us, though, instead of smiling, she looked nervous.

31

She walked up to the car and climbed into the back seat. She did not look happy that we were giving her a ride.

"*Hola*, Papi," she said.

"This isn't the way you normally walk home from school," I said. "And it's late—it's almost six. Where were you?"

"Nowhere."

"You must have been *somewhere* because nowhere isn't a place," I said jokingly. Isa didn't answer. She just turned up the music she'd been listening to so that I could hear it in the front seat even through her headphones.

This was the Isa I was used to—not the one from yesterday, when she'd been so chummy. I'd gotten used to the grumpy, distant one, but I couldn't help feeling sad that Isa was all shuttered again.

When we got home, my mom had reheated some of the chickpea stew Isa had made the day before, thrown together a salad, and put some bread on the table.

"Wash your hands, everyone," she said.

We all washed up and sat at the table. For some reason Isa refused to meet my eyes. I didn't know if I had done or said something to upset her. Was she mad that we'd picked her up?

That couldn't be it. It was cold out, and it was not a short walk home. Was it because she'd been someplace she didn't want us to know about? That seemed more likely.

Everyone else was eating happily, and I was surprised to find that Isa's stew tasted even better on the second day.

"This is really good, Isa," I told her.

"It is," she said. Then, after a beat, "Thanks."

After everyone had eaten enough, I decided it was time to make my announcement. After two tries at this already, I was pretty sure I knew how I wanted to handle this one. I was going to be calm, confident, and humble.

"Mami, Papi, I have something to tell you. There's going to be a singing contest for teenagers in Hamilton. The auditions are at the end of next week, and I'd like to try out."

I watched my parents exchange a glance and talk to each other with their eyes for a moment before they responded.

"A contest?" asked my dad. He sounded apprehensive, which seemed strange to me. "What kind of contest?"

"What do you mean? It's a regular singing contest. Kids come and try out with a song they choose themselves, and then the judges vote for a group of ten finalists." I didn't know if that was what he was really asking, since it seemed pretty self-explanatory to me. "Then the ten finalists get to sing on TV, and the viewers choose one winner."

"I see," said my mom. "Well, that sounds interesting. And it's open to anyone?"

"Anyone thirteen to eighteen who wants to go to Hamilton and audition," I said. I was really starting to get confused by all the questions. The Sprinkle Sundays sisters and my bandmates had not asked so many. They had just skipped right to the part where they'd been really excited for me. I could feel myself suddenly getting nervous.

"That could be a whole lot of kids," my mother continued. "How many do they think will show up?"

How many do they think will show up? What kind of question was that? Why weren't my parents just saying, "Go, Sierra! You can do it!"?

I took a deep breath and reminded myself to stay calm, confident, and humble. "Um, I have no idea," I said. "A lot, probably."

"And you're sure this is something you want to do?" my father asked.

At this point I needed help. I tried to meet Isa's eyes, but she wouldn't look at me. She was the one who'd given me the flyer and told me about it and gotten me all pumped up to do it! Now she needed to step in and say something. But clearly she wasn't going to.

I took another deep breath. My feelings were hurt, but I tried not to show it. I wanted to appear grown-up and professional, since I was asking to try out for something that seemed grown-up and professional.

"Are you guys saying you don't think I'm g-good enough?"

My voice broke a bit on the word "good." So much for grown-up. I sounded like a four-year-old.

It seemed to wake Isa from her mood. "Of *course* you're good enough, Sisi. You're a really good singer. And you're a natural! You've never even had real lessons. You should definitely try out."

And with that, she stared at our parents, as if daring them to contradict her.

"We know you're a wonderful singer!" my mom

said quickly. "I enjoy your singing every day, Sierra. It's one of my favorite sounds."

She looked over at my dad. He said, "It's just that we want to make sure you realize how highly competitive this is likely to be. It could draw contestants from all over. It's one thing to sing with your friends, but it's another to try out in a contest with many contestants, who are all terrific singers like you, and might be taking private voice lessons."

Then my mom said, "We're not telling you *not* to do it! That's your decision. And we're your number one supporters, no matter what. We're just helping you think it through, that's all."

I was quiet for a moment, thinking about my parents' words. By now I understood what they were really concerned about. They didn't want my hopes and dreams to be crushed if I didn't win. They wanted me to be brave but also realistic.

I felt much better.

"I get it," I said, my voice returning to normal. "I know it's going to be competitive and that everyone there will probably be a really terrific singer. But that's okay! I think it'll be a good experience. And I *love* singing. I want to find out if I really have some talent or not. And I think this will help me. I'm going to do it!"

Isa cheered and put her hands up in the air in a *V* for "victory."

My dad's face broke into a huge smile. "Of course you are, my sweet Sierra. And we'll all be there to cheer you on!"

I couldn't believe how relieved I felt. No matter what choice I made, it would never feel right unless I had my family's support. They were the most important people in the world to me.

"You've only got ten days until the audition, so I guess you'll need to get upstairs and practice right after dinner," said Isa. "I'll do the dishes."

I looked at her gratefully. Even though my twin could be distant, she also came through for me when it mattered.

Up in my room I began pulling out my homework, thinking it might be best to get that out of the way before I looked through my songs to see which one would be good for the contest. As I was working on my language arts assignment, I heard Isa come upstairs. Her mood had been all over the place this afternoon—weird and evasive when we'd picked her up, quiet at the table, then supportive to me with my parents, then generous in helping with the dishes.

"Isa?" I called out. "Can you come in here?"

Isa came to my doorway, surveying the absolute tornado that was my room. Even Marshmallow the cat seemed disgusted as she picked her way around the piles on my floor.

"This is bad, even for you," Isa said. She was the only member of the Perez family who preferred to be neat. Her room was always spotless, and she vacuumed it once a week like clockwork.

"Where were you coming from this afternoon?" I asked her, point-blank.

I could see her tense up.

"Nowhere. Why?"

"Isa! Why won't you tell me? I'm not going to get you in trouble or anything. What were you doing? Did you have detention?"

"Oh sure," she said. "Assume it was something bad! Something I'd get in trouble for."

That made me feel awful. I hadn't meant it to sound that way. "I just meant that your secret is safe with me. I'm your twin."

Isa shrugged. "Yeah, well, I don't have any secrets, so don't worry about it. You just focus on you, and everything will be fine."

I was definitely getting the brush-off. But I knew that being vulnerable was the one thing that could get Isa to open up sometimes. So I said, "Isa, I'm nervous."

"Good. It's healthy to be nervous." She turned and left, heading back down the hall. I heard her open the door to her room. A second later she called out, "You're a good singer, Sierra. I'd tell you if you weren't."

"Thanks, sis," I yelled back.

"You're welcome, Sunshine."

CHAPTER FIVE
PEG AND MARY'S ICE CREAM MUSEUM AND FACTORY

Between homework and thinking about which song to sing for the contest next week, you'd think I'd be too busy or nervous to take a field trip for a whole afternoon. But there was nothing that could stand in the way of me, my Sprinkle Sundays sisters, and a tour of the ice cream factory.

Mrs. Shear picked Tamiko and me up from MLK right after dismissal. Allie was already waiting in the back seat, as Vista Green got out twenty minutes before we did.

Tamiko and I climbed into the car, trying to maneuver our overstuffed backpacks so that all three of us could sit together in the back and still have room for our legs. It was a tough squeeze. We wiggled closer together.

I laughed. "This was easier when we were all eight, and a lot smaller!"

Mrs. Shear laughed as well. "You know, someone *could* sit up front with me. I don't have cooties. Or you can all pile your backpacks up here if you'd like."

That's what we did. We threw our bags into the front and buckled our seat belts, and then Mrs. Shear headed in the direction of the highway.

"ROAD TRIP!" yelled Tamiko, rolling her window down.

"We're going on a roooooad trrrrriiiiip," I sang loudly. I hummed a little tune to go with it. "This is a great opportunity for me to warm up for *you know what* next week."

Allie nodded and winked at me. I think she could guess that I didn't want to mention it to Mrs. Shear. I'd decided for the time being to just tell my besties, my band, and my family.

Tamiko drummed her hands on her lap. It was clear how excited we all were not only to be seeing one another on a Tuesday, which rarely happened, but also to be going on an adventure together.

"I thought about this *all day*," said Allie. "In homeroom Colin asked me if I had the notes from our life science class the other day, and I told him I had absolutely no idea. I couldn't even remember because all I could think about was this trip and the wonderful, amazing new flavors we're going to come up with!"

"I've planned ahead," said Tamiko, snapping the fabric on her legs. "I'm wearing realllllly stretchy leggings in case I taste-test too many flavors."

"That was smart," I told her. "I planned ahead too. I did some extra homework last night, so I can just relax and have fun today!"

Mrs. Shear put the radio on, and the three of us sang along to the music. I was good at staying in tune but not always good about remembering the lyrics to certain songs. That was Allie's strength—maybe because she was such a book-loving, word-loving person. She knew the lyrics to everything!

The drive was more than an hour, but with my two besties in the car, and school chatter and gossip to catch up on, the car trip flew by. It felt like no time at all before we were pulling up to a giant, hand-painted sign that read, PEG AND MARY'S ICE CREAM

MUSEUM AND FACTORY. We all let out a squeal.

There was a visitor's lot, and Mrs. Shear pulled in there.

"Are we ready, girls?" she asked.

"READY!" we replied as one.

"I think I was born for this moment," said Tamiko. "I can't wait to be inspired! I bet I can come up with three awesome new flavors after this visit. Maybe four."

Mrs. Shear patted her arm. "You always come up with brilliant ideas, Tamiko. Not to worry. We've just been in a dry spell."

We followed the signs to the welcome center. There was a thirty-minute guided tour of the factory, and a store where you could taste-test and also buy ice cream. We decided to take the tour first.

The tour was even more interesting than I'd thought it would be. Because Peg and Mary's was a national brand, they had a huge factory. The main room of the factory was enormous—with endless conveyor belts, huge commercial mixing vats, more vats filled with ingredients, and signs everywhere about wearing protective clothing and keeping your hair covered and how to improve employee safety. We could see employees in white coats walking around checking on things as the mixtures went down each conveyor belt to the final vat at the end, where it was mixed and then separated and put into containers. It was nothing like the small-batch production that Mrs. Shear did. It was overwhelming, really.

"This is fascinating," Mrs. Shear said. "And it certainly makes you think about where your food comes from, doesn't it?"

"Yes!" said Allie. "Who knew this many people and machines went into making one small pint of ice cream?"

As we strolled around the perimeter of the room, I started humming one of the songs we'd heard on the radio on the way there. It was the kind of pop song that got stuck in your head and wouldn't leave. I only knew the words to the chorus, but I thought maybe it would make a good audition piece for the contest.

"What are you humming, Sierra?" asked Tamiko. "Is it 'Too Good for You'? I love that song!"

I nodded. "Yes. I was just thinking about singing it next week for"—I lowered my voice so Mrs. Shear wouldn't hear me—"the *thing*. You know."

Tamiko gave me a funny look, as if wondering why

I didn't just say "the singing contest." Allie seemed to have understood earlier. And now that we were in the factory, I especially didn't want Mrs. Shear to think I wasn't focusing on the tour and the flavors and coming up with some new ideas. This was a work trip, and I wanted her to know I took it seriously.

Tamiko nodded at me vaguely and turned her attention back to the tour guide, who was explaining that the United States was one of the top three countries in the world in terms of ice cream consumption. No surprise there! She also told us that chocolate was the first flavor ever invented, not vanilla, as most people assumed, and that the average number of licks it takes to get through a one-scoop cone of ice cream is fifty.

"I'm learning so much!" Allie exclaimed. "I always felt like an ice cream expert, but I feel like an ice cream mega-expert now."

Next we were led into a room filled with ice cream toppings. It was absolutely beautiful. I didn't know where to look—there was so much to see! Many things I'd never even thought of as ice cream toppings before, like ground coffee, bacon, and saltine crackers.

"You guys have SO many toppings and

ingredients!" Allie said to the tour guide. "How do you keep track of your inventory to keep it fresh? I mean, do you ever buy too much, or too little? What happens when you make a mistake in your ordering?"

As soon as she'd finished speaking, Allie's eyes went wide. She added quickly, "Am I asking too many questions?"

The tour guide laughed. "I love all your questions, *and* your enthusiasm. And yes, of course, inventory and ordering are an imperfect science, even at a factory as large and busy as this one. So we don't think of the inevitable inventory fluctuations as mistakes—we look at them as a challenge to come up with brand-new flavors!"

"I love that!" I said. "I'm all about having a positive outlook."

Some of the others in our tour group were milling around the room now, but Tamiko, Allie, Mrs. Shear, and I were sticking close to the guide. I guess she could tell that we were truly interested in all the inventory talk, because she went on.

"Have you ladies ever heard of the book *Beautiful Oops!*?" she asked.

We all shook our heads.

"It shares a theory—an understanding, really—that anything that goes wrong while you're creating art can be turned into something *beautiful*. Now, let's say someone wants cherry vanilla ice cream but we've run out of cherries. We'll see what we do have and recommend something else, presenting it as, 'We're out of cherries, but how about trying our newest delicious flavor, vanilla banana peanut butter chip? It's sure to knock your socks off!'"

Allie laughed. "That's because you probably have lots of bananas and peanut butter chips, right?"

The guide nodded. "Exactly."

"Tamiko does that naturally!" I said, squeezing Tamiko's arm. "She's been beautiful-oops-ing without even knowing it."

Mrs. Shear smiled. "She has. And come to think of it, I've definitely had to beautiful-oops it myself a few times when I'm making some of our old standbys and I've run out of an ingredient."

The tour guide nodded. "I think it's a great thing to remember for life in general, not just for recipes. If something goes wrong, beautiful-oops it!"

I loved the idea of the beautiful oops. I was always getting into one tricky situation or another, juggling social commitments, sports, and academic groups. When I got in over my head, I just needed to find a way to make it work and carry on.

I started humming to myself again, thinking in the back of my mind what a neat concept beautiful oops could be for a Wildflowers song. I'd have to talk to Tessa about the lyrics, because she was so good at them.

I kept humming as we followed the guide to the next room. Tamiko and Allie were walking ahead of me, and I saw Tamiko lean her head toward Allie and whisper something. Allie quickly nodded and whispered something back. Then they turned around at the same time and looked at me.

I immediately stopped humming. "What's up?" I asked.

Allie shrugged and looked pointedly at Tamiko again, who smiled. Neither answered me. They just kept walking.

I followed, utterly confused. That was so weird! We were not the type of three-person friendship that kept secrets or talked about one another. That was part of the Sprinkle Sundays sisters code. And just now Allie and Tamiko had been *very* obviously talking about me.

I decided to push it out of my mind for now, because I was probably just paranoid or giddy from the nearness of so much ice cream. I focused on the Flavoroom instead, which included all the different flavors that Peg and Mary had ever made, including ones that they didn't sell anymore. They even had a clipboard where visitors could sign their name if they wanted a certain "dead" flavor brought back to life.

I moseyed up and down the rows, enjoying reading all the different flavors. I knew something would come to me if I just thought about it long enough, and I wanted to be able to give Mrs. Shear at least one really good new flavor idea before we left the factory.

Peppery Peach? Moroccan Mango? Peanut Butter and Jelly-icious? Nothing seemed quite right.

The song from the car ride, "Too Good for You," popped back into my head, and I sang it very softly under my breath as I wound my way around the room. I liked the tour, but I was pretty sure that after thirty minutes of nothing but *talking* about ice cream, I was ready to move on to tasting some of it. Visiting the ice cream store for tasting flavors and buying cones and pints was next. I was ready.

Still humming as I signed my name to the list for

the long-gone flavor Chunky Chunky Coconut, I happened to look up and see Allie and Tamiko whispering and eyeing me again. The second they noticed that I saw them, they stopped and started talking loudly about the Gotta Have Goat Cheese flavor.

"*Chicas!*" I said. "*What* is going on?"

Allie's face turned completely beet red, but Tamiko pasted on a big smile and said, "Nothing, Sierra! Just looking for inspiration."

There was a moment of total silence after she spoke. I knew she wasn't being truthful, and she and Allie knew that I knew it.

It was something about me. Had I been acting weird? I'd mentioned the contest a few times. But I hadn't made a big deal about it, had I? Was I boring everyone to death with it after just two days?

I supposed I *had* made a huge deal about it the day before when I'd made Tamiko video-chat with Allie during lunch so I could tell everyone at the same time. I'd acted like I had big news—like I'd already won the contest—when really all I'd done was find out about it and decide to enter. All I'd really done was read a flyer.

I didn't want to be a drama queen. Especially after

Tamiko's recent queen-of-everything phase. I just wanted to be my nice, sunny Sierra self. The one my friends didn't whisper about.

At last the tour guide announced that it was time to move on to the tasting.

But it no longer sounded enticing to me. My stomach felt queasy. Suddenly the field trip didn't seem quite as fun anymore.

I wanted to go home.

CHAPTER SIX
THE RIGHT SONG

None of us came up with the perfect new flavor for Molly's after our tour, but Mrs. Shear was really happy with how much we had all learned from it. She reminded us that sometimes ideas take a few days to "ferment." Then Tamiko suggested Fermented Froot Loops as a flavor, and everyone laughed.

Tamiko and Allie acted completely normal on the way home from the factory, so I tried to act normal too. But inside I was worried. I could tell when something was going on and I was being left out. Most people can sense things like that. And when you're dealing with two girls you've been best friends with for years and years, it's even easier to tell.

I didn't want to outright ask them what was up

again in front of Mrs. Shear in the car, because I thought that would make everyone uncomfortable, so I decided to just put it out of my mind until I saw them together again at Molly's on Sunday. If things weren't back to normal by then, I'd deal with it.

For the time being I had to focus on myself and preparing for the contest next week. Luckily, Reagan had confirmed with everyone in the band that we'd be having an extra rehearsal after school on Wednesday. I was really touched that everyone could spare an extra day to help me prepare. I knew they all had schedules as busy as mine, and homework as well.

I arrived ten minutes early for our practice, which was practically unheard of for me. But that's how much I cared about the contest. I'd even brought the snacks for the day, since Reagan's mom was usually the one to provide them, and I wanted to make sure that we could keep using her garage as our rehearsal space for a long, long time.

I'd stopped at a market on my way there and bought a bunch of muffins and some clementines. My mom always told Isa and me that vitamin C is good for the brain and the body, so I figured it might be good for brainstorming.

Reagan was already on the couch when I arrived, her math textbook open on her lap. "Hello!" she said. "Come in. I was just trying to get a head start on my homework."

I held up the bag of food. "I've got food!"

"Hurray!" she said. "I need it."

Tessa arrived a moment later, wearing her guitar case on her back, followed by Kasey.

"This is an exciting day!" Tessa squealed. "We're going to pick your audition song, which will help you win the contest, which will mean you get to appear on TV, and then you'll mention the Wildflowers, and then we'll get tons of requests for gigs, and we'll be so busy being rock stars that we'll have to drop out of eighth grade!"

We all laughed, Tessa included.

Kasey collapsed onto the couch, looking like she'd had a pretty long day. I handed her the pack of muffins and clementines, and she took one of each. "So, where do we begin?" she asked.

I threw my hands up. "I have no idea! I really need you all. I've had different songs running through my head for days, and I don't know how to decide which one would be the best for me to perform."

Reagan peeled a clementine, looking thoughtful. "Well, *I* think we need to strategize."

Kasey nodded. "I agree. This isn't just about picking a song you like. That's easy! This is a *contest*. This is about making an *impression*. What type of song will make the best impression? A trendy pop hit? Something more rock? An original, or a cover?"

Tessa shook her head. "I don't think it's about the specific song as much as finding the song that best suits Sierra's *voice* so that her voice is what they hear."

Reagan nodded. "I agree. Totally. It's about her voice."

I was just about to agree with Reagan, when she spoke again.

"Actually, now that I think about it, maybe it's *not* just about her voice. Maybe they're looking for someone marketable, too. So we need to present you as a *package*. You know, with a very distinct sense of style in your clothes, your voice, your song choice. Someone that they know could become famous at some point, so they can say they discovered you."

"That's true too," said Kasey. "But what's MOST important is that you leave them wanting more. You want them to say, 'Hey, that Sierra was really talented. I want to hear more from her.'"

"Okay, stop!" I said. "Now I'm totally freaking out! How can I possibly put together a style, pick a song that exemplifies my style, practice the song and sing it perfectly, and also exude star quality, all in just a week? I can't do it!"

I wedged myself into the couch beside Kasey and put my head in my hands.

Reagan put her arm around me. "Maybe we're taking things a little too far," she said. She rubbed her hand up and down my arm soothingly, like a mom. "How about for today we just have you sing a few of the songs that we all think you sing best, and we'll vote? And *your* vote counts the most, obviously." She grinned at me.

"That's right!" agreed Kasey. "All that other stuff doesn't matter if you don't love the song you're singing. The judges will feel that. What's your favorite song?"

"And try to make it a happy one," Tessa chimed in. "I do think judges give extra points to people who seem happy."

I racked my brain. Happy, favorite song. Happy. Favorite. Song.

I shook my head and buried it in my hands again. "I can't think of a single song!"

Reagan passed me her binder of original Wildflowers songs and covers that we've done, and I began flipping through it. There were so many great songs in there. How could I pick just one?

"You look like you're agonizing," Reagan said. "How about you do what Tessa suggested—sing something that makes people happy. Something sunny, like you. Then you can't go wrong."

If she'd said that to me first thing, and everyone had agreed and left it at that, then maybe I could have done that. But after hearing so many suggestions and ideas about what to prioritize in picking a song, and all of it sounding so *right*, I was truly and completely baffled.

I *had* to have the right song. That much was clear.

"If you have fun, they'll have fun," said Kasey. "For now let's just sing a few random songs and see if we can't loosen you up. Any practice will be good for your voice, regardless."

"Okay," I said. "That's doable. Let's start with 'Stand Up, Speak Up' because that song always makes me feel good."

For the next hour or so, we ran through a bunch of different songs. But while everyone agreed that most of them sounded fine, no one thought there was one that stood out in particular. Not even me.

So we wrapped up our emergency practice with our emergency unresolved. I thought about calling Allie and Tamiko and asking their opinion about what I should sing, but when I picked up my phone, I immediately put it back down again. They didn't know our song list as well as my Wildflowers bandmates, and there was still that yucky feeling in my stomach from them talking about me the day before.

It looked like I'd have to figure this out on my own.

My mom picked me up from practice and told me that dinner wouldn't be ready for at least an hour, so I went straight to my room to pore over my song choices again. I was hearing so many songs in my head at this point—from rehearsal and from the radio—that I was starting to go a little nuts.

I plopped onto my bed and started scrolling through my phone, looking at song titles. Then I heard something odd. It sounded like *me*, singing a

Wildflowers song from somewhere in the house. It was very brief—just ten seconds or so—but I heard it. Weird. Was Isa listening to a tape of me singing?

I opened my door and went out into the hallway. Isa's door was shut. I knocked on it.

"Who is it?" she called.

"The queen of England," I responded. "Seriously, Isa. Do you really have to ask?"

"Yes, I do," she said. I could hear the exasperation in her voice. "Come in."

I went in and found her sitting on her bed, her phone in her hand, just as I'd been sitting moments before. It was a common thing to do, of course, but I was still sometimes struck by our twin-ness showing itself in various ways when I wasn't expecting it.

"Did you come in here to stare at me, or can I help you with something?" Isa asked.

I rolled my eyes. "Knock it off, Isa. I came in because I heard myself singing! Were you playing a track of me doing a Wildflowers song?"

She shook her head hard. "*No*. The whole world doesn't revolve around *you*, Sierra. I was watching something on YouTube, though. Maybe it just sounded familiar."

She sounded overly defensive. Was what I'd asked so wrong? Or was Isa right—was I acting like the world revolved around me? I didn't *think* I was, but it was possible. And that theory made sense, considering what had happened with Allie and Tamiko the day before.

"I guess I was wrong," I said. "It's funny, though—it sounded just like me."

I turned to leave. Then Isa called, "Wait."

I looked back at her expectantly.

"Did you pick your song yet for the contest?" she asked.

Now it was my turn to sound exasperated. "I wish. I have *no idea* what to sing. I just met with the Wildflowers and we spent more than an hour going through songs, and no one could agree on what type of song I should sing, or if I should do a cover or an original, or focus on what suits my voice best, or which one makes me more of a 'package'..."

I let my voice trail off. I was pretty sure Isa was going to just nod and dismiss me, but instead she said, "You didn't ask me."

I stared at her. "You don't even like the kind of music I sing."

"Maybe I don't. But I *am* the one who told you about the competition. Don't you think I want you to do well? I'm your sister!"

Tamiko and Allie had seemed very happy for me the other day, but now something was up. So they were no help. My bandmates were wonderful and well-meaning and dying to help me, but they were too full of excitement to be very useful at the moment. Maybe I needed someone blunt and opinionated and practical like Isa to steer me.

"You're right. I *do* need you, Isa. I'm worried I'm going to try to be so many different things for the judges that I'll just end up a big, hot mess onstage and embarrass myself."

"We can't have that," she said, sliding her phone into the top drawer of her nightstand. "You represent Team Perez, and I'm not going to let Team Perez be embarrassed on TV."

"Only the finalists make it onto TV," I reminded her. I fussed with my hair nervously.

"Whatever. There will be tons of people at the audition, listening and watching. This is big, Sisi. Let's get to work."

CHAPTER SEVEN
WHAT'S THE SPECIAL?

Somehow the old Isa had returned. I didn't know if it was because she was proud that she'd found the contest and given me the idea to try out, or because she liked that I was asking her opinion about things again, or if she was just in a really good mood because her travel soccer team was doing well.

But every night that week after we were both home from our activities and had finished our homework and dinner, she came into my room and curled up on my bed with our two cats and watched me practice different songs. She listened intently, like she really cared, and offered interesting, honest feedback about each one. She was still Isa enough to tell me the truth and not fluff me up with compliments.

However, no matter how many times I asked her to, she refused to pick out my song for me. Desperate, I even went downstairs and sang for our parents a few of the songs I was considering, but they wouldn't pick for me either.

Everyone kept telling me that this was *my* audition, and it needed to be *my* decision. But I was getting more and more tired of trying to make this decision. I had my ever-increasing pile of schoolwork to do, my soccer and softball practices, I was doing the lighting again for the school play, and I wanted someone to just *tell* me what to do!

There was some good news, though. At school all week Tamiko was acting completely normally. She and MacKenzie and I ate and talked together every day at lunch, and I saw Tamiko between classes and in science, the one subject we had together. And it was like nothing weird had ever happened at the ice cream factory. Allie had been texting me normally too, sending me pictures of her incredibly delicious Vista Green lunches, like fish tacos and microgreens, instead of the same old sloppy joes we had at MLK.

So at least that was off my mind for the moment.

Well, maybe not off my mind, but it seemed like things were okay.

But when Sunday finally rolled around and it was time for my regular weekly shift at Molly's again, I was reluctant to go. I felt better about my friends, but the contest was just four days away, and I still hadn't chosen a song. As I was heading out the door to walk to work, Reagan texted me, Did you pick the song yet? Do you want to have another emergency practice?

I wrote back, No song yet. Please—just tell me what to do!

She replied, Whatever you pick will be great. You are great! But you need to pick ASAP. OKAY???

I sighed as I read her text and walked slowly across town. As I was crossing Main Street to turn off to the street for Molly's, I felt a funny little skip in my stomach. I turned around, wondering what it was that might be bothering me. And for just a second I saw a girl in all black with a baseball cap on her head walking into the Middle C music shop across the square. I felt the funny skip again when I saw her.

Could it have been Isa?

There were other girls who wore all black. And

Isa and I were both average height. Not many people had Isa's hair, though, which was a mostly grown-out fauxhawk with purple tips. But this girl had her hair up in a cap, something Isa never ever did. She liked hoodies, but she did not like hats.

Still, my old twin-tuition, which was what Isa and I called the special spidey-sense we had for each other, was telling me that it was her. What was she doing in the music store? Looking at instruments?

I shook my head and picked up the pace so that I wouldn't be late for work. Being late was something I was famous for, and it wasn't exactly like being famous for singing!

"I'm here!" I called as I breezed into Molly's. The bell over the door tinkled in greeting, and I saw that the clock read 12:45. Whew. Made to work exactly on time without a minute to spare.

Tamiko was serving a customer an ice cream cone as Allie wrote a new recommendation up on the daily pairings board.

"Try reading Roald Dahl's *James and the Giant Peach* with our Beaches and Cream flavor! Mmmm, beachy!"

"Great idea!" I told Allie, giving her a thumbs-up.

"Isa and I loved all the Roald Dahl books when we were little."

"Me too," said Allie. She glanced out the window at the beautiful sunny afternoon and said, "And doesn't today seem like a peachy day?"

I nodded enthusiastically, even though I didn't feel all that peachy inside. I was too worried about the approaching contest.

"Hey, has either one of you ever been in the Middle C music store across the square?" I asked.

Tamiko nodded. "Yes, I have. I used to take piano, remember? My parents bought all my sheet music there."

"I probably have too, just not for a long time. Why?" Allie asked.

I thought about mentioning seeing Isa, then decided against it. It seemed a little odd to say, "I thought I saw my twin sister, but I didn't go over to check and see if it was her. Do you guys think it was her?"

I should have just walked over there right then, but I would have ended up being late to work.

"No reason," I said. "I was just, um, wondering if they had a good selection of song music in there."

I busied myself straightening the napkins and plastic spoons. No matter how many times a day we tidied those, they were always askew.

"I guess that means you're still looking for a song to sing for the contest?" Tamiko said. "Maybe Allie and I can help. Sing a few of your favorites for us. Molly's is the perfect venue for an impromptu concert."

Allie nodded. "Sing something! There aren't any customers in here now. We might as well help you."

My face broke into a huge grin. My friends *did* want to help me! "Thanks, guys, but since we're at work, I probably should be focusing on work. Anyway, I've given it a lot of thought, and even though I WANT someone else to pick my song for me, I think it's best that I decide on my own."

Tamiko nodded. "I think you're right. That way, no matter what happens, you won't blame anyone else. . . ."

No matter what happens? Was Tamiko saying I'd lose and then blame someone else for picking my song? And did she not really believe I had a chance to win?

That hurt. I stayed silent, which was very unlike me.

Allie noticed immediately and jumped in. "She

didn't mean it like *that*, Sierra. Just that this is your audition, so you should make all the choices for it. Because you're representing *you*, you know?"

I nodded, still not trusting my voice. Tamiko's cheeks flushed, but she said, "Sierra knows I didn't mean it like that."

Just then Mrs. Shear came out into the front of the shop. She had a knack for appearing whenever there was a tense moment. I was pretty sure it wasn't a coincidence.

"Hello, lovely girls! Are you all just bursting with ideas for new flavors for Molly's?"

The three of us looked at one another sheepishly. None of us had even discussed it since our trip on Tuesday. I knew that I personally hadn't given the new ice cream flavor a single thought all week. I'd been much too preoccupied. I felt terrible.

Mrs. Shear pointed at the specials board. "Tamiko, what's going on? The specials board is still bare!"

Tamiko, who was never at a loss for words, opened her mouth, but nothing came out. Even if she had just hurt my feelings by accident, I felt the need to defend her.

"Um, well," I started to say. "Remember how

there was that neat room with the toppings? Maybe we could have a special just called Toppings, and it would just be . . . a cone full of toppings?"

Ugh. Even I thought that sounded weak.

Mrs. Shear smiled politely but shook her head. "That's creative, but it doesn't really help us sell our homemade ice cream, which is the goal. Other ideas? We need a real winner here, people!"

Then something odd happened. Allie looked over at Tamiko, and the two of them grinned at each other. Hugely. It was a weird, private grin, just like the one at the factory. I think Tamiko might have even winked at Allie.

Were they smiling about my dumb idea? *What was happening?* Whatever it was, there was some private secret that I was left out of. That much was for sure.

It felt like the ice cream factory tour all over again. And I wasn't imagining it—I could see it with my own eyes.

Uncomfortable, I looked down at the case full of bins of ice cream. I counted them over and over again, trying to calm my nerves. A minute or two passed and no one spoke.

"This isn't like you guys!" said Mrs. Shear,

shaking her head. "Tamiko, you always have something up your sleeve."

Tamiko rubbed her chin and looked thoughtful. "We could do design-your-own sundaes again. They were a big hit."

Allie nodded vigorously. "They were. We sold a ton!"

Mrs. Shear sighed. "I guess. I was just hoping for some of that Sprinkle Sundays sisters magic ... like with those mermaid sundaes, and Coffee and Doughnuts, and some of your other ideas."

"We'll keep working on it," I promised. I felt terrible about not having thought of the new flavor at all this week. Especially since Mrs. Shear had been so nice to take us on that field trip! "I promise. We'll come up with something amazing!"

Tamiko nudged Allie, and they looked at each other knowingly again. I wanted to shout, "WHY ARE YOU DOING THAT?" but I kept my mouth tightly shut until Mrs. Shear left on a run to the store for more walnuts and shaved almonds.

"Guys, what is going *on*?" I finally said. I did not like confrontation, especially with my two besties, but this was ridiculous. "You look like you have a secret, and I'm not in on it. If I'm being annoying about the contest or something, please—just tell me. I can take it. You guys are making me nervous."

"Oh, Sierra, no!" Allie said, sounding worried. "That's not it at all. We're totally pumped for you to try out for the singing contest. We just . . . Well, we have an idea about something, and we're still working on it, and we'll tell you when it's ready."

She looked nervously at Tamiko, who nodded confidently. "Yes, we'll tell you soon. Don't worry— it's nothing bad."

My dad once told me that when someone says, "Don't worry—it's nothing bad," it is *always* something bad, so he never ever says that to his pet patients' owners. He always says, "Here's what's going on," and just tells them the truth straight-out.

It seemed that there were a lot of secrets going on. Where Isa had been last week when Papi and I had picked her up, why she'd been going to Middle C instead of her soccer practice earlier, and why Allie and Tamiko were cooking something up without me when normally I was involved in all of their schemes.

I loved being busy and social and spending time with all my different groups of friends. And because I was so busy all the time, I did occasionally miss some things with my besties—like trips to the movies or study dates or whatever. But missing something and being left out of something were two very different experiences.

"Fine," I said at last, because Allie and Tamiko were watching me carefully, waiting for me to say something. And what else could I say? They weren't being mean. They just weren't being their usual selves. "Let's just get to work, I guess."

Allie started wiping counters, and Tamiko added, "Back by popular demand—design your own sundae!" to our specials board, even though we all knew it wasn't as good as coming up with something new and unique. And I got my phone out and put on a playlist of music that would be fun and cheerful for customers when they came in. It soon got busy, and I relaxed slightly. I was in my element, greeting customers and adding up their orders in my head without using the register. However, in the back of my mind, I couldn't help wondering what on Earth I was going to sing on Thursday for the audition, and why my two best friends were keeping something from me.

CHAPTER EIGHT
ISA'S SECRET

I walked home slowly from work, keeping an eye out for Isa. I seemed to see her everywhere lately, instead of nowhere, which was how it had been for months and months.

Allie and Tamiko had been mostly normal for the rest of our shift at Molly's, so I'd focused on being sunshiny Sierra—even though I hadn't felt like it—and making sure our customers were happy.

But I'd also made a decision. Tonight I would pick my song, no matter what, because I needed to spend the next few days singing it nonstop if I was going to be ready for the audition. Even if I had to put a bunch of song names into a hat and pick one out randomly, I was going to make a decision! Tonight!

When I got home, I could smell good things cooking in the kitchen. Sundays really were the best.

"*Hola!*" I called out.

Papi answered. "*Hola*, Sierra. I'm making masitas and rice. Dinner will be ready in an hour or so."

"Yum! *Gracias*, Papi." I thudded up the stairs and went straight to my room.

One hour was perfect. That gave me just enough time to look through my songs one more time and try to pick one. Then I could begin practicing it after dinner. And stick with it.

I flopped onto my bed with the Wildflowers songbook and began paging through it. The fact that my bandmates had all personally chosen each of these songs made the decision even harder. We loved all the songs to begin with, and on top of that I had special memories of us playing them together. They were *all* my favorite song!

I hummed a song, a pop hit from the radio, just something to warm up my vocal cords as I looked. When I heard a sound from the hallway, my head popped up, and there was Isa walking by with her laundry basket, only she wasn't wearing all black. She was in a black T-shirt, but she had blue jeans on with it. For her, that was unusual.

"Hey—were you wearing that all day?" I asked.

Isa paused in my doorway, holding the basket in front of her. "Huh?"

"Were you wearing black leggings earlier?"

"I don't know." She narrowed her eyes. "Maybe. Why?"

It was the new Isa, the infuriating one. "Never mind. I thought I saw you walking into Middle C at the main square earlier."

And then I saw it—Isa's entire face bloomed a bright red and she practically ran down the hallway.

"Isa!" I called. "STOP. Get back here!"

I ran into the hall and grabbed at her shirtsleeve before she could escape to the basement laundry room. "Come in here," I said, pulling her into my room and shutting the door.

Surprisingly, she let me.

"What's going on?" I asked. "And don't tell me 'nothing.'Why were you at Middle C? And why have you been acting so ... *Old Isa* lately? And where were you the other day when Papi and I picked you up?"

I fully expected her to say, "None of your business,

Sunshine," and run off again, but she didn't. Instead she put her laundry basket on the floor and sat down on my bed.

"Okay," she said. "I'll tell you. But you can't tell anyone—not even Mami and Papi. Promise?"

I felt my stomach drop. What was going on? Was Isa in serious trouble?

"I can't promise that," I said. "What if it's something serious or you're in danger? I'd have to tell them."

Isa burst out laughing. "In *danger*? Me? What do you think I've been *doing*?"

I threw my hands up, frustrated. "I have no idea! That's the problem!"

"Well, calm yourself." Isa lowered her voice and said, "I've been taking . . . singing lessons."

My jaw dropped to my knees. At first I was sure she was teasing, but her face was deadly serious.

"*Singing lessons?* That's the big secret?"

She nodded, looking solemn. "I found a teacher at Middle C, and he's giving me a discounted rate since I told him I'm paying for the lessons myself. I've been going for a few weeks."

"But . . . why wouldn't you tell us that? I think it's great that you're singing!"

Isa rolled her eyes. "Do you think I want everyone comparing us? You're in a band—everyone knows you're a great singer. I don't want to be the twin with the worse voice."

I thought about that. Isa and I both played soccer, but she played on a travel boys' team, while I played on MLK's eighth-grade girls' team. I knew that she was much better than I was, and while I was proud of her, I guess sometimes it did feel weird. Being identical twins makes a lot of things awkward.

"Yeah, I get that," I said. "I *love* that you're interested in singing, though. I'd be happy to practice with you. . . ."

Isa shook her head. "NO! I mean, not yet. Let me practice a little and get better. I'm still learning."

"Okay," I said. "That's fair." Then something occurred to me. "Hey, was that a recording of *you* I heard you playing in your room the other day? The one that I thought was me?"

Isa grinned shyly. "Yeah. I was singing one of your Wildflowers songs—just for myself, to see how it sounded."

"Isa! I can't believe you didn't tell me any of this. I think it's awesome. And," I said, pausing, not wanting to push too much, because Isa really didn't like to talk about personal stuff, "it seems to be making you *happier*. You've seemed much happier lately. Singing makes me happy too. I can express how I'm feeling using someone else's words."

Isa nodded. "It does feel good. I wasn't sure if I'd like it—I just wanted to try it—but now that I think I *do* like it, I want to ask Mami and Papi to help me pay for more lessons."

"I'm sure they will if you just tell them," I said.

"I'm not ready yet," she said forcefully. "So *don't* say anything. Got it?"

"Got it."

"Let's talk about you," Isa said. "You obviously don't have a song yet, right?"

I shook my head.

"Or an outfit?"

I shook my head again.

"Let's work on that. Start pulling stuff out of your closet and trying it on. I'll look at your songs."

It was a relief to not have to make these decisions myself. Even though Isa and I didn't share each other's tastes, she would never let me embarrass myself in public.

I laid a bunch of outfit options out on the floor to show her. "This yellow blouse is bright, so it will look good on camera," I said. "And this purple striped dress is good, because it's a dress, so it looks like I dressed up and I'm taking the audition seriously. And then I have this fun T-shirt that the Wildflowers and I made for one our shows—"

"Which outfit do *you* like best?" she asked.

I had no idea. I liked them all, and I said so. "I do get a lot of compliments when I wear the purple dress, though."

"Don't worry too much about what other people think. Which outfit would make *you* feel good, and make you feel the most like yourself? Because that confidence will help you perform better. If you're just wearing something other people like, you won't be one-hundred-percent comfortable, and it will show. I know, because everyone wants me to dress like you, in bright colors, but I know that I'm happier in black. Also, I look awesome in it."

She grinned, and I grinned back. I felt a huge swell of gratitude for my twin sister.

"C'mon, Sierra. Which outfit makes YOU feel good?" Isa said again. "Makes you feel the most like yourself?"

The answer to that was easy—it was the Wildflowers T-shirt I'd made with my band. I'd hand-painted it with wildflowers, and it had all my favorite colors on it. Plus, it was one-of-a-kind.

I pointed to the T-shirt. "This shirt makes me feel so happy, because it reminds me of my band and how much fun we have together! And I could wear it with a denim skirt and bright tights, to really make it a 'Sierra' outfit. What do you think?"

It was almost inconceivable—me asking Isa for fashion advice. But I knew she'd give me an honest answer.

"Sounds perfect, Sisi. That's exactly what you want—to be yourself and feel like yourself up there. That's what the judges want too. They want to meet the authentic you."

Suddenly a light bulb went off in my mind. I knew exactly which song would go with my outfit, and with me.

I grabbed the songbook off my bed and flipped through it until I found the page. I held it up and showed it to Isa.

"'Be Yourself'?" she read. "Ha! That sounds perfect! That is the exact right song to audition with.

Now all we have to do is have you practice it a few hundred times before Thursday."

"A few hundred?" I squealed. "Isa! I have to go to school."

"I'm not going to let you embarrass Team Perez. Let's get started. Stand up. Smile. Shoulders back. And . . . begin. . . ."

CHAPTER NINE
BE YOURSELF

Finally the day of the audition arrived. My mom picked me, Isa, and Tamiko up from school. Allie was already with her in the car. I was thrilled to have my best friends and my sister there to cheer me on. My dad had wanted to come also, but he'd had to stay at the veterinary clinic.

"I love your outfit," Allie said as I slid in next to her. "It's very Sierra."

I beamed. "That's exactly what I was going for! Isa helped me pick it out."

The three of us Sprinkle Sundays sisters squished into the middle seat of my mother's car, while Isa took the front seat. I was so glad that she wanted to come along. I was even more glad when Tamiko said, "I really like your earrings, Isa. Ear cuffs are huge in Japan right now. I saw a lot of people wearing them when I was there last summer."

Isa nodded and said thank you. I could tell she felt a little awkward around Allie and Tamiko, even though when we were younger, we all played together all the time. But she was trying, and they were trying, and I appreciated it.

The drive to Hamilton was only about twenty minutes, and when we pulled into the parking lot of the community center, it was already packed. A bunch of kids must have left school early in order to show up and get in line. I'd had a geometry test in the afternoon that would have been a pain to miss, but now I wished I'd tried to reschedule it. The butterflies in my stomach were flapping wildly as I looked at how many people were there.

"Stay cool," Isa said, even though I hadn't said a word. "It's just singing. You do it all the time."

"I'm cool," I said. Then I looked at my friends and sister. "No, I'm not! I'm terrified!"

Allie side-hugged me. "You're going to be great. Just . . . be yourself!"

Everyone laughed, and I was so glad that I'd finally settled on that song. It really did seem perfect for the occasion. I wished I'd decided on it sooner so I could have practiced it more, but I'd been singing it in my head all day at school, and at home in the evenings for my parents and Isa. I was as ready as I could be.

After we parked and walked up to the entrance, my mom went to scout out some information about where we should sign in and where we'd be waiting to audition, while Allie, Tamiko, Isa, and I stood in line.

"There are *so many people*," Allie said. "Can you believe it? I had no idea this would be so big."

I shot her a nervous look. "Don't say that! You're making it worse!"

Tamiko shook her head and said dismissively, "Half of these people have probably never sung anything in their lives. They've just watched those singing competitions on TV and decided they could do it too."

"Yeah," agreed Allie. "You're a *real* singer, Sierra. You're in a band!"

Their words were comforting, but I knew that plenty of these kids probably sang a lot as well, in a choir or lessons or wherever.

"You're a good singer, Sisi," said Isa quietly. "You really are."

I squeezed her hand quickly to say *Thank you.* Some of the kids in front of us were goofing around with their friends, talking about school and movies they'd seen and plans for the weekend. But some were holding sheet music and doing vocal warm-ups.

"Do you hear that girl?" I whispered to my crew, pointing with my head at a tall black-haired girl ahead of us in line. "She sounds like an angel. Did you hear that high C?"

Tamiko shrugged. "Angels belong in heaven. We want good singers here on Earth, like *you*, Sierra."

Allie nodded her agreement. "Yeah," she said. "So she hits a really high note. Big deal! Although I do like that boy up there with the raspy voice. He sounds different from everyone else."

"This is a great opportunity for you to sing alongside other good singers," Isa said. "It's just like soccer. Do you want to play against a team that's never won a game? Or play against a strong team so that you can get better?"

"Get better," I said, forcing a brave smile, but inside I was dissolving into nervous little pieces. Had I made a huge mistake deciding to come to this audition?

A person in a blue vest and a name tag that said VOLUNTEER finally made it down the line and handed me a number—eighty-four. I was number eighty-four to try out. And there were still tons of kids behind me. Who knew there were this many local teen singers?

Eventually the line started moving and we were ushered into a large recreation room that had been set up with rows of folding chairs. We could sit anywhere we wanted while we waited. The volunteers came in every so often to call kids in by groups of ten. So I had a while to wait.

I hummed to myself and did some quiet vocal warm-ups. I felt too shy to really belt it out in front of everyone in the room, especially since some of them were so good. So I chatted with Allie, Tamiko, Isa, and my mom, and tried to act as if I had everything under control.

"Want to practice your song?" Allie asked after we'd been waiting for more than an hour. "Or at least whisper-sing it?"

I shook my head. "Not in front of everyone. It'll just make me more nervous."

"You should practice it a few times," Isa said. "Go into the hall or the bathroom."

I looked at her in horror. "But then I might miss my number when they call it! I'd lose my chance."

"I could go in your place," Isa said, deadpan. "Then, when I won, you could go on TV and accept the award."

Allie and Tamiko laughed, certain she was joking, but I just looked at my twin. I wondered if she really *did* want to try out. . . . After all, she'd been taking the voice lessons, and she was the one who'd originally found the flyer for the contest.

I didn't answer for so long that Isa smiled and nudged me with her elbow. "I'm *kidding.* You know I couldn't do this."

"Numbers eighty to eighty-nine, please. Eighty to eighty-nine," someone announced over the microphone.

"That's you!" shrieked Tamiko. "Knock 'em dead, Sierra!"

"Break a leg!" said Allie.

My mom hugged me and whispered, "Good luck." And Isa gave me our secret Team P sign from when we were little—two thumbs-up but with the thumbs touching each other. I smiled.

"Be your sunshiny self," Isa said. "It's your best quality."

I followed the small group of people who'd been called along with me, and we were led into an auditorium. The judges all sat in the front row, while the singers lined up along the stairs at stage left and took turns going center stage, where the microphone was.

At least I've used a microphone before, I thought. *I'm ready for this!*

I was able to watch numbers eighty through eighty-three go before me. Number eighty was good but not particularly amazing. Eighty-one was very anxious, and he kept wiping his hands on his pants. I made a mental note not to do that myself.

Eighty-two couldn't carry a tune, and eighty-three was very, very good. I almost wished I hadn't listened to her. She had to be at least sixteen and was very poised, with a beautiful green print dress and bright pink fingernails. It was a good thing that I wasn't able to see the judges' reactions when she sang—I think that would have made me even more nervous.

"Number eighty-four!" one of the judges called.

I walked slowly up the steps and to the center of the stage. There were two women and one man sitting with clipboards and pencils, staring at me expectantly.

"What is your name and age?" asked the woman with brown hair.

I gulped. This was it. Time to turn on my sunshine and win over these judges. I could do it! I would just pretend I was working at the register at Molly's and trying to win over a grumpy customer with my charm.

"Hello!" I said boldly. "I'm Sierra Perez, and I'm thirteen years old. I'm in eighth grade at MLK Middle School, and I'm very glad to be here."

The male judge smiled back. In fact, all three of them smiled and looked a bit more jolly. "Great to have you, Sierra. What will you be singing for us today?"

"I'll be singing an original song called 'Be Yourself.' It was written by my band, the Wildflowers. We're all eighth graders, and we perform a mix of covers and original songs."

"Very impressive," said one of the women judges. "And I love original songs. They keep things interesting."

"Begin whenever you're ready," said the man.

I nodded and took two deep breaths. I even shook out my arms and legs for a second, which is something I do right before I perform with the Wildflowers. It's like I'm wiggling the nerves out so I can do my best.

Then I cleared my throat and began to sing.

"Be yourself! Who's better than you?
Be yourself! You're the only one who
Knows what you like,
Knows who you love,
Knows all your dreams and your secret
wishes too.
You don't depend on anyone else because
you need to
Just—be yourself!"

It was going great. My voice sounded strong, even though I hadn't warmed up much, and I made sure to keep a smile in my voice.

But then, as I was about to start the second verse, something awful happened. *I forgot the rest of the words.*

I stood there, frozen onstage, my mouth slightly open. I quickly smiled and acted as if this were just a natural pause in the song. After all, it was an original and the judges didn't know it. But I'm sure they could see the panic in my eyes.

Then, out of nowhere, I remembered what the tour guide at the ice cream factory had said. *Anything that goes wrong while you're creating art can be turned into something* beautiful. . . . Just beautiful-oops it!

I took a deep breath and started singing again. This time, though, I made up the words as I went along.

> *"Be yourself! Make a mistake and plow*
> *right through it!*
> *Be yourself! Betcha no one even knew it!*
> *Hmmmm mmm mmm mmm.*
> *Just. . . . Be. . . .Yourself!"*

When I was done, I gave the judges another huge smile and a bow. I acted as if I had planned for the song to go exactly as I'd sung it, and that I hadn't improvised and made up the second verse.

I had beautiful-oops'd it.

The judges were all writing and taking notes. One of them, the lady with the brown hair, smiled and said, "That was very nice, Sierra. You forgot the words for a moment there, didn't you?"

Uh-oh. I guess I hadn't pulled it off quite as well

as I'd hoped. I knew it was best to be honest.

I nodded. "Yes, I did," I admitted. "And I know the song! I think I was just so nervous about the audition. I'm sorry."

"Don't be sorry," said the other female judge. "I thought you handled it beautifully. You recovered very well."

"Thank you," I said. I kept the smile on my face, but inside I was kicking myself. There was no way someone who'd forgotten the words to their song was going to win! If I had just picked my song sooner, I could have practiced it more and known the words without even thinking about them.

Instead I would have to go back to the waiting room and tell Mami, Isa, Allie, and Tamiko that I had botched my big break.

Even worse, I'd have to tell the Wildflowers that I'd messed up one of our original songs! I couldn't believe it. I bowed again, stiffly, and walked offstage and back to the waiting room, where everyone was supposed to stay until the end, when they announced the finalists.

And just like that, the audition was over. Instead of feeling relief, I just felt mad at myself. Yes, I had made the best of it with my beautiful oops, but I hadn't been able to show the judges my very best singing or performance. And it was my own fault.

After so much buildup, my performance had been very, very disappointing, and there was no way to put a sprinkle of happy on that.

CHAPTER TEN
MELTED DREAMS

There was nothing left to do but wait.

I walked down the long hallway back to the waiting area and saw Allie, Tamiko, Isa, and my mother looking anxious. When I walked in, they all jumped up and down and clapped and congratulated me.

"Don't congratulate me," I said mournfully. "I messed up—big-time."

"What do you mean?" asked Allie. "What happened?"

"I choked."

"Literally?" asked Isa.

"Not, not *literally*. I performance-choked."

I explained to them how I'd started out smiling and happy and cheerful, and that the judges had seemed to like me. Then I'd started my song and completely blown it. I'd taken a long pause and then made up the second verse out of thin air.

When I was finished explaining the whole sad story to them, my mom gave me a huge hug, and everyone else piled on as well, until I was the center of a five-person hug. Everyone around us probably thought we were a little odd, but I didn't care. I was upset and disappointed in myself, and I needed my friends and family.

"Thanks, guys," I said. "It means a lot."

"At least you managed to beautiful-oops it!" said Tamiko. "I bet that impressed the judges a lot."

"I guess so," I said glumly.

"It impresses *me*," she added with a smile.

"I just have this feeling that you'll make the finals anyway," said Allie. "So you forgot the words for a second. So what? It happens! Probably ten people did that."

"Yeah, you can charm anyone, Sierra," said Tamiko. "I know you'll make it to the finals."

Isa was weirdly quiet. I knew that her twin-tuition was telling her how angry I was at myself, and she was feeling that pain like it was her own. That was the way it was with identical twins, even when they weren't very identical in personality.

The next two hours passed slowly. My mom went out and brought us back some snacks, and all of us sat and started our homework while we waited. I couldn't believe how long we'd been there, and I started to feel terrible that my friends were sitting there waiting with me for hours on a school night.

"Tell your parents to pick you up!" I told them. "My mom and Isa are here. You don't have to stay."

I didn't say what I was worried about, which was that, with the way they'd been acting lately, I didn't want them thinking I was some queen bee who expected them to spend an entire afternoon hanging around in a waiting room. I knew in my gut that my chances were slim, and getting the bad news after making everyone wait here with me for hours would just make me feel even worse.

"*Of course* we're staying," said Allie. "Don't be silly."

It felt like another hour went by, but it was probably only twenty minutes later when the judges finally came into the room.

The lady with the brown hair had a microphone, and she said, "Thank you all for coming out today to audition. Thank you also for your patience as we watched each contestant perform and took the time to give everyone careful consideration. We are very impressed with the talent here! You all have bright futures ahead of you."

Everyone clapped politely, but quickly, as we all just wanted to get on to the part where they told us who the finalists were.

The lady passed the microphone to the male judge. He said, "And now we'll announce our ten finalists, who will all appear on the show in a few weeks. Without further ado, our first finalist is . . . Alicia Freed!"

It was the girl in the green print dress who'd gone right before me. I watched her jump up and down and go up to the front of the room to stand by the judges. Her face was as pink as her nails, and she looked so, so happy.

I felt my stomach twist. I wanted to be up there so badly! And what were the chances that they'd pick me, when I'd performed right after Alicia and forgotten the words?

They called the other finalists' names one by one. Allie and Tamiko each held one of my hands, and they took turns squeezing my hand for support every time my name wasn't called.

Finally it was time for finalist number ten.

"And our last finalist is . . . Phillip Lum!"

Phillip ran excitedly to the front of the room. I counted and recounted all of the finalists and had to accept that my name had not been called. I was not in the top ten.

I knew it had been a long shot, but I felt just as disappointed as I would have if I'd had an amazing audition. I had really thought my singing ability was something special and that if I just had a chance to show it to the judges, they'd notice me.

My mother and my friends sat in stunned silence for a moment. No one knew what to say, least of all me. But I had to break the silence.

"Oh well. It was a good experience, right?" I said, trying for the old Sierra charm. "After all, it was fun to come and see all the contestants. And to try something different . . ."

"Let's get out of here," said Tamiko. "These judges don't know anything about talent."

Isa was still silent, and my mom gave me another hug. I felt terrible, and also, slightly embarrassed. Had

I really expected to make it to the finals in such a big, talented group of kids, most of whom were older and more experienced than I was? Now it seemed laughable that I was even here.

"Let's go," my mom said. "I'll drive everyone home."

The car was quiet on the way back to Bayville. I felt like I had let everyone down, even Isa, who had been so proud of me.

Maybe I didn't have what it took to be a star after all. It was a sad feeling.

It seemed like my dad had gotten home just before we did. He was washing his hands at the kitchen sink when we walked in. He looked hopeful and expectant, which meant that my mom had not texted him. So I had to break the bad news to him as well. It was hard to tell him that I hadn't made it, especially after he and my mom had warned me from the beginning that there would be many people trying out and it would be a very competitive process.

"It doesn't matter, Sierra," he said. "It was a good experience!"

I nodded mutely. Then the four of us worked

together to get dinner onto the table, and we sat down to reheated ropa vieja leftovers.

My parents kept up a steady stream of chitchat to distract me, but Isa had been eerily silent since we'd gotten the news from the judges. I don't think she had opened her mouth a single time in the car on the way home except to mutter good-bye to Allie and Tamiko.

When there was a break in my parents' overly cheery conversation, I said, "What's up, Isa? You haven't said a word."

Isa looked down at her food, which she was pushing around on her plate.

"Are you disappointed in me?" I asked. "Did I let Team Perez down?" My tone was teasing, trying to make light of a bad situation, but deep down I was pretty sure that that was how she felt.

Isa looked up at me, her eyes wide. "Seriously? That's what you think?"

"I don't know what to think," I said slowly. "I'm so mad at myself! I really blew it. And after everyone in my band and my friends and you all helped me and encouraged me. I thought I could be a star, and instead I'm just . . . well, just number eighty-four."

"You're *not* just number eighty-four," Isa said hotly. "You did something really brave, Sisi. You tried out! You showed up and stood in front of those judges and the other kids in your group and you sang. And then you messed up—and you *didn't* run offstage crying! You pulled it together and you kept on going. I'm really proud." Her voice broke a bit, as if she were overwhelmed by emotion. "I can't even . . ."

She didn't finish her sentence, just looked back down at her food. My parents exchanged looks with each other, and then with me, trying to figure out what was going on.

But I was pretty sure I knew. The way Isa had looked at the other contestants lining up when we'd been at the audition, almost hungrily, as if she'd wanted to join them. She was a competitive person. I'd watched her play soccer many times, and she was as aggressive as anyone else I'd ever seen. When her team lost, she sometimes kicked her water bottle or threw her jersey.

"You wish you'd tried out too," I said softly. And it wasn't twin-tuition that told me that. It was the look on her face.

Isa nodded, as my parents' expressions grew more and more confused.

"Isa! Why on Earth would you want to try out?" Papi asked.

"You don't even sing," said Mami.

Isa didn't reply. I had a feeling, though, that she wouldn't mind now if I explained for her. It seemed like she wanted to talk about it.

"Isa has been taking singing lessons," I blurted out.

You could have knocked my parents over with a feather. They both looked at Isa, their forks paused halfway between their mouths and their plates.

Isa's face turned red.

"Isa? Is this true?" asked my mom.

Isa nodded. "Yes. I've been taking them at Middle C and paying for them myself. I, um, really like singing too."

"Since when?" asked my dad. "Why didn't you tell us?"

Isa shrugged. "I don't know why. It started by accident, I guess. I was just always singing to myself when I listened to music. But then I started liking it more and more, and I thought about joining the choir at school, but everyone would be so surprised if I did that. . . ."

Isa didn't mention that her usual attitude of quiet, surly grumpiness and her refusal to join anything at school was pretty well known. She was right—it would have seemed really out of character for her to suddenly join the choir, and she would not have wanted all that attention.

"Anyway, I'm not trying to be like Sierra." Here she paused and looked at me pointedly. "She has her band, and that's *her thing*. I just like to sing and would like to get better at it. That's all."

Mami's face broke into a huge grin. "Well! How lucky are we to have TWO musical daughters in the family!"

"Very lucky," echoed Papi. "And I am so proud of you both. Sierra, I'm proud of you for trying out today, and doing something truly courageous. You are a talented girl, and if you continue to work hard, good things will happen! I promise. And, Isa, I am proud of you for following your passion, because I can tell you have been beating yourself up about it. Don't! Never be afraid to be who you are."

Isa laughed loudly. "Papi, are you telling me to *be myself?*"

"Be yourself!" I sang. "Who's better than you? Be yourself! You're the only one who . . ."

And then Isa jumped in and sang along with me.

"Knows what you like!

Knows who you love!

Knows all your dreams and your secret

wishes too.

You don't depend on anyone else because

you need to

Just . . . beeeeee yourrrrsellllllf!"

Our parents burst into applause, and Isa and I stood up and took a bow together. "Team Perez," I said, grabbing Isa's hand.

"Team Perez," she repeated.

CHAPTER ELEVEN

TUNE IN TONIGHT

It was a huge relief that I hadn't told anyone else at school about the audition except for MacKenzie. She and Tamiko were incredibly nice and sympathetic at school Friday morning, while also understanding that I did *not* want to talk about it, and I particularly did not want anyone else to find out about it.

I made it through the school day focusing on my schoolwork and teachers and trying to be my normal, cheerful self. But inside, I couldn't wait for the bell to ring and for it to be the weekend.

I let myself sleep in on Saturday morning, which I rarely do, because usually I'm off to a soccer game, or a lighting rehearsal for the school play, or a band practice. But today was one of those magical

Saturdays when I didn't have any obligations. I stayed in my pajamas and read a book in bed for a while. Then, when I finally got up, I made myself some tea and toast and sat in the kitchen watching TV on the tiny set in the corner. The next day I had to work at Molly's, but today I could just *relax*.

The house phone rang while I was cleaning up my dishes. I waited to see if one of my parents would get it, since the home line meant it was probably one of the vet techs from their clinic calling or one of my grandparents. But after three rings no one had answered it, so I picked up.

"Hello?"

"Hello! May I speak to Sierra Perez, please?"

It was a woman's voice that I didn't recognize. Definitely not the clinic or one of my grandparents.

Something in her tone sounded extremely professional and important. I cleared my throat before answering, "Yes, this is Sierra. Who's calling, please?"

"Sierra, this is Cynthia Meadows. I was one of the judges at the Who's a Star? contest. I'm not sure if you remember me. . . . I was wearing a navy-blue jacket."

Did I remember her? Of *course* I remembered

her! It was my first-ever audition for a TV singing program, and there had been only three judges. The question was, why was she calling *me*?

"Yes, I remember you, Ms. Meadows," I said. "How are you?"

"I'm well, thank you," she replied. "I'm calling because I happened to see your face after we announced the finalists, and I saw how disappointed you were."

I felt my cheeks flush. She was calling because I'd looked so pitiful? That wasn't exactly flattering.

"Um, yes, I suppose I was," I admitted. "Not that I'd had expectations or anything. I was just, you know, hopeful. But I'm okay, Ms. Meadows. You didn't have to call—"

Ms. Meadows cut in. "I know I didn't have to. I wanted to, Sierra. For several reasons. One, I want to make sure you turn on your TV tonight and watch the promotion for the show, which will be airing at eight o'clock. And two, I wanted to have the chance to tell you privately that I think you have a beautiful voice."

I gulped. She thought my voice was beautiful? I felt my insides turn to goo. "Really?"

"Really," she said. "Your voice is terrific. The other judges agreed. We just felt that you need more time to work on your composure. You were so nervous, which is natural, of course, and you are very young. But the more you sing, the more relaxed you'll become."

"Yes, of course," I said. "I plan to keep singing! Don't worry about that."

"Good. Because I also wanted to say that I hope you continue to work on your music and take it seriously. And I hope you'll consider trying out for the Who's a Star? contest again next year. We had so many contestants come out in the Hamilton-Bayville area that it seems clear this will become an annual thing!"

They were going to do contest tryouts here again! I would have another chance. It was the best news in the world!

"Thank you, Ms. Meadows. That means so much to me. I will definitely try out again next year! Wild horses couldn't stop me."

Ms. Meadows laughed. "I'm glad to hear it. Now don't forget—watch the show's promotion tonight at eight o'clock. And you might want to tell your friends and family to watch too. All right?"

"Yes, I will. I'll tell everyone, *and* I'll be cheering for all of those finalists. Thanks again for calling!"

I hung up the phone, feeling significantly more cheerful than I'd been when I'd picked it up. Ms. Meadows had called me personally to tell me to keep singing. Me! Maybe I wasn't a star yet, but that didn't mean it couldn't happen someday.

I couldn't help but wonder, though, why she'd asked me to watch the promo for a show I wouldn't be on. Would it have details for next year's contest? Or did she just want a lot of people to tune in and drive up ratings? I hoped it wasn't the last reason. I grabbed my phone to text Allie and Tamiko. For half a second I thought about *not* telling them because of their weird up-and-down behavior toward me lately. But they'd been so supportive at the audition the other day, and they were my best friends. I wanted them to know. I started typing.

Hey! One of the judges from the contest called me and told me to watch the promo for the show tonight at 8pm. She told me to tell my friends to watch too! So, you know, WATCH!

Allie wrote back immediately. She called you personally? Sierra, that's amazing! Of course I'll watch.

A few minutes later, Tamiko sent me the thumbs-up emoji and Can't wait for 8!

Next I texted my bandmates. I had given them a very brief summary of how my audition had gone, not wanting to make too big a deal out of my beautiful-oops moment, especially since Tessa was the one who had written the words to the song.

We'll ALL be watching, Reagan promised. Want to come over and the whole band can watch from my garage?

I'm not on the show! I reminded her. It's probably just info about next year. I just wanted to tell you guys because you're the best bandmates ever and the judge told me to spread the word. Thanks for all of your help preparing!

And lastly, when my parents got home from the clinic later that afternoon, I told them and Isa that we had to watch the promo that night after dinner.

"Of course," said Papi. "I want to know all about this contest! I think it's great news that they'll be doing it again. You have a whole year to practice."

"I don't understand why she'd call you to tell you to watch a promo for a show you're not on," Isa grumbled. "That just seems mean to me."

"She didn't," I said. "She called to tell me to keep working on my singing, and that there would be another contest next year, *and* that I should watch the promo."

I was defending Ms. Meadows because she had been so nice and complimentary on the phone, but the truth was, I had no idea why I was telling everyone to watch the promo either.

"Who cares?" said my mom. "I would watch it anyway just because I'm curious about how this contest will work, and I want to see the kids who were finalists. I'm very proud of every single kid there who tried out."

My mom's tone was so matter-of-fact that the discussion ended there, and turned to the chocolate Labrador retriever my dad had examined earlier in the day who had eaten a mango pit.

After dinner Isa, my parents, and I cleaned up the kitchen and headed into the family room to hang out while we waited for the promo to come on. I felt jumpy and excited inside, even though I didn't have any idea what there was to be jumpy and excited about.

Then the texts started coming in.

I've got my TV on, texted Reagan. Remind me why we're watching?

Ready to watch! said Allie. Did you make it onto the show and tell us you didn't, just to have a big reveal? Those shows LOVE a big reveal!

No reveal ☹☹, I texted back. And, I have no idea why we're watching!

"Stop texting, Sierra!" said my mom. "Look, here it is!" She grabbed the remote, turned the volume up, and looked at the screen intently.

The promo started with a shot of the outside of the community center. The camera panned on the line of kids outside waiting to go in. Before I could even see if I was in that line, the promo switched to another shot of everyone in the waiting room, holding their numbers and warming up their voices.

"It was our biggest crowd ever for a Who's a Star? audition!" said the announcer. "So many amazing young singers turned out for this audition. We'll definitely be returning to the Hamilton-Bayville area next year!"

Then the view switched to a shot of a boy trying out. It was the one with the deep, raspy voice who'd been ahead of me in line.

"Hey! I remember him," said Isa. "I can't believe he didn't make it. He was really good."

"They were all good," said my mom, looking over at me hastily, as if she were worried that seeing the promo would get me upset again about not having made the show. But I wasn't upset. It was fun to watch, and I actually felt a little proud. I had been a part of this!

Then, suddenly—there I was. On *television*.

"SIERRA, THAT'S YOU!" shouted Isa, who ran up to the TV to get closer, blocking our view.

"Move, Isa!" my dad said.

My jaw dropped as I stared at myself on the screen, singing.

"Be yourself! Who's better than you?

Be yourself! You're the only one who . . ."

It was the beginning of the song, and I sounded pretty good! I felt myself puff up slightly with pride. I *had* done okay in the beginning. Then, just before I blanked on the words, the scene cut to the judges discussing me.

The male judge said, "I don't think this young lady is ready for the show just yet."

"I agree, but it would be great to see her again when she's older," said the second woman judge.

Then Ms. Meadows said, "For sure. She has a

special quality." She looked down at her clipboard and wrote something. Then she turned to the other judges and said, "Sierra Perez. Remember that name. She could be a star someday."

The promo then cut to another kid's audition.

There was a ringing in my ears, and I was so happy that I almost felt faint.

She could be a star someday. She'd said that about *me!*

"That was you!" Isa yelled, jumping up and down. No one was paying attention to the rest of the promo anymore. "That was you, Sisi!"

My parents were both red-faced and smiling. They hugged me and hugged me again. "Our daughter! We are so proud of you!"

My phone started lighting up with text message after text message.

Ah!!!!!!!!!!!!!!!!!!!! Tamiko wrote.

Allie's text was more eloquent but just as enthusiastic: FUTURE STAR SIERRA PEREZ!

The Wildflowers group text also exploded. And I could see that I was getting messages from classmates and club mates that hadn't known I had auditioned.

I looked up from my phone, a little teary-eyed, and smiled at my family. "I couldn't have done it without all of you," I said. "My family and my friends and my bandmates."

I looked at Isa, who had an uncharacteristically large grin on her face. "Especially you, Isa," I continued. "You helped me so much, getting ready for the audition. Maybe Team P will sing together someday. What do you think?"

"Really?" she asked.

I nodded. "Really."

Isa grinned. "Well, we do have a lot of talent in this family. Two veterinarians . . . Why not two singers? Team P can do anything they set their minds to!"

CHAPTER TWELVE
STAR POWER

On Sunday, I was excited to get to Molly's. I always looked forward to going to work, because my job was scooping ice cream with my friends, but today I was extra excited, because I was still tingling about the fact that Ms. Meadows had said I had what it took to be a star.

Maybe it wouldn't happen for a long time, and maybe it wouldn't happen *ever*, but the fact that a talent judge had said that about me meant the world.

I skipped through the door of the ice cream shop a full sixteen minutes early, which was practically unheard of for me. Allie was already there, of course, since she always came early with her mom or got dropped off by her dad if she was staying at his apartment.

"Yay! It's Sierra—my only famous friend who's been on TV," teased Allie.

I took a huge bow and pretended to be very grand and fancy. Then I checked the trash cans—one of my regular tasks—and saw that they were nearly filled to the top.

"This TV star is going to take the trash out," I said. "I'll be back after this commercial break."

Allie giggled and got her chalk out, ready to put up the day's book and ice cream pairing. The specials board was blank again.

We were really letting Mrs. Shear down. I resolved to spend today's entire shift thinking of the perfect new ice cream special. I owed a lot to Molly's. Not only was serving ice cream a great job, but Molly's was a fun, happy place to work, and I got an automatic date every single week with my two best friends, one of whom I probably wouldn't see very often because she now lived one town away.

Molly's was a huge part of my life.

When I came back inside from the dumpster, Tamiko had arrived and was putting on her apron. She clapped when she saw me and gave me a huge hug. "I knew you could it," she said. "I just knew it!"

I was confused. "Do what? I still didn't make the show!"

She waved her hand. "I know. But you made a *name* for yourself! You introduced Sierra Perez to the world. And you did it really well!"

I smiled. "Thanks, Tamiko. That means a lot."

The bell for the door tinkled, and an older couple came in with what looked to be their grandson. It was time to get to work.

"Hello!" Tamiko said cheerfully. "Welcome to Molly's. What can I get for you today? We have some very special Mint Lemonade ice cream this week, and one of our most popular flavors, Honey Lavender!"

"Mmm-mmm," said the woman. "I'd like a double-scoop sugar cone of the Honey Lavender, please."

"And how about you, Mitchell?" the man asked the little boy. "What do you want?"

"Brownies," he mumbled. "I want *brownies.*"

Uh-oh. This was going to be tough.

"I'm afraid we don't have any brownies today. How about I make you a black-and-white milk-shake?" Tamiko suggested.

The boy shook his head at Tamiko, disgusted. He wanted *brownies.*

Then the man stared at me. He squinted his eyes. He elbowed his wife and whispered something into her ear.

Self-consciously I tucked my hair behind my ears and smoothed my apron. Had I forgotten to wash my face or something? Was there food in my teeth? A huge stain on my shirt that I couldn't see?

"You're that girl!" said the man finally. "From the Who's a Star? contest. We watched the commercial for it last night and we heard you sing. You were great!"

I blushed furiously. It was one thing to have my friends and family know about it, but to be recognized by a stranger was very different. He'd seen me on TV!

"You were terrific," the woman said. "And I can't wait to watch the show when it comes on in a week or two. I just love those singing competitions."

I looked at Allie and Tamiko for help, partly because I was embarrassed and partly so that they would see that I wasn't taking this too seriously.

But they were exchanging a look between them—just like the looks I'd seen before at the ice cream factory tour. I felt flustered all over again.

"Thank you! Um, how about trying our Cocoa

Coconuts flavor?" I suggested. "It's really chocolaty, just like a brownie. But it's even more fun."

The man nodded. "Sounds perfect. We'll get two single cups of your Cocoa Coconuts, please. And sign our cups . . . if you wouldn't mind."

"Coming right up!" said Allie. "Sierra, you sign first, then hand me the cup to scoop, please."

I felt myself blushing even more as I took a marker from the drawer under the counter and signed my name on their ice cream cups. No one had ever asked for my autograph before. I wondered if it would ever happen again.

I handed the cups to Allie, who set to work scooping. Tamiko stood quietly, which was unusual for her.

When the customers left and we were alone again in the shop, I whirled around to face Allie and Tamiko.

"Okay, guys. Spill it," I said. "What is with all the looks between the two of you? Do you think I'm getting a big ego or something? I'm not! I promise. In fact, I was crushed last week after the audition. It really shook my self-confidence. But then, after Ms. Meadows's call, I started to feel better. And seeing the promo helped. But I don't want you thinking that I think I'm so great or something. Because I *don't*, okay?"

"But you *are* great," said Allie. "That's what Tamiko and I think! You've always had that special, bubbly Sierra charm. And that's what we called it—your charm! But I think Ms. Meadows was right. You're a star in the making. It's your star power."

Tamiko, who looked like the cat that ate the canary, pulled out a piece of chalk and walked over to the specials board. "The reason you've noticed us exchanging 'looks' as you called them is because Allie and I came up with the *perfect* new special for Molly's two weeks ago. It's called the Sierra Sundae! We didn't want to tell you about it, because we wanted to save it as a celebration after you won the Who's a Star? tryouts."

"A Sierra Sundae?" I repeated, shocked.

"We thought you'd win for sure, because we had no idea how many people would try out . . . ," Allie said hesitantly.

Then Tamiko jumped back in. "And then were worried when you *didn't* make it, because we didn't want the idea for the special sundae to hurt your feelings. . . ."

Tamiko and Allie both paused and looked at me. I was so floored, it took me a second to realize that they were worried I wouldn't like the idea. "I love it! I'm just really surprised! Thank you!" I said, beaming at my BFFs.

"Good! Now that you were on TV and that lady said all those nice things about you, it's perfect!" Allie jumped up and down and squealed. "I'm going to make a Sierra Sundae now to put out on social media."

Tamiko reached up with her chalk and wrote, "Who's a Star? Ask about our new Sierra Sundae!" on the board, using her beautiful, curly handwriting and adding tons of little yellow stars.

I couldn't believe it. I had been stressing out about my friends' looks, and about not having an idea to present to Mrs. Shear. But the big secret my friends had been keeping from me was that they'd come up with an ice cream special—*about me*! Allie was scooping and shaping and working her magic, and Tamiko put on some music. When Allie was done, she handed me an absolutely beautiful creation—it was a sundae with a star-shaped cookie on top, and plenty of our signature sprinkles.

"The ice cream flavor is Star Anise, because we think you're a star!" Allie said.

"We're so proud of you," Tamiko added.

I had tears in my eyes, and I knew I had to record this moment. I took a picture of the sundae and sent it to my parents and Isa and my bandmates. Then I grabbed an eraser and Tamiko's chalk and rewrote what she'd written on the board.

"Each and every one of us is a star! Try our new Star Sundae today and reach for your dreams!"

"That's perfect," said Allie. "I love it!"

"It's amazing. Maybe you should be the marketing person instead of me, Sierra," Tamiko joked.

Then Tamiko took one of her fancy pictures of the sundae, using all the special photo filters, and posted it on Molly's social media accounts, with the blurb **We are all STARS! Come try our new Star Sundae!**

Business started to pick up then, and some of our regular customers came in. A few had seen the promo for the singing contest and congratulated me. And then, just when the line we'd had for more than a half hour was starting to get under control, my parents and Isa came in, followed by the rest of the Wildflowers.

"Sierra!" my bandmates yelled. "You're a star!"

"Anyone can be a star here at Molly's," I said. "Just try our new Star Sundae!"

Everyone in my family ordered the new special, and so did Kasey and Tessa from my band. But Reagan said she didn't like the taste of star anise.

"It tastes like licorice, which I also don't like," she said. "But I'm in the mood for some plain old vanilla. I'd like a double scoop of that, please."

"Coming right up!" said Allie. "We don't keep it out here in the case, because it's not as popular as our more unusual flavors. But we have some in the back."

Allie disappeared backstage while I waited on new customers and chatted with my family and friends. It was turning out to be one of the best days at work I'd ever had.

It was funny how things worked out sometimes. I had thought that the only positive outcome of auditioning for the singing contest would be to make it onto the show and be a finalist. But instead the contest had brought me much closer to my twin sister, shown me how much my friends cared about me, and given me the confidence in my abilities to keep singing, knowing that maybe I *did* have a future in music someday.

And I'd gotten all of that from a contest that *hadn't* picked me! Life was pretty amazing sometimes.

"*Psst* . . . Sierra."

Allie was whispering at me from the doorway to the back of Molly's. By the look on her face, I could tell that something was wrong.

I walked over to her and said quietly, "What is it?"

"We're out of vanilla! I can't believe it. Mom used it up yesterday when she was trying out a new flavor. You know how I hate telling a customer we're out of something . . . especially vanilla!"

Allie looked mortified. We had all these customers in the store, and they would hear her tell Reagan that we didn't have a basic flavor. Mrs. Shear would be disappointed too. She liked every customer to be 100 percent happy when they left her store.

Tamiko looked over at us urgently from the cash register. That was normally my job, so I could tell she was stressed and unhappy that I'd left her there. Her eyes said, *Hurry back, please!*

"There's only one thing you can do," I told Allie. "You're going to have to beautiful-oops it! Make her a double scoop of the Elderberry Flower, and put a load of crazy toppings on it, and call it our other new special . . . the Wildflower!"

Allie's face broke into a huge smile. "Right! Of

course! I'll beautiful-oops it, just like you did the other day. Great idea!"

Allie got to work, and when she handed the cone to Reagan, she said, "I know you asked for vanilla, but this is a custom cone just for you. It's called the Wildflower!"

Reagan's face lit up like a sky full of fireworks. There really is something magical about ice cream. Just the right flavor can change your day from a good one to a spectacular one. And it has the power to keep friendships going strong.

"Don't forget your sprinkle of happy," I said, adding some multicolored sprinkles to her cone.

It was such a nice afternoon that everyone stayed and ate at the tables outside or milled around inside the store, talking. Allie, Tamiko, and I were busy, but so happy to be together with our friends and family there.

"I think Molly's is my favorite place in the world," said Allie, sighing with contentment.

"Me too," said Tamiko.

"Me three," I agreed. "Sprinkle Sundays sisters forever!"

Still Hungry?
Here's a taste of the first book in the

series, *Hole in the Middle.*

Donuts Are My Life

My grandmother started Donut Dreams, a little counter in my family's restaurant that sells her now-famous homemade donuts, when my dad was about my age. The name was inspired by my grandmother's dream to save enough money from the business to send him to any college he wanted, even if it was far away from our small town.

It worked. Well, it kind of worked. I mean, my grandmother's donuts are pretty legendary. Her counter is so successful that instead of only selling donuts in the morning, the shop is now open all day. Her donuts have even won all sorts of awards, and there are rumors that there's a cooking show on TV that might come film a segment about how she started Donut Dreams from virtually nothing.

My grandmother, whom I call Nans—short for Nana—raised enough money to send my dad to college out of state all the way in Chicago. But then he came back. I've heard Nans was happy about that, but I'm not because it means I'm stuck here in this small town.

So now it's my turn to come up with my own "donut dreams," because I am dreaming about going to college in a big, glamorous city somewhere far, far away. Dad jokes that if I do go to Chicago, I have to come back like he did.

No way, I thought to myself. Nobody ever moves here, and nobody ever seems to move away, either. It's just same old, same old, every year: the Fall Fling, the Halloween Hoot Fair, Thanksgiving, Snowflake Festival, New Year's, Valentine's Day and the Sweetheart Ball . . . I mean, we know what's coming.

Everyone makes a big deal about the first day of school, but it's not like you're with new kids or anything. There's one elementary school, one middle school, and one high school.

Our grandparents used to go to a regional school, which meant they were with kids from other towns in high school. But the school was about forty-five minutes away, and getting there and back was a big pain, so they eventually decided to keep everyone at the high school here. It's a big old building where my dad went to school, and his brother and my aunt, and just about everyone else's parents.

Some kids do go away for college. My BFF Casey's sister, Gabby, is one of them. She keeps telling Casey that she should go to the same college so they can live together while Gabby goes to medical school, which is her dream. It's a cool idea, but what's the point of moving away from everything if you just end up moving in with your sister?

Maybe it's that I don't have a sister, I have a brother, and living with him is messy. I mean that literally. Skylar is ten. He spits globs of toothpaste in the sink, his clothes are all over his room, and he drinks milk directly from the carton, which makes Nans shriek.

My grandparents basically live with us now, which is a whole long story. Well, the short story is that my mother died two years ago. After Mom died, everyone was a mess, so Nans and Grandpa ended up helping out a lot. Their house is only a short drive down the street from us, so it makes sense they're around all the time.

Even their dog comes over now, which is good because I love him, but weird because Mom would never let us get a pet. I still feel like she's going to come walking in the door one day and be really mad that there's a dog running around with muddy paws.

My mother was an artist. She was an art teacher in the middle school where I'm starting this year, which will be kind of weird.

There's a big mural that all her students painted on one wall of the school after she died. The last time I was in the school was when they had a ceremony and put a plaque next to it with her name on it. Now I'll see it every day.

It's not like I don't think about her every day anyway. Her studio is still set up downstairs. It's a small room off the kitchen with great light. For a while none of us went in there, or we'd just kind of tiptoe in and see if we could still smell her.

Lately we use it more. I like to go in and sit in her favorite chair and read. It's a cozy chair with lots of pillows you can kind of sink into, and I like to think it's her giving me a hug. Dad uses her big worktable to do paperwork. The only people who don't go in are Nans and Grandpa. Dad grumbles that it's the one room in the house that Nans hasn't invaded.

Sometimes I catch Nans in the doorway, though, just looking at Mom's paintings on the walls. Mom liked to paint pictures of us and flowers. One wall is covered in black-and-white sketches of us and the other is this really cool, colorful collection of painted flowers with some close up, some far away, and some in vases. I could stare at them for hours.

I remember there used to be fresh flowers all over the house. Mom even had little vases with flowers in the bathrooms, which was a little crazy, especially since Skylar always knocked them over and there would be puddles of water everywhere.

Sometimes when I had a bad day she'd make a special little arrangement for me and put it next to my bed. When she was sick, I used to go out to her garden and cut them and make little bouquets for her.

I'd put them on her night table, just like she did for me. Nans always makes sure there are flowers on the kitchen table, but it's not really the same.

Grandpa and Nans own a restaurant called the Park View Table. Locals call it the Park for short. They don't get any points for originality, because the restaurant is literally across from a park, so it has a park view. But it seems to be the place in town where everyone ends up.

On the weekends everyone stops by in the mornings, either to pick up donuts and coffee or for these giant pancakes that everyone loves. Lunch is busy during the week, with everyone on their lunch breaks and some older people who meet there regularly, and dinnertime is the slowest. I know all this because I basically grew up there.

Nans comes up with the menus and the specials, and she's always trying out new recipes with the chef. Or on us. Luckily, Nans is a great cook, but some of her "creative" dishes are a little too kooky to eat.

Nans still makes a lot of the donuts, but Dad does too, especially the creative ones. Donut Dreams used to have just the usual sugar or jelly-filled or chocolate, which were all delicious, but Dad started making

PB&J donuts and banana crème donuts.

At first people laughed, but then they started to try them. Word of mouth made the donuts popular, and for a little while, people were confused because they didn't realize Donut Dreams was a counter inside the Park. They instead kept looking for a donut shop.

My uncle Charlie gives my dad a hard time sometimes, teasing him that he's the "big-city boy with the fancy ideas." Uncle Charlie loves my dad, and my dad loves him, but I sometimes wonder if Uncle Charlie and Aunt Melissa are a little mad that Dad got to go away to school and they went to the state school nearby.

My dad runs Donut Dreams. Uncle Charlie does all the ordering for food and napkins and everything you need in a restaurant, and Aunt Melissa is the accountant who manages all the financial stuff, like the payroll and paying all the bills. So between my dad, his brother, and his sister, and the cousins working at the restaurant, it's a lot of family, all the time.

My brother, Skylar, and I are the youngest of seven cousins. I like having cousins, but some of them think they can tell me what to do, and that's five extra people bossing me around.

"There's room for everyone in the Park!" Grandpa likes to say when he sees us all running around, but honestly, sometimes the Park feels pretty crowded.

That's the thing: in a small town, I always feel like there are too many people. Maybe it's just that there are too many people I know, or who know me.

Right after Mom died I couldn't go anywhere without someone coming up to me and putting an arm around me or patting me on the head. People were nice, don't get me wrong, but everyone knows everything in a small town. Sometimes I feel like I can't breathe.

Mom grew up outside of Chicago, and that's where my other grandmother, her mother, still lives. I call her Mimi. We go there every Thanksgiving, which I love. I remember asking her once when we were at the supermarket why there were so many people she didn't know. She laughed and explained that she lived in a big town, where most people don't know each other.

It fascinated me that she could walk into the supermarket and no one there would know where she had just been, or that she bought a store-bought cake and was going to tell everyone she baked it. No one was peering into her cart and asking what she was making for lunch, or how the tomatoes tasted last week. Nans always wonders if Mimi is lonely, since she lives by herself, but it sounds nice to me.

Everyone in our family pitches in, but I officially start working at Donut Dreams next week for a full shift every day, which is kind of nice. I'll work for Dad. He bought me a T-shirt that says THE DREAM TEAM that I can wear when I'm behind the counter.

We have a couple of really small tables near the counter that are separate from the restaurant, so people can sit down and eat their donuts or have coffee. I'll have to clean those and make sure that the floor around them is swept too.

Uncle Charlie computerized the ordering systems last year, so all I'll have to do is just swipe what someone orders and it'll total it for me, keep track of the inventory, and even tell me how much change to give, which is good because Grandpa is a real stickler about that.

"A hundred pennies add up to a dollar!" he always yells when he finds random pennies on the floor or left on a table.

Dad will help me set up what we're calling my

"Dream Account," which is a bank account where I'll deposit my paycheck. I figure if I can save really well for six years, I can have a good portion to put toward my dream college.

So we're going to the bank. And of course my friend Lucy's mom works there. Because you can't go anywhere in this town without knowing someone.

"Well, hi, honey," she said. "Are you getting your own savings account? I'll bet you're saving all that summer money for new clothes!"

"Nope," said Dad. "This is college money."

"Oh, I see," she said, smiling. "In that case, let's make this official." She started typing information into the computer. "Okay. I have your address because I know it. . . ." She tapped the keyboard some more.

See what I mean? Everyone knows who I am and where I live. I wonder if people at the bank know how much money we have too.

After a few minutes, it was all set up. Afterward Dad showed me how to make a deposit and gave me my own bank card too.

I was so excited, not only because I had my own bank account, which felt very grown-up, but because the Dream Account was now crossed off my list, which meant I was that much closer to making my dream come true. I was almost hopping up and down in my seat in the car.

"You really want to get out of here, don't you?" asked Dad, and when he said it, it wasn't in his usual joking way. He sounded a little worried, and I immediately felt bad. It wasn't as if I just wanted to get away from Dad.

"You know," he said thoughtfully, "I get it."

"You do?" I asked.

"Yeah," he said. "I was the same way. I was itchy. I wanted to go see the big wide world."

We both stared ahead of us.

"I don't want to go to get away from you and Skylar," I said.

Dad nodded.

"But think of Wetsy Betsy."

Dad looked confused. "Who is Wetsy Betsy?"

"Wetsy Betsy is Elizabeth Ellis. In kindergarten she had an accident and wet her pants. And even now, like, seven years later, kids still call her Wetsy Betsy. It's like once you're known as something here, you can't shake it. You can't . . ." I trailed off.

"You can't reinvent yourself, you mean?" asked Dad.

"Exactly!" I said. "You are who you are and you can't ever change." I could tell Dad's mind was spinning.

"So who are you?" he asked after a few more minutes.

"What?" I asked.

"Who are you?" Dad asked. "If Elizabeth Ellis is Wetsy Betsy, then who are you?"

I took a deep breath. "I'm the girl whose mother died. I sometimes hear kids whisper about it when I walk by."

I saw Dad grimace. I looked out the window so I wouldn't have to watch him. We stayed quiet the rest of the way home.

We pulled up into our driveway and Dad turned off the car, but he didn't get out.

"I understand, honey. I really do. I understand dreaming. I understand getting away, starting fresh, starting over. But wherever you go, you take yourself with you, just remember that. You can start a new chapter and change things around, but sometimes you can't just rewrite the entire book," he said.

I thought about that. I didn't quite believe what he was saying, though. In school they were always nagging us about rewriting things.

"But you escaped," I said. "And then you just came back!"

"Well, you escape prison. I didn't see this place as a prison," Dad said. "But Nans as a warden, that's ..." He started laughing. "Seriously, though, I left because I wanted an adventure. I wanted to meet new people and see if I could make it in a place where everyone didn't care about me and where I was truly on my own. I never had any plans to come back, but that's how it worked out."

"So why did you move back here?" I asked.

"Because of Mom," said Dad. "She loved this place. I brought her here to meet everyone and she didn't want to leave."

"But Mimi didn't want her to move here," I said, trying to piece together what happened.

I had always thought it was Dad who wanted to move back home. Mom and Dad met in college. She lived at school like Dad did, but Mimi was close by, so she could drive over for dinner. Mom and Dad hung out at Mimi's house a lot while they were in college.

"Noooo," Dad said slowly. "Mimi wasn't too thrilled about Mom's plan. She didn't really understand why Mom would want to move out here, so far from her family, and especially where there weren't a lot of opportunities for artists."

"So she changed her mind?" I asked.

I never remembered Mimi saying anything bad about where we lived, but Dad would always tease her, saying, "So it worked out okay, didn't it, Marla?"

She came to visit twice a year and always seemed to have a good time. "It's a beautiful place to live," she would say, smiling.

"Well," said Dad. "It took Mimi a while to change her mind. But she saw how happy Mom was and how much everyone here loved Mom, so she was happy that Mom was happy. That's the thing about parents. They really just want their kids to be happy, even if they don't understand why they do things. If you decide to move away from here, I'll miss you every day, but if that's what you want to do and that's what makes you happy, then I will be there with the moving truck."

"So if I tell you I want to move to Chicago for college, you'll be okay with that?" I asked.

"If you promise to come home and visit me a lot," said Dad, grinning.

"Deal!" I said.

"I love you," said Dad.

"I love you back," I said.

"Okay, kiddo, let's go in for dinner. Nans goes mad when we're late."

"Dad, isn't it correct to say that Nans gets angry? Because, like, animals go mad but people get angry."

"In that definition, Lindsay, I think that is an entirely correct way to categorize your grandmother when you are late for dinner. She gets mad!"

I giggled and opened the car door.

"Ready, set, run to the warden!" said Dad, and we raced up to the house, bursting with laughter.

First Day of Work

The plan was that I'd start working at Donut Dreams two weeks before school started. That way I'd get into my regular routine and not have to adjust to a job at the Park and a new school at the same time. For the school year, I'll work after school two days a week and one day on the weekends.

But since much of the waitstaff take vacations at the end of the summer, it was all hands on deck, according to Grandpa, and the whole family was taking full-day shifts at the restaurant.

Mornings were always way complicated because things start early in the restaurant business. Even if the Park didn't open until six thirty in the morning, that meant everyone, including the cooks, the busboys, and the waitresses, got there by five o'clock to start prepping the food, brewing coffee, sorting the daily bread deliveries, and making sure the ovens were on.

Since we own Donut Dreams, everyone just assumes that we eat donuts at every meal, and that they're stacked everywhere in our house. But we actually eat like everyone else, and Nans only lets us have donuts on the weekends, just like Mom did.

So Monday morning I put on my Dream Team T-shirt and got downstairs early. Nans already had my fruit and juice at my place at the table. Since she got up early to make the donuts, by the time Skylar and I got up, she joked that she should be making lunch. Dad had to be at the restaurant early in the morning, so after Mom died, Nans was the one who came back home from the restaurant to stay with us when Dad had to leave.

Nans was making me scrambled eggs and I was surprised to see Skylar, still in his pj's, eating his cereal.

"What are you doing up?" I asked. "It's not like you have to go to work today."

"Nans woke me up," he whined. "We have to drive you to work. So even if I don't have to go to work, I still have to get up."

"You can get in the car in your pajamas!" Nans said, exasperated. "I just can't leave you here alone while I run Lindsay to work!"

Skylar rolled his eyes. "Well, can I at least get a donut while we're there?"

Nans sighed. "Sure," she said with a grin. "On Saturday."

It probably seems weird to eat breakfast before you go to work in a restaurant, but working in a restaurant is hard, and you don't get a lot of breaks. It's not like you can stuff snacks in your apron pockets either. You're on your feet the whole time and running around, and you can barely sip a drink, let alone eat. During slow times the staff will grab a plate in the kitchen, but as soon as you have a customer you have to put it down, so no one ever has a leisurely burger or anything.

Nans jingled her keys, and Skylar sighed loudly and pushed back his chair. I took one last look in the mirror before we left, and then Nans drove down the curvy road toward the restaurant.

I could ride my bike to work, especially in nice weather, but Mom would never, ever let us ride on Park Street. She said people went too fast around the curves.

It's kind of weird that even though Mom died, some of her rules are still here, and nobody has tried to get rid of them. At first we did things like staying up really late because everyone was so distracted, and nobody seemed to notice. Plus, there were, like, hundreds of people at the house and stopping in at all hours.

But one night at dinner, Dad said, "Okay, life as we know it is going to be very different, but there are ground rules that stay the same."

After that we had bedtimes and regular meals and all the old rules seemed to kick back in.

When we pulled up to the restaurant, it was six fifteen. You could tell Nans was torn, because she wanted to go in and check things out and get a few things done in the office, but Sky was scowling.

Nans glanced in the back seat. "Sky, do you want to go say hi to your dad?"

But before he could answer, Dad came bounding out of the restaurant. "A fine family morning!" he bellowed, smiling at me. "Look at this wonderful employee on her first day at Donut Dreams!"

He actually looked really proud, and I kind of blushed a little.

"She's going to be spectacular, as always!" said Nans, smiling.

"And I get to see my boy!" said Dad, reaching in to give Sky a squeeze.

"I had to get up early," Skylar whined.

"Good practice for when school starts!" said Dad. "And since you made the very big effort of getting into the car, I have a little treat for you." He handed Skylar a bag.

"Donuts!" screamed Skylar, and Dad laughed.

"First-day-of-work exception," Dad said. "Don't get too used to it!" He gave Skylar a kiss on the head and added, "Have fun at camp!"

Then he turned to me and opened the car door. "And you, my dear, are mine for the day. Let's get to work!"

My cousin Kelsey was also working behind the counter at Dreams, and she gave me a quick wave when I came in.

Kelsey and my other four cousins all work at the Park and Dreams. Kelsey is only older than me by a month and a half, but she always tells people I'm her younger cousin.

"You know what to do?" asked Kelsey.

I nodded and slipped behind the counter with her and put on an apron. Dad was talking to the manager of the restaurant about something, so I turned around and stared at the rows of donuts, making sure they were all lined up and that the shelves were clean.

When Mom was alive I went home right after school, but after she died, Dad would pick Skylar and me up and bring us to the restaurant so we could be near him. We'd hang out at a table and do our homework or color for a few hours before Nans would take us home for dinner. I had watched the counter at Dreams for a few years, so now I knew exactly what had to be done.

If you look around, a restaurant is kind of a fascinating place. It's usually busy—if it's a good restaurant, that is—and there are people sitting and talking about stuff, and if you pay attention, you can learn a lot. And most people don't stop talking when someone comes over to the table. So even if I helped clear a table or dropped off a glass of water, I could really get an earful. That's what I loved most, picking up little pieces about people that you wouldn't normally know.

Grandpa loves to go around and talk to everyone,

and he stops and chats with the regulars, especially the ones at the counter in the morning. He knows everything that was going on in town, but he never spilles it to any of us, which drove Mom crazy.

"Oh, come on," she'd say. "I know they were probably talking about it at the Park. What's the dirt?"

And he would just smile and shake his head and say, "I just pour the coffee. What do I know?"

But Grandpa never misses a beat, so you have to be on your toes. I once saw him correct people for not properly wiping down a table, or not setting it right, or sloshing a glass of water when they put it down.

I know that he likes things tidy, which is hard when you sell donuts, because some of them have sprinkles or are crumbly. So when you lift them off the tray, you get crumbs everywhere—on the shelf, on the floor, and sometimes on the counter.

At Dreams there's a lot of wiping and sweeping, because if Grandpa sees sprinkles all over the glass counter, he won't be pleased. He'll say, "Is that counter eating those sprinkles?" So the first thing I did was wipe down the counter, which was already clean.

"Ugh," whispered Kelsey, "it's the East twins."

The East twins were running up to the case and

putting their fingers all over the glass front. The two boys were adorable, but every time they came in, they made a huge mess.

"Hi, Mrs. East," said Kelsey. "What can we get you today?"

Mrs. East always looked like she'd just run through a windstorm. There were always papers coming out of her bag, and her clothes were usually wrinkled or stained.

But she was really nice, and after Mom died she made us a lot of dinners and brought them over. She even came over with a picnic lunch one day for me and Sky and took us to the park.

"Oh, let me get the boys settled here," she said, lifting them into chairs. "Jason, please stop hitting your brother!"

"That one, that one!" the boys started yelling, waving their little hands at the donuts.

"Boys!" said Mrs. East. "Use your manners! And Christopher, stop screaming!"

The boys scrambled off their chairs and ran back to the counter. Luckily, there was no one else waiting, because it took them a full ten minutes to choose their donuts.

I had one hand over the chocolate iced one when Christopher yelled, "No, no, no, not that one!" and I had to move my hand around the shelf until it was hovering over the "right" one.

"Thank you," said Mrs. East. "You girls are amazingly patient! And I'm more frazzled today than usual. We just got back from vacation with my mom, and even though we love them, moms can be such a pain sometimes. Right, girls?"

She looked up as she was handing us the money for the donuts and froze. Her eyes went wide as she looked at me, remembering, and then her hand flew over her mouth.

Kelsey shifted from foot to foot nervously.

This happens a lot. People will say things and then be really scared that they said the wrong thing in front of you. Before Mom died, even when she was sick, all of a sudden everyone was really careful about what they said around me. For a month after Mom died, my friends wouldn't even talk about their moms in front of me.

I talked to Aunt Melissa about it, because she was who I went to for a lot of stuff these days.

"Honey, people are trying to be considerate. But

sometimes you have to help them, too," Aunt Melissa told me.

Poor Mrs. East looked a little like she might cry. Kelsey looked at me expectantly.

"Yeah, you should hear Kelsey complain about Aunt Melissa," I joked.

Kelsey opened the cash drawer and smiled. "Yeah, but she's got nothing on Nans, and you basically live with Nans."

We laughed, but Mrs. East still stood there, silent. I could tell she still felt awful.

"That'll be five fifty, please," said Kelsey, and Mrs. East suddenly looked down and realized she still had the donut money in her hand.

"Oh thank you, honey," she said.

She took the donuts to the boys, who shoved them into their mouths in five seconds flat. Then she walked back over and grabbed some extra napkins.

"Sometimes you take things for granted," she said to me, I guess as an apology. "How was your summer, Lindsay? You excited for your first day at Bellgrove Middle School? Oh and the big Fall Fling is soon, right? Did you do any dress shopping this summer?"

Fall Fling is, I guess, a big deal. It's the fall dance at

the middle school, and everybody goes. I think they go because there's not much else to do, but kids start talking about it around the Fourth of July.

My BFF, Casey, had already started looking online for a dress, and she's been poking me to go shopping. The thing is that shopping for school is a little weird these days. Usually Aunt Melissa takes me and Kelsey to the mall that's an hour and a half away and we stock up, or we just order stuff online.

"I'm not ready to start thinking about school," I said. "It's still summer!"

"You're right!" laughed Mrs. East. "You enjoy every last drop of summer!"

Then she went over to try to wipe the boys' faces, which were covered in donut icing. It was also in their hair.

"So did you pick out a dress yet?" I asked Kelsey.

"Not yet," she said. "I found a few online that Mom said she'd order so I can try them on. Here, I'll show you."

She grabbed her phone from behind the counter, which was a big no-no. Grandpa did not let anyone have a phone when they were "on the floor," which meant out in the open in the restaurant.

Legendary IRELAND

'The hunger that we feel at the loss of contact with the natural world and its ancient stories is not a physical one, but a kind of spiritual and emotional starvation. Yet feeding this hunger may involve nothing more difficult than walking out into the landscape and looking at it with the eye of the imagination. The power of the human capacity to imagine, to see beyond, reaches us through century after century, and draws us again and again into the indivisible trinity of story, place and people. A landscape will survive as long as there are people to love it, and a story is never quite over as long as there are people to tell it.'

THE AUTHOR

EITHNE MASSEY was born in Dublin, studied at
University College Dublin and the National University of
Ireland, Maynooth, and currently works as a librarian.
Previous publications include short stories and a study of
Prior Roger Outlaw of Kilmainham, a Hospitaller who played
a key role in the Kilkenny Kyteler witchcraft case. Having
travelled all around Ireland, north and south, Eithne
Massey blended her interests in mythology and the old
and secret places of Ireland to create a vivid and original
portrayal of the Celtic sites and their legends.

THE PHOTOGRAPHERS

JACQUES LE GOFF was born in Paris but has lived in
Ireland for the past twelve years. His lifelong interest in
the art of photography and his love of the Irish
countryside were the impetus behind his involvement in
this publication – a decision made before he discovered
that the author possessed no navigational skills whatsoever
and was as likely to lead him, and his dog Jess, into the
middle of a bog as to the site of an ancient monument.

PIP SIDES specialises in black and white photography.
He also employs infra-red photographic film which lends
a ghostly romantic effect to his studies of what he terms
'spiritual Ireland': its castles, stone circles, burial tombs
and natural landscape. Pip's work can be viewed at his solo
exhibitions, in his own gallery in the Buttermarket Craft
& Design Centre, Enniskillen, or online at:
www.pipsides photography.com
A native of Cavan, Pip divides his time between
his studio in Enniskillen and his retreat in west Clare.

Legendary
IRELAND

A Journey through Celtic Places and Myths

EITHNE MASSEY

THE UNIVERSITY OF
WISCONSIN PRESS

The University of Wisconsin Press
1930 Monroe Street
Madison, Wisconsin 53711

www.wisc.edu/wisconsinpress/

5   4   3   2   1

A Cataloging-in-Publication record for this book is available from
the Library of Congress
ISBN 0-299-19800-6 (cloth)

First published by The O'Brien Press Ltd, Dublin, Ireland

Editing, typesetting, layout and design: The O'Brien Press Ltd
Front cover photograph: Grange Stone Circle, Lough Gur,
County Limerick by Pip Sides.
Back cover photograph: The *Lia Fáil*, Tara, County Meath,
courtesy of The Irish Image Collection

Printing: L.E.G.O. Spa, Italy

This book is for my parents, William and Eileen Massey

Acknowledgements

The author would like to thank the Head of the Department of Irish Folklore, University College Dublin for permission to use material from IFC S 575: 172–356 in the section on Lough Muskry. Thanks are due also to the staff of the Department, the staff of the National Library, UCD Library and Dublin City Library Service for their assistance during the research for this project. The staff at O'Brien Press and, in particular, Susan Houlden have my gratitude for their support during the making of LegendaryIreland.

I would like to thank the following people for their hospitality: Frances Crickard, and Davy and Leon Mc Govan in Antrim; the Murphy family in Cork; the Poole family in Donegal and Maureen Massey and Johnnie Doyle in Kerry. Thanks are also due to those who accompanied us on various site visits: Maura Leahy, Catherine Groves, Conall Mac Riocard, and Maureen, William and Donal Massey. I would also like to thank all those unknown people who assisted us on our travels during the past year. We encountered nothing but kindness from Tory Island to Béara. A special thank you is due to Michael Lavelle, and Michael James Gaughan and crew, for getting us to Inis Glora when we thought the cause was lost.

Finally, I would like to thank my sister Fidelma Massey for her perceptive comments on the introduction, and indeed all my family and friends, who helped us out with everything from advice and encouragement to dog-minding during the time this book was written.

Picture Credits

The author and publisher would like to thank the following for permission to reproduce photographs: Dúchas The Heritage Service: p55; The Irish Image Collection: p22, 46, 134, 175, 185; Jacques Le Goff: pp2 (author and self photographs), 18, 84, 99, 112, 139, 146, 158, 191, 197, 203, 211; Peter Mulryan: p39; Pip Sides: pp1, 2–3 (background and self photographs), 6–7, 8, 31, 34, 62, 68, 77, 79, 91, 92–3, 105, 119, 126, 152, 169, 218. The engravings reproduced in this book were taken from Hall's Ireland vols I–III and Grose's Antiquities, Vols I and II. The author and publisher have endeavoured to establish the origin of all images used, and they apologise if any name has been omitted.

Table of Contents

Introduction

Ireland is an island of stories, some of which stretch back over many centuries and have their roots in a tradition that goes back even further. Many of these legends have close associations with particular places. This book retells just some of these legends and links them with the places from which they grew. Place and story are inextricably bound together, and so in the arrangement of the stories I have followed a geographical sequence rather than the traditional division into four cycles.

However, these traditional divisions do provide a useful context in which to gain a sense of the richness of the world of the Celtic legends. The first of these, the Mythological Cycle, tells the tale of the very origins of human life in Ireland. The stories deal with the successive invasions of the island, the great battles between the tribes of the Tuatha Dé Danann (the divine people of the goddess Danu) and the Fomorians, the demonic tribe who competed with them for control of Ireland. They also include the stories of the Sídh (those mythical beings which share human passions but not human sickness and age), such as that of the lovers Midhir and Étaín. The second cycle is the Ulster Cycle, which has at its heart the great epic of the *Táin Bó Cuailgne*, (*The Cattle Raid of Cooley*). The central story of the battle between Conchobhar, king of Ulster, and Maeve, queen of Connacht, encompasses the exploits of the great hero, Cú Chulainn. This cycle includes associated stories such as that of Deirdre. There has been much dispute between scholars about the period in which the Ulster Cycle is set. Conchobhar, King of Ulster, was said to have lived in the first century AD, and the nature of the society portrayed – warrior-like and tribal – seems close to our perceptions of the Celtic Iron Age. But Maeve, for example, has her roots as a goddess figure much further back in time, as do many of the figures woven into the tapestry of the stories. Similar uncertainty surrounds the stories of the Fianna Cycle. These stories deal with Fionn and his hunter companions, including the epic

Opposite:
Statue of Cú Chulainn carrying the dead Ferdia, Ardee, County Louth.

pursuit of Diarmuid and Gráinne. The Fianna Cycle stories take place in the natural world rather than in the courts of the kings, and the 'fian' actually existed as a group of young warriors who lived in small groups outside society. The stories are set at the time of Cormac Mac Airt, who was said to have reigned as high king in the third century AD, but the genesis of the figure of Fionn is probably far older than this. The fourth cycle, known as the Historical Cycle or the Cycle of the Kings, has its stories set in a later period, and some of the characters involved are based on actual historical characters living in a Christian society. However, here, as in all the legends, different worlds and different periods intertwine and historical characters drift in and out of the landscape of legend. It is impossible to establish a clear and consistent chronology, all the more so as the stories were written down many centuries after they had already had a long history as part of an oral tradition. This oral tradition indicates that while extant texts date from no earlier than the eleventh and twelfth centuries, many of the stories were originally written down up to four centuries earlier. The Ulster Cycle tales may have been written down as early as the seventh century and they portray a world that is undeniably pre-Christian in its ethos. Irish literature is the earliest vernacular literature in western Europe and, while scholars have argued over the historical existence of its heroes, and queens and kings, whatever human existence these characters may have had has long been concealed under the layers of a thousand re-tellings. I therefore make no apologies for telling these stories once again in contemporary language, or for the slight liberties I have taken with some of the texts. Every society retells its myths in a slightly different form and the texts we have of the tales are the products of a medieval Christian society where the stories were recorded by clerics who added their own gloss to the versions they wrote.

Having said this, I must add that the amount of loving effort the scribes put into producing and preserving these beautiful manuscripts indicates how important these stories were to their society. And through all their re-tellings the stories retain a distinctive sense of the sacredness of the natural, sensual world; they celebrate it in its entirety, from the joy of the blackbird's song in spring to the cold beauty of winter. St Colmcille is said to have been more frightened by the sound of the axe in his beloved oak grove at Derry than of death and hell, and early Irish lyrics, many written by monks, include many lovely celebrations of the natural world. This close connection with the natural world and with the features of the landscape is also found in the poems of the *Dindshenchas*, the lore of places, which gives us the stories associated with the names of particular places and is a major source for Irish legends. Other important sources are the *Leabhar Gabhála Éireann* – commonly known as *The Book of Invasions*, and the *Leabhar Laighean – The Book of Leinster*, both compiled in the twelfth century, together with the *Leabhar na hUidhre* or *The Book of the Dun Cow* which is late eleventh or very early twelfth century. The original texts are inaccessible to all but Gaelic scholars but it is worth looking at some of the translations to get a sense of the complexity and beauty of the original language.

Although one might hope to be on firmer ground when dealing with the physical places and the man-made structures associated with the stories, in reality the situation is almost as confusing. Structures such as burial chambers and earthen mounds have been neatly classified by archaeologists, but as in the stories, scholarship can classify but cannot fully explain. Some of the sites visited in this book show evidence of settlement as far back as 5,000 years ago, dating from the New Stone Age or Neolithic period; while in other cases the structures are as late as the tenth century. A great many of the sites show evidence of layer upon layer of settlement, and in many cases there is no consensus as to what their purpose was. The only generalisations that can be made are that many of the structures mentioned in the book were used as tombs of one kind or another, or at least show evidence that burials were carried out there, while others seem to be places where the community gathered for defence or celebration.

The categories used by archaeologists divide the period of prehistory into various time spans. These divisions are based on cultural change rather than strictly on timescale, and sometimes vary from place to place – for example, one community might still be living a Neolithic (i.e. New Stone Age) existence while another nearby might be using bronze and have developed corresponding social structures.

Human occupation in Ireland dates from 9,000 years ago when people lived by hunting, fishing and gathering wild plants. This way of life was fairly widespread over Ireland at sites such as Mount Sandel, County Derry, and Ballyferriter, County Kerry. The hunter-gatherers left no traces of field monuments although a controversial date from a passage-grave in Carrowmore in Sligo suggests that they may have begun to build monuments for their dead by the end of the Mesolithic period.

It was the people of the Neolithic period who left their mark on the early landscape, as they settled down to till the land and rear cattle. The great walled fields in north Mayo known as the Céide Fields indicate how they organised their land and how important stock-rearing was to their society. They honoured their ancestors and the dead, and some of the most spectacular Megalithic tombs in Europe are the work of the early farming community in Ireland. There are about 1,450 of these monuments, and many of them became the focus of the lore of places and of the stories which are the subjects of this book. The most famous of them are at the Bend of the Boyne (*Brú na Bóinne*), now a UNESCO World Heritage site with the greatest collection of Neolithic art in Europe. The great cult centre at Tara, County Meath, also has its origins in Neolithic times and has continued for millennia to be a sacred place and a setting for stories of gods and kings. The hundreds of portal dolmens which dot the landscape and are often known locally as *Leaba Dhiarmada agus Gráinne*, are another legacy of the Stone Age builders.

The Bronze Age from *c.*2000BC brought to Ireland's society the use of metal and the beginnings of trade. This was a warlike society, but also a very creative one, which crafted exquisite weapons and jewellery in gold and bronze. Such wealth needs to be defended, so structures such as the great hill-forts began to be built – Dún Aonghusa on the Aran Islands had its beginnings in this period. Standing stones and stone circles were ritual sites for these Bronze Age people and the first *crannógs*, or defensive lake-dwellings were built.

Around 300BC the first Celts arrived in Ireland and ushered in the Iron Age. Hillforts continued to be built and the coast was fringed with defensive promontory forts. Royal sites which also served as great cult and tribal centres were built and are still impressive today. These are at Tara in County Meath, Rathcroghan in County Roscommon, Dún Ailinne in County Kildare and Emhain Macha in County Armagh. They are the buildings of an aristocratic, tribal and violent society which has clear connections with the world portrayed in the *Táin*. This society is one where certain values are held in common, particularly courage, strength, generosity and faithfulness to one's companions and to one's tribe. It is a multi-theistic society, where heroes swear by the gods their people swear by. It is one where music, poetry and rich colours were held in high regard, as were feasting, fighting, racing, hunting and hospitality. In general, however, the attempts that have been made to match the evidence of archaeology or actual historical events with the accounts of the history of Ireland in the *Leabhar Gabhála* or the *Táin* have met with little success. There are no clear patterns and neat correspondences; rather, the world of the stories is a world that is larger inside than it is outside, and where time may be circular as well as linear, possessing the shape-shifting, mutable qualities of the Sídh.

Because of this, a mental shift is needed to enter fully the world of the legends. The stories are the myths created by people – many people over a very long time – from their history and geography, from time and place. Myths have been described as the dreams of the tribe and, like dreams, they take what happens in time – history – and transfigure it. In this world, events may be inconsistent, even contradictory. Because they do not fit into a rational world view, in the light of day their importance can be denied. However, to live without myth is to live without the healing power of dreams and the imagination.

At the same time, the raw material on which the imagination works is rooted in time, in a specific place and in the physical features of the landscape. In the stories, this natural world merges with the world of the collective imagination. So, the emotional power of the stories adds resonance to our encounters with place, and place itself can embody a story in a similar way to that in which the ancient Irish could see a hill as a goddess, or a lake as the embodiment of a god. The word *sídh* can thus mean both a magical being and the mound in the earth where that being lives. A further shift in perception is needed to accept that the same member of the Sídh can have his or her home in many different places – the guardian spirits are very local ones. Many of the people of Ireland, well into the twentieth century, believed that certain trees and wells and hills were under the guardianship of their local otherworld being and each of these enchanted places was protected accordingly. There was an element of fear as well as awe in this relationship, for at certain times, notably at Samhain (Halloween) and Bealtaine (May Eve), you could slip easily from one world into the other.

This feeling of respect for the natural landscape and the ancient remains it holds is under threat. WB Yeats once said that 'places may begin to seem the only hieroglyphics that cannot be forgotten', but in present-day Ireland, the letters are being erased from the landscape. Driving through Ireland during the first two years of the new millennium, there were times when it felt as if

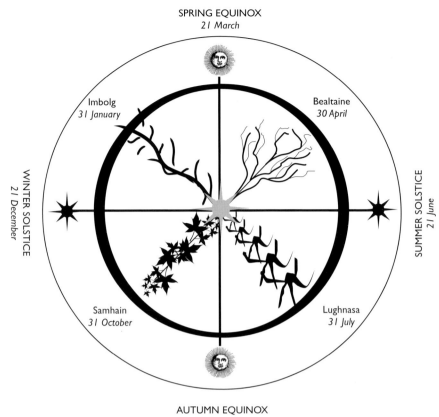

SPRING EQUINOX
21 March

Imbolg
31 January

Bealtaine
30 April

WINTER SOLSTICE
21 December

SUMMER SOLSTICE
21 June

Samhain
31 October

Lughnasa
31 July

AUTUMN EQUINOX
21 September

Above:
Celtic wheel of
the year.

the entire countryside had been placed under siege – home-made posters protested against plans for super-dumps, or satellite masts on historic hills, or road-widening schemes set to destroy ancient sites. Nor was all the violence against the landscape on the part of outsiders; land improvement is a particular threat to earthen monuments such as raths and we saw more than one beautiful place hosting its own private super-dump with its antiquities defaced by mindless vandalism. In some cases too, attempts to 'develop' a site as a tourist attraction had in fact damaged it beyond repair. There is a definite irony in encouraging people to visit sites which at present owe much of their appeal to the fact that they are largely unvisited. However, unless there is a deep communal appreciation of the worth of the places in this book, we can no longer afford the luxury of assuming that they will resist destruction. Recent reports indicate that, in spite of the legislation introduced to protect these monuments, the rate of their destruction is increasing rather than decreasing. In order for these places to survive, those with power over the landscape – whether they are local landowners or government departments – need to become guardians as well as exploiters, and this relationship needs to be supported by the whole community. There is a Greek myth about a character called Erysicthon, the Earth-Tearer. Erysicthon cut down a grove of sacred trees in order to build his banqueting hall. Demeter, goddess of the fertile fields, at first warned him gently against this sacrilege, but when he threatened her with his axe, she cursed him. He became eternally hungry, and never satisfied. In his greed, he ate filth and became thinner and thinner, hungrier and hungrier, poisoned by his own waste.

The hunger that we feel at this loss of contact with the natural world and its ancient stories is not a physical one, but a kind of spiritual and emotional starvation. Yet feeding this hunger may involve nothing more difficult than walking out into the landscape and looking at it with the eye of the imagination. The power of the human capacity to imagine, to see beyond, reaches us through century after century, and draws us again and again into the indivisible trinity of story, place and people. A landscape will survive as long as there are people to love it, and a story is never quite over as long as there are people to tell it.

When the Sons of Míl, one of the early peoples of Ireland, came to its shores, they asked their poet Amairgen to quiet the waves which were preventing them from landing. The poem with which he did this is an invocation of Ireland:

I invoke the land of Ireland:
Much-coursed be the fertile sea,
Fertile be the fruit-strewn mountain,
Fruit-strewn be the showery wood,
Showery be the river of waterfalls,
Of waterfalls be the lake of deep pools,
Deep-pooled be the hill-top well,
A well of tribes be the assembly,
An assembly of kings be Tara,
Tara be the hill of the tribes,
The tribes of the sons of Míl,
Of Míl the ships, the barks,

Let the lofty bark be Ireland,
Lofty Ireland, darkly sung …
I invoke the land of Ireland.

From *Ancient Irish Tales*, Cross and Slover

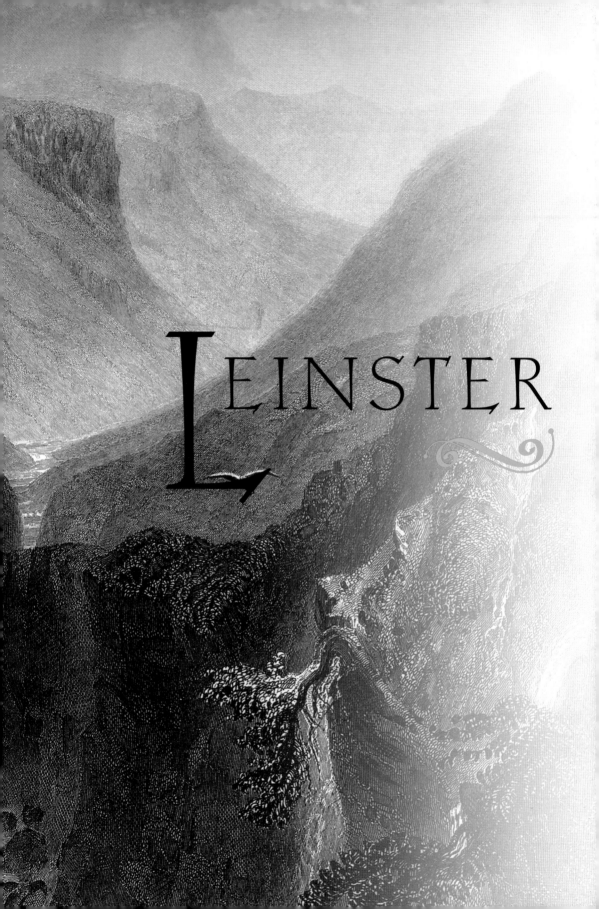

LEINSTER

Howth Head,
BEANN ÉADAIR
Dublin

Pages 16-17:
WH Bartlett's nineteenth-century engraving depicting the 'Head of Glenmalure', County Wicklow.
Opposite:
Aideen's tomb, a portal tomb in the grounds of Howth Castle.

Despite its proximity to Dublin, Howth Head retains its sense of being a place apart, particularly if you choose the time of your visit carefully. The best time to visit Howth is on a weekday when the weather is dull and the place is not full of crowds of people trying to get away from the city. This rocky peninsula, once an island, is steeped in history and legend. The original name for the peninsula, *Beann Éadair*, 'the Peak of Étar', is said to come from the name of the great warrior, Étar, who died for the love of Áine, the goddess of Knockainey. Diarmaid and Gráinne came here, fleeing from Fionn, and Deirdre and the sons of Usna rested here during their flight from the jealous king Conchobhar.

Howth is an attractive village and the harbour still functions as a fishing port, although these days you are more likely to meet a golfer than a fisherman as you

and dejected, a man wandering in a mist. He had left the feasts of Tara and had come to be alone with his thoughts, looking out over the sea where his son, Connla, had been taken away by a beautiful woman of the Sídh many years before. At the time, he had wept, but his wife had consoled him, saying: 'Yes, it is hard to lose a child to the land of the Sídh; but look you, we have yet one son, Art the Lone One, who is as clever and brave and good as ever a child could be, and likely to be a great king when you and I are gone.'

However, now that his wife too had left him, Conn found no comfort in his son's company. Art reminded him too much that strength was with youth and that he himself was no longer young; that there were to be no more great battles and marvellous adventures in love and war. His skills now were those of an old man – diplomacy and wiliness. Conn looked eastwards into the rising sun, as if it could bring him salvation with the daybreak. He thought of his wife's wise words and of her even temper that had saved him from many a hasty action; and he thought, most painfully of all, of her arms around him in their bed, and her small feet wrapping themselves around his legs for warmth during the cold nights of winter. The king blinked through his tears and rubbed his eyes. Coming towards him over the silver waves was a coracle, a coracle that seemed to move without oar or sail, and standing in it was a figure that glowed in the light of dawn. As it came nearer, Conn realised that it was the most beautiful woman he had ever seen.

Bécuma of the Sídh, she of the Fair Skin, smiled her secret smile as she watched the figure on the shore shade his eyes with his hand to watch her approach. She knew who he was, and although she found his son, Art, more to her liking, she had decided that she was in no position to be choosy. She would start with the father and, in time, no doubt the son would come to her. Bécuma had never left herself in want of anything, which was why she had been banished from the Many-Coloured Land; she had betrayed her husband and the choice had been death by fire or banishment to the mortal realm. She had chosen banishment, but her people had warned her not to attempt to enter any of the *sídh* of Ireland, for their doors were closed against her. Her silver coracle brought her to land, and she heard Conn's gasp as she stepped onto the shore, lifting her red satin cloak and grass-green gown out of the water as she did so. Her hair was yellow-gold, her eyes a clear grey, her skin like the first snow of winter. Now she was close enough for him to smell her perfume, which seemed to Conn like the scent of whitethorn on a warm summer's day. He opened his mouth to ask her who she was, but before the words were out of his mouth, she

Left:
Howth Head and Dublin Bay.

said: 'I am Dealbhchaem. The fame of your son Art has spread to the Many-Coloured Land and I have come to seek his love.'

Conn frowned. 'You wish to marry my son then? Indeed, that is not good news to me.'

'Who shall I marry then?' she asked softly.

'Why, none but myself,' said Conn.

Bécuma bowed her head and put her hand in his.

'If it is your wish, so it shall be,' she said. 'But grant me something in return. It would not be right to have Art at Tara so soon after we are wed, for I would wish to forget him. Send him away for a year.'

The king was perturbed. 'I would not wish to banish my own son for no reason,' he said.

Bécuma sighed and raised innocent grey eyes to the king's. Conn paused. Perhaps the maiden was right; his son, so young and strong, might not be a good person to have around them so soon after their marriage.

'It could hurt him to see you in the place of his mother,' he said thoughtfully. 'I will do as you wish.'

The pair travelled to Tara; there, Conn made the order to send his son from the kingdom, not even stopping to bid him farewell. For the first few months, he was deliriously happy with his beautiful young wife. Every day, Bécuma charmed him further. So enchanted was he that at first he did not notice how badly things were going with the land of Ireland. The cows gave no milk, the corn did not grow, the bees made no honey. Blight fell on all of nature so that even the women bore no children and the people began to murmur that there was a curse on the land. The poets and magicians met together and by their arts discovered that their new queen was not, in fact, Dealbhchaem, but Bécuma who had been banished from the Many-Coloured Land for her misdeeds; they told the king that he must send her away.

'I do not care if her name is Dealbhchaem or Bécuma or the Morrigan itself,' said Conn. 'She is my beloved wife and I will not send her away. Find another way to rid the land of this blight.'

So the magicians conferred again, and they came back to the king with the news that if the son of a sinless couple could be found, and his blood mixed with the soil of Tara, the land would be made fertile again. Conn said that he would go on a quest to seek the sinless one. His magicians told him that it might be better to send his son, Art. But Conn had grown so tired of looking at the sad faces and listening to the hungry, crying children who surrounded him that he said angrily: 'No – it is my task to save the land.' He went to Beann Éadair, where he found Bécuma's coracle and went away over the sea. He left the rule of Ireland under the stewardship of Art.

Conn returned, after many months, with a young boy from a magic island; Segda was the child of a sinless couple and the king had tricked him into coming with him back to Ireland, planning to murder him so that the land might prosper once again. However, there was much dissension that a sinless child should suffer for the fault of the king, and, at the last moment, Segda was rescued by his mother, a woman of the Sídh. She appeared before the king and the nobles and said, 'I tell you that it will make no difference whether you kill the boy or not; your evils will not leave you until the cause of evil herself has left.'

At this, the old woman fixed a steely eye on Bécuma, so lovely in her green robe and red-golden crown.

'As long as Bécuma stays in the land, it will have no luck.'

Then she took Segda's hand and they both disappeared.

Ireland continued to suffer, and Conn, though he still was enslaved by Bécuma, grew greyer and more disconsolate. Meanwhile, Bécuma thought more and more of how handsome his son was in comparison, and how nobly he had ruled the land during his father's absence, so that she began to seek him out, to ask him to ride with her, to sing with her, to play chess. However, Art avoided her all he could, and when he looked at her there was nothing but coldness in his eyes, for he saw her as the blight of the land and the destroyer of his father's honour. Things went on thus until, one day, Bécuma came upon Art playing chess with Cromdes the Magician on the lawn before Tara. She demanded a game with Art, for stakes to be chosen after the match. Then she deliberately lost the first game. As a prize, Art demanded from her the wand of the great magician, Cú Roí. With the help of her foster sister, Áine, Bécuma managed to get the wand. When she brought it to Art, she asked, 'Are you impressed, then, with my power?' but he said nothing.

So Bécuma said, 'Well then, sulky boy, I demand a return game.'

Art had no choice but to agree, and, as they played, Áine of the Sídh moved one of his pieces so that he lost.

'I did not move that piece,' he said angrily.

Ardee, Louth
BAILE ÁTH FHIRDIA

The eye of faith is needed to appreciate the connection of Ardee with one of the most moving stories of the *Táin Bó Cuailgne* (*The Cattle Raid of Cooley*), the great epic of the Celtic Iron Age. The tale tells of the efforts of Maeve, queen of Connacht, to gain possession of the Brown Bull of Cooley. Great battles were fought and many heroes died, but at Ardee there is not much to see of the old heroic days, apart from the small River Dee and a few stones marking a ford. However, as the poet Patrick Kavanagh said when he talked of the hills around his home, 'gods make their own importance', and so too do heroes. Ardee lies at the centre of Muirtheimhne, the territory of Cú Chulainn's birth and one that played an important part in the power struggles of the Iron Age.

The stream flowing on the outskirts of this comfortable and prosperous town

was once the site of the epic battle between Cú Chulainn and his foster brother, the great hero of Connacht, Ferdia, who is commemorated in the town's name, *Baile Áth Fhirdia*, 'The Town of Ferdia's Ford'.

It marked one of the boundaries of Ulster – a province cut off from the counties to the south by bogs and mountains – and for many centuries was one of the heartlands of the Gaelic tribes. By the reign of Elizabeth I, Ulster was a separate, impenetrable area, almost immune to the English monarch's control. By this time, however, the town of Ardee had become a town of the Pale – a community which existed well within the borders of English control. The walls, gates and castles of the new settlers had replaced whatever settlement had been there in pre-Norman times.

The county of Louth has preserved much of its medieval heritage, and the castle in Ardee, built in the thirteenth century by Robert de Pippart, has recently been restored. Both James II and William of Orange lodged at the castle on their way to the momentous Battle of the Boyne in 1690.

The ford is easily reached by following the left bank of the river from the Dublin side of the bridge on the N2. Close one eye to block out the modern houses and factories and try to hear the noise of the battle above the roar of traffic going through the town – not an easy task. To be fair to the good people of Ardee, a park has been made on the banks of the river and the fine stone bridge has been carefully preserved, unlike many Irish towns where the demands of traffic have been put before respect for such venerable structures. On the banks of the river, the people of Ardee have even erected a statue of the two heroes of the combat, with Cú Chulainn holding Ferdia in his arms as he sings his lament for his dead companion.

Ardee is also a good central point for touring Louth and neighbouring Meath, including the Boyne Valley complex. Within easy distance lies the village of Slane, with its dramatic approach from the south and its magnificent castle. Other small towns and villages in the vicinity, such as Castlebellingham, demonstrate a palpable sense of pride in their past. These towns hold the echoes of a Norman rather than a Celtic history. The land is good and has been cultivated for a long time; the houses are old and have been in families for generations. If this heritage lacks the dramatic power of the wild heroes of the legends, it is nonetheless equally worthy of preservation.

THE FIGHT AT THE FORD

The curse of Macha had come upon the men of Ulster. In their time of greatest need, they lay helpless on their backs, screaming and writhing in the pains of childbirth as the warrior goddess had prophesied. Only one man was free of it – this was Cú Chulainn, the warrior known as the Hound of Ulster, who though he was still but seventeen was already the greatest fighter the land of Ireland had ever known. The armies of Maeve of Connacht were marching forward, intent on capturing the Brown Bull of Cooley from Conchobhar Mac Neasa of Ulster, so that the queen's herd could be as fine and finer than that of her husband, Ailill. She sent hundreds of men against the hero Cú Chulainn and he killed them all, as effortlessly as a bull flicks away flies on a hot summer's day. Then, loath to lose so many good men, she chose great champions to meet the defender of Ulster in single combat where he held her army at bay at the ford on the River Dee. However, every day her champion was slain, and Cú Chulainn hurled insults at her across the river from where he camped with his charioteer and a small group of followers.

Maeve consulted with her council, and they all spoke with one voice – the only champion capable of defeating Cú Chulainn was Ferdia, who had trained with him at the warrior-queen Scáthach's school in Alba. However, when Maeve called Ferdia to her, he refused point blank to fight with Cú Chulainn, for not only was he the Hound's foster-brother, suckled by the same wet-nurse, long-time sharer of his secrets and his dreams of glory, but

he loved the champion with the love of those who have suffered and fought together, in a bond closer than that of blood. Ferdia remembered their sense of comradeship as they ran wild through the woods in the glory of young freedom, before they took on the warrior's code; he remembered the mock battles that always ended in laughter, and although Maeve promised him gold and jewels and her own ripe body, he shook his head. In desperation, Maeve arranged a great feast. Whole cows were roasted, the finest of boars and the most succulent of deer. There was ale and wine, and Maeve's own special drink, mead – sweet and heavy as the honey from which it was made. Maeve plied Ferdia with good things and turned his head with praise, and finally she said, 'You need not worry about your friend sharing your scruples, Ferdia. I have heard it said that he has mocked you, saying that it would not worry him to skewer you as well as the rest of the champions, and it would take no effort for him to do it.'

Ferdia, fuddled with drink and flattery, shouted out, 'Indeed, then I will fight him and change his tune.'

So Maeve smiled coolly, and, promising him a great brooch and the body of her fair daughter, Fionnabhair, she left him to sleep off his hangover and remember his promise in the cold light of morning.

After all the court had retired to sleep, Fergus Mac Róich lay tossing and turning in his bed. Fergus had joined the Connacht camp because of Conchobhar Mac Neasa's treachery against the Sons of Usna, but he loved Cú Chulainn as a son. Finally, he got up and crept from the camp. He crossed to the other side of the river and warned the Hound that Ferdia was coming against him. Cú Chulainn lamented bitterly that he should be forced to fight his friend, but Fergus said, 'Do not let your affection blind you. Ferdia will be the hardest of your enemies to defeat, for he wears the great skin of horn that shields him from every weapon.'

'And do I not have the *Gáe Bolga*?' said Cú Chulainn proudly. 'The great mace that goes into a man's flesh and splits into thirty darts, punching holes throughout his inside? Who can defeat that?'

And Cú Chulainn went that night to feast and sleep with his wife, Emer, in her fort at Dún Dealgan, so that none should say that he was afraid of the contest on the morrow.

In the pink and gold dawn, the champions faced each other through the mist on the river. They were dressed in their finest armour – the bronze and gold and silver glinted in the sun; their sleek horses whickered in welcome when they saw each other, and their charioteers called greetings over the water. When Ferdia, tall and brown-haired, saw the beloved face of Cú Chulainn, he bowed low, and Cú Chulainn, small and broad and dark, returned his bow.

'Greetings to you, Ferdia,' said the Hound.

'And greetings to you, Hound of Ulster,' said Ferdia.

'How shall we fight today?'

'Let us use the throwing spears and darts,' said Ferdia.

So they fought, each one as skilled as the other. At first, it seemed to them almost like one of the games in Scáthach's training camp. They pitted skill against skill, each one knowing the tricks and feints that the other put forward. However, as the battle became more serious, they began to shout insults at each other. They dredged up all the old, hurtful names from the past …

'You were my little servant, Cú,' whispered Ferdia as he held Cú Chulainn's neck in a vice-like grip. 'My little bed-maker, my little shadow, copying me when I practised my skills, often not able to keep up with me.'

'That was then; this is now; and it was only because you were years older than me,' responded Cú Chulainn furiously, wrenching his neck out of the other's grasp and forcing him onto his knees in the river-bed. 'Now I am the stronger, and you have lost many of your skills and half your strength through drinking mead and sleeping with loose women like Fionnabhair. Did Maeve promise you her? Sure that bitch is promised to every dog in the camp …'

'Is she indeed? Well, there's not so many women will want to sleep with you by the time I am finished with you, you black-visaged squint eye!'

'Ah shut up, bladder breath!'

'Gorse head!'

'Old lard-belly!'

But then Ferdia was wounded, and he caught and ripped open the Hound's arm; and by the time the sun went down, both champions were bleeding and exhausted. As they parted that night, they kissed each other fondly, and Cú Chulainn sent medicines over to the other side of the river to his friend, while Ferdia sent the best food from the Connacht camp to Cú Chulainn. Their horses shared the same paddock and their charioteers sat together at the same campfire. The next morning, the two champions rose and greeted each other across the bank. On this day, Ferdia gave Cú Chulainn the choice of weapons, so that they fought with javelins and spears. And that night too, Ferdia sent food, and Cú Chulainn sent healers to chant incantations over Ferdia, for

their wounds were so severe that salves or medicines could no longer heal them.

On the third day, they fought with swords, with such ferocity that the river stopped in its course, and those who watched from either side of the bank were covered in the blood of the champions as it sprayed from their veins. Most of the watchers fled in terror, and those who stayed could see little, only a whirling cloud of dust and blood, and sharp flames when the swords crashed against one another.

That evening, the two men did not embrace one another, but turned as soon as the sun went down and made their way wearily to their camps. There was no sharing of food or medicines, and the horses and charioteers stayed on opposite sides of the river. In the grey morning, the warriors made no greeting to each other as they watched each other perform feats of arms. Then they moved closer and closer to each other, so that they were fighting hand to hand, and only the charioteers had the courage to stay to watch the flesh and blood fly. They fought in utter silence.

As the evening drew in, they fought more and more furiously, so that their great bronze shields burst as they crashed together; and as this happened, and before Laeg, Cú Chulainn's charioteer, could hand Cú Chulainn another, Ferdia forced his sword into Cú Chulainn's chest, lifting him into the air on its point. He threw him towards the northern bank of the river, shouting, 'Go home for your bone, Dog!'

Laeg, fearing that Cú Chulainn would be defeated, shouted. 'Look you, Cú – he has tossed you like a mother tosses her baby!'

Then the battle fury came upon Cú Chulainn. He called to Laeg to bring the *Gáe Bolga*, and he whirled around with war demons circling him like black crows. Within seconds, the great mace had plunged into Ferdia's chest and pierced through the hide that covered it. He fell to the water, screaming in his last agony.

A moment later, Cú Chulainn, the battle-rage passed, had fallen beside his friend and lifted him in his arms, watching the life fade from his face. Ferdia's charioteer came forward to take the body, but Cú Chulainn dragged it, crawling himself and grievously wounded, onto the Ulster side of the river. The charioteer called, his voice broken in sorrow and shame, 'Is it his weapons and armour you want? Take them then, but leave us the body so that it will not be mocked and shamed by the Ulster army.'

Cú Chulainn looked up from where he lay on the ground, his face twisted with rage and grief: 'Get away from this river before I kill you too, man. Ferdia will be buried with the honour of a prince and a great warrior; I will wash his fair body myself for the ceremony. It is not for the spoils of war I have taken him, but because I need to hold his head in my arms a last time, and a last time tell him how dear he was to me. No one could have had a truer friend or a braver companion. It is to me now as if I have killed a part of myself. I had thought of war as an honourable thing, not this bloody mess, brought on by the whims and greed of the great ones, and turning friend against friend. It seems to me now that every battle I ever fought was nothing – was the game of a child – compared to this one I fought with Ferdia, my beloved brother.'

Cú Chulainn continued to defend Ulster against the armies of Connacht until the Ulster warriors were able to fight once again. For the origin of the Táin, see 'Pillow Talk'; for the end, see 'The Battle of the Bulls'. For the reason behind the sickness of the Ulstermen, see 'Macha's Curse'.

said that a prince brought his bride to the site and told her to look around her – that everything she could see was part of his possessions. Unfortunately, she looked the wrong way, could see only a few feet in front of her, and died of the shock! Not far away, on the grounds of Ballymascanlon Hotel golf course, is one of the finest portal dolmens in Ireland, the 3.6-metre (12-foot) high Proleek Dolmen.

The name Louth is said to come from Lugh, the many-skilled Celtic god who brought the Tuatha Dé Danann victory at the Battle of Moytura. This part of the county is very different from the area around prosperous Ardee, but the people still speak with the same slow musical accent, and still seem to take a long time in considering a basic question such as a request for directions. Perhaps such hesitation is a result of having been so long a people of the borderlands, between North and South, between Celt and Norman, between a world of quiet farms and lovely hills, and one of great heroism and tragic battles.

THE BATTLE OF THE BULLS

The last battle was over. The *Táin Bó Cuailgne*, the long war-tale that poets would recite for many centuries to come, had reached its end. Ulster was victorious over Connacht, although Queen Maeve, devious as ever, still had a trick or two up her sleeve. The smoke of funeral pyres covered the skies over the battlefield of Garach; the air was filled with the stench of burning bodies and the cries of ravens, who called to their comrades that red meat was littered on the battlefield, fresh for the taking. The war goddess Morrigan shrieked high above the smoke, while her sister Badbh took the form of a scald-crow and rejoiced in the mindless carnage that had come upon all who had fought that day. Men had slipped and slid in the blood and gore that covered the green fields; their heads had been cut off them where they lay. Bones and gobbets of flesh lay scattered like bloody stars over the black earth; skulls lay split in pieces; bodies had been dismantled into their component parts; and now arms and legs and feet and hands lay yards from each other, as if they had never been attached to the same living, breathing person. Here and there, a headless torso was sprawled, spitted with spears. It was too soon for those who had been in the battle to feel sorrow, for all anyone wanted to do was to get away from the smell of rotting and burning flesh and the shrieks of those who had not yet met with the mercy of great Donn, the Lord of Death.

Long-faced Maeve had begun her journey back to her palace of Cruachain

Above:
*The Cooley Peninsula,
County Louth.*

at Rathcroghan in the west, defeated by the armies of the north and having had her own life saved only by the mercy of Cú Chulainn. She left widows and orphans wailing behind her and brought back to her people in Connacht news of many deaths, but she walked with a proud step, for had she not managed to take the Donn of Cooley back with her? The night before the final ignominious battle with Conchobhar, Maeve had sent the Donn to Rathcroghan with his fifteen heifers, by hidden ways and through trackless wastes. She had looked around at the battlefield and called it a shame and a shambles, but deep within her heart, she did not feel grief, for she had the bull – the greatest bull in Ireland, perhaps in the history of the world. The storytellers would speak of his prowess for years to come – how his back was broad enough to take thirty lads on it; how he could fill fifty heifers in a day, and, if they did not have a calf by the following morning, they would burst from the power of his seed within them.

As they made their way through the blue hills and brown bogs, Maeve began to hum gently, already planning her revenge on Cú Chulainn. The sun was shining and her head was full of plans to build up her army again. Her husband, Ailill, walking silently beside her, almost tripped over a severed head. It was one left behind from their journey north – one of the thousands of Connachtmen killed by Cú Chulainn. It was now staring at Ailill with empty eye-sockets. From the red hair and the golden torc at the throat, he recognised his sister's son. He turned off the trail and was sick.

Back at Rathcroghan, the bull was led to where the white bull, Finnbheannach, was held within an earthen compound. No one would venture in to feed Finnbheannach, for all through the battle he had been like a wild thing. He was as broad as the Donn of Cooley, though perhaps his horns were not as massive. He had never been defeated by another animal. When the Donn was brought into the stockade, he stood staring in front of him, pawing the ground as if he recognised him.

The two bulls faced each other. Somewhere, deep in their animal brains, each knew the smell of the other. They had been swineherds together many lives before they had taken the form of bulls; through centuries they had battled with each other in myriad different bodies – as fish, as stags, as warriors, as ghosts, as dragons, as maggots together in the one stream, swallowed by a young cow, and so, finally, taking the form of bulls. The people of the court of Cruachain stood around the top of the stockade, waiting to see what would happen. Who knows what goes on in an animal's head? Perhaps after centuries of war, even they become as sick of slaughter as humans. Whatever the reason, the Donn of Cooley went and placed his hoof gently on the horn of Finnbheannach, so that the white bull's head bowed to the ground as if to his master. He stood like that for a long time, and the people grew weary of waiting. Ailill, thinking of the warriors lost, called out: 'Will you not give us something to see, Donn of Cooley? Men have died on both sides because of you.'

At that, the brown one bellowed out and the two beasts locked horns. It was as if a great storm had erupted out of nowhere – the noise like thunder, the earth flying on all sides whipped up by the giant hooves. The bulls crashed through the stockade, killing Bricriu, the satirist who was looking on to judge the fight, and then churned earth under their hooves as, horns locked, they began their battle through the length and breadth of Ireland, leaving lakes dug from the soil and hills raised with their fighting.

There was terror throughout Connacht, for many thought that the world had come to an end. There was no possibility of sleep, because of the noise of the fighting bulls. All who heard it could never forget it, for it seemed as if the sky was filled with the sounds of angry gods bellowing their rage. The battle lasted for a day and a night; finally, at dawn, the people at Cruachain saw the Donn passing with the great body of his rival caught on his horns. However, the Donn himself was sorely wounded, spilling blood with every step he took, leaving hoof prints filled with gore. He staggered into the lake near the *dún* as if to try to wash off the carcass of his rival, but came out with the liver and shoulder blade and loins still caught on his great black horns. It seemed to Ailill's troops that they might now be able to take the bull and kill him, but Fergus Mac Róich, the Ulster warrior who had fled to Connacht when the sons of Usna were killed, roared out: 'The Brown of Ulster is the victor, and half-dead already. All of you leave him in peace and let him go back to his own place now, or be answerable to me.'

And it seemed to all that Fergus's eyes followed him in some deep sorrow as the Donn made his way back towards the north; and that Fergus himself felt like a bull trapped in Connacht, kept in a stock house to service Maeve.

As the bull raged onwards, he dropped parts of Finnbheannach on his journey. The great beast had only one instinct – to get back to his own place, the soft Cooley peninsula with its gentle hills and the fresh smell of the sea. Yet, even when he reached there, his frenzy did not leave him. In his madness, he killed all that stood in his way. Many of those who had survived the battles and famine and sickness, and now thought that quiet times could come again, were crushed underfoot by his hooves. Finally, he reached the place now known as Druim an Tairbh, the 'Back of the Bull'. He turned his face towards the north and rushed into the flank of the mountain before him, as if he thought it was yet another rival to vanquish. But his horns locked into the soil and the rock, and his heart burst in his chest like a nut cracking. He fell to the earth, his spirit leaving his body with a great bellow of rage and pain. It was many days before even the ravens dared to approach his great carcass to feed on the rotting flesh.

Cú Chulainn was finally killed through the machinations of Maeve. At his death, he tied himself to a stone so that he would die upright, facing his enemies.

Tara, Meath

TEAMHAIR

Tara is probably the most famous legendary site in Ireland. Its name, *Teamhair*, means 'Lofty Place'. It is associated with days of glory: with heroes and beautiful women, with great priest-kings who ruled a land that in the legends was always fertile and contented. Yet by the time these legends were being written down by Christian scholars, Tara was already no more than grass-covered mounds. Its glory days were long over and its secrets hidden under the earth. Nonetheless, standing on these mounds and looking over the magnificent views of Meath to all sides, you get a sense of the power of the old kings – for Tara was the heart of all that symbolised royalty and prosperity to the ancient Celts.

Tara is an important location in many of the most important stories of Ireland, including tales of both love and war. Here the kings mated with the goddess of

sovereignty at the beginning of their reign. Here every year on the three days either side of Samhain – the feast of the dead at the Celtic New Year in November – the doors to the other world swung open and here, every third year, a great assembly was held. Here Conn of the Hundred Battles stood on the Stone of Destiny, the *Lia Fáil*, which cried under his foot because he was the rightful king. Here Cormac, the great high king of Ireland, found the path to the realm of Manannán, the god of the sea, and here began the tragic story of Diarmaid and Gráinne, Cormac's daughter who fell in love with Diarmaid at her wedding feast. Here too reigned Niall of the Nine Hostages – tradition says that it was he who brought Patrick to Ireland as a slave. When Patrick returned many years later as a missionary, he defied the power of Tara and King Laoghaire by lighting a fire on Easter Sunday on nearby Slane Hill. Then he and his followers, magically transforming themselves into a flock of deer, made their way secretly up onto the hill of Tara, into the sacred space, and challenged the king's druids to a combat of magical powers. (This transformation is the reason why the prayer 'St Patrick's Breastplate' is also known as 'The Deer's

Cry'.) Patrick's victory gave him the right to preach the gospel in Ireland, and the power of the old ways was weakened forever. The final desertion of Tara is said to have been the result of the place being cursed by a saint.

Tara is entered through a gate leading to the nineteenth-century church which replaced a much older church on the site, and is now used as an interpretative centre. The climb up the hill is a gradual one, the grass kept cropped by sheep. The Fort of the Synods, Ráth na Riogh, Teach Cormac, Ráth Gráinne and Ráth Laoghaire – the names given to the monuments on the hill – date from a later period than the monuments themselves, but the *Lia Fáil* is said to be the same stone which called out when Conn touched it.

Modern excavations have been carefully limited in order to preserve the integrity of the site, but ongoing archaeological surveys reinforce the image of Tara as a hugely important ceremonial site, which by the Iron Age had become associated strongly with royalty. The Mound of the Hostages covers a 4,000-year-old passage grave – the remains of 200 cremations were found here. As in so many places in Ireland, the spiritual power of the site came from its having been considered sacred for thousands of years, and built upon by generation after generation. In historical times, the Uí Néill clan claimed Tara as the site of the high kingship. There are two wells near the site, and an ancient hawthorn tree where people still tie rags as an offering and make their wishes. On the River Odder nearby, King Cormac is said to have built the first mill in Ireland for his mistress, Cernat, to save her the pain of grinding corn when she was carrying his child.

There is layer upon layer of ancient ritual embodied in this landscape, but the feeling of Tara is not of the weight of centuries, but of free air – of a green landscape smiling upwards with the promise of a good summer. Close to the great ceremonial centre of the Boyne, where forces older than human ones hold sway, this is the heart of a civilised, almost courtly, prehistory.

'She was the sacred place on the road of life' – so runs the scholar Edward Gwynn's translation of the *Dindshenchas*, the lore of place. In other poems, Tara is described as the noblest of hills, a rampart of glory and gold, a centre of feastings and battles. There are times, especially at those ancient lynchpins of the Celtic year, the first day of May (Bealtaine) and at Halloween (Samhain), when Tara is still visited by those trying to make a connection with its glorious past. However, most of the time, Tara is a quiet, green hill with a view of stud-farms and lazy cattle, of a blue, hazy distance and a quietness broken, not by the call of the land to its sovereign, but only by the sound of birds singing.

THE MAGIC BRANCH

The great high king of Ireland, Cormac Mac Airt, stood and looked over the fair green of Tara. It was a pleasant prospect on this May morning, for the dawn light changed the pastures to the colour of gold, and a land of plenty stretched before him – a rich, contented land of fat cows and fast horses, of valorous deeds and great hunts. It was a land of sweet music, of songs which celebrated the feats of heroes, but it was also a land full of the quieter music of mill wheels and spinning wheels, of easy prosperity. Cormac had little cause for complaint, for had he not a son growing in strength and courage, and a fair daughter whose gentleness and dignity would make her a fitting wife for any hero? Had he not a clever wife, whose beauty had not faded with the years, and even a small, dark-eyed mistress who asked no difficult questions and let him lie with his head on her lap while she sang to him for hour after hour? Why then was he, in the prime of life and at the height of his power, dissatisfied and weary, as he looked over the flower-covered green? Was it because there were no more battles to fight and no more women to win? He had won them all – he had tasted wine and blood and kisses – and here he stood, watching the sun rise over the lands that lay under his control like some sweetly smiling woman, and wondering why he felt empty greyness in his heart. He stood, stroking his dark beard, wishing for something to which he could not put a name.

Then he heard it – a sound like no other sound he had ever heard, in either the banqueting hall or the forest; a music that seemed to sound in stillness rather then in movement or time, with a sweetness that filled his heart so that he felt it contract in his chest. The music grew louder and he saw a young man coming towards him. He was tall, with golden hair, and he was clad in a purple cloak with green and silver lining that caught the sun and seemed to sparkle as he walked. In his hand, he held a silver branch with three golden apples on it, and as he shook it gently, it seemed that the music came from it. Cormac greeted the stranger courteously.

'Fair youth, you are welcome here to my kingdom. What is your name and station?'

The stranger smiled and shook the branch again, so that all rational thought went from Cormac's head, and he thought only that he would die if he did not have the source of that wonderful music.

'Fair youth,' he addressed the stranger again. 'Tell me what I must give you

Above:
The Lia Fáil, *or
Stone of Destiny at
Tara, which cries
out at the touch of
the rightful king of
Ireland.*

to have that wonderful branch. From where does it come?'

Now the young man spoke, and his voice had the music of the apple-branch in it.

'It comes from the Isle of Apples, from the Pleasant Plain, from the Land beneath the Waves. It comes from the kingdom of Manannán Mac Lir. It is a branch of great power, for when you shake it, everyone who hears it forgets the sorrow of the world in the delight of its music. And you may have it, if you grant me three wishes.'

Cormac did not stop to consider. He said, 'That I agree to; only let me have the branch.'

The stranger smiled and put the branch in the high king's hand. Then he said, 'I will come back to you in a year to ask for my first wish.'

A year later, to the very day, Cormac went out onto the green and saw the youth coming towards him, looking as young and as fine as ever. When he reached Cormac, he said, 'I have come to ask for my first wish.'

'Speak then,' said Cormac, who had had time to consider and was a little nervous of what the stranger might ask.

'I will have your daughter come with me,' said the stranger.

Cormac paled, for he loved his daughter, Ailbe, as pastures love the soft rain after a hot day's sunshine.

'I will give you fields and fine horses and bondmaids. I will give you gold and jewels and the treasures of my palace. Ask me anything, but do not ask for my daughter.'

But the stranger shook his head to all of Cormac's promises, and when he realised that he had no choice, the king called his daughter from the hall and embraced her tenderly, weeping as she left with the stranger.

'I will return next year for my next wish,' said the youth. There was great mourning in Tara until Cormac shook the magic branch, and all sorrow was forgotten.

The next year, Cormac met the stranger again, and this time he asked for his son, which made the king weep bitterly, for he loved his son, Cairbre Lifeachair, as the pastures love the sun after a long winter's cold.

'I will give you all my kingdom,' he said, 'if you will only let my son stay.' But the stranger shook his head, so Cormac sent his son with the stranger, and went back to the manor of Tara, where he and his wife wept long and hard; and all the people of Tara wept, until he shook the branch with the golden apples, and he could no longer hear their weeping.

The third year, the stranger asked of Cormac his wife. The king bent his head and wept, for he loved his wife, Eithne, as the pastures love the sun and the rain together; and he said, 'Take my life; for I have nothing if my children and my wife are gone.'

But again the stranger smiled and shook his head, and said, 'Why do you not use your branch to forget your sorrow?'

Cormac said, 'I will give you back your branch if you will give me back what I love. No magic nor music can heal sorrow and regret – it only makes us forget them for a time. If you will not give me back my family, I will go to your palace and die in the attempt to bring them home.'

The golden-haired man said nothing, but merely smiled and took Cormac's wife's hand to lead her away.

And so Cormac followed the stranger into the mist that formed around him as he left the green of Tara. He walked for many miles, with the stranger striding ahead, leading his wife, and Cormac following, always following, over harsh mountains and rough bog, past fields of rushes filled with golden light, and always southwards into the sun, so that the two figures ahead seemed to walk in a halo of light.

He saw many wonderful sights as he made his journey, for he had stepped across the border into the land of the Sídh. He saw white horses race as easily across the surface of the sea as they would over the plains of Tara. He saw magical islands with castles and herds and brave, noble people. Finally, he came to a beautiful silver house, thatched with the feathers of white birds. In the courtyard outside there was a great fountain, and from it five streams of silver flowed. Over the fountain there were nine hazel bushes and five silver salmon swam in the waters below. A couple sat on high thrones behind the fountain; one was a glorious queen with golden hair and a crown of golden fishes with ruby eyes, and the other was the young man who had led Cormac's wife and children away.

Cormac saluted them and said, 'What is this kingdom, and where am I?'

The queen smiled and said, 'You have come to the Isle of Apples, the Pleasant Plain, the Land of Truth, Cormac of Ireland. This is where your family is; and you should know that they have been safe and happy since the time they came here. It is to them as if they have passed no more than a day with the people of Manannán, Ruler of the Ocean and the lord who sits here beside me.'

Cormac bowed to her; for he knew that he was looking on the great goddess, Áine; and then, turning to the young man, he said, 'Know then, King, that I would return to you this magic branch and all its wondrous music if you would give me back my loved ones. For not all the music in the world can make up for the loss of those who are dear to us. Or if you will not return them to me, I will stay here and give up my kingdom to be with them.'

Then Manannán, who changed as he spoke from a young man to a man of great years and wisdom, bearded and white-haired, and with a crown of prancing silver horses with sapphire eyes, said, 'No, King. Go back to your own place, and learn to be a wise king as well as a powerful one. You have been led here to learn what your next task is, which is to seek true judgement through the last years of your life. Take your family with you, for now you have learned to value them also. I will let you keep the Branch of Sweetness, but I will give you another gift also, the Cup of Truth, which will break in three pieces when three falsehoods are spoken over it, but become whole again when three true things are said.'

Cormac and his family feasted that night with the god and goddess, eating their fill and listening to poets and musicians and talking to each other.

When Cormac awoke the next morning, he found himself on the green outside the ramparts of Tara. The air was full of the scent of cowslips and bluebells, and the sound of small birds singing in the dawn. The wonderful branch was there by his side, and the cup that had stood on Manannán's table; and all his family were with him, each one changed and made wiser by their sojourn in the Isle of Apples. After this time, Cormac became known as Cormac of the Long Beard, one of the greatest kings Ireland had ever known, wise and merciful; and during his reign Ireland was a golden land, rich and peaceful and full of music. For added to the music of spinning wheels and mill wheels and the clarion calls of hunts and quests, the deep music of the king's good judgement was heard in every valley in the land.

And there are those who say that even still, the deep sigh which cows make when they lie down on the grass on a fine summer's evening is one of regret and remembrance for those happy days when Cormac ruled over Ireland.

Newgrange and the Boyne Valley, Meath

BRÚ NA BÓINNE

I f Tara is air and the flight of birds, Newgrange is wood and stone and water. If Tara is the sovereignty of the king, Newgrange is the sacred space far more powerful and more ancient than any sovereign's power. The concentration of great tombs at the bend of the River Boyne in County Meath (*Brú na Bóinne*, 'The Mansion or dwelling Place on the Boyne', also translated as 'The Bend of the Boyne') constitutes one of the most important centres of Neolithic antiquities in Ireland, and indeed in Europe. To reach Newgrange, you move slowly down roads which follow the bends of the river, past old stone farmhouses half-covered in green moss, through a landscape that has been cultivated by man from a time beyond time – a rich land, a quiet people; long before Maeve led her armies towards Ulster in battle for a great bull, the people here herded their cattle quietly, paying homage to the Bóinn, the cow-goddess of the river. The remains at Newgrange are from long before the time of the Celtic warrior society that produced the stories of the *Táin*. Knowth and Newgrange have been dated through excavation to around 2500BC, making them older than Stonehenge, Mycenae or the pyramids of Egypt. The Newgrange site remained sacred, a burial place for pre-Christian kings, and known and honoured at least until Roman times, but at some point after this the secrets of the mounds were lost. Newgrange became part of the possessions of the monks of Mellifont Abbey, a grassy hill for grazing cattle. The great tombs slipped quietly into the quiet land of Meath, and were left without interference until the beginning of the modern age. Then, at the end of the seventeenth century, a local landowner was quarrying stone, and stumbled onto the entrance to the chamber of the great mound at Newgrange.

Since then, the mound has been continuously studied, and, in the middle of the last century, Newgrange was excavated and the exterior reconstructed in line with the evidence available. Now the great mound is a sparkling white quartz-covered circle on the green hillside. Newgrange is one of many mounds in the Brú na Bóinne complex. It is the largest and most dramatic of the tombs, sited on a hill looking down towards the river, with its entrance aligned towards the mid-winter solstice sunrise. Before the archaeologists had discovered the alignment of the roof-box over the entrance to the great passage, situated so that it lights the

Below:
The River Boyne.

furthest recess in the tomb at dawn on the winter solstice, they had been told of a local tradition that held that the rising sun at some point in the year lit those same three spiral stones. The astronomical and engineering skills of a people who lived almost 5,000 years ago have also resulted in a structure that keeps the inner space as dry as a bone and silent as a tomb, where the temperature stays at a steady 10 degrees.

The other main ritual centres of the Boyne complex are Knowth and Dowth. Unlike Newgrange with its single mound, at Knowth you can spend time wandering through the ritual area marked by seventeen satellite mounds scattered around the central tomb. It is now also possible to visit the inside of this central mound. While Newgrange has one passage leading into the burial chamber, Knowth has two long passages leading into the centre under the great mound. Its orientation is hotly disputed, with theories put forward of equinoctical or possibly even lunar alignment. It should be visited as part of a trip to the complex, not least because the carved stones here are incredible examples of Megalithic art – in fact, the Knowth tombs constitute 30 per cent of the known Megalithic art of Europe. Newgrange and Knowth can be visited only as part of a guided tour from the excellent interpretative centre, and as there is limited access, it makes sense to come very early in the day.

Below:
Plan of the gallery at Newgrange, County Meath.

The visitor centre supplies a wealth of archaeological information. The archaeologists can tell us that while there is evidence of burials in the mounds, it

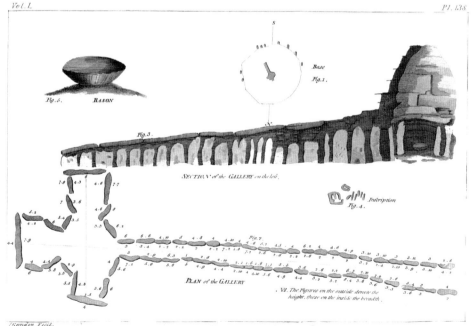

seems highly unlikely that these huge, complex structures were built as individual tombs. They can also give us a great deal of information on how these structures were made. However, what they cannot give us is definitive answers as to the meaning behind all this human effort. The experts cannot say *why* these people carved rocks with spirals, with lozenges, and, in one case, with a single fern. They cannot say why the stones were painstakingly shaped and carried from districts far away. Why did these people make the bowl-like depressions in the recess stones, which may have held some form of liquid? Are the carvings on the stones astronomical maps or messages in some lost shamanistic language that we can no longer read? Is the carving on the stone marking the western entrance of the main tomb at Knowth, resembling so closely a human face with an open, screaming mouth, the 'guardian stone' as it has been named, or something else completely? In the absence of definitive scientific answers, theories abound.

What is sure is that these places acted as treasuries for the people who lived 5,000 years ago – treasuries not of material wealth, but of their deepest feelings and thoughts about how the cosmos functioned. If we take our leave of the archaeologists and go back to the legends, we are told that Aonghus, the young god, the god of lovers, brought the beloved dead to the Brú. Here he took Diarmaid and breathed life into him for a time every day so that he could converse with him in the dark house of the dead. Here, in this same chamber, light breaks in on the darkest day of the year. Here, by some power of love – whether human, emanating from the memory of the tribe, or divine, emanating from the power of their gods – here, in some sense, the dead lived and spoke to the living.

Close to Newgrange and a further integral part of the Brú na Bóinne complex was the royal house of Cleiteach, although there are conflicting theories about its exact location. Some authorities site it near Stackallen Bridge, which is located some miles from Newgrange on the Boyne. This is the theory put forward by the great nineteenth-century Gaelic scholar and place-name expert John O'Donovan, who suggests this place as a possibility in his Ordnance Survey letters. However, O'Donovan was not at all adamant about this theory; originally he sited Cleiteach at Clady, a hill on the northern bank of the Boyne, one mile north of Bective; later, he admitted that this must be wrong, and walked the length of the river trying to find the site. It was then that he put forward the possibility of Cletty being one of the mounds on the river near Stackallen at Broadboyne bridge. Later in the century, William Wilde, father of the famous Oscar, suggested either Clady or Assay as possible sites. There was little further investigation until Elizabeth Hickey, in 1965, made a convincing argument about the location of Cleiteach, based on geographical features and the physical landscape linked with the written sources, suggesting that the site of Cleiteach might be at Rosnaree House, near Newgrange itself.

Rosnaree, the wooded headland of the kings, is the place where the great high king, Cormac, is believed to be buried. He moved to Cleiteach from Tara after he gave up the high kingship because of physical disability, and died there when a salmon bone caught in his throat. At his funeral, as he was carried across the River Boyne, it rose up, refusing to let him be buried with the pagan kings at Newgrange. According to some accounts, Cleiteach is also the place where the god Nuadhu lived when banished from Newgrange by Aonghus Óg, and also where Fionn tasted the Salmon of Knowledge and gained the power of foreseeing.

Perhaps the specific site of the original Cleiteach, which was destroyed in a great fire in the sixth century during the reign of Muircheartach Mac Earca, is not really so important. The course of the River Boyne itself has been much altered by canalisation and by dredging. Its leafy banks, however, still repay the visitor with a sense of luxuriant, slow-moving power. Because it can sometimes be hard to connect with the ancient power of Newgrange, surrounded as we are by other people during the visit, it is worthwhile to spend time at the quieter places along the banks of the river. To visit the ancient graveyard at Ardmulchan, for example, when evening light turns the grass to a golden green, and to watch the river as it curves past the Norman castle and Celtic crosses, is to feel something akin to the kind of power that one feels at Knockainey in Limerick. In both these places, the land is rich and has been cultivated for a very long time, and the goddess that was honoured here is one associated with fertile land and herds. In one story, Bóinn, the goddess of the Boyne and mother of Aonghus, the Lord of Newgrange, was drowned and became the river when she opened the well of Segais. This mythical well was the source of wisdom where the nine hazel trees grew and dropped their nuts and berries in the water, there to be swallowed by the salmon of wisdom, the salmon which gave Fionn his powers of foreseeing. Bóinn flowed past Brú na Bóinne, one of the most important access points to the otherworld. And it had been at the Brú that she had betrayed her husband Elcmar when she lay with the Daghdha. On a night which the Daghdha made last for years, their mating engendered Aonghus. The *Dindshenchas*, the lore of places, calls on Bóinn as one of the great ones, the rulers of the landscape. Her name associates her strongly with cows (*bó* being the Irish word for cow), and there are echoes of her power well into the nineteenth century when O'Donovan recorded that local farmers drove their cattle through the River Boyne as a charm against the powers of the Sídh.

In historical times, the river was the site of the famous and bloody Battle of the Boyne between James II and William of Orange. Walking along its quiet banks, it is hard to imagine any violence or hatred disturbing the peaceful realm of this gentle goddess. However, the following story shows that things could be otherwise.

THE REVENGE OF SÍN

When the great king, Muircheartach Mac Erca, came back from a hunting-trip with a strange and beautiful woman, there was much talking among his people, for it was whispered that she had appeared out of nowhere while he sat apart from his companions on the hunting mound at the Brú. Many thought that she must be a fairy woman come out of the mounds, for her beauty seemed not of this world. It was a dangerous thing to do – to hunt alone at the time of Samhain, when the leaves were turning and beginning to fall in fiery drifts, and the great forests on the banks of the Boyne were transformed into a copper and crimson melting pot. Outside the houses, cold air solidified into a mist when man or beast breathed out, mingling with the vapour that rose from the river. Inside the houses, there were great fires and feasts, and songs celebrating a king whose victories had brought all the tribes under his power, who had left dead bodies as countless as the leaves that fell from the trees, crushed underfoot into the earth. A tall, dark-haired man with a heavy beard and a searching eye, Muircheartach was generous and hospitable; his house at Cletty was always full of guests, of poets and musicians and brave warriors.

The people loved and trusted their king; so although they whispered when the woman came to Cletty, they did not demur. However, when Muircheartach put his wife, Duaibhseach, and his own children out of the house, his people began to worry that he was under an enchantment that would bring evil to the realm. And while the woman, Sín, was indeed beautiful, with her slanted amber eyes and bronze hair, it was a strange, sly beauty, a beauty without gentleness, and her power over the king was such that he could do nothing but watch her while she moved or spoke or sang. Then the king commanded that, at his beloved's request, no cleric should enter Cletty while the lady Sín resided there.

Duaibhseach, proud and a princess in her own right, went, red-eyed, to the hermit Cairneach and complained of her treatment, and he went and stood in front of the great house – one of the finest and strongest in Ireland – and cursed Muircheartach for his evil-doing.

However, Sín, looking from the ramparts with Muircheartach, laughed and said to the king, 'Do not worry about the curse the greasy cleric puts on you. He cannot harm you with his bells and his books while I am here to protect you, for my magic is stronger than his.'

Muircheartach looked at her lovely form, and thought of the knowledge that she had, which he thirsted after as he might after wine or her body, and asked the question he had wanted to ask from the first moment he had seen her: 'Are you human, then, or a woman of the Sídh?'

Sín smiled and said, 'I am human like you, but I have knowledge that could make wonders happen before your eyes. I could make the Boyne water into wine, and change the very stones on the hills into flocks of sheep, and the ferns that grow all around Cletty into fat swine. Ask me what you will.'

So Muircheartach asked her to perform these deeds, and before his eyes she changed the stones around the *dún* into blue men who battled with another army which she made from goats – a horrible goblin crew which had kept their animal heads, horns and all, but had the bodies of warriors. It was a brave battle the couple watched, and when it was over, Sín brought the king and his household inside and took three casks of water which she changed into a wine the like of which the king had never before tasted. Then she fed the host with magic swine which she had created from ferns. It was a wild feast that night, but one that gave those that partook of it no nourishment. The next day, the king and his army could hardly move from their beds, for their strength had been sapped by the enchanted food and drink.

Now, Sín had power over the king and all his court, so it seemed to them that battalions of the blue men and other creatures without heads were attacking the house, and the king and his warriors went out to do battle with this phantom army, not realising that the witch had made the demons of stones and sods and the green growing things of the riverbank. So it continued, with the king moving further and further into a world of dark enchantment – feasting at night on magic food that left him weak in the morning, and further weakened during the day by the senseless battling with the goblin army created by Sín. The clerics tried to cure him of the enchantment, but as soon as he returned to Sín, his eyes were blinded once again.

This went on, then, until the Wednesday night after All Saints' Day, when a winter wind came over the land, and Sín called out her names of Sigh and Wind and Winter, Storm and Grief. First, thunder and lightning flashed, and then she made a great snowstorm come down, which enveloped the house at Cletty and the sleeping king. He awoke screaming in the darkness, having seen fire and destruction, forewarning him of the fate that he was bringing upon himself. Twice he awoke from nightmares but each time the lady Sín gave him enchanted wine and he fell back into a drugged sleep. The third time, he awoke to find the house ablaze, and all his retainers fled, for as he slept, Sín had lit red fires in every corner of the mansion. She had put each weapon in the place with its point facing inward and had set a demon army battling outside, so that the king thought that the house was surrounded by enemies. Fire burst from every doorpost and window ledge. Muircheartach ran around in frenzy, trying to find a way out, but everywhere was blocked by flame and crashing timbers. The flickering leaves of the fire fell on his head and his shoulders, and terror came into his heart – a terror that he had never known in battle. Yet still the frenzy that Sín had put on him clouded his brain and his eyes, so that everywhere he looked he saw someone ready to attack him, and he fought the very tables and benches wildly, as if they had been mortal enemies.

Muircheartach begged Sín to save him, to make a path for him through the flames, but she turned her back and disappeared. With her cloak of invisibility about her, Sín stood and watched, until the flames grew too hot and bright and she left Muircheartach to his fate. He ran screaming through the house, the flames biting at him like angry teeth. Finally, in desperation, he climbed into a cask of wine, but the flames fell on his head, and burnt it, leaving the rest of his body whole. So it was said that the king was both burned and drowned.

Cairneach buried Muircheartach with the respect due to a great king. Duaibhseach came to her husband's graveside and lamented, and they say that she finally fell dead from grief. Then the clerics saw a most beautiful lady approaching them – so lovely that some of them turned their eyes to the ground to keep their minds from evil thoughts, while others could not look away from her. Long red hair fell over a green mantle with a silver fringe, and her beautiful countenance was made even lovelier by the loneliness and sadness of her face.

'Who are you?' they asked.

'I am Sín, daughter of King Sige. I am the one who brought this king to his death.'

'And why did you do this?' they asked.

'Muircheartach, dead here before you, killed my father and my mother and my sister at the battle of Cerb; he destroyed all my family, all the old tribes of Tara, and took the land of my people away from them. I was only a child when that happened, but I swore that I would gain vengeance on him and I learned the skills of magic so that I could do so.' She paused, and the face she turned to Cairneach was the bleakest he had ever seen.

'But despite all my knowledge and foreseeing, what I did not know was that I myself would fall under a spell – that I would love this man for his strength and his courage, his kindness and generosity; for his smile and the way the hair curled at the back of his neck. That is the revenge fate has had upon me.'

It is said that then she too died, from her grief at the death that she herself had brought about, and that although she had been an enchantress and the murderer of a great king, because of her beauty and her sorrow, Cairneach took pity on her and buried her in hallowed ground.

Hill of Uisneach, Westmeath

UISNEACH

Uisneach Hill has always been considered the centre of Ireland in both physical and metaphysical terms. In legendary terms, it stands in the province of Midhe, the mythical fifth province which touches all of the four others. The hill is located in Westmeath, a county that has been described as Meath's less fortunate twin, for here the land is not so rich. Uisneach is not a high or commanding hill, standing only 181 metres (594 feet) above sea level. Yet the view encompasses the central plain and, like at Tara and Cruachain, it is not necessary to climb very high to see very far. The hill was excavated in 1926 and a layer of ash found at the southern end of the ring ditch, indicating that great fires were lit here over long periods, from Neolithic to historical times. Excavations have shown that Iron Age structures were also built here, but most of the remains on the hill are little more to the naked eye than mounds and earthen circles. The hill's most impressive feature is not man-made at all, but the great boulder on the south-west side of the hill, known as the Catstone. This huge, cracked limestone boulder was left in the valley after the retreat of the ice, and is 5 metres (16 feet) high – all the more dramatic because it is surrounded by green fields. The stone is easily reached from the Mullingar–Athlone road, on a track which on our visit in early autumn led past blue flowers and pink thistles, reddening hawthorn berries and already ripened blackberries. It is a quiet place without the great dramatic beauty of the west, but it is also mercifully unspoilt by any development, and its sense of apartness was increased by the fact that when we visited there were no animals grazing on the hill. The Catstone's ancient name was the Stone of Divisions or *Aill na Mireann*; it marked the true centre of Ireland and is reputed to be the place where Eriu (also called Éire) is buried, the goddess from whom Ireland gets one of its names.

The hill has one of the greatest concentrations of legends in Ireland. In some accounts, it was on this hill that the god Lugh was attacked by three enemies – the three brothers who married the triple goddesses of which Eriu was one part – and fled to drown in a nearby lake. It was also the place where Connla the Fair, son of King Conn and brother of Art, was tempted into the other world by a woman of the Sídh. Despite the attempts of Conn's druids to defeat her, she threw the young Connla an apple, which placed an enchantment on him so that when she reappeared to him he sailed away with her, never again to be seen by his family. Eochaidh Ollathair, the horse god and consort of the goddess Áine, was also said to have a residence on Uisneach, and Geoffrey of Monmouth claimed that the stones of Stonehenge came from the hill, brought to England through the magic power of Merlin. Fintan the Sage had his home here.

Below:
Ancient Irish druids in traditional dress. The figure on the right is an arch-druid with gold chain, cap and wand.

One of the strongest traditions, however, is that of the sacred fires of Uisneach, lit every Bealtaine or May Eve. The fires continued to be lit here long after St Patrick had cursed the hill. A great gathering was held on the hill at the time and cattle were driven through the twin fires to protect them for the coming year. Large quantities of animal bones were also found during the excavations at Uisneach, indicating either great feasting or animal sacrifice, or perhaps both. There is a holy well further west along the road from the Catstone and a tradition says that there is a further, hidden well on the hillside. The *bile* or sacred ash tree of Uisneach was one of the four great trees of pagan Celtic Ireland. Thus the hill encompasses all of the traditional physical attributes of a sacred landscape – rock and water, tree and ritual fire.

I had a strange experience on the evening after my visit to Uisneach. After a very long day which had included a lot of driving, I was travelling from Cavan to Dublin, along a stretch of minor road which was totally unknown to me and which was, after a couple of wrong turns and missed signs, beginning to seem endless. It was a rainy dusk, but the sky was still streaked with light. The road wound its way through hedges, hills, trees, and fields, each part of the route seeming very like the one before. I found myself passing through a valley with sloping hills on either side – a valley that seemed very familiar. In my tiredness and disorientation, it seemed to me to be the same valley where I had stopped earlier to view the Catstone. For a crazy moment, I wondered if I had strayed so far from my route that I had found my way back to Uisneach; I even began to look out for the black and white cows I had noticed on the hill opposite earlier on. Then I passed a huge house built of raw red brick, which I knew I hadn't seen before, and the strange feeling passed. But it made me wonder if that was part of the secret of Uisneach's centrality – not just that the stone touches each of the provinces while owing allegiance to none, but that where it is located could be a place anywhere in Ireland – a green hill, with ditches and dikes and small blue flowers, with gorse and hawthorn growing over it; a place that in terms of political importance is 'nowhere' but that is, in some sense, everywhere.

FINTAN THE SEER

Fintan the Seer was brought from his home at Uisneach before the king and nobles at Tara and they asked of him how the land should be governed and divided, for he was the oldest and wisest man in Ireland. They asked him first who he was, what his lineage was and how long he had lived.

He answered them: 'I am the son of Labhraidh and Bóchna. When I was fifteen years of age, I came with Cessair and Buan and fifty women to this shore, at Bun Suaine in the south. That was forty days before the deluge, and I was the only one to survive the great rains, for I hid in a cave at the mountain of Tounthinna near the Shannon. When I came from that cave, I

Above:

*The huge, cracked
limestone boulder known
as the Catstone, or the
Stone of Divisions, on the
Hill of Uisneach.*

was the first man to see the new land with the waters gone. That is five thousand and five hundred years ago, and since then I have taken many forms. I have been the one-eyed salmon at the falls of Assaroe, and have given wisdom to those who came to me. I have talked to the hawk of Achill, who is nearly as old as myself, and heard many stories from him. I have been a falcon, flying high over the hills where Fionn and the Fianna hunted. I have been an eagle, watching the kings and queens at Tara come to greatness, and then dying, one after the other. I have seen forests grow up from seeds, and fall and become trackless bogs. I have seen generations cut the forests and build palaces and temples, and I have seen those houses crumble to the same dust as those who built them. I have seen the tribes invade, and conquer those who were here before them; I have seen them be defeated by new tribes in their turn. What all my years have taught me is that all living things change – the land, the water, the people. Even the great rocks crumble in time.

'I planted one of the five great trees of Ireland – the Ash of Uisneach – and I have watched it fall and grow again from its seeds. Because I have seen so many things, I know how the land should be divided and the ways that those who rule should disport themselves.

'Let me tell you this, and make a record of it, so that generations to come should know it. Let there be Knowledge in the West, Battle in the North, Prosperity in the East, Music in the South, Royalty at the Centre. The royal centre is not only here at Tara, but also at Uisneach, for at Uisneach is the Stone of Divisions that touches on every province of Ireland, and so partakes of all their virtues. Tara and Uisneach are like the two kidneys of a beast, of equal necessity for the health of the people and the land. Tara is great – it is the place of governance; but keep the knowledge of Uisneach and the harmony of the land will continue.

'Let it be recorded that a ruler should have no blemish on his spirit, for if he has, the land will fail and the people go hungry. Let there be justice rather than might in ruling the land, and no bloodshed or battles in the struggle to hold it. Treat the land as your mother, and it will continue to feed you. Treat it as a slave to be used, and it may rise up in revolt. Let the great ones keep in mind that every ruler who lives will die, and every race give way to a new one.'

Thus spoke Fintan, the oldest and wisest one, as wise ones have spoken before and since. And the kings and the nobles and warriors seemed to listen, and his words were written down; though whether any of those who heard paid much heed to them is another matter entirely.

Glencree, Wicklow

GLEANN CRIOTHAIGH

S cholars have claimed both Glencree and Bohernabreena as the location of the famous 'hostel' – *Bruiden Dá Derga* – where King Conaire met his death. The site was certainly somewhere in the Wicklow or Dublin mountains as this was the route of the Slí Cualann, one of the great roads from Tara. Eugene O'Curry was the first to suggest Bohernabreena, as, according to the story, the hostel was built over the Dodder and the place name incorporates '*Brú*', or 'hostel', and *Bóthar*, or 'road'. In 1935, Henry Morris made the case for Glencree as the site, with the hostel situated over Mareen's Brook, which flows into the headwaters of the Dodder, while Ferguson had previously suggested Donnybrook. Given this uncertainty about the location, I have decided to take Glencree as the most likely situation – it is certainly the most atmospheric of the suggested locations and a perfect gateway to the Wicklow mountains. Its name means 'The Glen of the Marshy Place'.

The county of Wicklow is the youngest in Ireland – it was established only in 1606 when it was 'shired', in an attempt to rout out the Gaelic rebels who lived in the hills and constantly raided the south and west of the Dublin suburbs. Wicklow, with its high mountains, deep glens and dark forests, was bandit country – the home of the rebel, the fugitive and the hermit. It was also a place of escape from the city of Dublin, and so it continues to this day; with its bogs and heather-covered hills, its isolation and its beauty. Much of the county is now preserved as a natural park, with woodland walks and trails through unspoilt countryside. The great woods of Wicklow have been re-planted and it is now one of the most forested areas in Ireland – although there is some concern that the mechanical planting and logging may have an adverse effect on the native wildlife and the archaeological remains of the county. Most of these prehistoric remains are situated in the gentler hills and valleys to the north-west of the county, towards the Kildare border. The wilder land of the high mountain ranges has always been less hospitable for settlement, which is why rebellion continued to be fomented here as late as the beginning of the nineteenth century. Glencree was so heavily wooded in medieval

Below:
The Wicklow mountains.

times that it was made a Royal Deer Park and enclosed in the thirteenth century, but by Tudor times it had fallen back to wildness, and a concentrated effort had been made to clear its forests so that they could not act as cover for the wood kerne, the Irish rebel soldiers. Later, the military road was built over the mountains – the same route which still links Glencree with Aughavannagh. At the same time, a barracks was built in the valley at Glencree – a building which later became a boys' reformatory. Glencree is also the site of a burial ground for German airmen who crashed in Ireland during the Second World War, and an iron cross marks the site where the body of a young republican was left by his killers during Ireland's Civil War. When swirling mists part to allow the strange conical top of Knockree, the Hill of the King, to be seen, the presence of the dead in this valley can feel more powerful than that of the living. In nearby Glenasmole, the lovely valley of thrushes, Oisín, the son of Fionn, fell from his horse on his return from the Land of Youth.

The young king, Conaire, felled by the swords of his foster-brothers and their allies; Oisín, falling from his horse; airmen, falling from the sky; men and trees falling before the axe – these are dark stories for such a lovely place. But the Wicklow mountains are equally famous for another exile from society who came to these isolated glens in search of a different kind of refuge. St Kevin was a saint who loved wild things far more than humans. It was said that once he stood still for so long that a blackbird laid her eggs in his hand and he waited in that position until the young birds were hatched. After he had founded the great monastery of Glendalough, he grew tired of the crowds who followed him there, and made his way over the mountains to another lonely valley, north of Glencree – a place that is now known as Hollywood Glen. Here, he refused to cut any timber, either to clear his way or to build a shelter, and when he came to the great forest, the trees, out of love for him, moved aside and made a path for him through the wood.

DA DEARGA'S HOSTEL

Frost and ice covered the mountains from the glens of Dún Bolg to the sea. It was a hard, cold, black night with no lights showing in the vastness of the high moors of the mountains by Áth Cliath. A band of warriors travelled through the pitch darkness, guided only by the stars, for the moon was still no more than a faint bow in the sky, and it seemed reddish – soiled with blood. At their head was Conaire, the young, fair-haired king of Ireland. Despite his great youth and the fact that he had not been bred as a king but in exile, until very recently his reign had been one of plenty – poets said that from Bealtaine until

Samhain, no wind strong enough to stir a cow's tail disturbed the peace of the land. He was a kindly king, with sleepy grey eyes and an air of seriousness about him despite his youth. They said that his father had been a bird spirit of the Sídh, who had come to his mother in secret and lain with her. His mother, Mes Buachalla, was the granddaughter of the fair Étaín, the most beautiful woman in Ireland. Though Étaín had been taken into the mounds of the Sídh long ago, the poets still used her beauty as the ultimate standard of loveliness in women; and those who looked at Conaire saw that beauty take the form of a man.

However, recently, things had changed. It was said that the king had broken the *geasa*, the solemn prohibitions that had been put upon him at his coming to the kingship. Strange signs had been seen in the sky; crops had failed; and winter – a winter so bitterly cold that it froze every river and lake in Ireland – had set in. And, most ominous of all, ships had started to land on the east coast, coming from Britain and full of sea pirates. Incgel, the British marauder, had joined with Conaire's foster-brothers, who had been sent into exile for their raping and raiding in Ireland. It was said that they were joining with others who did not want to see Conaire's peaceful reign continue – for in times of peace, there is little loot for those who love war.

Conaire was now seeking shelter with an old friend and companion, Da Dearga, the Red One – the most generous host in the land. The king was weak and weary, but knew that he had to keep near the ocean to defend his land against the threat from the east. He already felt a sense of doom, for earlier that day, when they had been climbing steadily from the coast in the red glow of sunset, three riders had swept past them. At first, Conaire had thought that it was the sun that turned them to the colour of flame, but then he realised that everything about them was red – their hair, their skin, their clothes, their horses. He remembered yet another of his *geasa* – 'Do not let the Three Reds go before you to the house of the Red One.'

Conaire sent a messenger to try to catch the horsemen and ask them to wait so that he could go ahead. The messenger had offered great gifts in exchange, but they had answered:

'We are the sons of Donn, riding the horses of Donn. Though we are alive, we are dead. There shall be much feasting this night in the house of the one of the dark face; many shall come to partake of his feast. We ride together. The three red ones stop for no one, neither king nor peasant.' And they spurred on their horses and rode even faster, westwards towards the hostel of Da Dearga.

Above:
Grotto at Glencree.

The march continued, interrupted only by the calling of the wolves in the hills. A strange pair passed the troop – a man and a woman, one more ugly and twisted than the other, and the man with a pig on his back, a pig that was half-roasted but still alive and squealing. Finally, they reached the hill where the hostel stood. Lights blazed from the window, for Da Dearga always welcomed travellers weary of the bleak terrain around his home. Mac Cécht, the king's closest companion, looked fearfully at Conaire, for was that not yet another of the *geasa* – that his king should never spend the night in a dwelling where light showed outside the walls? But Conaire's usually cheerful face was sunk into his cloak, and his grey eyes were dark. Da Dearga welcomed the company nobly, providing food and drink and warm fires, and they cheered a little as they sat by the glowing hearth. However, soon there was another interruption – a black, twisted woman, demanding entrance, though it was well after sunset. They brought her before Conaire, who asked her name. 'Cailb,' she said.

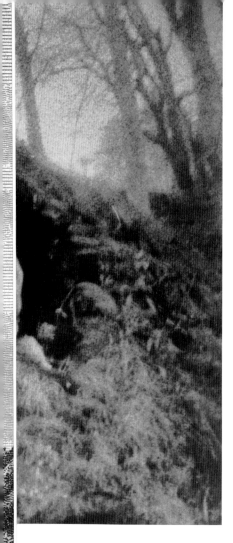

'That is a short name,' said Conaire.

'I am also called Sind, and Sinann and many other names.' And the woman began to give such a list of names – many of them people of the Sídh – that Conaire raised his hand to stop her.

'And what is it that you want?' he asked.

'A night's lodging, with the king's company, which you will agree is not much to ask.'

'I would give you anything but that, woman,' said Conaire. 'But it is my *geis* not to allow a visiting woman into my dwelling after sunset. Instead, let me send you good food and drink and a fire outside.'

'Is that the way the king treats a poor old woman?' asked the hag indignantly. 'Indeed, it is a fine state Ireland has got into with a ruler like that.'

She continued to berate him in this vein, so that finally Conaire sighed and said, 'Very well, come in then and stay.'

So was the last of his *geasa* broken. But as the servants led the crone away, she turned to Conaire and said, in a voice loud and clear for one so old and bent, 'No flesh of yours shall escape this place you have come to – save what the birds carry away on their claws. Many will take the long drink of death this night in Da Dearga's hall.'

The evening seemed long. Although the company was weary, they sat up together by the fires, fearful of the darkness outside; fearful also of attack from the east. Sometimes the wind rose up, and the company stirred, thinking of warriors creeping over the gorse of the hills; sometimes wolves called. Conaire remembered when he had last visited Da Dearga, when the hostel had been filled with the sound of birdsong and singing streams – a heavenly place in summer, full of life. Now all was death and stillness and frozen air.

While the king sat, he pondered on what had led him to this cold place in

the tale of Suibhne.

Eorann began: 'My husband, Suibhne, was always a hasty man, and on many occasions I have had to stop him before he acted unwisely. But a braver or kinder husband you could never find. I loved him dearly, and bore him a daughter and a son. Then – and I do not know how it happened – during the great battle of Moira, he lost his mind. The priests have told me that it was because he insulted the cleric Rónán – my husband never cared for Christian ways – but I have always thought that it was the battle itself that sent him mad: the noise, the destruction, the smell. It was a dreadful, bloody fight; the crows gathered over the corpses for days afterwards, feasting on their flesh. In any case, his friend, Loingseachán, told me that in the middle of it all, Suibhne began to scream and to whirl around in circles, and the next minute he had leapt into the highest branches of a yew tree.

'He would not come down, even after the battle was over and the corpses had been carried away; it was as if he no longer wanted to have anything to do with humans. I went to try to call to him down, but he only leapt away, going west towards Donegal. For months, he lived by jumping from tree to tree, his feet never touching the ground, his hair unkempt and his clothes gone to rags. His sweet mouth was stained with the herbs and grasses he lived on.

'In the end, Loingseachán tricked him into coming down out of the trees and he came home to me. But he was changed. He told me that he no longer wanted to be king; that he could not stay or settle in one place, even for a night, for the sights and screams of the battle were always with him and movement was the only way to get away from his visions of the horror. I begged him to let me go with him, saying that I would rather live in rags and in cold and hunger with him than with rich jewels in a palace without him; but the madness overtook him again, and he left me one night, travelling far to the woody glens south of our home. I consulted with Loingseachán, and we agreed another trick to try to get him home again – telling him that his family was dead. He fell to the ground in grief and was caught and carried to his palace but, once again, the madness overtook him. He saw phantoms, he said, in his dreams, screaming and crying and fighting with one another. The horrors would wake him in the night, and even when he was with me and I held him as tightly as I could, it made no difference – he bucked and screamed in my arms like a wild thing. So it went on like this. He left me again; then he came back to me again, but by that time I was with someone else. He berated me, but as I said to him, what was a woman to do? He had

his mad friends in the forest; he had the company of wild things and the joy of the green crown of trees around him; I had nothing to hold me but the arms of a man. And so he went away again, and I cried long and hard, but I swore that it would be for the last time.

'I was in bed one night when he came to the tree outside my window, and made a poem. That poem was the loveliest thing that I have ever heard. He sang of the forest – the clear springs so full of fish-life, the call of the thrushes and the other wild things, the belling of the great stags in winter. It made me weep to hear him, but the poem made me realise that he was lost to me forever, lost to the forest and the world of the wild woods and the trees and the birds. He could no more come back to being a human king than I could fly through the trees with him. So I rose up and went to him and said, "You are back now, but I know you will go again. You cannot stay in the company of other humans; now your companions are the creatures of the wild. So, as I know that all it will take is a clear night or the call of the north wind to make you leave me, I ask you to leave me now. Go, and do not come back."

'That was the hardest thing I ever had to say. There was silence from the hazel tree outside my window, and then his voice came again – oh, his sweet voice: "I will be gone then. Let me tell you: the cry of the grouse on the mountainside is in any case far sweeter to me than the voice of my wife lying beside me."'

The woman paused and looked down at her hands.

'That is the last time I have seen him or heard his voice. I have wept every night since then; and all I want to know now is that he is safe and has found some peace in his poor head.'

Muirgil took her hands gently. Although this woman was a queen, Muirgil felt nothing but compassion for her grief and a sense of her own wealth and happiness in comparison.

'I think,' she said, 'that holy Moling may have given him some kind of rest. I think that he has found refuge and healing here in this place of trees and water.' She paused and looked over towards the wood.

'Look,' she said. 'The shadows are lengthening. He will come soon for his milk. Would you like to try to talk to him when he comes?'

Eorann shook her head. 'No, I do not want to speak to him or let him know that I am here. But if I were to stand in the shadow of the hut, I could perhaps see him when he comes.'

Muirgil filled a pail with warm milk and went to the edge of the forest.

She thought that she saw something move in the shadows to the west. Then she saw Suibhne, running in from another part of the forest. The birds sang softly. She smiled her sweetest smile, encouraging him to come closer. Perhaps it was that smile that brought her husband, watching from the shadowy trees, over the brink into his own madness.

There was a flash of steel in the slant of the sun, and a cry. Suibhne fell, his body pierced by the spear of Mongán. Mongán's sister had told him that his wife loved the man of the woods, and now, driven to frenzy by the thought that his wife had slept with the mad king, he had killed him. Mongán stood in the shadows, staring at his hands. Muirgil dropped the pitcher and ran to where the king had fallen, calling out for St Moling to come and help her. The blue-robed woman moved out from the shelter of the hut and walked slowly towards her husband's body as the light died over the western woods.

MUNSTER

Lough Muskry, Tipperary

The Glen of Aherlow with its surrounding mountains is an area of Tipperary which deserves to be better known. The banks of the River Aherlow are beautifully forested and steeped in history, while the walks on the mountains to hidden lakes and panoramic views are the equal of any in Ireland. Lough Muskry is one such hidden lake, situated high in the mountains and not accessible by car. The walk to the lake and back should take no more than three hours from where the road ends in the forestry south of Rossadrehid village. The walk is quite steep but is not overly difficult, as there is a trail for the full extent of it, and the views of the surrounding mountains and of the lake itself make it more than worthwhile. Much of the early part of the route is through planted forest, with the latter part moving onto open moorland. One of the best times to undertake the walk is in the very early morning, when on sunny days you will have the experience of seeing the thick white mist clear from the river valley below, leaving bright blue skies and magnificent views of the glen. While the lake itself is not visible from the track, it is easy to identify the rim of the corrie in which it lies. The towering cliffs which surround the lake form a natural amphitheatre, the rocks gouged as if slashed by a knife. The water of the lake is dark and very cold looking, and there is little bird life around it. However warm the day, one is unlikely to be tempted to cool off in its green depths. To the north is Knockastakeen, where the strange rock formation, the *Fir Bréaga* or 'False Men' stands out clearly.

The lake was formerly known as *Lough Béal Séad* – the Lake of the Jewel Mouth – but it has also been identified as Loch Béal Dragan, the lake of the Dragon's Mouth. Its present name, Lough Muskry, comes from the Múscraighe sept who lived in the south of Ireland. The lake is said to have been formed on the spot where Cliach the harper stood for a year to serenade his beloved, the daughter of Bodhbh of Slievenamon. The tradition continues that a *piast*, or serpent, emerges from the lake on stormy nights. Another local tradition has it that if a special grass grown near the lake is eaten, it will cure scurvy. This tradition has been upheld by botanical studies of the lakeside which have shown that scurvy grass is present in the area. Material collected by the Folklore Commission in the 1930s demonstrates the range of legends attached to the area of the Glen of Aherlow and the Galtee Mountains. This manuscript collection contains stories of buried treasures (often

Pages 80–81:
'The Lower and Torc Lakes, Killarney', *engraving by WH Bartlett.*

Above:
*On the mountain path to
Lough Muskry, County
Tipperary.*

'Danish gold'); of holy wells moving location because they had been ill-treated by a user; of houses being left undisturbed after their owners died because the living did not wish to disturb the dead; of festive Lughnasa journeys into the hills to collect bilberries, on the last Sunday of July. Further back in time, William Le Fanu, the brother of the celebrated writer, Sheridan, walked across the Galtees in 1838. A fog came down and, for a time, the members of the party were completely lost, wandering in the mist and unable to get their bearings. They finally found shelter but when they mentioned that in their travels they had seen a chestnut horse running alone across the hills, they were told that they were lucky to have come back alive. The 'yellow horse', they were told, was a fairy steed, which usually foreshadowed the death of those who had seen it.

We saw no fairy steeds on our trip; nor were there any swans with golden collars gliding on the lake. But on a warm May morning, the walk to Lough Muskry was idyllic. Stonechats darted and squabbled at the side of the track, and lambs, white enough to act as advertisements for washing powder, scrambled across the path and down the rocks, plaintively calling for their mothers. The valleys stretched away into a blue haze, and the larks that sang seemed to celebrate the return of the sun and the beginning of summer – at least for a day.

THE VISION OF AONGHUS

Aonghus, the child of youth and the god of love and beauty, lay sick in his bed in the Brú, and no one could say what ailed him. He fell in and out of a sleep that seemed to do him no good, for he moaned and called out while he slept, and awoke weeping. The people of the Sídh began to fear that he would never recover and dreaded the darkness that such a fate would bring to them.

For it was Aonghus who protected lovers everywhere, who came with the spring with his bright cloud of singing birds. Yet still he would not say what ailed him, but only begged to be left alone so that he could sleep.

Finally, after a year, his mother, Bóinn, the goddess of the great river Boyne, became desperate. She sent for one of the greatest and wisest of the druids. He came to where Aonghus lay on his bronze bed and took one look at him. Then he said, 'Easy it is to see what ails the lad.'

The court waited expectantly.

'He is in love, and his beloved appears to him while he sleeps. He will never be well until he finds out who this girl that he is dreaming about is and gets her as his wife.'

Aonghus raised a pale head from the pillow and smiled. 'In truth,' he said, 'I did not know my sickness until you told me of it. But so it is: the most beautiful girl in the world has visited me in my dreams and sings to me in the night. I will never be well until I find her. She has cheeks the colour of the yew berry and hair the colour of the dark night. Her eyes are bright lakes and her neck is white as a swan. She will not let me touch her; when I try to grasp her in my arms I wake up. Tell me how I may find her.'

The druid replied: 'You must seek her all over Ireland; for she, like you, is one of the Sídh, and she must love you, for why else would she come to you when you sleep?'

For many months, Aonghus's mother and his father – the great Daghdha himself – searched for the maiden with whom Aonghus had fallen in love. Their search grew more frantic as the months went on and the youth grew paler and weaker, and the flowers faded early in the fields, and the birds were silent on bare branches. Finally, they spoke to Bodhbh, the great otherworld king of Munster, who had his *sídh* in Slievenamon. He told them of a girl who was as fair as Aonghus's vision. She was Caer Iobharmhéith, the sweet yew-berry, the daughter of Ethal Anbhuail of the Munster Sídh. She had been sent by her father to live at Crotta Cliach in the Galtee mountains, by the lake known as Loch Béal Dragan, a high, hidden lake in the wild mountains. The girl was under an enchantment; she went in the form of a girl and a swan in alternate years, and she was the only one who could choose which form she took. To find her, Aonghus must go to the lake on the next Samhain eve.

At the beginning of November, Bodhbh and Aonghus travelled from the Brú over bogs and river-valleys, wide plains and high, silent mountains. It was not until they had reached the edge of the lake that they could see it at all, for it was hidden in a cup in the hills. As they climbed the last slope, Aonghus listened intently, hoping to hear the sound of his beloved's voice. But all was still and silent. Gliding over the surface of the dark waters of the lake was a multitude of shining white birds; fifty of them were attached to one another by chains of silver; but one, the most beautiful and graceful of them all, had a chain of gold.

Aonghus stood at the lakeshore, saying nothing. He did not see the shape that had enchanted him in his dreams; he saw only white swans. How could he be sure that his beloved was here? How could he know her? Standing beside him, Bodhbh said nothing. Aonghus reached out to catch the swan with the golden collar, but she flew away from him, across the water. The evening was darkening and the moon rose over the black lake.

Then the silence of the mountains was broken by Aonghus's voice, calling the girl to him, telling her of his love. Aonghus sang of how he had dreamed of Caer for many long months, of how his life was worth nothing without her by his side.

'Come to me!' he sang. 'Whatever form you take, I will cleave to you; wherever you go, I will follow. I will not oppose your will, whether you be swan or maiden; if you come to me on land, I will not hinder you from going again into the water. Only come to me now!'

And so, finally, she came, breaking the chain that bound her to her handmaidens. As the white bird set her foot on dry land, Aonghus saw that she was indeed the girl with eyes full of light who had come to him in his dreams. And at the moment of recognition, there was a further transformation. Aonghus himself stepped forward into the dark water, and in that moment he too changed; he became a great white bird, a swan to be a swan's mate. He and the girl embraced and, as swans, took flight over the water. They circled the lake three times, and then, linked together by the golden chain, they flew northwards, over the moonlit mountains towards Brú na Bóinne. As they flew, they sang a song of such beauty and joy that all who heard it fell into a deep sleep. The inhabitants of Ireland, Sídh and human, slept for three days and three nights and had such dreams that their lives were transformed when they awoke, each one finding a world made new, full of enchantment. Caer was the wife of Aonghus from that day on, and, as part of his bridal gift, Aonghus gave her four kisses, which he forged into singing birds.

Slievenamon, Tipperary

SLIABH NA MBAN

S lievenamon (*Sliabh na mBan*, 'The Mound of the Women', or *Sídh Femen*, 'The *Sídh* of the Women'), a mountain bordering Tipperary and Kilkenny, was one of the most important *sídh*, or otherworld residences, in Irish tradition. Nowadays, the nineteenth-century song, 'Slievenamon', is still sung, having acquired the status of a local anthem. The mountain dominates the surrounding landscape and there is a clearly defined track to the cairn near its summit. The small village of Kilcash nestling on the slopes of the mountain is a pretty, sleepy place with a Romanesque church and a ruined Butler castle nearby. There are magnificent views from the summit, although the mountain has long been cleared of its original forests. The early nineteenth-century 'Lament for Kilcash' mourns not only Lady Margaret Butler, but also this lost world, where the great woods symbolised a past nobility:

What shall we do now for timber?
The last of the woods is down.
Kilcash and the house of its glory
And the bell of the house are gone.

'Caoine Cill Chais', (anon), translation Frank O'Connor

The cairn on the mountain is the traditional home of Bodhbh Dearg, one of the great otherworld lords, who was given this *sídh* when Manannán divided the underground palaces between the Tuatha Dé Danann after they had been defeated by the Milesians and driven into the mounds. The Fianna hunted here, and in the forests that covered the mountain they must often have held their rituals. This was the mountain on which Fionn and his companions finally stopped after their wild chase from Tory in the north, hunting a magical deer. On Slievenamon, snow surrounded the Fianna and they found themselves inside the fairy mound, guests of the Lord Donn, who asked for their help in a battle against other members of the Tuatha Dé Danann. Here also lived Cnú Dearóil, the marvellous musician only four fingers high who played music that could break the hearts of listeners. From here too, according to the ancient text, *Agallamh na Senórach*, came another musician, Cos Corach – perhaps Cnú in another form – whom St Patrick blessed for the beauty of his music. It was to here that Midhir,

one of the Tuatha Dé Danann, fleeing from King Eochaidh, brought his beloved and long-sought-after Étaín, before the couple made their way to Midhir's *sídh* at Brí Léith in Longford.

Yet another tradition says that Slievenamon was named 'The Mound of the Women' (*Sliabh na mBan*) because a great troop of women raced to the top to gain the prize of Fionn as a husband. In some accounts, Fionn was given his magical powers on Slievenamon, when he followed a beautiful woman and caught his thumb in the doorway as she disappeared into a *sídh*. From that time on, when he put the thumb into his mouth, he could see far into the distance in space and time. The tradition of fairy women associated with the hill survived well into the last century. In the story of the fairy spinners, for example, a woman's cottage is invaded by the Sídh; but she runs in screaming that Slievenamon is on fire, and the fairy women leave in a great rush to save their homes. However, there have been darker manifestations of belief in magic than the common folk motifs of mysterious lights appearing on the mountain or fairy troops seen crossing a traveller's path late at night. As late as 1902, William Murphy was brought to court for trying to bewitch his neighbour's cows on 1 May. There is also the story of Bridget Cleary, a young woman from the village of Cloneen in the foothills of the mountain, who in 1895 was burnt to death by her husband, Michael Cleary, in an attempt to drive away the fairy being he thought was possessing her. The case made headlines at the time and children sang a rhyme for many years afterwards: 'Are you a witch or are you a fairy/Or are you the wife of Michael Cleary?'

In general, the music of Slievenamon is not so harsh. Listen to it. It is there in the memory of the deep humming of the Fianna ritual trances, a chanting that is echoed in the buzzing of the bees in the heather. It is there in the soft accents of the local people, in the sighing of the breeze and the songs of the hidden birds in the trees around the ruined walls of Kilcash. It is heard late at night in the villages under the mountain, when local musicians come in to play tunes which seem to have their roots in other worlds.

THE BIRTH OF OISÍN

The slopes of Slievenamon are known to be enchanted, but whether this enchantment comes from the presence of the great *sídh* of Ard Femen or from the beauty of its forest of hazel and alder, of slender birch and copper

beech, cannot be said. Whatever the reason, of all the places in Ireland where broad-faced young Fionn loved to hunt, the slopes of Slievenamon were among the most beloved.

It was a spring dawn, a cold one with a fresh wind – on such mornings, Fionn loved to begin his hunts, watching the deer flee before him through the bright green branches, almost always sure of capturing them with the help of his hounds, Bran and Sceolan. The woods were still wet with dew when suddenly, from a thicket, a doe started out and the hounds began a tremendous baying. The fawn – as white as milk or freshly fallen snow – raced through the branches, but before it did so it cast a glance back at Fionn, the only person near enough to see it clearly. The look made him stop in his tracks, for it was not that of a frightened animal but of a human being, pleading and proud at the same time. He shook the thought off and followed his hounds to where they ran close on the heels of the fawn. They ran through glades of hazel and oak, and as the day wore on, and Fionn and the hounds still followed the deer, they left the forest and went further and further up the slopes of Slievenamon, into a high silent valley that Fionn had never seen before. There, having left the rest of the hunt far behind, the doe suddenly stopped dead in her tracks and lay down quietly by the edge of a stream. 'They have her now!' thought Fionn exultantly; but instead of attacking the fawn, the two dogs put their ears down and cowered before her, whimpering, as if half-afraid and half-delighted. When Fionn came up to her, he raised his spear; but when he looked into those deep and liquid brown eyes, he slowly put it down. For the first time in his life, Fionn found that he could not kill. So, instead, he put his hand gently on the doe's head and she nuzzled it, licking it with a soft, pink tongue.

'You must be a beast of the Sídh,' said Fionn.

When the rest of his companions joined him, Fionn ordered that no harm should come to the doe, but that they should bring it back to Almiu, his great palace at the Hill of Allen in Kildare.

That night, all but one of the deer was roasted on the great fires of Almiu. The Fianna feasted and sang and told stories and Fionn went late to bed. He had not lain there long when he heard someone entering his room. He immediately reached for his sword, but put it down when he heard a gentle laugh and he saw that what was before him was not a warrior but a beautiful young girl. Her skin was as white as milk or newly fallen snow; her hair was as dark as midnight; her eyes brown, as gentle as a deer's.

'Who are you?' he asked gently. 'And why do you laugh?'

'I am laughing,' said the maiden, 'because I have finally found my heart's

Below:
The castle ruins at Kilcash,
County Tipperary.

desire, and I was afraid I might be killed by him, though death at his hand would be preferable to life at the hand of another. And who I am is Sadhbh, called also Blái Dearg, for my father is the magician Dearg, who does not love you, and therefore would not let me come to you. I had no lover in the people of the Sídh, but one wanted me, the Fear Dorcha, and that Dark Man has pursued me night and day in my form as a doe. Will you give me your protection, for I have looked for you for a long time to ask you to do so?'

'I will not just give you my protection,' said Fionn, drawing the bedclothes aside. 'I will give you my love and make you my wife.'

Fionn loved Sadhbh with all the passion of his young and passionate nature. He could hardly bear to be from her side for a moment, so when the day came when he had to go to battle against his ancient enemies, he found it difficult to drag himself away.

'I will look out for you from the ramparts of Almiu,' said Sadhbh. 'And as soon as I see you coming, I will run out and greet you.'

'Do not run too fast, my love,' said Fionn, laying his hand gently on her

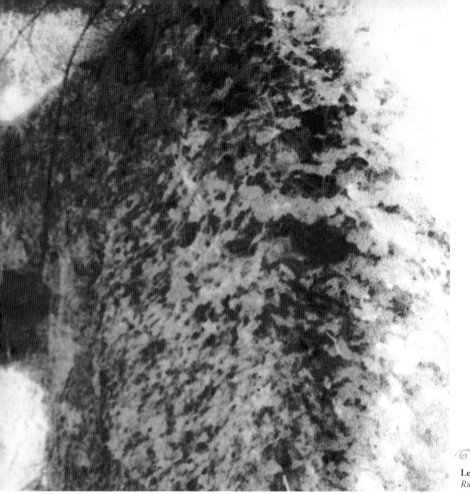

stomach. 'For I do not want you to harm the child.'

However, when Fionn returned victorious from battle, he found no one running to meet him. The *dún* was in chaos, with servants running to and fro, calling each other names and trying to shift the blame from one to another. Finally, he managed to get some sense from his steward: 'My lady is gone,' he said, stuttering over the words. 'She was up on the *dún*. She was watching eastwards from where she knew you would come, And then it seemed as if someone with your countenance and bearing appeared, with two great hounds by his side. Before we could stop her, she had run out towards you, her arms outstretched, and you know yourself, my lord, how fleet of foot she is – none of us could catch her. But as soon as she drew near to the man, it seemed that his appearance changed to that of a dark man in a black cloak, and the dogs with him were not Bran and Sceolan, but two great dark hounds who came towards my lady and dragged her by her gown to where he stood; and then ...' The servant paused, looking fearfully at his master.

'Well, and then what?'

'Then he raised his rod – it seemed to be of hazel or some such wood – and touched her. And in the place of our lady there was a doe, which tried to run towards the *dún*. But every hound in the place set up such a howling and barking and strained to get at her, and the dark man's hounds pulled and nipped at her, so that she was forced to go with him. He led her away into a mist that suddenly came down, though it had been a bright day before that. We have not seen her since, but we have sent our people far and wide, looking for some trace of her. It is as if the ground had swallowed her.'

Fionn said nothing. He went to his own room and lay on his bed, which still held a faint woodland scent on the sheets. He knew that it was the Fear Dorcha who had found his wife and taken her away.

For the next five years, Fionn hunted like a man possessed – every glen and forest in Ireland rang to the calls of Bran and Sceolan; every hillside echoed with his halloos. Whether it was deep winter or high summer, Fionn hunted – not for the shy, brown deer or the angry boar to feed the bellies of his men, but for his lost beloved. As time went on, hope faded, and Fionn became older and colder and he took other women to his bed, but he never forgot his sweet, early love.

Then, one day in early spring, when the Fianna were hunting on Ben Bulben, a mist came down, separating Fionn from the rest of his band. Only Sceolan and Bran and their three pups, who were bidding to become as great dogs as their dams, were with him. They ran ahead of Fionn into a narrow valley that reminded him of somewhere, though he was sure he had never been there before. As he made his way carefully along, the mist began to clear a little, and he could see the five dogs standing in a circle and baying joyously. They moved apart so that he could see what they were guarding, and there in the centre of the group was a small boy. The child had skin like milk or newly fallen snow, and long dark eyes, as liquid and gentle as Sadhbh's. But the boy's golden hair was the colour of Fionn's and his nose and jaw had the set, even at four years of age, of that hero. There was a tiny tuft of soft, brown hair on his forehead – the shape that might be left from the gentle lick of a doe. Fionn, although he would never find Sadhbh again, had been given his son, who would become a poet and one of the great ones of the Fianna. He named him Oisín, which means Little Deer.

Béara Peninsula,
BÉARA Cork

This is a landscape without compromise, especially in winter – a landscape of jumbled rocks, grey and white and black. On the summits, the rocks are striated, as if scratched with a witch's claws. The fields are full of russet ferns, copper reeds, and grass the colour of blood that has been dry for a very long time. This wild and mountainous region is entered through gateways which are deceptively fertile and gentle – Glengarriff, full of tropical plants and heavily planted with trees, so that in the misty rain, the twisted pines and rocky islands look like something in a Japanese print; or on the other side of the peninsula, Kenmare, folded into its mountains and straddling the lovely Kenmare River. However, beyond each of these places is the Béara Peninsula, home of the *Cailleach Bhéarra* (Hag of Béara) – glorious in summer, but perhaps most itself during the cold days of winter. The hard rocks – the bones of the land – are revealed under buffeting wind and driving rain; and the presence of the sea, both preserver and destroyer of the people who have settled here for thousands of years, is a constant, angry presence in our ears.

The people of the past are remembered in the rich folklore of the region. There are the stories of the Gaibhleann Gabha, the mythical smith – an appropriate presence in an area which was once rich in copper and silver, and has a tradition of mining going back centuries. The name Béara is traditionally said to come from the name of a Spanish princess, who married a local chieftain, but no single character is more associated with the peninsula than the Cailleach or Hag of Béara. This ambivalent character is likely to be a surviving form of an ancient land-goddess and the ritual consort of human kings. The imagery associated with her is sombre. Sometimes she is said to be the wife of Manannán Mac Lir, god of the sea, but she is also connected in the stories with the lord of death, Donn, and she appears in various forms all over Ireland. In some areas, she was associated with the harvest, so that the last sheaf cut was known as the *cailleach*. In Scotland, she was the protector of wild animals. On the Béara peninsula, she is associated most strongly with the cow, and it is possible that her original name, *Boí* or *Buí* comes from the old word for cow. Dunboy and Inis Boí – an ancient name for Dursey – hold echoes of that connection, as do the rocks beyond Dursey – the Bull, the Cow and the Calf. The Bull Rock is one of those places known as the House of Donn, the palace in the west where the lord of death called the dying to him.

Bere Island, a short ferry ride from Castletown Bere, the main town on the peninsula, was inhabited from early prehistoric times. It has a wealth of antiquities – wedge tombs, ringforts, holy wells, standing stones and promontory forts. Indeed, the whole peninsula is covered with the remnants of very ancient times, and at Ballycrovane, on the northwestern side of the peninsula, you can find the tallest ogham stone in Ireland, set against a magnificent backdrop of small islands on one side and great mountains on the other. The Ring of Béara corkscrews through these mountains, each one more dramatic than the last, and then opens out into views of sea and rock and silver light. The more sheltered valleys are miracles of green, and the two-storey traditional farmhouses that they hold sometimes seem to be suspended, swimming in the rivers of mist which surround them, or perched like nests on impossibly rocky heights. Not far away from Ballycrovane, at Coulagh, a rock jutting out from a cliffside is known as the Cailleach. She faces into the sea and wind, turned to stone by St Catherine because of a dispute over a prayer book. As you approach from the road, the rock does indeed seem like the shape of an old, hook-nosed woman, her body half submerged in the earth. Offerings of coins are still left here.

Just outside Castletown Bere, with its busy port, its pubs, its restaurants and its industries, there lies another such place where centuries seem to meet and mingle. Dunboy, the site of Dónal Cam O'Sullivan's castle, is now a lonely ruin, facing out into the sea. Defeated by the English forces under Carew, the last chief of Dunboy set out from there on the last day of 1601 to make the long journey northwards to Leitrim, where he hoped to find refuge and allies. One thousand men, women and children accompanied him on that harsh winter journey. Out of that number, thirty-five survived to reach Leitrim. Inland from the shell of the castle lies another ruin, that of a glorious nineteenth-century mansion burnt to the ground during the War of Independence. In Dunboy's small harbour, the wind plays through the bare ribs of a boat, long ago wrecked and left to be stripped by the elements. And perhaps the Cailleach looks on, remembering old battles lost, and white bones that have been picked as clean as the wrecked vessel, to become part of her skeletal landscape.

THE HAG OF BÉARA

Cold darkness. Even in the pain and the panic, the thought came into his head: 'So this is death.' He had often wondered about death, although he had seen little of it, for he was a prince and he had led a sheltered life. A dog of his had died – a small red dog killed by his father when she became too old even to take comfort in lying by the fire or taking scraps of meat from his hand. His father had said, 'She is better off so; she was only suffering.' But he had not believed him. Surely life was always better than death.

So now he fought for his life, struggling against the black waves and the wild wind, calling out for help, though no one sailed this stretch of water between the island of Béara and the mainland, haunted as it was with tales of hags and witches. And then the blackness overcame him.

'Once I slept with princes, stronger and wealthier and far, far fairer than you. But that was long ago.'

The old woman stirred the fire and the young man huddled closer to it. The cabin smelled of damp and old age, of drying seaweed and sulky turf. The fire gave little heat, and the boy shivered. After unconsciousness had come upon him as his body sank deep into the waves, he could remember nothing. He had woken to find himself in this hovel, being fed a thin green soup that seemed to be mostly dirt-coloured water with a few strands of cress floating in it. Yet, although the soup made his stomach churn, at least it was hot, and he was alive. The boy peered at the crone opposite him. He could hardly distinguish a face behind the acrid smoke that filled the cabin and the grey veil that the hag wore. He wondered how her rheumy eyes could see beyond the thick cloth at all, and shivered slightly as he remembered stories of the Hag of Béara, the Cailleach who could just as easily kill a man as rescue him.

The woman cackled as she caught him staring.

'You do not know who I am? Am I no longer known by the men of Ireland? I have had many names. Once my names were almost as beautiful as I was myself. I was called Boí, the Cow-woman, and I had herds of fine beasts grazing all over this peninsula. I could fly through the air over the mountains; I could run in a hare's shape through the golden cornfields; and I drank mead and wine with the great kings. I had so many lovers they could not be counted; to each one I was as generous with my body as I was with my treasure. I had fifty foster-children whom I raised to greatness. One of my greatest lovers was Fothadh Canainne, that mighty warrior. He feasted only when there were dead men present at the table, and his head still spoke to me after it had been taken from his body by treachery. How he loved my long, golden hair – you see now, there is not much left, and what there is is grey and thin.'

She pulled a strand of greasy hair out from behind the veil. The young man said nothing, for he could think of nothing to say. The woman cackled again, as if amused at his discomfort.

'It is as well that I wear a veil in these days. The tide is ebbing now – can you hear it call? Now, there is greed in men's hearts rather than valiant deeds, meanness and treachery instead of hospitality and courage. There is no nobleness left in this land. You do not know what it was like, in the days of the kings when the gods walked with us, and any moment we could be visited by one of the great lords – by Aonghus or Donn or the great Daghdha himself. In those days, any woman could be the mother of a god, and any man the lover of a woman of the Sídh. If you had seen me dressed in the richest of cloth, with white gold at my ears and my neck, and yellow gold plaited in shining balls

Above:
*A standing stone on Bere
Island keeps watch over the
Atlantic Ocean.*

THE RETURN OF OISÍN

I am fallen here, in this Wicklow glen, like a dead leaf on the floor of the forest. I am the dried husk of summer, waiting to be crushed into the earth, unable to move without the help of those who, a moment ago, thought me some kind of god. They look down at me, horrified; one minute they were seeing a fine warrior on a white horse, the next minute an ancient withered man, transformed as soon as I touched the soil of Ireland. The people's faces are coarse and cowardly, their limbs puny; I have seen no one here that has a quarter of the strength or nobility of my companions of old. But every one of them is stronger than me now.

Yet the summer is as sweet as it ever was, though the noise of the forest is torture to me now, in this woody glen, so full of life. Full of sap rising, birds building, bees humming, linnets, thrushes, and ringdoves. All is flowering, all is alive and full to bursting. And the bells of the Christian priests tell me over and over again that my world has gone.

It was in another such beautiful glen, in autumn, that I hunted with my father, Fionn Mac Cumhaill, and my son, Oscar, near Loch Leane in the south. In autumn, that place has the saddest beauty, the beauty of a world about to change. It was a clear, cold morning that we started out.

'Oisín,' my father called out. 'You take your company down by the lake. I think there are the tracks of a young fawn down there.'

I nodded, although I resented my father telling me how to go about the hunt. I knew I still had things to learn from him about woodcraft and magic, but he was no longer the man he had once been; bitter lines had been etched on his mouth since Diarmaid's betrayal of him and his of Diarmaid. Lines were on his forehead from the long battle with his old companion, Goll. Yet still I felt as if I walked in his shadow. But as I made my way down towards the lakeside, I forgot him in my joy in the beauty of the mountains and the water and the excitement of the hunt.

Then I stopped, for riding towards me over the hillside was the most beautiful woman I had ever seen. Her skin was whiter than a white rose. Her hair was the gold of the sun, her eyes the colour of a thrush's egg. She rode a fine white horse, with golden reins and saddle, and as she came towards me, I could see that her eyes were shining with joy.

'I have found you at last,' she said as she approached me. 'Oisín, I have sought you long, and come so far to find you, for I have seen you in dreams

Opposite:
Killarney woods.

and I know that you are my heart's match.'

I could say nothing. I, Oisín, the great poet and teller of tales, was struck dumb by her loveliness.'

'Will you come with me?' she asked sweetly. 'I am Niamh, Princess of the Golden Hair, and I have come from the Land of Pleasure to take you back there with me as my husband. Will you come with me?'

I was so overtaken with desire for this lovely woman that had she asked me to go with her anywhere in this world or any other, I would have left without a backwards look. I saw nothing, neither my father nor my son coming up behind me, calling me. I went to her, and she pulled me onto her horse. We rode like the wind away from that place, leaving my companions calling behind me. The journey took us over seas and plains and mountains, and far beyond the land of Ireland; finally, we reached her father's place. They treated me with great honour there and I lived with my sweet bride for what seemed to me to be three years, and had a son and a daughter by her. I lived a life of pleasure – of hunting and feasting and laughter. But one day I awoke with a longing in my heart to see my companions again, and my son Oscar and the fair land of Ireland, and even my father; for I thought that now I should no longer feel that I lived in his shadow, having lived so long in the bright sunlight of the other world. I imagined the stories I would have to tell them, how they would listen to me in wonder. So finally I went to Niamh and said, 'My sweetheart, you know I love you better than life itself, but I feel that I must visit my family and my companions. Will you come with me that you may be welcomed by my people as I have been welcomed by yours?'

Niamh's hands fell from her needlework.

'Oisín,' she said. 'Let me ask you not to do this. I cannot come with you and I fear that you will not return if you leave me to visit Ireland.'

'My love,' I said firmly. 'Nothing would keep me away from you. If you will not come with me, let me go alone. I will return before you know that I have gone.'

My wife nodded. 'So the day I dreaded has come. So be it, then. But take the white horse we rode on to come here; and promise me one thing – that you will not dismount from his back no matter what happens. Promise me that, if nothing else.'

I laughed a little – so this was her trick to make sure that my visit was a short one! But she looked so disconsolate that I promised what she wished.

The white horse carried me like the wind to Ireland; but it was not the

Ireland of my youth. It seemed as if a race of dwarfs – ugly, misshapen weaklings – had taken over the island. I rode through the valleys asking the people for news of Fionn and the Fianna, but no one seemed to know what I was talking about. Everyone looked blank, except for one very old man who said that he had heard stories of such heroes who had dwelt in the forests three hundred years before. Slowly, I began to realise that what had passed for a year in the Land of the Young was a hundred years in the world of mortals; my father, my child and my companions had long since become white bones, rotted into the land itself.

Yet still I rode through the countryside, for although the people had changed, the land remained familiar, and I hoped to find the traces of my lost world. Finally, I came here to Gleann na Smól, the valley of thrushes, where I met a group of men trying to shift a heavy boulder. They begged me to help them, for like the rest of the inhabitants they were a puny lot. I leaned from the back of the white horse to shift the stone, and as I did so, a bell rang out from a neighbouring valley and the horse bolted, throwing me to the ground. As soon as I touched earth, I felt my flesh wither, my eyes fade, my strength seep from me. Within seconds, I was an ancient heap of skin and bones, and the white horse had galloped off, back to the fair princess I would never see again.

Always, those who leave expect to come back to the same world. They want it to be unchanged – the same companions opening their arms to welcome them; the girls they left years before as young and pretty as ever; their friends gathered together, agog to hear stories of adventure. But those who leave never come back to the same place. Indeed, now I sometimes wonder if that lost world really existed – if my memory has recreated it in brighter colours than the ones it actually held. When I tell these people of how the world was when I was young, I can see that they only half-believe me. They smile behind their hands to see me weep, but I will weep my fill, because Fionn and the Fianna are no longer living. They look at my withered flesh and offer to bring me to the man who is preaching of a new god. His name is Patrick and he talks of something called the soul and promises eternal life.

I do not want eternal life. I would sell what the Christians call my soul to have only one day of my youth again – to be alive and strong and a part of the green world, to hear the hounds baying in the forest, the sweet note of the blackbird, and my companions calling me to the hunt.

Caherconree, Kerry
CATHAIR CHONROÍ

The Slieve Mish mountains act as the barrier to an area that has one of the richest local heritages – in terms of archaeological remains, language, folklore and music – in the island of Ireland. The Dingle Peninsula, or *Corca Dhuibhne* (named for one of the septs who lived here in ancient times), is also one of the most astoundingly beautiful places in the country and, as a result of this, has become something of a tourist fly-trap in recent years. However, within a few miles of where a United Nations of visitors eat in restaurants with cuisine (and prices) comparable to the capitals of Europe, there are high and lonely green valleys, cloud-covered for much of the year, where the old ways have not changed greatly and the feeling remains of another world.

One such valley is that of the Finglas River, which leads to the base of Slieve Mish and is one of the starting points for the approach to Caherconree hill-fort. The fort is situated on a spur of Baurtregaum mountain, 683 metres (2,241 feet) above sea level. The climb to the fort is not an easy one, and should be attempted only in good weather – the best route to take is to turn off from the Castlemaine Road to the south where the ascent is marked by red and white poles, a route which avoids the worst of the bogs. At the fort, the views are magnificent, incorporating much of west Munster. Be aware, however, that the mists can come down suddenly and surround you completely, leaving you imprisoned in a grey, swirling world of stone and water-laden air. The hill-fort, which has not been dated exactly but was certainly in use by the Celtic Iron Age, is what is known as an inland promontory fort, with cliffs falling steeply to the north, south and west, and a 110-metre (360-foot) line of massive sandstone blocks stretching fully across the mountain spur and acting as the defence to the east. It was thus almost impregnable – with no entrance apart from the two gateways in the line of rocks.

The location of the fort indicates that it acted as a defence or marker between two tribes; it still forms the boundary between the baronies of Corkaguiney and Trughanacny. There are the remains of a number of stone huts inside the walls and there was also originally a stone trough which was removed in the nineteenth century. However, little else remains to give evidence of the life within the fort. Historically, Caherconree was said to have had seven battles fought around it, but probably, because of its situation, had completely fallen out of use by the time of

the Normans. By the nineteenth century, there was even some dispute as to whether anything remained of the legendary *cathair*. For the legends endured – Caherconree was still famous as the stone fort of the great warrior magician, Cú Roí, from which its name comes.

Cú Roí is an important figure in the stories of the Ulster Cycle, acting as a wise judge and arbitrator in some of its tales. It was he who judged who should receive the champion's portion. He did this by fighting the three great heroes of the Red Branch – Cónal, Laoghaire and Cú Chulainn – in the form of a demon outside his fortress. He eventually awarded the prize to Cú Chulainn, though their relationship was to sour badly in later years. Cú Roí seems to have been associated with the sun. He was said to be a great traveller who returned to his fortress in the evening. He could make the fortress revolve, and so no one could gain entrance to his shining, spinning palace after sunset. But when he was angry he could become terrible. When he helped the men of Ulster in their raid on Iuchar's fortress and he was not included in the sharing of the spoils, he took a terrible revenge.

In legendary terms, the Slieve Mish mountains are also associated with the coming to Ireland of the sons of Míl. They landed at Kenmare Bay on Bealtaine (May) eve and fought their first battle with the Tuatha Dé Danann here. Scota, their queen and wife of Míl, died in the battle and was buried at the place known as Scota's Grave near Tralee. Another Milesian princess, Fas, is buried in nearby Glen Fais. On Slieve Mish, the Milesians met Banba, one of the three queens of Ireland after whom the island was named. As well as having a wealth of legends associated with it, the area is also exceptionally rich in the physical remains of the past – in the early 1980s, an archaeological survey, carried out on the Corca Dhuibhne area, listed no fewer than 1,572 sites of interest. These included rock art, tombs, standing stones, cairns, ring-barrows, promontory forts, ogham stones, holy wells and a large number of wedge tombs dating from the Bronze Age, when the district as a whole seems to have experienced a population explosion.

The slopes and valleys around the Slieve Mish mountains are thinly inhabited today, and the isolation of these valleys may be one of the reasons for their association with madness – Glanagalt (*Gleann na nGealt*, 'The Glen of the Mad People'), the valley where it was reputed that all the insane people of Ireland (including Suibhne or Mad Sweeney) felt compelled to visit, is a little to the west, and Mis herself, after whom the mountain range is named, was said to be a princess who was driven to insanity by the death of her father in battle. When the mist comes down and the valleys become as isolated as islands, it is easy to understand these associations.

If the mist and rain do come down, and Cú Roí's fortress refuses to show itself, spend time around the village of Camp and in the Finglas valley. Finnghlas, the white speckled river, is known as such because of the milk poured down by Cú Roí's wife, Bláthnaid, as a sign to her lover that the time had come to rescue her from her prison in the clouds. The river winds its way through woods of oak and holly, the dark greenness broken only by the vivid colours of montbretia and fuchsia – a world away from the high bleak beauty of the mountainside.

THE DEATH OF CÚ ROÍ

A clear day on the mountain, and a girl with nut-brown hair was carrying a bucket of milk in from where three white cows were pastured. The birds that played about the cows circled her head, unafraid, for the cows were Iuchar's, and Bláthnaid, the flower-like one, was the daughter of that same king. A tall man in a dark grey cloak came down towards her.

'Leave it, my love. Let one of the servants do that.'

The girl smiled, and said in a voice as soft as music, 'Are not all the servants down helping out with building the palace that you are making for me, the greatest palace in Ireland? Are not all the men at arms and bondmaids and builders working down there, and the harpers along with them to keep them cheerful? Are we not the only ones left up here on the mountain?'

Cú Roí, the great king and even greater magician, laughed. His face was like that of a blazing lion, though his curling mane had long ago turned as grey as his cloak.

'Indeed they are – they are all doing your bidding, sweet one. All but Feircheirdne, who is going to play music for us; his tunes are too good to labour to. Let us lie in the sun and listen to him. Ah, here he is. Feircheirdne, play for us.'

Feircheirdne was a fair-haired man with grey eyes that were soft only when he played his music, or sometimes, but even then rarely, when he looked at his king.

'I have a new song, King,' he said. 'I have made it in honour of Bláthnaid, your new wife. It tells the story of how the men of Ulster would not share their spoils with you after you had helped them in their raid against Iuchar, king of the Isle of Man. It tells of how you took Bláthnaid and Iuchar's three cows and the magical cauldron away from the men of Ulster. It tells how you defeated that beardless youth, Cú Chulainn, the young pup they call the

Hound of Ulster, and shaved his head and daubed his skull with dung when he tried to fight you and steal her back from you. They say that he is still skulking around, ashamed to show his face until his hair grows again. It is a mighty song.'

'She is not so new a wife, for it is nearly a year now that I have her,' said Cú Roí fondly. 'But she is all the dearer for that, for a sweeter girl was never born. She it is who calls me back here from all my wanderings. She is the one who holds all the secrets of my heart.'

Bláthnaid put her hand on her husband's arm and said something softly into his ear. Cú Roí's ruddy face became redder and he smiled.

'Well, Feircheirdne, it seems that my wife would like to be alone with me today. Take the chariot out and go down to see how the work is progressing at the fortress.'

be
gl
ra

we
ag

re
to

of
ju
in
th

ci
st
th

se
bl

Feircheirdne looked as if he might be about to protest, but he caught the glint in his master's eye and turned away, giving a peremptory bow to the lady. Bláthnaid drew her husband to the steps of the fort, where they could look down into the valley, blue and hazy on this summer's afternoon, the sea glinting in the distance no bluer than the girl's eyes.

'Let me look for lice in your head, beloved,' she said. 'I saw you scratching yesterday.'

Cú Roí lay with his head in the girl's lap, content in his power and in his love for this captive princess. It seemed that the gentle hands wove their own spell over his grey curls, and she sang gently to him so that he almost slept. In his daze, he did not notice that men were gathering in the glen below Caherconree.

When the sun had risen to its highest point, Bláthnaid said, 'Let me go and heat water for your bath. I will wash you and clean your hair, and then we will lie down together and take some rest.'

'Can we not rest now?' said Cú Roí. Bláthnaid laughed. 'No, let you wash yourself first, you old goat. Go inside and I will bring water.'

Should anyone have been watching Bláthnaid when she went to the stream, they would have seen that she did a curious thing. She took two buckets with her, and while she filled one bucket with water, she poured the contents of the other into the spring. The milk from the marvellous cows coloured the water white as it mixed with the stream. She watched as it flowed downwards to the green valley – that place full of oak trees and holly and small flowers, so different from this cloudy palace where for most of the year she lived in a world enclosed by mist, a thick, grey mist that made her a captive of Cú Roí as effectively as bars and padlocks. Her father's small island had been like the valley, low-lying and fertile, not a the god, Donn, lord of death. Fairy hares, Donn's pets, were often seen on the hill. To the north is Slieve Phelim, another legendary site; to the south, the Harps of Cliú on the Galtees; to the east, the fairy mountain of Slievenamon. There is a sense of richness in these places, both in the physical sense of green life and in the emotional sense of layer upon layer of myth and history embedded in the landscape.

In the village of Knockainey, a dog's bark is the only sound breaking the evening stillness. He stands at the gate to the ancient church and graveyard, daring the stranger to enter and disturb the sleeping dead. Cows graze in the shadow of a ruined stone castle, and the doors of the houses are open, soaking in the last of the sun. The open doors of houses give a glimpse through the darkness to white-painted panelling, a holy water font in the shape of the Virgin Mary, an oilcloth covering a table where pink ham and green lettuce have been laid out for tea. This is deep Ireland.

Above:
'Cromlech on Galtee More', by TC Croker.

ÁINE OF KNOCKAINEY

The bright one, the honey mouth, the wife of the sea god and the great sky-horse, Echdae – she has appeared to so many, from the earliest times to the recent past. She is generous to those who serve her but merciless to those who do not show her respect. She is the child of the sun. She is Áine of Knockainey and Lough Gur.

Strange then, that she should appear by moonlight.

Ailill of Munster, king of the south and the man who would become known as Ailill Ólom, huddled in the lee of a rock. He wondered how he had allowed Fearcheas to convince him to come out once again on Samhain night, the most dangerous night of the year. This was the night when all sensible people kept within doors for fear of the Sídh. He sighed; he had no one to blame but himself, for he had been the one to go to the Leinster druid Fearcheas for advice. But he had been frightened by the great magic he had

Above:

Grange Stone Circle at Lough Gur, County Limerick.

seen on the Samhain morning of the previous year. That Samhain eve, he had been out on the hill, tending his horses, and had fallen into a deep sleep. When he awoke at dawn, he found that the hill had been stripped of its grass during the night and his horses were around him, hungry and dazed on the bare slopes. Ailill's motto was 'What I have, I hold.' Knockainey, for all they might call it a Sídh residence, was within his realm, and he wanted no host of the otherworld people denuding it of its rich grazing. So, protected by the druidic spells from sleep and from the magic mist that allowed no one to see the people of the mounds, he waited with Fearcheas to see what would happen. The moon rose, a sickle-shaped silver boat sailing gently across the sky. Shadows formed around the rocks of the hill and Ailill shivered. Despite the fact that this was the beginning of winter, there was a faint scent of hawthorn in the air. The two men waited.

When the moon had reached the pinnacle of her rising, music filled the air. It seemed to Ailill and Fearcheas that it came from inside the hill, and grew steadily louder. The scent of hawthorn grew stronger in the darkness. And then, where there had been smooth grass, there was an opening, with brightness streaming from it. A herd of cattle came forth, shining gold and silver in the moonlight, and began steadily to crop the grass of the hillside. Two people appeared out of the hill. Dazzled by the light at first, the king and the druid could not make out who the figures were; but as they came closer, they saw that it was an old man with a grave face, and a young and beautiful woman whose golden hair seemed to brighten the air around her to daylight. She was playing on the strings of a bronze *timpán*, and it was from this instrument that the wonderful music came. Ailill was suddenly filled with desire for her, and made towards her. As she turned from him, he grasped her roughly. The old man, meanwhile, began to struggle with Ailill to pull the girl away. Fearcheas threw his spear, piercing the old man through the heart. The woman cried out and dropped her *timpán*, then turned savagely to Ailill, who felt as if he had been set on fire by the warm, beautiful creature in his arms.

Minutes later, it was over. Ailill had, as ever, held what he had – he had violated the girl, and now she stood over him where he lay moaning. In her hands, she held two bloody ears.

'Well may you moan,' she said. 'But you who would not listen are better off without these ears to hear with. Know that you will be cursed for generations to come. You will lose your kingdom and your honour; your foul mouth will become poisonous through your own fault; and never again will you hear the sweet sound of music. Know that you will be called Ailill Ólom – Ailill of the Bald-Ears – from now on, and men will mock you and women laugh behind their hands when you pass. Know that you will know neither rest nor pleasure again.'

Ailill feebly raised his spear, trying to drive it through the woman's heart, but she laughed and drew herself up to her full height so that she seemed no longer a young girl but a woman in the glory of maturity.

'Do you think that you can stop me from rising every morning? Do you not know that every day I arise, new-made, from my bed in the sea-king's kingdom? And although I seem to weaken with winter, do you not know that I rise from my cradle in the earth like the yellow corn every summer? You stupid mortal, do you still not know who I am?'

Behind her, the sky lightened and the first birds began their song. Though it was the first day of the harsh winter, though the lady was pale, and her face as cold as November ice, Ailill could be in no doubt, as the light flowed from her and encircled her head in a nimbus of glory. He was looking at the great lady Áine, goddess of the green hill and of the brightness of the sun.

almost to the extent of hypnotising the wanderer. As you walk through the Burren, the light shines back off both land and sea, and the trinity of light, stone and water has an effect which is quite literally stunning, bringing on a feeling of dislocation which is very hard to describe unless you have experienced it. The Burren is also where some of the major Megalithic remains of Clare are found, including the Polnabrone Dolmen. In contrast, the charm of the area around Doonbeg and the southern part of west Clare lies in its miles of yellow sands, its feeling of openness to wind and water and its cheerful, bucket-and-spade towns like Kilkee and Kilrush. Inland, there are green hills and fertile valleys.

However, every part of Clare shares a wealth of tales associated with ancient heroes such as Cú Chulainn, the Fianna and the Tuatha Dé Danann. Folk tradition has always been very strong in Clare and it has one of the richest musical traditions in the country. In the early twentieth century, the scholar Thomas Westropp recorded many of Clare's traditional stories, including one of the banshee, or fairy woman, which has its origins at least as far back as the eleventh century. Near Killaloe is Craglea, a great rock which is home of a great lady of the Sídh, Aoibheall. She appeared to the high king, Brian Ború, the night before the Battle of Clontarf (1014) and in the fourteenth century to the Norman knight, Richard de Clare, as he made his way to the battle of Corcomroe where his soldiers were slaughtered. On the latter occasion, she was seen washing the bloody armour of the troops at a river. Clare retained these traditions of magic into modern times – Biddy Early, the wise woman of Feakle, practised her magic until her death in 1873, and a mermaid was reportedly seen off Miltown Malbay as late as 1910.

One of the most persistent traditions of this part of the country is that of the fugitive island in the ocean to the west. The islands have been sighted from Liscannor Bay to Loop Head. Sometimes the island is the home of the dead. Sometimes it is Hy Brasil, or Manannán's Many-Coloured Land, the Land of Youth. In Liscannor Bay, the magical island is called Kilstruiteen, a place of gold and silver towers and wooded slopes which sank below the waves thousands of years ago and is seen only once every seven years. It was said that when boats passed over the place where the island was, the passengers could smell the flowers still growing under the water. This mirror-image of a lost land is one of the most powerful in Irish tradition, and, looking out towards the sun setting in the western sea, it is easy to understand why. As the day changes to night, on the deserted sands at Doonbeg, the beach becomes a liminal zone between two states of being, the tide changing the landscape even as one walks upon it. The light transforms the shapes of clouds over the water into towers and forests and valleys, and wakens some deep instinct to believe in that world, where those who are lost are talking and laughing and listening to music – the guests of an otherworld king.

DONN, LORD OF THE RED PALACE

The horns of the moon have risen over the dunes of Doonbeg, and the Lord of the Dark Face watches over the shadowy waves from his red palace, the home of those who have left life and gone to their ancestors. Kings and warriors and old wise men, smiling mothers and proud queens, mourning widows and merry girls – all of them come home to Donn's house, far to the southwest of Ireland.

The waves are still tonight, and Donn has not yet made his journey to summon those whom he will take to his home. He is the lord of shadow, of storms and shipwrecks and those who die with blood upon them. Unlike the Morrigan, however, he does not glory in slaughter. He is the god of truth as well as death, for death is the inescapable last truth. His sister is the goddess Áine of Knockainey, the goddess with the face of the sun. He knows that even the people of the Sídh, bright and powerful as they are, will finally come to his shadowy house. He watches and waits quietly in the darkness.

And tonight, someone has come to beg a boon of him.

Fionn is known by all as a great hunter, a great warrior, a great womaniser, a great giver of gifts and hospitality, and an even greater boaster about his own past. He is fair-haired and broad-shouldered and, when the two men stand together, it would seem that he should be the one granting the favours. But that is not the case – Fionn has come to plead for a gift for one of his companions. For, in addition to his other attributes, Fionn has great loyalty to his friends. He has made the journey to the House of Donn out of concern for one beloved to him.

'Lord Donn,' Fionn says, bowing very low. 'My musician, Cnú Dearóil, is a sad and lonely man, for he has no wife. Usually, this would not be a problem, for I could easily find one for him from the numerous princesses, fairy-women, messengers and seers that gather around me and the Fianna, like bees around honey. But there is a problem, my lord. Cnú Dearóil is no taller than four of my fists, though he is the greatest musician the world has ever known. Gracious Lord Donn, if you were to hear him play, even you would be impressed. Warriors suffering from the wounds of battle and women in labour fall asleep when Cnú Dearóil plays his lullabies. So I have come to you,

great lord of the otherworld, to beg for a wife of a suitable size for my friend.'

Lord Donn considers for a moment, and then nods his head graciously. 'I will see what can be done,' he promises.

And he is as good as his word, for within his realm he finds the musician a wife as fair as a May blossom. She is called Bláthnuit, meaning 'Little Blossom', and she is no bigger than Cnú Dearóil himself. The pair live together for many happy years, travelling on Fionn's horse on his journeys throughout Ireland, taking refuge from the rain under his cloak. When they die, they too are welcomed into the House of Donn, and Cnú Dearóil plays the music that lets the dead forget their past sorrows.

In his dealings with the great ones, with warriors like Fionn and kings and princesses, Donn was often generous. But Donn was not generous only to the rich and mighty. He has been seen wearing a black silk hat, giving alms to a widow who went outside her house so that her starving children should not see her weep on a hungry Christmas Eve. He saved the cattle of a local herdsman from theft. His horses are often heard at *Cnoc an tSodair*, the Hill of the Trotting, near the shore at the dunes, and his lights are seen over the same dunes where those he has brought home feast with him, listening to the music made in his dark tower. He gives the best to his guests – the willowy girls and blue-eyed athletes, the grey-haired widows and toothless, tired old men. For the Lord of Death is courteous, and not just in giving the gifts of life. Sometimes, and not rarely, when he calls those who have lived too long or have suffered too much, he is more than courteous – he is kind.

CONNACHT

Dún Aonghusa,
the Aran Islands,
ÁRAINN MHÓR Galway

I f certain places have their defining myths – the story that seems best to embody the experience of the place and of the people who have lived there – the myth of the Aran Islands must be one of survival. Survival against the harshness of the elements, the wild western sea and ferocious winds coming in over the Atlantic; survival in a hard and inhospitable landscape. The islands are made up of the same grey carboniferous limestone pavement that covers the Burren, and what little soil there is is the result of back-breaking effort on the part of the human population. The tiny, stone-walled fields were created from sand and seaweed and broken shells. Because there are few trees – what there are are low-lying hawthorn and hazel – and no turf, at one time even fuel was at a premium, ferried in from Galway on the famous hookers. It was not an easy existence, but the community survived.

And what also survived were ancient customs, an ancient language, and one of the most impressive monuments of ancient Ireland – the great fort of Dún Aonghusa.

The fort is situated on the largest of the Aran Islands, Inishmore. It dominates the island. Its situation is one of astounding natural drama and beauty. Built on the edge of cliffs almost 100 metres (328 feet) above sea level, the stone fort is made up of three widely spaced horseshoe-shaped walls. The walls are massive and the complex covers 4.5 hectares (11 acres) of land. One of the most impressive features is the middle rampart of *chevaux de frise*, where jagged limestone rocks form an impenetrable barrier to the inner area. There is a single entrance through this army of stones to the open spaces of the innermost court and the natural stone platform near the edge of the precipice.

In mythological terms, Dún Aonghusa does not seem to have any connection with the god of the Tuatha Dé Danann, Aonghus Óg. The fort was said to have been built by another Aengus, the last king of the Fir Bolg. The Fir Bolg were one of the ancient tribes of Ireland who were gradually driven to the extreme western shores of the country before their final defeat. There has been ongoing controversy over the function and dating of Dún Aonghusa. The huge effort put into the defences may suggest a refuge, although some archaeologists have dismissed this

Pages 128-129:
Abbey of Cong, County Mayo.
Above:
An engraving of the stone fort of Dún Aonghusa, the Aran Islands, Galway.

Above:
*The great stone fort
of Dún Aonghusa,
the Aran Islands,
Galway.*

It was a changed Ireland, for the conquering Dé Danann had themselves been defeated by the Sons of Míl, and a new king reigned at Tara. King Cairbre had at first welcomed the Fir Bolg, but as time went on, he had become more and more wary of their power and had imposed heavy taxes on them. Finally, the Fir Bolg had fled west and set up their kingdom on Galway Bay. Their realm had stretched from Black Head to Ballyvaughan, and they had built great forts along the line of their jurisdiction.

However, Cairbre had been watching from the east, fearful of their power, and had finally sent warriors against them. Bloody battles had been fought, with great losses on both sides, until Aengus had sent his three brothers and his son, Conall, to fight the four mighty warriors who led the enemy: Ceat Mac Maghach, Conall Cearnach, Ros Mac Deadha and the great Cú Chulainn himself. Aengus's beloved son, Conall, had fought against the Hound of Ulster, and had been killed by a blow from the *Gáe Bolg*, the fiery bolt which was Cú Chulainn's invincible weapon.

Conall had been young, and had held the promise of being a great king.

Why hold on to my kingdom, thought Aengus, if there is no child to hand it on to? Why try to lead on a people who are dying all around me? Why try to hold my name when there is no one to pass it on to?

He looked to the sky, waiting to hear the voice of the Lord of Storms, waiting to see the sky split open and the heavens descend in a deluge of water and wind. But there was only the sea; blood red as the sun sank into it. And the white stone all around him – hard, ungiving and silent.

There was water in his eyes – whether from the spray of the ocean or something else Aengus was not prepared to question – and a smell of salt and blood on the wind. The king looked down to the pale rocks under his feet, to where the delicate white bones of a seagull lay crushed, and beside them the remains of the broken egg of some bird. Then he arose and went to buckle on sword and shield and take up his spear, for all that was left for him to do was to die fighting the enemies of his people. In a time as short as the wink of a god's eye, nothing would be left of him or his race but a fortress of stone on the edge of the world, carrying his name and the bloodline of a dark race.

Lough Corrib, Galway

LOCH COIRIB

Lough Corrib, the lake sacred to the god Manannán, is situated north of Galway city and touches Mayo on its northern flank. It is the second largest lake in Ireland and is bordered by a variety of landscapes. Approximately 56 kilometres (35 miles) long, it varies greatly in width and is dotted by no fewer than 145 islands. It is said that Manannán, taking on the shape of a mortal called Oirbsiu, was killed by Uillen Red Edge at the battle of Cuillen. Loch Corrib rose where his blood spilled, bringing his mortal flesh back into the watery, immortal world that is his realm. If that is the case, and god is dead, the lake is a worthy tomb. Rushes, sacred to this particular god, grow around it and it changes shape and character as often as a cloud blows across the sun and shadows cross this world of water and mist and wooded islets. Manannán himself was a trickster, changing shape as often as water – sometimes an old man in a grey cloak, sometimes a great warrior riding the waves like horses. He was called Manawyddan in Wales and was also the three-legged solar god from which the Isle of Man takes its name. His wives were Áine, the sun-goddess of the south (though some say that she is his daughter) and Fand, the woman of the Sídh who loved Cú Chulainn so desperately. He shook his cloak between Fand and Cú Chulainn so that the memory of their mad love should fade from their hearts. He had many children, and his daughter lakes are Sheelin and Ennell, Owel and Derravaragh. One of his sons was the great king Mongan, the shape-changer; one of his foster-sons was Lugh, the many-skilled god.

He gave the Sídh the gift of invisibility and shape-changing, and some say that it was he who divided the palaces in the hollow hills among the Tuatha Dé Danann after their defeat by the Milesians. It was he who instigated the feast of Goibhniu, where food never runs out, and the people of Danu are renewed and made young again. The pigs of Manannán, when killed and eaten, rise up the next day, ready again for the feast.

The eastern side of Manannán's lake is flat and less beautiful than the west, although there are still interesting sites to visit. One of these is Annaghdown, a village with a substantial complex of ecclesiastical remains, and the site of the drowning of Annach Cuan. The story of this tragic drowning gave rise to one of the loveliest songs in the Irish language, 'Annach Cuan'. Knockma, the home of the fairy king, Finvarra, is also near this part of the lake.

In contrast to the east side of the lake, its north and western perimeters border Connemara, which has some of the wildest and most dramatic scenery in Ireland. It is this mixture of landscape – pasture and woodland, rock and bog, islands and lake – which give the lake its unique character. One of the most beautiful parts of the lakeshore is around the villages of Cong and Clonbur on its northern tip. The towering mountains are relieved by the presence of the lovely wooded slopes of the river which flows through Cong. Cong itself is a tiny village and, although it is heavily frequented by tourists, it is still, with a fine Augustinian priory, a beautiful place to visit. The monastic settlement here originally dated from the seventh century. The underlying rock in this area is limestone, and is fissured with caverns and underground rivers – a world of constant subterranean activity. To the north of the village is the Plain of Moytura – the place claimed by William Wilde, the famous Oscar's father, as the site of the first battle of the Dé Dananns against their enemies the Fir Bolg. Most authorities now assert that both battles took place at the site near Lough Arrow in Sligo, but Wilde's theory was supported by the very large number of prehistoric antiquities – particularly cairns – in the surrounding district. Early Christian remains are also plentiful; some of the most atmospheric are on the island of Inchagoill, which can be reached by ferry from Cong. This wooded graveyard was in use until relatively recently, and there are substantial Romanesque ecclesiastical remains. There is also the Stone of Lugha, which is one of the earliest Christian inscriptions in Ireland.

Below:
Ruins of Cong Abbey,
County Mayo.

Travelling on the lake is probably one of the easiest ways to get a sense of this watery, woody landscape. Another, slightly more difficult one is to hike up into the mountains around Clonbur and Cornamona. Here one enters a world of shifting mists and unexpected sunlight, of rain that covers the patchwork of bright fields in a watery haze and then, just as suddenly, passes over. Our minds stained by our technicoloured culture, we find the effects almost too much. How can these colours, this light, be real? Is Maureen O'Hara about to come tripping over that emerald-green hilltop? Where is the Hollywood cameraman hiding – the master of illusion who just this second decided to light up that particular island with yet another rainbow? Or was that improbable band of colour beaming in a message from that other great trickster – was that really a sign from Manannán's Many-Coloured Land?

MANANNÁN AND THE CRANE BAG

A fine, mackerel-skied evening over the silver sea, and the Son of Lir was out riding his great horse, Waterfoam, skimming over the waves, surveying his realm. To him, the ocean is a purple-flecked pasture of flowers, the salmon its lambs, leaping high in the water. He is equally at home over and under the waves, bringing some chosen ones, like Connla and Bran and the great King Cormac, to visit him in the Apple Isle, the Land of Promise. In his kingdom, blue and crimson horses graze, gold and silver birds sing in trees with shining leaves, and there are houses of white bronze, set with jewels and crystals and thatched with white feathers. This day he had been out hunting, with his spear and his bow in his hands, scanning the skies for birds to bring home to the feast. Now it was evening, with a golden sky to the west, and he had turned in towards the mountains, hoping that there he might capture an eagle or a sparrowhawk.

He narrowed his eyes against the setting sun – surely there was a bird, an exceptionally large and beautiful one, flying high over the lakes in the valleys

landscape of high mountains, rocky passes, and most of all, blanket bog. This stunning but desolate landscape is barely relieved by a house, much less a village. Boglands have a particular atmosphere which is all their own. No crops can be grown there; no animals can graze there. They contain great riches of plant life but the overriding feeling of travelling through such a landscape is one of desolation. It has a strange, slightly uncomfortable beauty. The bogs are the Irish equivalent of the desert – a desert made up of brown earth and water and open skies; a place in which the individual feels very small against the vastness of a landscape that seems untouched by humanity. The boglands are also preservers – indeed petrifiers of the past, a growing and living memory of the race. When the tracts of bogs at the Céide Fields in Mayo were excavated, extensive remains of a highly organised prehistoric landscape of fields and structures was discovered under the blanket of turf. The dark tower of Bellacorrick power station stands out in harsh contrast to its surrounding bog, the source of its fuel. One wonders if in future years our descendants will look back on the stripping of the bog in the same way that we look back in sadness at the clearing of the great Irish forests.

Perhaps the feeling of loneliness in Mayo is increased by the knowledge that this

Below:
View of Clew Bay and Croagh Patrick, County Mayo, by FW Fairholt.

is not a countryside that was never settled, but one that once had a much higher population than it has now. Mayo was one of the counties that suffered most from the disasters of the

FAIRHOLT

BASTIN

nineteenth century, particularly the Great Famine and the ensuing mass emigration. Up until very recently, a huge percentage of its young people were still being leached from its soil. Now, however, the empty landscape is beginning to be filled with new houses – during the past five years, Belmullet has seen growth and prosperity probably unknown since its hey-day as a market town in the mid-nineteenth century. Yet, despite its new wealth, the smells of turf smoke and seaweed still linger in its small harbour.

Inis Glora, however, has lost its human community, possibly forever. Like the neighbouring Iniskea islands, it was inhabited until the mid-1930s, but the island community was shattered in 1927 when ten of its people were drowned at sea. Up until more recently, fishermen lived on the islands during the summer and worked the seas off their coasts, but this too has ceased. There is no regular boat service to Inis Glora, and if you wish to visit it, you must make your arrangements well in advance – it was only the native courtesy and sense of hospitality of the Mayo people which got us there at all.

If you can manage it, make the journey. The island is about 3 kilometres (less than 2 miles) offshore and is only about 27 hectares (66 acres) in size. There is no pier so you would need to be reasonably agile – and wearing wellingtons – for the scramble onto the rocky shore. On the island, there are the remains of a Celtic monastic settlement said to have been founded by St Brendan. You will also find the remnants of a stone church and some beehive huts, together with various other enclosures, including the church of the women. It was said that bodies buried in the soil here did not rot, because the place was so sacred.

The island is deserted now except for sea birds and some sheep. There are no beaches, but lovely golden and pink stones veined with silver line the shore and long ridges from old potato crops, like giants' graves, cover much of the interior – a record of the lost community. During our visit there, a gull circled noisily overhead, as if warning us off her property. She became particularly vociferous as we walked to the southern end of the island, away from the Christian section. Here there are mounds of broken stone, littered with the bones and feathers of birds, with sheep skulls and brown pools between the rocks. The patterns of the bright tawny lichen on the stones are uncannily like the spirals and semi-spirals, the circles and cup marks of the Megalithic art found at Knowth.

Even if you do not make it to the island, the peninsula itself is a beautiful place to visit. It is covered in extensive early Christian and Megalithic remains. It was the reputed home of Fliodhas, the wife of Fergus Mac Róich and an ancient goddess of wild things, especially deer. The Mullet is a place of long, deserted beaches – pale dunes filled with small singing birds and long grass bending in the wind. In summer, the shades of blue on the distant mountains darken into black and purple; and the lighter greys and silvers also constantly shift and change. These are some of the most beautiful views in Ireland, towards the deceptively gentle line of mountains to the south, with the cliffs and mountains of Achill and the southern coastline of Mayo. Achill is where the great Hawk of Achill, who lived for thousands of years, was said to have had his home. To the south, beyond Achill, is the holy mountain, Croagh Patrick, one of the most revered places in Ireland, where a pilgrimage is still held in July every year – a continuation of the ancient Lughnasa rite. St Patrick is said to have been tormented by black-winged birds on 'the Reek', and then comforted by angels with white wings, who came to him in multitudes – one angel for every soul saved in Ireland.

In the townland of Cross on the Mullet, Cross Abbey stands on the coast facing towards Inis Glora at the closest point to the island. Beside a long white beach there are still the remains of a monastery and graveyard. The monks from Inis Glora moved here after they had left the island. Close by, you can visit Cross Lake, which is said to have been a refuge of the Children of Lir during wild winter weather. If you make the journey to the lake in winter, when it becomes the haunt of barnacle geese and whooper swans, you may see white wings flying out towards the lonely island in the west.

THE CHILDREN OF LIR

The moment of transformation – from fair day to storm, from maiden to wife, from good woman to demon, from white-limbed child to swan. Four pairs of grey eyes staring at me in horror as I transformed myself before their very eyes from loving mother into wicked witch. The eyes that looked at me were my sisters' eyes, and my own eyes, for everyone said that we were as alike as three peas in a pod, the fair daughters of Bodhbh – Aobh, Aoife and Ailbhe. Why did Lir not choose me in the first place? My father offered him the choice; but he chose my elder sister, seeing in her wisdom and nobility.

He did not hear me calling silently to him, 'Choose me, Prince. Choose me.'

My sister Aobh did not have time to grow old and wise, for she died when she bore her second set of twins, Conn and Fiachra. The eldest pair, Fionnuala and Aodh, were still not much more than babies. And then my father called Lir to him again and offered me to him – Aoife, the second sister, the second best – and he agreed to take me then, but his face and his heart were closed against me.

I loved my husband and I loved my sister's children, and for many years, I was a good wife and a good mother, while I waited to have my own child – a child to whom I would be the first, the most important one, the real mother. When that did not happen, it seemed that nobody cared very much. Lir had his four children – three sons and a fine daughter – and my father his grandchildren. As they grew up, it seemed that Fionnuala was set to rival my sister in the love she inspired in all who had dealings with her. It is hard to be always second choice. The children made their own self-contained little world: two sets of twins, indissolubly linked, unheeding of my pleas to let me into their tightly closed circle. And that was perhaps why I became bitter and sick, and I lay in my bed for a year and waited for someone to notice. Something grew and hardened in me during that year. Lir would come and ask me how I felt, but did not listen for my answer. Fionnuala would come with the boys, shushing them to be quiet so as not to disturb me. I could hear their relieved laughter when they left me. Life went on around me.

One autumn morning, I got up and called the children to me. I told them that they were going to visit their grandfather, and they were delighted – all but Fionnuala, who looked at me strangely and when I asked her what was the matter, said that she had not slept well, a night of bad dreams.

I took them in my chariot to Lake Derravaragh, and told them to bathe, for although it was the end of the year, the air was mild and the water warm. As I watched them in the water, their white limbs dancing in the low sunlight, splashing and playing and singing and laughing, I knew that I could not kill them. So I took my wand and pronounced their doom, and looked on as the white feathers sprouted on their flesh, their necks growing longer, their feet becoming webbed and their legs short and unwieldy.

'You shall spend the rest of your days as swans,' I said. 'Three hundred years you will spend here at this lake, then three hundred years on the Sea of Moyle. Do you know the Sea of Moyle? It is one of the wildest and coldest seas in the world. Your webbed feet will freeze to the rocks, so that when you

Above:

*The ruins of Cross
Abbey standing on the
coast, facing towards
Inis Glora, County
Mayo.*

try to get loose, you will tear your feet, and when you swim, the salt water
will be agony.

'The last three hundred years you will spend on Inis Glora, in the western
ocean. You shall not be released from this spell until the man of the north
marries the woman from the south. But I will give you one boon – during all
this time, you will retain your human minds and your human voices, and you
will sing such music that all who hear you will be astounded, and however
sad they are, they will be comforted.'

And then I could look at them no more, but made my way to my father's
palace. His face dropped when he saw that I was alone, and the bitterness in
my heart increased. Of course, it was not long before the people of Danu
discovered my evil-doing; and my own father in his great anger turned me
into a demon of the air, condemned to fly and wander in exile forever,
terrifying all who saw or heard me.

The moment of transformation – from good daughter to shrieking demon,
from one of the tribe to the one who will always be an exile. Fionnuala,
Aodh, Conn and Fiachra had an easier time of it than I did, for during their
three hundred years on the lake, the Danann came and listened to them and

cheered them; and their music comforted all who heard it – all, that is, except me. But then they went to the Sea of Moyle, and that was a hard time for them, for the storms beat their soft feathers, and the ice froze their feet to the sharp rocks, and the wind drowned out their singing; and no one was within miles to listen to their music in any case, except poor sailors blown off course who covered their ears for fear of the treacherous songs of mermaids. Fionnuala would try to shelter her brothers under her wings and at the pin-feathers of her breast, and it was only the heat of the four bodies that kept them alive on many, many nights. Often, though, they would be blown apart, separated from each other, and each one found those wild, lonely nights the hardest – not knowing if they would meet again.

How do I know this? I know because I was there, hating them still, but still their mother, watching over them – needing to know that they still suffered. Those wild nights were the only ones where I myself escaped my pain. For, buffeted by wild wind and crashing waves, I was released from the anger that burnt inside me. The wildness of the storms carried me to some other place where I no longer needed love, and my rage was called back to me in the wind and the water.

However, that too finally ended, and the four swans made their way westwards, passing over their father's *sídh* at Sídh Fionnachaidh. They called aloud as they passed over, and the Danann looked up at the four magical birds, so white against the blue sky of autumn; they waved at them but the four children did not stop, for the times had changed. The Sídh now disguised their palaces as grassy mounds, hiding them from the eyes of the new race that lived in Ireland. The Place of the White Field seemed to the swans no more than green mounds and furze and crops of nettles – not jewelled palaces and lovely orchards; not houses thatched with white feathers. The song they sang then was so mournful that I think if I had had any heart left, it would have been broken by the music. Meanwhile, below, the Danann called to them in frantic voices to come home, come back to their loved ones. They flew on, unable to hear, far to the west and to the shores of the great ocean.

And there, on Inis Glora, they found a lake on an island, where they made their last home. Their music was such that it drew birds from everywhere around. And after another three hundred years had come and gone, I heard new sounds on the island – the chant of Latin and the tolling of a bell. A hermit came there – a gentle man who listened to the birds every evening, and they told him their tale. He made silver chains for them, which held them together, so that no matter how wild the storms were, they could never become separated. I hid in the trees by the lake, silent and watchful, knowing that the day would finally come when the enchantment would end.

A princess from the south married a prince from the north, and, having heard of the wonderful music of the four swans that lived on Inis Glora, she demanded them as a bridal gift from her husband. But when the prince came to fetch them, the hermit Mochaomhóg refused to give them up. The prince became angry and made to take them by force from where they stood by the altar in the hermit's tiny church.

And then again, the moment of transformation — from swan to human. Not to godlike children, on the verge of blossoming, but to four withered old people, bent and broken, ready for death – children who had never grown up, had never known the pain of not being loved enough; children who had found love even in the shape of wild swans; children who were nearly a thousand years old.

Then Fionnuala said, in a cracked voice that was hardly above a whisper, 'Brother Mochaomhóg, our time is not long. Baptise us now, and bury us together in the churchyard of your god. Bury Conn on my right and Fiachra on my left, and place Aodh before me, for it was so we used to stand on the rocks of the Sea of Moyle when the wind buffeted us, during so many cold and bitter nights.'

So the children of the Sídh were transformed into good Christian corpses and buried far from the mounds of their people. The hermit mourned them greatly. He still goes to the lake in the evening, but it is silent now except for the harsh call of the gulls; all the birds that sang there once have fled. My voice has called to him once or twice, but he does not even hear me above his prayers. I continue to live, without the mercy of death. I suffer more than the children ever suffered. They have found release in their last transformation – to bleached bones buried beside a priest's cell. I am what I have always been. With no hope of rest or change, I make my cries, shrieking my pain over barren islands, limitless oceans, salt foam white as a swan's wing.

Rathcroghan, Roscommon

CRUACHAIN

The road between the small Roscommon village of Tulsk and the town of Ballaghadereen travels through the site of one of the most important ancient ritual centres on the whole island of Ireland. It is easy to pass by without realising this. Perhaps the sight of a green mound on the side of the road might stir a memory of ancient Cruachain, home of the warrior queen, Maeve; or perhaps, passing through Tulsk, you might stop for a coffee at the Heritage Centre and discover that there is a world of ancient magical places surrounding the village. Even among those interested in mythology and archaeology, Rathcroghan is surprisingly little known and explored. The site covers 6 kilometres (almost 4 miles) and includes over 80 different pre-Norman features. There are monuments dating from various periods – Megalithic tombs, Bronze Age cairns and forts of the early Christian period. Within the complex, there are acres of unexplored mounds and a cave reputed to be the entry to the otherworld.

Above:
*Tulsk Abbey, County
Roscommon.*

Detailed surveying of this huge site began only in the 1980s, and excavation of the features is still in the early stages. Many of the structures remain a mystery but some certainly date back to 3000BC. *Ráth Cruachain*, or Cruachain Fort, the largest mound in the complex, is easily accessible from the road, and this is traditionally held to be the place where the quarrel between Ailill and Maeve began over who had the greatest wealth. This was the quarrel which started the *Táin*, Ireland's great epic. As with so many of these sites, Iron Age dwellings were built on the site of much older structures, often graves, because these places had been held sacred over many centuries. Ráth Cruachain is not a high mound, but like Tara, it gives the sense of altitude and distance – of imperial powers looking over acres of land and claiming it as a kingdom. The sky is wide and the surrounding land flat, but not boggy – this is good, fertile grazing land.

To the south of the mound, there are traces of an ancient avenue, running east to west, which was probably used in the ceremonies held here at Samhain, the cusp of the new year, when Maeve would consult with her druids as to what the future year might bring to her and her people. During my visit on a bright winter's day, the outlines of the hills seemed etched in some hard, bright metal – silver or perhaps iron – and the land itself, with its smooth green mounds, leaves a sense of a landscape little changed over long centuries. It is easy to imagine the herds of cattle and flocks of sheep, the horses and pigs and dairy cows, being herded before Maeve and Ailill, and the people moving backwards and forwards from their wattle

huts, sheltered by earthen mounds and wooden fences. As the red sun sets in the sky, it is also easy to imagine the warriors gathering, filling the plains as far as the eye can see, readying themselves for their march to Ulster and to death.

Rathnadarve or *Ráth na dTarbh*, the Fort of the Bulls, is a large ring-barrow, situated near Ráth Cruachain at Ballymacthomas. According to local tradition, this is the circular earthen stockade where the Brown Bull and the White Bull were herded together to fight their last battle. Nearby is Oweynagat or *Uaimh na gCat*, the Cave of the Cats, a place steeped in local folklore and myth. Access to the cave is possible, though wet-weather gear is essential. In 1779, it was still known as the Hell-Mouth of Ireland, a tradition that had survived for thousands of years. In this cave, the war-goddess, the Morrigan, was said to live, and, at Samhain, magic pigs and bronze-beaked birds issued forth from it. The great hero, Nera, entered the underworld through Owneygat. A further legend links the cave with a tunnel connecting it with the caves of Keshcorann in Sligo, another home of malevolent female deities. Mirroring this site of otherworld power, at Carnfree, south of Tulsk, there is a centre of earthly power which, in historical times, was the inauguration site of the O'Conors, kings of Connacht.

Cruachain continued as an important centre of assembly well into the beginning of the Christian era; it may have been deserted as late as the beginning of the ninth century. Legend has it that Christianity came here with St Patrick, who met the two daughters of the King of Leinster as they were learning the ways of magic from the Cruachain druids, at Ogulla or Clebach well, southwest of Tulsk. As was usual with these stories, the two maidens enthusiastically embraced the Christian faith and died directly after having received baptism. The well is still the site of a local pattern and is well cared for by the people of the village. In fact, Rathcroghan has been fortunate in that the population has respected the monuments enough to keep them preserved through many centuries. The local community has now established

an excellent interpretative centre which helps greatly in putting the locality into context. However, nothing can really compete with visiting the mounds themselves and watching the flocks of birds blown across the plains by a wind as fierce and relentless as the will of Connacht's ancient queen.

PILLOW TALK:
The Beginning of the Táin Bó Cuailgne

The marital bed at Rathcroghan was vast and deep, and Ailill Mac Máta never questioned who his wife and consort, Queen Maeve of Connacht, brought into it. She had married him not only because he was a king in his own right, but because he was a man who would not be mean, or cowardly, or jealous; she boasted that she never had one man without another waiting in his shadow. Ailill had reason to know the truth of this, for at the moment he was quite sure that his wife was sleeping with Fergus Mac Róich, the Ulster warrior who had taken refuge in the court of Cruachain after Conchobhar Mac Neasa had tricked him into betraying the Sons of Usna. Fergus was an embittered man, but nonetheless a great warrior and a clever counsellor; still, Ailill wondered if his wife really had to give him the friendship of her thighs as well as that of her court in order to keep him in their camp.

He looked down at her while she slept, her straight yellow hair loose on the fine pillows, her grey eyes closed; for once, her long face was peaceful, but Ailill knew that just as soon as she woke there would be plots and dissension and sometimes, and not rarely, false promises coming from that lovely mouth. However, times had been quiet lately and the land rich in herds, the rivals to their power lying low before the combined strength of Maeve and Ailill. They knew the ruthlessness of Maeve – she had killed her sister in order to rule at Rathcroghan and she would kill, sell or barter any of her loved ones to keep it and to keep her power. Ailill's face was tender as he looked at her, for she held her husband's devotion like she held her great wolfhounds, tight to her side on a short leash, easily brought to heel. Yet, deep down, he thought to himself that she was lucky to have him, for there were not many who could have put up with her scheming and her temper.

As he watched the sunlight streaming down on his wife's face, she opened one eye and looked at him. Maeve, when she awoke, awoke like a warrior, fully alert and ready for battle.

'What is it?' she asked, 'What are you thinking of?'

'Ah, nothing really,' said Ailill.

'Go on, then,' said Maeve. 'You must have been thinking of something.'

Ailill answered at random: 'I was just thinking that you were a lucky woman to have married me.'

Maeve sat up against the pillows and narrowed her eyes.

'And what do you mean by that?'

Ailill shrugged. He was beginning to regret that he had started this conversation.

'Only that you are better off now than the day you married me.'

'Am I indeed? And are you not better off that I took you still young and brought you to my bed and gave such gifts to you? I was the highest and mightiest, the bravest in battle of my father's six daughters, and that is why I rule in his place. Look at the soldiers I have and the common men and the herds and the bondmaids and the gold. Do I not rule over this great land with wealth enough without you to be called one of Ireland's great queens? I have heard them say that you are no more than a kept man really, husband dear.'

Ailill rose from the bed and began to buckle on his sword.

'That is not the truth and well you know it, woman. I have brought you great wealth.'

Maeve rose also, and pulled her sword towards her.

'Well, then, prove it – let us each count our wealth and see who is the richest.'

'Let us do that, so,' said Ailill.

The counting of the goods took many days. First of all, the household goods were piled in great heaps and counted – everything from buckets and tubs to golden rings and bracelets; clothes of all colours; slaves and servants; swords and shields and bronze-tipped spears. But Ailill and Maeve were equal in all that their households held.

Then they started on the animals – the pigs, the sheep, the rams, the lambs, the mares and foals and stallions – but again there was no difference between what they possessed.

Finally, they counted the herds of cattle. They walked around the stockades listening to the bellowing within while all the calves and cows and bulls were counted. And once again, they were equal – except for one thing. Ailill had the great bull Finnbheannach, who had left his wife's herd to be with that of the king.

Maeve's pale face went white with rage when she saw that her husband had something that she did not have, for truly the beast was magnificent. Fifty young boys could play on the breadth of his back, and when he stamped the earth, he dug a trench of thirty feet. The very palace of Cruachain shook when he bellowed.

Maeve felt all her pleasure in her wealth turn to ashes in her mouth, and she demanded of her counsellors where she might find a bull the equal of Finnbheannach. She was told of such a one, the Donn of Cooley, who was owned by the farmer Dáire. She called her messenger, Mac Roth, to her. 'Go to Dáire,' she said. 'And tell him that in exchange for the loan of his bull for a year, I will give him such gifts as he will never have seen before – bondmaids and gold, cattle and horses, and my protection for life. Promise him anything, but come back with the bull.'

Mac Roth returned some days later, but without the bull. Maeve came to meet him in her chariot, her face set with anger when she saw no sign of the Donn.

Mac Roth stood before Maeve with his eyes cast down and told his tale: 'When we arrived at the house of Dáire, we were welcomed with much honour. I put forward your proposition and the farmer, who is an excitable man, was so delighted that he burst his cushion underneath him, bouncing up and down with glee. He called for wine and fine food to seal the bargain.'

Mac Roth paused, then continued in a lower voice. 'Some of the company drank too deeply of the good wine put before us. Their tongues were loosened and they began to boast that it was as well Dáire had agreed to let us have the bull, as if he had not done so, it would have been no difficulty for us to take the Donn away from him by force.

'By this stage, Dáire too had been drinking; and he became angry. He told us to go back to our mistress and tell her that he would let no bull of his stray into Connacht.' Mac Roth paused.

'Continue,' said Maeve icily.

'He said also …' Mac Roth swallowed. 'He said to me to tell my mistress that if she is in need of a bull let her come to him and see what the men of Ulster can do for her.'

Maeve's face was set with rage.

'So be it,' she said. 'We will go to Ulster. We will go into Ulster with such a hosting that the men of Ulster will bow down before us in terror. We have Fergus Mac Róich and he will lead us through the gap of the north and we will slaughter every mother's son of them. I will call on all my allies from the south and the east and we will make these proud Ulstermen eat their words. And then we will take this bull into Connacht to be part of my herd.'

She stopped, for she had suddenly noticed that there was a girl sitting in her chariot – a golden-haired girl, armed with a spear and dressed in a speckled green cloak. The girl had not been there the moment before.

Maeve spoke quietly, for she knew by the triple irises in the girl's eyes that she was in the presence of a member of the Sídh. 'Who are you?' she asked.

'I am Fedelm the prophetess,' the girl answered.

'Tell me then,' said Maeve. 'Do you see a great victory for me over the Ulstermen?'

The girl's eyes met Maeve's.

'I see crimson; I see red,' she said.

'But do you see me bringing the Donn back to my herds?'

'I see crimson; I see red,' said the girl again.

'Do you see me leading my army, victorious and proud?'

'I see crimson; I see red,' said the girl.

So Maeve turned from her and asked her no more, but began to plan how she would gain allies. She would promise gold and riches, land and bondmaids to those who fought with her, and if that was not enough, she would promise her daughter, Fionnabhair, to the warriors of Ireland. She would even promise her own body to those who would work with her to destroy the forces of Ulster, to beat every warrior of the north into the ground. She would win such a victory that all who heard her story would say that she was the greatest ruler in Ireland. She planned how she would watch, laughing, while Dáire, who had dared to insult her, had his head and his privates cut off and placed on a stake. She counted her finger rings and thought about how many more she could pile in her coffers. She had long ago given up wearing an extra one for every king killed, for there had been so many, but she would be sure to get more to store for her daughter's dowry. She sniffed the air, smelling blood, and watched as a scald-crow took flight from the body of a dead calf, its black shape cutting through the gentle blue sky.

And so began the *Táin Bó Cuailgne*, The Cattle Raid of Cooley.

The story of the Táin *is continued in 'The Fight at the Ford' and 'The Battle of the Bulls'.*

Ardagh Hill, Longford

BRUIDEN BRÍ LÉITH

The *Brú of Midhir* is Ardagh Hill, otherwise known as Slieve Golry or Slieve Callery – a word that comes from Calraighe, the name of one of the ancient tribes which inhabited the area. It is a partially forested hill near the village of Ardagh, County Longford. This is the heart of the midlands – a place of small villages and reasonably good farmland, but prone to flooding in the winter months; some fields remain under water for weeks on end. It is not a place of great dramatic beauty; nor is it a place where much is made of a glorious past. However, this is also the ancient Plain of Tethbha, and Ardagh Hill, rising to no more than 198 metres (650 feet), dominates the surrounding flat area. *Bruiden Brí Léith* means the 'Dwelling Place of Liath'.

This hill was the site of the main dwelling of Midhir of the Sídh. Midhir was a wise

judge, the foster-father of Aonghus Óg, god of love, and the father of the war-goddess, Macha. His *sídh* was said to be guarded by three cranes, which had only to look on warriors in order to rob them of the will to fight. There are no obvious remains of the *sídh* on Ardagh Hill, and the locals seem more interested in promoting the Oliver Goldsmith connection of the village than its association with one of the more complex and beautiful of the love stories of Ireland – *The Wooing of Étaín*.

The village itself is an unusually pretty one, with rows of well-kept stone cottages, and a sense of an orderly, almost eighteenth-century existence. The ancient cathedral, St Mel's, which is associated with St Patrick, stands in the grounds of the Church of Ireland church. St Mel and his sister, Eiche, both founded monasteries in the area; Eiche was reputed to have been able to carry hot coal in her apron as a sign of her purity – a tradition later attributed to St Brighid, who also has strong associations with the area. According to Patrick Logan in *The Holy Wells of Ireland*, there is a legend of three nuns with a big spotted cow being seen near Brighid's well at Ardagh.

Legends associated with Ardagh Hill were collected by the Folklore Commission in the 1930s, and many of them are recorded in Máire Mac Neill's book, *The Festival of Lughnasa*. Midhir lives on in these traditions, as the 'giant' Midas, who lives in the centre of the hill in a great palace. Unwary children, collecting bilberries here on Lughnasa Sunday at the beginning of August, were warned not too stray to far from their friends as they might fall down the giant's 'swallyhole' and never be seen again. In one tale, the giant took his revenge on the foolish individual who tried to quarry the hill by piling sods and stones onto him. Perhaps the most moving story is that of the man who got lost while crossing the hill one night. When his companions searched for him, they found only a flat stone, with blue flowers and grass around it, quite unlike anything else that grew on the hill. For thirty years, these strange flowers grew around the stone, until one day, at a time when the lost man would have been about seventy years of age, they disappeared. Many said that the man had been living under the hill for all that time, sending signs to the upper air, but was now dead. However, the hill was associated not only with disappearances and death, but also with lovers – on Bilberry Sunday, the last Sunday in July, young people gathered the berries and celebrated on the hillside, and the fruit was used to make a special wine which was supposed to act as an aphrodisiac – linking the hill once again with one of the most powerful of the ancient Irish love stories.

The hill is a little outside the town, and much of the ascent can be made by car. From high on its sides, there are panoramic views of the surrounding countryside, but the hill itself seems remote from the village and from the farmland surrounding it. Close by is Frewin Hill, or Dún Fremu, the *dún* of Eochaidh, the Horse King, the Ploughman and the human lover of Étaín. Here he retired, troubled in mind, when Midhir played his final trick on his human vanity and he lost the fair Étaín forever.

The famous Ardagh Chalice has no association with the village – it was found in a place in Limerick of the same name. The hidden gold in Ardagh Hill is not that of metal. In the forest, light flickers through green leaves, and reflects in the pools and peat streams of the hillside. As it flows down through the trees, the water seems to capture the late afternoon sun, shining gold. That gold is all that remains of the hair of Étaín, as she stood on the green in front of Brí Léith on a May morning and waited for her story to begin once again.

THE FINDING OF ÉTAÍN

The great feast of Samhain, the beginning of winter and of the new year, was being celebrated at Tara, and Eochaidh Áireamh, the new high king, had brought a bride to celebrate with him. She was Étaín, the daughter of Étar. Eochaidh Áireamh had searched high and low to find the loveliest and most virtuous of women to become his wife, and when he had come to the pool at Brí Léith, where Étaín was standing with her long, golden hair unbound as she washed herself in a silver basin, he knew that his journey was over. The poets had already made a song about the meeting – telling of Étaín's skin as white and as soft as snow, her cheeks as red as the foxglove, her side long and slender, her eyes the colour of hyacinths and her eyebrows and lashes the blue-black of the beetle's shell. The ladies in the court looked on her with envy but not with hatred, for it was impossible to hate someone so still, so calm – a pool of water that reflected only sunlight.

However, in the midst of all the celebrations, there was one who looked on in agony. This was the king's brother, Ailill Anghubha, who had fallen so much in love with Étaín that he could look at no one else while she was in the room. His love was such that he fell into a terrible sickness, and the druids and the healers could do nothing for him. Eochaidh loved his brother, and although he had to leave the court to make his progress through the country, he said to Étaín, 'While I am gone, be sure to look after my brother Ailill; anything he needs to help him recover, make sure that he has it. And if he should die – the gods forbid it – make sure that he is buried with the proper ceremonies of a prince.'

It did not take long for Étaín to discover the reason for Ailill's sickness, and, out of a desire to heal him, she agreed to come to his bed one morning. She left the palace at dawn and made her way to the trysting spot, and when she arrived there, she found a man who looked like Ailill. Yet somehow she knew that it was not he. So she turned and left the man without speaking. This happened again the next day and the next, and on the third day, she challenged the man, saying, 'Who are you, and what right have you to come to meet me here, stranger?'

At this, the man no longer looked like dark-eyed Ailill, but took the form of a tall, fair-haired young warrior with burning grey eyes and a noble appearance.

'No stranger I am to you, fair one, and my rights to be with you are greater than those of Eochaidh,' he said. 'I am your husband from your past life in the fairy mounds. Midhir of Brí Léith am I; and sit yourself down, while I tell you the tale that you do not remember.'

Étaín could not deny that there was something that seemed familiar about Midhir; so she sat down on the grass in the early sunlight and listened quietly while he told his story. By its end, the birds were singing and it was full light, and small memories were coming back to Étaín: of a place of such beauty that it made the breath catch in her throat; of hunts and feasts and music and glorious troops, of immortal lords and ladies.

'You were born Étaín, the daughter of King Étar of Echrad, the loveliest lady of the Sídh. Many tasks did my brother Aonghus perform in order to win you for me. We lived happily in Brí Léith, until my first wife, Fuamnach, became jealous of my love for you. As I held you in my arms one day, I felt you change, soften, fall from between my fingers – she had transformed you into a pool of water; I caught the pool in a silver bowl. That same water I kept in the sun of my chamber, until out of it came a tiny worm, which in turn grew into a marvellous butterfly, with multi-coloured wings – wings the colour of your eyes and hair and lips and black brows. The fly stayed at my side always until my wife sent a wind to blow you away, over the ocean; you were beaten by winds and storms, until finally you found your way back to Brú na Bóinne, where Aonghus kept you safe in a sunny tower of glass. But again you were driven out by the jealousy of Fuamnach, and blown overland until you fell into the cup of King Étar's wife. She drank you down, and nine months later, Étaín, you were born again to live a new life, as fair and as gentle as you ever were. So will you come to me, away to my palace, back to your own people, away from the griefs of humankind? Will you come to live in bliss once more?'

Étaín thought for a moment.

'Is Fuamnach still there?' she asked.

Midhir laughed and shook his head. 'No, she has left me; you would be my one true wife, queen of Brí Léith, where winter never comes and no harsh words are spoken.'

Étaín thought again: 'I will go with you, for it seems that I remember things now I did not know were part of my memories; but I will go only with the consent of Eochaidh, for I would not set up dissent between him and the people of the Sídh.'

Midhir bowed deeply and said, 'So shall it be, lady – I will win you from Eochaidh.'

When Étaín went back to Ailill, she found him cured of his sickness. He said that each dawn, when he had tried to go to meet her, he had been overcome with a great tiredness, unable to move. However, now he no longer felt the madness of longing for her, and they could tell the king what had happened. Eochaidh was pleased with the care Étaín had shown for his brother, and Ailill took the name of Ailill One-Stain, for the only bad deed he had committed was to love his brother's wife. Étaín said nothing to her husband about Midhir's promise.

At Bealtaine, the beginning of summer, a tall, grey-eyed warrior appeared before Eochaidh and challenged him to a game of chess. At first, Eochaidh refused, saying that the board was in his wife's chamber and that he did not wish to disturb her, but Midhir – for it was he – produced a wonder from his bag – golden pieces and a silver board, and they sat down to play.

Eochaidh won every game, and, as a payment, he demanded that Midhir perform many great tasks including to clear the rocks and stones from the plains of Meath, so that, from that day, cattle could graze on the most fertile land of Ireland; and to cut down great forests and remove the rushes around his palace of Tethbha. Finally, he asked Midhir to build a causeway over the bog of Lamrach. Midhir completed all these tasks, but he stipulated that none should watch him while the tasks were done. Eochaidh's steward, however, watched the ploughing of the land for the causeway, and, the next day, when the task was completed, Midhir came angrily to Eochaidh.

'You have broken your pledge,' he said. 'None was to watch while I worked for you. You are a man of no honour and you are not worthy of the great gifts you have been given. I demand the right of one last game.'

The king looked around at his soldiers – should he call them in to overcome this impudent man who dared to criticise the king? Then he thought of the deeds that Midhir had done – the great magical forces at his command, and he looked to where his wife was standing, watching him, expecting him to do the honourable thing. He nodded.

This time the game went very differently – within nine moves, the king was defeated. He held up his hands and asked, 'What is your prize, then, warrior?'

'I ask for a kiss from the fair Étaín,' replied Midhir.

Eochaidh went pale. He was silent for a time, furious with himself – for is it not always the case with a wager that it should demand the thing most beloved of the loser? Finally, he said, 'Very well. Come back in one month for the payment of the debt.'

When Midhir came back the following month, the palace was surrounded by legions of soldiers from every corner of Ireland – all there to ensure that Midhir would not carry Étaín away with him. But Midhir smiled as he stood before the king, saying, 'I have come then, for the kiss from Étaín.'

Étaín stepped down from her seat beside the king to where Midhir stood in the centre of the great hall of Tara. Around her on all sides were warriors and ladies and all the people of the court, watching. She cast one half-smiling glance to where Ailill stood, and a final serious one at Eochaidh; then she went into the embrace of Midhir's arms. As she did so, the couple rose above all the assembled company, higher and higher into the air, until they flew through the smoke-hole in the centre of the hall. A great cry rose up from the people and they raced outside. But all they could see were two beautiful white swans flying away in the blue sky, linked by a silver chain around their necks. Eochaidh sat in the hall with his head in his hands, thinking of his lost beloved, and the lost child that she carried within her.

Some say that Midhir and Étaín lived happily from then on, man and wife as they had been fated to be from the dawn of time. However, there are others who say that Eochaidh razed all the fairy palaces in Ireland, searching for his lost bride. It is said that he finally came to Brí Léith, and Étaín, tired of the violence and destruction that the king was inflicting on the Sídh, convinced Midhir to go out to parley. Eochaidh demanded his wife back, and Midhir told him to return in a month when Étaín would go with him.

'But if you are to have her, you must show that you know her, the way that I have always known her through all her transformations. And if you do not know her, you must swear that you will stop the destruction of the *sídh*.'

Eochaidh laughed. 'Of course I would always know my beloved – her fair head, her white side, her red lips. Your terms hold no terror for me.'

When Eochaidh returned, he found fifty women of the exact appearance of

Étaín standing in front of him, each smiling the smile of his wife, each speaking in her gentle tones. He looked at each one intently, trying to find something that would mark one of them out as his true wife. But what he had always seen when he looked at his beloved was his own image reflected and magnified in her eyes – and here were fifty maidens, all gazing at him with that same look. Midhir's smile widened and he urged Eochaidh to choose.

Eochaidh stood, watching the maidens, unable to say who was his own Étaín. He asked them questions, but they all seemed to know the answer; he danced with some, but they moved with the same liquid charm as his wife. Finally, he said, 'There is one act that no other woman could do with the grace of my wife – I would ask each of these maidens to serve me wine.'

So, each maiden took a cup and a jug, and served wine to the king; each one did it with great skill and grace, until all but two had done so. Then one of the last two moved forward, smiling, lifted the jug to pour the wine, and carried it to the hand of the king.

'This is my Étaín,' shouted Eochaidh. 'This is the one I will take.'

Midhir smiled again, and the last remaining woman, with a glance over her shoulder, made her way into the *sídh*. With great rejoicing, Eochaidh brought back Étaín to Tara, and she was soon with child by him. However, one day, as he sat with his wife in his arms, and his new daughter in the cradle beside them, he asked her, 'And tell, me, beloved, what happened the first child you bore?'

'This is the first child I have had,' said Étaín. 'Why, since I was born in the *sídh* at Brí Léith, I have known no other man but you.'

Then Eochaidh realised that he had chosen wrongly, and had taken his daughter instead of his wife from the Sídh. In a great rage, he commanded his servants to kill the child that the second Étaín had borne. But the little girl had the beauty and charm that was the gift and curse of all the Étaíns, and, in pity for her and her mother, the servants did not kill her, but instead hid the baby in the forest. There she was found by a cowherd and his wife, and fostered by them in ignorance of her noble birth. In time, this third Étaín, Mes Buachalla the cowherd's fosterling, became the wife of a prince and bore Conaire, who became one of the noblest kings of Ireland. Despite King Conaire's greatness, he too was fated to be punished for his grandfather's destruction of the *sídh* of Ireland – but that is another story.

Conaire's story is told in 'Da Dearga's Hostel'.

Keshcorann Caves, Sligo

CÉIS CHORAINN

The caves of Keshcorann are easily accessible, located halfway up the western slopes of Keshcorann mountain. They are situated on the road from Ballymote to Boyle, just before the village of Keash. The caves are clearly visible from the main road, and a side road to the left brings you within a short, although very steep, climb to the caves themselves. If you continue the climb up the mountain, you will find a cairn and the remains of a ringfort at its summit. There are seventeen caves and, although very little evidence of human habitation has been found in them (excavations found only the bones of hares, foxes and bears), they are an important site in terms of their legendary associations. The mountain range on which they stand is called the Bricklieves, or Speckled Mountains, and from the slopes of the caves there are fine views over the

surrounding countryside. Some of the caves link into each other, and wet-weather gear is essential for exploring them, as the floor is covered in a heavy brown slush which seems to contain a large percentage of liquefied sheep manure. In one cave to the left of the range, however, the interior is a vivid green world. Here, the rocks are spilt with tiny fronds of fern and psychedelically bright algae.

Keshcorann gets its name from Corann, a poet of the Dé Danann whose music calmed the rampaging sow, Caelchéis (*Céis* means 'The Wicker Causeway'). In gratitude for saving the people from the beast, the lands were granted to him, to hold his name forever. This connection with the ancient mythical sow suggests that, as at Ben Bulben, some form of very ancient animal worship or sacrifice may have taken place here. The caves on the hill were one of the resting places of that ubiquitous pair of lovers, Diarmaid and Gráinne, and also the home of the magical smith, Lon Mac Líomtha, the master craftsmen who had only one leg and one eye, but in recompense had three arms. In one of the caves, a she-wolf suckled the infant Cormac in the days before he took up his rightful place as high king of Ireland. Until relatively recently, the caves were visited on Bilberry or Garland Sunday, the last Sunday in July, in an echo of the ancient Lughnasa rite.

On the other side of the mountain is Lough Arrow, the site of the famous Second Battle of Moytura, when the Tuatha Dé Danann defeated the race of the

Fomorians, their rivals for the control of the land of Ireland. Myth and history mingle on the shores of the lake, for this is the location of Carrowkeel, Sligo's second great Megalithic graveyard and ceremonial centre. Carrowkeel is one of the most impressive ancient landscapes in Ireland. Many of the tombs predate Newgrange and may be from as early as 3800BC. The complex contains wedge, passage, portal and court tombs. Pottery from the passage tombs has given its name to a pottery type, Carrowkeel ware.

At the time the Carrowkeel complex was built, the slopes of the hillside at Keshcorann would have been heavily forested in elm, hazel and oak, honeysuckle and holly. Now there is long, slippery grass and a dotting of golden furze and white hawthorn. Sure-footed sheep graze around the caves and the view is over placid, cultivated countryside. This area is a quiet one, with small friendly towns — many, such as Tobercurry, with a strong tradition of Irish music. Near Tobercurry is another famous mountain of the Sídh, Knocknashee. In Castlebaldwin there is an information centre which would make a useful start to any exploration of the area. The countryside here is less dramatic than in north Sligo, and few people visit the caves. When we visited the site on a wet June Sunday, we met only one other person — a writer who had come from Australia because of the myths associated with Keshcorann. For most of the time, the caves are undisturbed, silent places of transformation and mysteries long ago forgotten.

THE HAGS OF WINTER

Fionn, the great warrior and hunter, ran through woods on the steep slopes on Keshcorann, delighting in the brush of branches against his arms and legs, the sharp smell of early winter, the call of the hounds and the shouts of his men. He was bound, he felt, for an adventure, a tale to tell during the long winter evenings around the blazing hearth of Almiu. Only his hounds and his companion, Conán, were with him, for he could still outrun all of the Fianna, even his son and his grandson; the only one to match him on any day was Caoilte Mac Rónáin. However, although the adventure that was about to befall Fionn would be told at many a fireside in years to come, it was not Fionn who would be the hero in it, but the man who would become his bitterest enemy — Goll Mac Morna.

Suddenly, the forest disappeared. A thick mist had come down; the dogs began to whine. The two men forced the hounds onwards, for they had been on the scent of a deer and were determined not to let it escape. But another smell was taking over from the scent of the deer – a smell of darkness and decay. The way up the hill was steep and very slippery underfoot. Fionn fell once and cursed as he tried to wipe off the brown, stinking mud clinging to his knees and hands. As the mist cleared slightly, the two hunters found themselves at the mouth of a cave where the smell grew stronger. Just discernible in the darkness were three old women. Each was uglier than the next; each was misshapen and wrinkled. Each had crimson hair, bristling out like the bristles of a boar; each had a stubbly beard and their black lips hung down to their withered breasts. Worst of all were their eyes. Each one of the six eyes gazing on the warriors was a blank white space, faintly veined with blue, with no iris or pupil. The three creatures were spinning, and as they spun, they hummed. Curious, Fionn and his companion pushed back the holly bush that grew at the mouth of the cave, and made their way inside, calling on the dogs that had hung back behind them, shivering and whining. As they passed the bush, the two men felt a great weakness come upon them and they fell to the ground. The spinners were witches, the daughters of a sorcerer; they were called Camóg, Cuilleann and Iornach. They were set to take revenge on Fionn on behalf of their father, who hated to see the wild things of his woods disturbed by the hunting of the Fianna. The three old women wound the great Fionn and his companion in their threads and they lay there, trussed up like babies, while the hags cackled at each other in victorious joy.

Soon, the rest of the Fianna appeared, drawn to the cave by the howls of Bran and Sceolan, the wise dogs who had refused to enter the enchanted place. When they saw their leader bound and gagged, the Fianna rushed forward into the cave, but they too were overtaken by the magic, and left as weak as kittens, trapped like flies in the spinners' webs. The smiles of the hags became even wider, and they were about to start stringing up the Fianna onto their cooking spits when an almighty bellow came from the mouth of the cave. It was Goll Mac Morna, who had slain Fionn's father and who would, in turn, one day be slain by Fionn. Goll had never lost his loyalty to his companions in arms. Cleverer and older than the rest of the men, he did not put one toe beyond the holly bush, but waved his sword and challenged the hags to battle.

'There's three of us and one of him,' said the eldest. 'Let's shut him up.'

The three witches came forward and set upon Goll like angry hornets, but he spun around with his sword flashing in the weak winter sun, so that,

half-blinded, they put their hands to their eyes. In an instant, he had managed to split two of them with one sword-stroke. The third hag was so aghast at losing her sisters that she threw herself down before Goll, promising to remove the enchantment from the Fianna if he spared her life. This he did, and Fionn and the Fianna came from the cave, rubbing their eyes, their legs still shaking. But just at that moment, a fourth sister witch appeared, yowling in rage. In an instant, Goll had lifted his sword again and killed her also.

They left the bodies of the witches at the cave for their father to find, but they took home the young deer that the Fianna had slaughtered.

In gratitude for his rescue, Fionn offered Goll his own daughter, Sgannlach. She was a good wife to Goll, and stayed faithful to her husband even after enmity had broken out again between the two men. The couple were hunted by Fionn the length and breath of Ireland; finally, they ended on a barren rock far out to sea on the west coast, with Fionn on their tail and a great army ready to destroy them. There, far from the fertile valleys and bird-filled forests, Goll begged his wife to leave him and save her own life. But this she refused to do, and so they died, side by side, bound together by ties even stronger than the magic of the witches of Keshcorann.

Ben Bulben, Sligo

BEANN GULBAN

The distinctive, scooped-out edge of Ben Bulben faces out towards the coastline of Sligo and acts as a signature to a county which not only contains a wealth of folklore, archaeology and history but is also rich in stunning natural beauty, encompassing wild sea and high mountain valleys. *Beann Gulban* means 'The Mountain Peak of Gulban' but it is not known who or what Gulban was. This countryside is haunted by the ghosts of William Butler Yeats and his brother, Jack, both of whom were possessed by Sligo – its scenery, its folklore and its people – throughout their lives. Reading any of Yeats's poetry – particularly the earlier works – gives one a feeling for Sligo in a way that no prose can, as does looking at a Jack Butler Yeats painting such as *Memory Harbour*.

The ascent of Ben Bulben should be undertaken only by those with good

Above:

*An engraving depicting
the distinctive outline of
Ben Bulben on the horizon.*

navigational skills, and, as usual in Ireland, mist can come down suddenly, so suitable clothing and footwear should be worn. The top of the mountain is particularly boggy. There are several routes which can be taken to the trig point marking the summit. Unfortunately, one of the most picturesque of these at the Gleniff Horseshoe has most of the routes blocked off by anti-access notices which must be among the most aggressive in Ireland. Those who do make the climb will be rewarded by magnificent views over the surrounding countryside and numerous sightings of what look like caves but which are, in fact, the remains of the workings of the now-defunct Ben Bulben barytes mines, which closed in the late 1970s. The mythical boar of Ben Bulben has had many stories told about it and may be a link to a time when animals were sacrificed as a way of communication with the gods.

Those unwilling or unable to do the climb can find consolation in the drive up to and around the Gleniff Horseshoe – particularly lovely when the evening light comes in from the west – or the less arduous trek to the top of Knocknarea, where the gigantic cairn is said to cover the grave of Queen Maeve. Not far away from the cairn is the Carrowmore complex of tombs, which is possibly the oldest in the country. It is estimated that some of the monuments in the huge complex date from as early as 4000BC. Unfortunately, many of the original 60 monuments were destroyed – some, even more unfortunately, by careless early excavation. Despite this, it is a unique experience to walk through a landscape filled with strange humps and lumps, which turn out to be cairns and tombs. Houses and fields mingle in among the relics of ancient days, and the line between ancient past and the present blurs. No wonder Sligo was such a rich ground for stories of the Sídh – the other world literally rises up before you on every side.

Some of the tombs, such as Listoghil, are now part of land owned by Dúchas, and there is a good interpretative centre where you can buy a map of the site. Like Rathcroghan, this is a place where it is well worth while giving yourself plenty of time to wander around. Part of the joy of the experience is that this can be done without being surrounded by crowds of people. The only groups that you are likely to meet are the assemblies of ancient stones, which from a distance can seem like the backs of grey-cloaked men and women, huddled together for a gossip that has lasted thousands of years.

THE STORY OF DIARMAID AND GRÁINNE

Cormac Mac Airt sat in his hall with his head in his hands. Despite his reputation as the wisest king Ireland had ever known, he had no idea what to do. His problem was his youngest daughter, Gráinne – a girl as fair as a lily but as wild as a hare. No scoldings from her mother nor threats from her father could stop her from eyeing up the warriors as they practised on the green at Tara, and he was afraid that she would present him with a grandchild before he could marry her off to a prince, making her another man's problem. He groaned slightly, and the old warrior Fionn, who was sitting opposite him, asked him if he had had too much wine the previous night.

'It's not my head that is my problem,' said Cormac. 'It's that child of mine, Gráinne. I need to get her married off quickly before she disgraces me with some stable-boy.'

Fionn put down his drink and looked speculatively at his high king. 'Gráinne is the blonde one, isn't she?' he asked. 'She's a fine girl.'

'Ah, she's lovely enough,' said Cormac. 'But she has a will like iron. No young man can get the better of her tongue.'

Fionn smiled slightly. 'Well, if no young man can manage her, why not try for a not-so-young one?' he suggested. 'A man with years of experience of dealing with the female sex.'

Now Cormac put down his cup also. 'And would you be thinking of anyone in particular?' he asked.

So it was agreed that Gráinne should marry Fionn, and, strangely enough, when her father broke the news to her, she did not scream and roar as she had at any of the other suggestions he had put to her. Maybe, he thought to himself, the pot-bellied old boaster was right, and an older man would suit his headstrong daughter.

Perhaps Gráinne had been misled by the stories of Fionn's prowess into thinking that he was still a young and handsome warrior. In any case, when she saw the grizzled and hoary man that she was to marry, her face dropped. And what is also certain is that the night before the wedding, Gráinne disappeared with the flower of the Fianna, and one of Fionn's most beloved warriors, Diarmaid Ua Duibhne, Diarmaid of the Lovespot.

Fionn was furious when he awoke at noon to find his head aching and his bride fled. Like himself, all of the Fianna, with the exception of Oisín and Oscar, had been put into an enchanted sleep by a draught from Gráinne's hand. It did not help his mood when Oisín told him that Gráinne had originally suggested that he himself become her lover.

'You are well shot of her, my father,' he said. 'She will lead poor Diarmaid a merry dance, for although she is beautiful, he did not want to go with her

at all. But she mocked him and then put a *geis* upon him, so he had no choice. She caught him like a rabbit in the trap of his own honour.'

However, Fionn had been looking forward to bedding Gráinne. Moreover, he hated to be crossed by anyone, so that, even more than lust, anger drove him, and hatred, fuelled by the fear that his powers were failing and that the young lovers had made a fool of him. He began the great hunt for Diarmaid and Gráinne which would lead the Fianna all over Ireland.

When Diarmaid and Gráinne left Tara, they went west of the Shannon, and then southwards towards Slieve Luachra. Always, Fionn pursued them, though his greatest warriors, Oscar, Oisín and Caoilte, held their companion Diarmaid in such affection that they hindered rather than helped Fionn in his angry quest. The lovers could never eat where they cooked nor sleep where they ate. They were pursued through forests and over mountainsides, onto islands and through bogs. They knew the freezing cold of winter and the relentless sun of midsummer. Ireland is marked with hundreds of dolmens called 'The Bed of Diarmaid and Gráinne'.

All the time they travelled, Diarmaid refused to betray Fionn by making love to Gráinne, though she did not make it easy for him; for while she had thought him handsome when she saw him in the banqueting hall, the trials that they went through together made her truly love him as well as desire him. Every night, Diarmaid would put a fishbone between himself and Gráinne as they slept, so that if one of them rolled over towards the other it would stick into them and keep them apart. Then, one spring day, after Diarmaid had fought his way through an army of the Fianna and they had made their way over a mountain stream, Gráinne stood on the bank and mocked Diarmaid as he pulled back the hawthorn for her to make her way into the safety of the thicket.

'Look, Diarmaid Ua Duibhne, you who are called the great lover of the Fianna. Look how the water has splashed up onto my thigh. Despite all your courage in battle, that water is braver than you in terms of where it dares to go.'

Then Diarmaid, who had desired Gráinne for many months, pulled her into the thicket and he made love to her; and he let Fionn know by secret signs that he had done so.

So the lovers' adventures continued for sixteen years, with the pair sleeping in bothies in the green woods and living off the nuts and fruits of the land. Winter followed summer, and always they moved on, unable to rest for fear of Fionn. Sometimes, Gráinne would sleep on rushes, and Diarmaid on sea-sand, so that Fionn's magic thumb would not be able to tell him whether they were on the mountainside or the seashore. They had friends in their wanderings, especially Aonghus, the god of love, who was foster-father of Diarmaid, and loved him like his own child. It was he who finally made peace between the exiles and Fionn. It was agreed that Diarmaid and Gráinne should live far from Fionn and the Fianna in Sligo; but although Fionn pretended to have forgiven the lovers, he bided his time and waited for revenge. Fionn never gave up the hunt.

One fine summer's morning, Diarmaid awoke after a restless night and said that he would go hunting on Ben Bulben.

'Do not go, my love,' said Gráinne. 'For I fear for you – you were calling out in your sleep and I am afraid that your dreams mean that something evil will befall you. And besides, I would like you to help me with some work in the house.'

However, over the years, Diarmaid had learned how to ignore Gráinne. He left the house with his spear and his hound. He climbed the great flank of the mountain, and, near the top, he came upon Fionn, sitting on a hillock. His face had become fleshy over the years, his eyes small and mean, but he was smiling. Diarmaid knew that smile of old – it was the one that Fionn always wore just before he put his spear through the heart of a deer after a long day's hunting.

'Well, old companion,' said Fionn. 'You have picked a good day for the chase, for the wild boar of Ben Bulben has been seen out on the hillside today.' He sighed. 'But of course it is not up to you to hunt it, for is there not a *geis* on you not to kill a pig? And I am sure that your wife would not like it if you took such risks. How is the lovely Gráinne?'

Diarmaid said quietly, 'Gráinne is as lovely as ever. But do not tell me where or what I can hunt. I have never turned back from the chase yet.' And he left Fionn and began to search for the boar's tracks.

He heard it before he saw it, rampaging through the gorse, snorting its fury. It appeared through the brushwood, its hide as thick as iron, its cruel tusks and angry red eyes squinting as it came into the sunshine. Diarmaid ran towards it, sinking his spear into its flank, as his hound tried to dig its teeth into its thick hide. The beast threw off the great hound as if it were no more than a fly, and the dog fell onto its back yards away, whimpering miserably. But Diarmaid's spear had gored the creature's skin and now he held it fast.

The great beast ran all over the slopes of the mountain, trying to buck

Diarmaid off his back. So it went on, with Diarmaid hanging on for dear life, sometimes wrestling the boar with his arms caught around its neck like a lover, sometimes just barely holding on to the end of his spear as the creature dragged him through gorse and heather and bracken and scrub, up and down the steep mountainside. Finally, the boar gave a massive buck, and Diarmaid fell on the earth. The beast dug one of its tusks into his tormentor's flesh, goring his belly from hip to shoulder. Diarmaid lay there and, with one last burst of strength, pushed the hilt of his sword deep into the boar's belly. The beast fell, dead from battle wounds and exhaustion. Nearby, Fionn sat saying nothing. By now, the rest of the Fianna had arrived, and Oisín said angrily to his father: 'Do something now, for Diarmaid, our dear companion of old, is near death. You know that you can cure anyone, no matter how badly wounded, with a drink from your hands.

Fionn strolled over to where Diarmaid was lying in agony.

'Not looking so well now, are you, Diarmaid, beloved of women? Of course, I'd love to help, but I'm only an oul' fella with bad eyesight. I can see no water near here.'

Diarmaid groaned, 'I have seen a fresh stream no more than a few feet away, Fionn; and for the gods' sake, help me, for I have always been a faithful friend to you. It was only because Gráinne put a *geis* on me that I went with her, as you well know. And it was so long ago ... I know you have planned this; but have mercy now and save my life.'

'And what about the kisses you gave to her in front of me and my men when I found you? And your life with her and the children she bore you – are not these a mockery of me?'

Fionn stood staring down at Diarmaid, but Oisín came up and shook his father's shoulders, shouting, 'Old man, if you do not go now and get water for Diarmaid, I will kill you with my own hands. You know that we cannot let a companion die like this. Go to him now!'

Fionn shrugged. He went slowly to the pool and filled his cupped hands with water, but when he drew near to Diarmaid, and saw how handsome he still was, and thought of how he and young Gráinne had made a fool and a cuckold of him for so many years, he let the water trickle through his fingers. Twice he went to the well and took water in his hands to bring to Diarmaid, but twice, as he returned to where the hero was lying, his jealous memories got the better of him and he let it pour to the ground.

Oisín was shouting at his father now, telling him to move quickly and help the dying man who was lying in his arms, shaking uncontrollably. So, finally, Fionn took the water all the way to where Diarmaid was lying. But at that moment, the hero died.

Gráinne gave a great cry of pain when she saw the Fianna returning from the mountain with Diarmaid's hound limping beside them and a body carried on a bier made of green branches. For years, she planned a revenge on Fionn, training her children in the ways of battle. When Fionn heard of this, he came to her, and, in spite of all the slights and insults she piled on him, he stayed with her, calling her his honey tongue, his sweetheart, until one day she looked in the mirror and saw that although Fionn was an old man, she herself was no longer young. And she thought that although she would never love anyone as she had loved Diarmaid, there was a lot to be said for being the wife of a great leader. She knew that even though Fionn was silver-haired and red-faced, he was reputed to be a great lover, so that even the fairy-women came out of the *sídh* to sleep with him. Finally, she went with him to Almiu.

When the couple arrived at Almiu, the Fianna, whom Fionn had commanded to come out to greet his bride, shouted out their derision. They called to Fionn to mind his wife well this time, so that Gráinne dropped her head in shame. But she held it up again when she saw the rich robes and jewels prepared for her, the servants ready to do her bidding, and the lordly bed with its red silk hangings, so different from the bothy of branches she had slept in when she had run away in her wild youth with sweet-lipped Diarmaid Ua Duibhne.

Ulster

Grianán of Aileach, Donegal

GRIANÁN AILIGH

The Grianán – or sun-palace – of Aileach is a circular stone enclosure, a cashel, situated 244 metres (800 feet) above sea level and visible from miles around. It is easily accessible, as a road leads to the top of the hill on which it is situated. Around the massive stone enclosure, with its single entrance leading through the thick walls, there are three concentric earthen banks. The Grianán was built on the site of an ancient tumulus which may date from Neolithic times – it was certainly already in place by the Bronze Age. The present structure probably dates from the Iron Age, and was heavily restored in the nineteenth century. The edifice is an impressive one, and the surrounding views are staggering, stretching over five counties and encompassing mountains, lakes, beaches, cliffs, pastureland, the loughs Swilly and Foyle and the wild Atlantic. Derry, St Colmcille's city where it was said that the angels were as numerous as the leaves on the oak trees, can be clearly seen to the southeast.

This is the centre of one of the ancient kingdoms of Ulster, and kings were ceremoniously crowned at Aileach until the twelfth century. The Uí Néills in the fifth century and later the O'Donnells reigned from here. Inside the cashel, there is relief from the howling presence of the wind, and smooth, green grass, with the layered walls rising in a circle around the inner court. The place acted as sanctuary, as an inaugural centre and as a palace. It was said that in its heyday the building was covered in red yew, in gold and bronze and in precious stones so that it shone as brightly in the day as in the night. Outside the cashel are the remains of an ancient roadway and a holy well.

The Grianán was the target of attack from the enemies of the king, notably the Danes in 937. After 1101, it was no longer used as a royal residence, having been destroyed by Murtagh O'Brien, the king of Munster. In revenge for the destruction of Kincora in 1088, Murtagh was said to have told his troops to take a stone each from the structure, so that it could never be rebuilt. The Grianán was, however, used again – not by the nobility of the land but by the peasantry in the eighteenth century, who took shelter in it to attend forbidden masses.

There are many legends associated with the Grianán – particularly in relation to the building of the palace. Some say that the great Daghdha himself built the original structure. Others say that, in the fourth century, a master-builder called Friguan eloped with the daughter of the king of Scotland and built the sun-palace in her name. There is a further association with St Patrick, who is said to have baptised King Eoghan here. Of more recent date is a folktale which associates the site with the Irish hero, Hugh O'Donnell. It is said that a man passed over the hill of the Grianán one night and saw a bright light shining from it. When he looked inside the light, he saw a great company of horsemen with swords and shields and shining armour. They sat

 upright on their horses, yet seemed to be sleeping. One of them opened his eyes and said to the man, 'Is it time yet?' holding his horn to the ready. The man ran away in terror, knowing that what he had seen was the sleeping company of Hugh O'Donnell, waiting for the moment to come to do battle for the land.

Pages 180-181:
WH Bartlett's engraving of 'Dunseverick Castle', standing on the ancient site of Dún Sobhairce, one of the four royal roads which led from Tara.

THE GODS OF THE HILL

The Daghdha, the Lord of Plenty and the great builder, sat strumming his harp as he looked over the northern ocean. Behind him was the Grianán, the sun-palace of Aileach. It was almost completed, this work of giants, and the great mother Danu would be pleased, for here was a fitting residence for the shining ones. The Daghdha was satisfied because he knew that his work would last well beyond even his long reign as All-Father of the Tuatha Dé Danann. Feasts would be held here, celebrations of Samhain and Bealtaine, contests and races and tourneys. The children of the Sídh would be born here, and grow to adulthood, and live out their thousands of years. All would move in an ordered pattern, like planets in their allotted spheres. He himself would be the great gift-giver and protector; Manannán would rule the kingdom of the sea; Áine the sun; Donn, the gentle king, the shadowlands of the dead; Brighid the flocks and the wild things; Eochaidh the herds of swift horses; and Lugh would be their many-skilled defender and their king. Even those other ones, those who were less kindly but still part of the immortal family – the Morrigan and her sisters, Badbh and Macha – had their part to play.

The Daghdha's smile grew broader – truly, his mating with the Morrigan had been a magnificent one, as she had stood with one foot on either side of the River Uinsinn. He prided himself that he could fill a woman's womb as well as his cauldron could fill a belly – leaving none dissatisfied. And her assistance at the battle had been a decisive element in their great victory. The children of Danu had finally defeated the evil Fomorians at the Battle of the Plain of the Two Pillars, Moytura.

Now the song that he played told the story of that struggle – of how the shining ones had driven the forces of darkness from the land. The battle had been long coming and hard fought. Years before, the Tuatha Dé Danann had fought the Fomorians and defeated them. But during that battle, the great leader, Nuadhu, had lost his arm and had thus had to give up the kingship, for the leader of the realm had to be without blemish. Bres, half Fomorian and half of the race of the Tuatha Dé Danann, had become the new king, but he had been a tyrant, forcing the gods into slavery and conniving with the Fomorians, especially with the giant, Balor na Súile Nimhe (Balor of the Evil Eye). The Daghdha sang of how the physician, Dian Céacht, had made a new arm of shining silver for Nuadhu, and he had taken back the kingship of the Tuatha Dé Danann, and the leaders had met and decided to finish the fight

Above:

*The sun sets over the Grianán
of Aileach, County Donegal.*

with their enemies for once and for all.

The Daghdha sang of the preparations for the second great battle, when, led by Nuadhu, the smiths and wrights and carpenters had forged magical weapons and built battle-chariots. He sang of the death of Nuadhu, and of how the shining Lugh of the Long Arm had killed his grandfather, Balor, with a stone from his sling shot through the giant's malevolent eye. He sang of how Goibhniu the smith had made magical weapons that mended themselves overnight, however badly they were broken during the battle, and how Dian Cécht had cured those who had been wounded. He sang of how the Fomorians and their allies, the Fir Bolg, had been routed and had fled to their ships, and how the body of Nuadhu of the Silver Arm had been taken to Grianán. He was now buried under the great stone enclosure, and the hero, Lugh, had taken his place as king of the tribe of Danu.

Finally, the Daghdha sang of how his days of servitude to the Fomorians were over. Now he could concentrate on what he wanted to do, on what he did best – building great palaces that would last for as long as there was life in Ireland. The treasures of the Tuatha Dé Danann would be kept there – those treasures taken from the four magical cities in the north of the world – the sword of Nuadhu, the spear of Lugh, the stone of Fál and his own cauldron, which was never emptied no matter how many were fed. There was no reason why the Dé Danann should ever give up their hold on this green and fertile land.

He continued his song, and did not see the sails that were coming over the horizon from the lands to the east; nor did he hear the calls of the Sons of Míl as they came nearer to the mountainous shores far to the south of Aileach. Despite the enchantments of the Tuatha Dé Danann, who had covered the shores of their island in a magic mist so that no one should find it, a new race had seen the land of Ireland and coveted its beauty. The Daghdha, great as he was, did not foresee that the children of Danu would be banished to the world under the green hills, hidden from human sight. Despite his power and wisdom, he did not hear the song the Sons of Míl sang as their sages landed – a song invoking a power older and greater even than that of the children of Danu. As their small crafts scraped onto the shingle, the Milesians called on the land of Ireland itself – its forests, its rivers, its hills and its lakes, its broad plains and forested glens – to welcome a new tribe to its shores.

Tory Island, Donegal

TORAIGH

There is a traditional Irish dance called 'The Waves of Tory'. It is a fast-moving, communal dance, which can get pretty wild late at night at a *ceilí*. The wilder it gets, the closer it comes to its name, for the waves of Tory have to be experienced to be believed. Tory Island is the most isolated of the inhabited islands off the coast of Ireland, not because of distance – it is no more than 12 kilometres (7 miles) away from the nearest point on the Irish coast – but because of the wildness of the seas which separate it from the mainland. Because of this isolation, the people of Tory have always been a race apart – indeed, one translation of the name Tory links it to the Irish word for pirates. The most commonly accepted interpretation of its name, however, is that Tory means 'Towery Place', and, approaching the island's distinctive profile from the sea does give one the feeling of moving towards a battlemented fortress.

As recently as the middle of the 1980s, there were plans to evacuate the island and relocate the remaining families on the mainland – this was after the winter of 1974 when the island was cut off from the mainland for over seven weeks. The people of Tory fought back, however, and now the island has a regular ferry service, plans for a small airport, and a thriving school of local artists. It is also an island whose people have fiercely guarded its traditions, its music, its monuments and its folklore.

The island is 5 kilometres (3 miles) long and at its widest no more than 1 kilometre (half a mile) wide – in places, it is much narrower. It is bare and treeless, made up mainly of rock and bog, with some pasture lands. Despite this, it manages to support a variety of bird life, including water birds such as swans, and sea birds such as puffins and gannets. In summer, it is also the home of the now rare corncrake – in the evenings, their rasping calls from the low hedges and long grass make it seem as if Tory itself is calling out. The island is never silent – between the calls of the birds and the noise of the wind and the sea, there is a feeling of ceaseless movement and turbulence.

The turbulence is reflected in the folklore, for the island was the fortress of the great giant, Balor na Súile Nimhe (Balor of the Evil Eye) – the greedy and merciless giant who could murder with a glance. Balor's Soldiers (also called the Eochair Mhór) are the sea cliffs which form a line of serrated rock on the northeast of the island, some distance out to sea. Directly aligned with the coast, they act as a second rocky wall of defence for the island at this point in the coastline. This is the

I.WAKEFIELD.

highest point of the island, and here its beauty is harsh and uncompromising – unsoftened by any greenery. This peninsula forms the area known as Balor's Fort, and there are the remaining traces of an Iron Age promontory fort. Four embankments acted as defence from the rest of the peninsula, and the remains of a well and twenty huts have been found here by archaeologists.

The most obvious archaeological remains on the island are, however, the Christian ones. Legend has it that St Colmcille, Donegal's patron saint and the founder of Iona, founded a monastery here, which flourished for a thousand years – from the sixth to the sixteenth century. There are many legends concerning St Colmcille's deeds on the island, and there are still impressive remains of a round tower and an unusual Tau or T-cross. Other remains include the bed of the holy woman whose body was washed up on the island – clay from this site is still said to contain magical properties. Parts of the island's magical heritage were less benign. It is said that the cursing stone, now hidden away from human use, was put into action against the frigate, *Wasp*, which had been sent with a garrison to enforce payment of taxes by the islanders in 1884. The ship sank off the coast, leaving only six living, and the soldiers whose bodies were recovered were buried in the Protestant graveyard.

In direct contrast to the harshness of their island environment, the people of Tory are friendly and humorous. They have a ruddy, scrubbed look – a natural result of living in a place which must be the organic equivalent of a washer-drier, constantly buffeted by waves and wind. You may well be welcomed to the island by the king of Tory himself, for the islanders have managed to hold onto the tradition of having their own king – a man who acts as a spokesperson for the island in the world of bureaucracy on the other side of the water.

Contact with the mainland is easier now than it has ever been; in West Town, the houses are festooned with satellite dishes – rusty links to the outside world during the long, dark nights of winter. However, the ferry ride can still result in green faces and unsteady legs, even in the height of summer. Visitors come to the island and swear that they will never repeat the trip, but find themselves returning again and again. One such visitor was the English artist, Derek Hill, whose hut on the northern cliffs of the island stands out starkly against a desert of grey rock. Between the clefts in the expanse of rock are crumbled smaller stones, so that the fissures look like mouths with broken teeth. It is hard to imagine a place more exposed to wind and water. Climbing here in the evening, with the wind crying and the sea beating against the rocks at the base of the cliffs, it is easy to imagine the yellow beam of the lighthouse as an all-seeing eye – closing, then opening again in a steadfast rhythm. The lighthouse is Balor's eye in reverse. This eye shines out not to destroy, but as a comfort and guide to those at the mercy of the waves of Tory.

THE BIRTH OF LUGH

A princess, as lovely as a summer's dawn over the great Atlantic, stands at a tower window, looking over the treacherous sound which separates her island from the mainland. In the distance, she can see the clear line of hills that is Ireland, no more than a few miles from her fortress on the rocks. But it might as well be a different world, for she is locked here in a tower by her father, Balor of the Evil Eye. The wind and the sea are her companions; they talk to her ceaselessly – in a whisper sometimes on the calm days of summer; in a shriek on the wild nights of winter. Her companions are kind to her, for she is easy to be kind to – her nature is sweet and her face is lovely. How strange, her ladies say, that such a mother as the witch, Ceithlinn of the Crooked Teeth, and that hideous monster, Balor of the Evil Eye, king of the Fomorians, should have produced a child as fair as Ethlinn. She is their only child. Balor was told at her birth that his fate was to be killed by his grandchild, so, from her birth, he had his daughter locked in a tower on this lonely island, far away from the eyes of men. Sometimes he comes to visit her – he knows that she draws back from him, frightened by his ugliness, frightened most of all by the great eye-lid that hangs down over the single eye in the middle of his brow. If he were to lift that eye-lid, she would die, burnt to a crisp in an instant. Yet though he sees nothing, Balor likes to think that he sees all, and he knows that his vigilance must increase now – now that his child is a young woman. Her companions are warned at pain of death to let no man onto the island, and, in particular, into the stone tower.

However, it is lonely out here on the island of the towers, and the ladies long for company. So, they are happy that today two gentlewomen have

landed on the island. One is old but sharp-eyed, the other one young and muscular with ruddy cheeks. The two ladies explain how they were shipwrecked and are in need of shelter from the wind and waves. Ethlinn's companions bring them up to introduce them to their mistress, warning them, with giggles behind their hands, not to mention the word 'man' – for their innocent mistress thinks that the world is made up entirely of females.

But what has the older woman taken from under her green cloak? Some kind of silver branch, it seems. She shakes it and its little bells make such a lovely sound that all the ladies fall asleep. For once, there is silence on the island; every gull, every meadowlark, wader, pipit, stonechat, every raven and peregrine and rasping corncrake – every one is silent. The swans in the lakes, the puffins on the cliffs – they all put their heads under their wing, hiding their eyes as if it was the dead of night instead of a summer afternoon. The hares sleep in their burrows; even the wind and the sea are silent – every watching eye is closed. Except the eyes of Ethlinn, who looks on in surprise as the young stranger divests herself of female clothes and starts to tell her how lovely she is – what a pearl beyond price. It is not unpleasant, however, to sit here and talk to this strange creature, and soon the sensations that she is introduced to are even more pleasurable than talking. The old woman, meanwhile, takes herself off for a walk along the cliffs, telling the young man – for so he has described himself to Ethlinn – that they must leave before the sun comes up over the eastern sea.

All evening and all night long, the couple lie in each other's arms. The young man tells the princess that his name is Cian and that he has come to the island to find the cow that Ethlinn's father stole from him. Biróg the enchantress carried him in the air over the water.

'And have you found it?' asks Ethlinn.

'Forget about the cow,' he replies. 'I have no more interest in it now that I have found you. Will you come with me, away from here?'

'I am afraid,' says Ethlinn. 'For you know my father can kill anyone he looks at with one glance of his eye.'

At that moment, Biróg returns to the tower. 'We must go now,' she says. 'The sun is rising and there is no time to waste.'

'But Ethlinn will come with me, or I will not leave,' protests Cian, holding the princess more tightly.

Biróg shakes her head. 'I have not the strength to carry both of you in the air. You must leave her now.'

Cian demurs, but Ethlinn gently pushes him towards Biróg, saying, 'Go with her. If you stay here, you will die, and if I have to see you die, I will die from grief. I know that you love me, and even if I am forced to stay here for the rest of my life, watched and guarded by my father, I will have the memory of your love with me. Look to the future – all bad things will come to an end. It is for the best.'

So, finally, Cian is persuaded to leave, and only just in time, for Ethlinn's companions are beginning to stretch and yawn as they awake from their long sleep, and there is the sound of thunder in the air as Balor arrives.

He sniffs. 'Do I smell a man here?' he demands. The companions laugh, and Ethlinn asks innocently, 'What is a man?' It is lucky that Balor does not open his eye, for his daughter's face is pink and her eyes are shining.

Nine months later, Ethlinn bears three babies. This cannot be hidden from her father, and he takes the tiny ones from her, where she lies, clutching them to her and screaming, and casts them from the sharp battlemented rocks out into the wild waves at the east of the island.

But Ethlinn, who has pulled herself to the edge of the cliffs, determined to throw herself into the waves after her children, sees what he cannot see. Before the precious bundle sinks under the water, a female figure skirts over the silver waves, and lifts one of the children above the waters, carrying it southwards towards the land of Ireland.

'What will you do now?' asks one of her maidens as she sits on the rocks and stares southwards into the eye of the noontime sun.

'I will watch the sea,' Ethlinn says. 'My father will still raid ships, kill sailors, demand the tribute of every third child from the people of Ireland. But I know that out of my father's dark blood will come a light for the land. As I watch the tide go in and out from my small window to this great ocean, I will know that every time it does so, the time is coming nearer when I will need to wait no more. Each tide brings me closer to the day when my child will kill the tyrant who tried to kill him, and will free the land of Ireland from his harsh servitude.' She raises her voice and calls over the water, to where she can see the figure of Biróg bringing the baby safely to his foster-mother, Tailtiu.

'His name is Lugh,' she calls. 'He is the bright one – the gifted child. Look after him well.'

Lough Neagh, Tyrone

LOCH nEACHACH

The shores of Eochaidh's Lake (from which the name Lough Neagh is derived) are tranquil, edged with farmland and small fishing craft. There is often a haze on the water so that you cannot see even to the far side of the lough. At these times, the vast stretch of water (the largest in Britain and Ireland) might almost be a sea. On days like this, is hard to imagine the lake rough and tempestuous, but it has claimed the lives of many who did not respect its moods. According to a local tradition, the lough claims one victim each year. The long shoreline is flat, lacking the dramatic beauty of Lough Leane in Killarney, and without even the small hills that encircle Lough Gur in Limerick. Like Lough Gur, this lake has great treasures of myth and story attached to it – many of them associated with how it came into being.

In one version of the story of its origin, Lough Neagh was formed when the giant Fionn got himself into a rage and tore up a huge piece of earth, throwing it towards an enemy in Scotland. The resulting vast hole became filled with water and formed the lake. Other legends claim that it marks the place where the lovers Eochaidh Mac Maireadha and Eibhliu went when they fled from her husband Mairidh, Eochaidh's father. Aonghus, the god of love and foster-father of Eibhliu, assisted the lovers by giving them a magical horse, but he told them that it must not be allowed to urinate anywhere. When the pair stopped and made their home in Ulster, however, it did so, and caused a spring to come up, which Eochaidh quickly covered. However, after a time, a woman went to the well and left the spring uncovered, so that the waters rose to drown all of the tribe, with the exception of a single girl, Lí Ban, the daughter of Eochaidh. In mythology, Eochaidh was a horse god, and the name Lough Neagh comes from the title of the descendants of Eochaidh who were the sept who lived on its banks. Other more recent folklore tells of the magical city that can be seen under the water of the lake at certain times of the day – an alternative, underwater universe, which is a mirror image of that of the living people who inhabit the banks of the lake.

Although it has been established that the area around Lough Neagh was one of the earliest inland sites of habitation in Ireland, there are relatively few ancient remains on the shores of the lake. Those antiquities that remain are for the most part from the period of Celtic Christianity rather than from earlier times. At Ardboe in Tyrone, on the southwest shore of the lough, there is one of the finest High Crosses in Ireland. Tradition has it that this Celtic church was founded by St Colman, who mixed the mortar for the building with the milk of a magic cow. This was also a traditional site of Lughnasa celebrations, where the people of the five counties surrounding the lough met at the beginning of August. In addition to saying the rosary in the ancient graveyard, it was traditional to wash feet, hands, face and head in the lough, as if its waters held a special power at this turning point of the year. Like many lakes in Ireland, these waters have been under threat in recent years from the levels of sewage and fertiliser run-off from the surrounding farmland, resulting in a build-up of phosphorus and nitrates and the growth of thick, choking algae on the surface of the lake. This is a threat not just to the wildlife but to the livelihood of the fishermen of the lakeside – Lough Neagh is famous in particular for its huge stocks of eels, which come here from the Sargasso Sea. Measures are being taken to counteract this pollution, and work is being done to preserve the area's environment. Such measures are welcome, for the power of this place lies in the water and the surrounding vegetation, rather than in monuments made by man. Lough Neagh is a place to visit for its natural riches – its wealth of waterfowl and plant life, and its tranquil, sheltered loveliness.

LÍ BAN THE MERMAID

A fisherman sat in his boat, far out on Lough Neagh, looking into its silver water. Muirchiú was glad that he was too far away from land for anyone to see his face, for he was weeping. His beloved had left him for a soldier, whose tales of wars and great adventures had stolen her heart and turned her head. What did it matter that Muirchiú himself was a fine, strong, young man, with black curls and ruddy cheeks, and that his father's family had fished from these shores since time before time? How could his quiet life compete with that of one who had known battle and feasting and adventures? He should have listened to his sour old uncle, Conleth, who had told him that there was no trusting women. Hadn't one of them even been responsible for the creation of the great loch itself? The lady Neagh, in her pride and arrogance, had visited the magic fountain of her people and left the cover off, and so the waters had flowed out of it until the great lake was formed, drowning all living things under its blanket of water.

There was a pull on the net and he moved swiftly to grasp it. Perhaps, he thought, he would be lucky enough to catch an eel ... He tugged and tugged but whatever was caught in the net was heavier than any fish. As he pulled, determined not to lose his catch, or his new net, he began to feel worried in case it was some kind of monster – one of the great worms that live in many of the lakes of Ireland – which would pull his boat over and into the water. The thought went through his head that it would serve his sweetheart right

Above:
The waters of Lough Neagh.

if he were washed up dead on the shore. She would be sorry then. As the creature thrashed around, Muirchiú seemed to catch a glimpse of a silvery tail, the flash of fin. Finally, red in the face with exertion and panting and cursing, he managed to pull the net into the boat – and there, caught in its coil, with a look of pure fury on her face, was the most beautiful woman he had ever seen. She had silver hair, the colour of the lough water at sunset, and wide aquamarine eyes under delicate black brows. Her lips were red and the curve of her neck was as sinuous and graceful as an eel. From head to waist, she was delicately formed and bare of covering as a newborn babe, but from the waist down, she had a huge fishtail of silver and gold scales, like that of a salmon but a hundred times bigger.

'Put me down, you great oaf,' said the lovely creature, thrashing her tail angrily. 'Or it will be the worse for you and your children.'

'And your children's children,' she added as an afterthought.

The fisherman held fast but, with one final buck, the creature flipped itself out of his arms and lay on the bottom of the boat, panting nearly as heavily as Muirchiú himself.

Muirchiú finally found his voice: 'What class of a creature are you?'

'I am not,' said the creature in her curiously accented, archaic Gaelic, 'any class of a creature, but the Princess Lí Ban, the Beauty of Women, the fairest daughter of Eochaidh Mac Maireadha and of the royal house of Ulster.'

Muirchiú began to speak, but was interrupted by the woman's anxious voice.

'Oh, look – there is Dogeen. He's coming up to look for me.'

At the side of the boat was an otter, swimming furiously around the stern, making whimpering noises that did indeed sound like the cries of a distressed dog. The fisherman reached over and pulled the little creature into the boat, where it jumped onto the mermaid's lap and started to lick her face furiously. She tried to pet him through the coils of the net, and then said, 'Would you let me out of this tangle of threads? It's very uncomfortable sitting in them.'

Muirchiú considered for a moment, eyeing her shrewdly. 'Will you promise, then, not to jump out of the boat?'

Lí Ban sighed. 'I promise to sit here quietly for as long as the lake is calm.'

Muirchiú, like all fishermen, could tell what weather was coming by the smell of the wind and the shape of the clouds travelling across the sky. When he saw that the lake was as still as a pond and the evening sky was clear, he nodded and helped the mermaid out of the net. She settled herself down on the seat opposite him and immediately began smoothing her hair.

'So how did you end up half-fish?' asked Muirchiú, curiously.

Lí Ban grimaced. After three centuries, she was getting tired of telling the same story to every fool who caught her.

'When the fountain was opened and the waters came and drowned all my people, I was in my bower, with my little lapdog,' she began briskly. 'The water did not come into the bower, and I found myself face to face with the god Manannán, who told me that I was under his protection. I said that if I was doomed to live underwater, I might as well be a fish, and so I found myself a salmon, and my dog an otter, and sometimes I am fully fish and sometimes fully woman, and, then again, sometimes I have the upper shape of a woman, and I have been roaming the seas and the lake of Ireland these three hundred years. And very little of interest have I seen there, and certainly no one as handsome as you.' She smiled and Muirchiú blushed furiously.

Lí Ban gave the young man a shrewd look. 'I have rarely been foolish enough to be caught by a human, but I thought I heard someone weeping and was curious to see what it was about, so I came too close to your net.'

Muirchiú looked sheepish. 'That was me. Don't mind what I was wailing about. It was only some silly girl, but you are twice as beautiful as she is.'

Lí Ban looked unimpressed. 'Don't start getting any ideas, now. A daughter of a king would not be interested in a fisherman, no matter how handsome,' she said sharply. 'Anyway, I'm too old for you, by a few hundred years at least. But I will give you a kiss.'

She leaned towards him; her lips touched his and her pale arms pulled him towards her; her long hair seemed to draw him into a net of cool softness. At first, it was like diving into deep water – he was drawn down, down into depths beyond which he had never swum. There was music down there, the deep sound of the bottom of the ocean. Then it was as if he was caught in the coils of a great eel – it was pulling him, touching him, burrowing into secret places, arousing him more and more. As his passion increased, it seemed as if the water darkened and the waves rose, and he went further and further down into the dark depths of the lake.

When he opened his eyes, he was back on land, with a crowd around him praising God that he had been saved from the water.

'What happened to you at all?' they asked. 'And how did the boat manage to come back to land through such a tempest?'

'What tempest?' he asked, still fuddled.

'The one that blew up in a minute and was gone just as quickly,' replied one old man, eyeing him closely. 'The ones they say the mermaids call up by their singing.'

But Muirchiú was not listening – realisation was dawning as he saw the empty boat, and a faint, mocking voice came into his head. Lí Ban was saying, 'I only swore to stay while the water was calm, fisher-boy.'

Ever after, Muirchiú would tell the story of how he had almost captured the most beautiful woman in the world. Indeed, he told the story so well that his girlfriend came back to him, begging to know if her kiss was as sweet as a mermaid's. Many years afterwards, Muirchiú heard that Lí Ban had been captured again – this time by a cleric, at Inbhar Ollarbha. The story was that a dispute had broken out between the cleric and another priest over who had the rights to the mermaid's soul. Muirchiú laughed at this, for he would not have cared about Lí Ban's soul if he could only have had her body. The word got around that the dispute had been settled by the appearance of two magical stags who had taken Lí Ban to a church where she was baptised and, in the way of the Sídh who have taken to Christianity, died immediately. But Muirchiú was not so sure of the truth of that part of the story, for he often thought, when out fishing on the lough, that he could hear the sweet, faint call of her voice, singing over the water, and even, sometimes, the echo of her clear and mocking laughter.

Ballycastle,
BAILE AN CHAISLEÁIN Antrim

lthough the story of Deirdre and the Sons of Usna begins and ends at the court of King Conchobhar at Emain Macha in Armagh, perhaps its strongest connection is with the glens of Scotland, where Deirdre made her home after fleeing with her lover. The lament Deirdre sings when leaving these glens has the same emotional depth as the one she sings when her lover is killed. However, Scotland lies beyond the scope of this book, so instead we look to the extreme northeast coast of Antrim for the site of this story, to the landing place where Deirdre returned after her few short years of happiness. Tradition has it that this landing place was Ballycastle Bay, just under Fair Head. The beach at Ballycastle is a pleasant one with magnificent views towards Rathlin and Manannán's Rock. Ballycastle is a lively seaside town and the site of Lammas Fair in August, a gathering that has its roots in the Lughnasa festival. At the east end of its beach, there is a cluster of flat rocks, known as Pan's Rocks because, in the past, salt-panning was carried on here by the local people. It is said that Deirdre protested to the very end against landing here, wanting to land on Rathlin Island where at least they had the security of the sea as a barrier between themselves and the jealous Conchobhar.

The sea journey to Rathlin Island is well worth making, not just for the experience of a beautiful and peaceful island, and the numbers of sea birds which make the island their home, but also for the friendliness and kindness of the people who live there – there is nothing quite like the feeling of staying on such an island when the last of the day visitors have left and the island sinks into its world of quietness. Folk tradition says that Rathlin was formed when Fionn's huge mother tripped and dropped a pile of stones in the bay, on her way to Scotland to buy whiskey – she lies drowned under the water, and, in stormy weather, people say, 'The old witch is kickin''. The idea of the *Cailleach* or Old Witch as creator of the landscape links this northeastern point of Ireland with that extreme southwestern one – Béara.

Not far from Ballycastle is Torr Head. It was there that the traitorous warrior Barach forced Fergus Mac Róich – who had taken on the safety of Deirdre and the Sons of Usna as his personal responsibility – to leave his charges and dine with him at his fort. The journey around the coast from Ballycastle to Torr Head passes by Fair Head, where there are signposted walks on the cliffs. The small valley of Lough na Cranagh holds a *crannóg* in a lake hedged by green hills. Here, the trees and the gentle hills give relief from the sometimes overpowering drama and tempest of the coastal views. Fair Head is also the site where yet another giant has his residence – not, in this case, a figure from mythology, but a character from local folklore, known as the Grey Man. This cloaked figure may be seen striding along the cliffs, looking out towards the sea when a storm is brewing. Perhaps this figure is

Above:
*'Fair Head',
County Antrim,
by T Creswick.*

connected with the grey-cloaked god, Manannán, for the rock that bears his name is not far out to sea, in the wild Sea of Moyle where the Children of Lir spent the most miserable part of their time in exile. Here you feel closer to the Mull of Kintyre than to Ireland; and indeed, at those times in the past when land travel was made difficult by bogs and great forests, Scotland would have been more easily accessible than many parts of Ireland. It is on Fair Head that during the reign of Elizabeth I, the old Gaelic chieftain, Sorley Boy, screamed his madness and grief when he heard the shrieks coming across the sound from Rathlin. He had sent the women and children of his clan there for safety but an invading fleet, led by Drake and Norris, landed on the island and butchered every one of them.

This is country that can best be appreciated by those prepared to do some walking, to immerse themselves in hidden valleys and wild headlands. Not far away is Cushendall and the site of Oisín's Grave – a Neolithic court grave on Tievebullagh mountain. This is the country of Fionn and the Fianna, of hunters racing with their hounds and their horns down narrow glens towards the sea. If Deirdre's ghost wanders here, it is a lonely one, continually looking eastwards across the sea towards the glens of Scotland.

THE TRAGEDY OF DEIRDRE

I was there at her birth, and I was there at her death. And if I had known what I know now, at the time of her birth – if I had known of the sorry destruction that her lovely face would bring on us all – I might have taken that little crying baby and held her tight against me, and stopped her crying by stopping her breath at my breast. And I would have done it for love of that little one, and for the honour of our king and the safety of our world.

She was born to sorrow – in the middle of the feasting, when her mother was crying out in pain in the birthing-room, the prophecy made by Cathbad was that this child's beauty would be such that it would bring great sorrow to the land of Ireland. So there were many would have agreed with me if I had taken her and killed her gently then; but the king laughed, and said no, for he was one who always wanted the best of everything and why should he not have the most beautiful woman in the world as his bride? So he sent Deirdre away into hiding, with no companion but me – Leabharcham, an old woman poet – to look after her in her house in the forest. There she grew more beautiful every day, and more gracious, but always a little serious for want of the companionship of others of her age. And while her hair grew blacker and her eyes bluer, the king, Conchobhar, grew greyer and grosser in his palace at Emain Macha, and it tore my heart to think of his lewdness in taking my sweet nursling to his bed.

He would come and visit her and sit her on his knee and try to make her laugh, but she looked at him with big, solemn eyes and not a smile on her lips. And I could see that the time was approaching when her beauty would be such that Conchobhar would wait no longer. So I cannot tell whether it was more by design than by chance that my tongue slipped one day, when Deirdre, watching the snow fall from the window of our lonely fortress, said, 'Look, Leabharcham – there is a raven feeding on a dead calf in the snow. I would wish that I should meet a man with such black hair, such red lips, and such white skin.'

And I, busy with my spinning, and my mind on my work, said, 'In truth, Conchobhar is not such a one – though I knew him when he was a handsome enough lad, before age and greed made him as he is. But such a one is Naoise,

Deirdre, and the sons of Usna were killed by their former companions, the three of them standing in a circle around her, protecting her with their shields. Deirdre, to her great sorrow, did not die on that day. She spent a year with Conchobhar, being used by him as a bull uses a cow, and never once did I see a smile cross her lips. It is true that at the beginning he tried to cajole her, to tempt her with presents and sweet words; but her look was the same to him whether he beat her or begged her – she had nothing to give him but dull and stubborn hatred. At the end of the year, he asked her, 'Who is it that you hate most in the world, my Queen of Sorrows?'

She shrugged and answered him: 'Apart from yourself, King of Shame, it would be Eoghan Mac Durthacht, for it was he who struck the blow that killed my beloved.'

So Conchobhar told her that she would spend the next year with Eoghan, and perhaps after that she would be sent to another warrior who had helped to kill the sons of Usna. He took her in his chariot with Eoghan, and brought me along to punish me by seeing her pain, and they travelled the great road from Emain Macha. It was a snowy day. The sky was bright blue and only the black shapes of the forest broke the whiteness of the hills. Deirdre had scratched her face with her nails, trying to ruin her beauty, and she stood slumped in the chariot like an old woman, but Conchobhar, having brought her to this, still could not leave matters alone. He said, 'That face you have on you, woman, between me and Eoghan, is like the look of a ewe when she is caught between two rams.'

He and Eoghan both laughed loudly. Deirdre said nothing. I saw what she was going to do, but I did nothing to stop her, for I thought that in death her spirit might find its way to the blue hillside in Scotland and to her beloved Naoise. She flung herself from the chariot against a great rock that was beside the road there. Conchobhar's laugh was stopped in his throat and he stood silent, looking down at her body in the snow, where the red blood flowed over white skin and black hair.

Giant's Causeway, Antrim

CLOCHÁN NA BhFOMHARAIGH

Established as a UNESCO World site in 1986, the Giant's Causeway and the area around it on the north Antrim coast has long been a favourite site for tourists to Ireland. It was 'discovered' by polite society at the end of the seventeenth century and was not marked on maps until 1714, despite the fact that some of the earliest settlers in Ireland are likely to have lived on the north Antrim coastline, as the flint-factories on Rathlin Island testify. From the time of its discovery, the causeway became increasingly popular, so that by Victorian times, any traveller to Ireland considered it a compulsory stop along their route. Visitors such as William Thackeray and the Halls gave detailed descriptions of it. Some of the travellers, having seen the somewhat exaggerated prints of the wonders of the causeway, may have been a little underwhelmed. While the black basalt rocks, which

Above:
*WH Bartlett's engraving, 'Scene
at the Giant's Causeway', County
Antrim.*

make up the causeway, are interesting in a geological sense, the area they cover is not a huge one. Nevertheless, there are estimated to be 40,000 of these rocks, and they are set in stunningly beautiful surroundings of magnificent cliffs which have formed their own strange shapes and columns.

Tourism, with the guides, postcards, boat-trips and hawking, while providing an income for local people, also brought its own dangers of overcrowding and, before safeguards were put into place, in some cases involved the actual removal of rocks from the causeway. Now, access to the causeway and cliffs is better controlled and, while there are still crowds in summer, a visit during spring or autumn, preferably in the early morning, can be made with nothing but dozens of sea birds for company. At any time of the year (with the possible exception of wild winter days, when the cold wind can cut through any number of layers of clothing), the cliff walk is well worth making, with magnificent views to the west to Donegal and eastwards towards the blue outline of the Scottish coast.

The causeway (*Clochán na bhFomharaigh* — 'the stepping stones of the Fomorians'), once believed to be the work of giants, is in fact a totally natural formation. Sixty million years ago, lava flowed towards the sea, cooling to become black basalt and, in the meantime, cracking to form the honeycomb of shaped rocks — in a similar way to the way in which mud cracks when it dries. Many layers of lava flows resulted in the variety of shapes and sizes, from the tall columns and the misshapen cliffs to the flatter causeway itself. While Thackeray described the causeway as 'a remnant of chaos', in some ways it is the very opposite — an example of a natural wonder that seems so regular and ordered as to have to be man-made, the work of some demented and obsessive giant. And so the stories go. According to local stories, the giant Fionn Mac Cumhaill, transformed by folklore into a comic figure rather than the great and jealous warrior he comes across as in the legends, built the causeway as a route to fight a giant in Scotland. When he reached Scotland and saw his enemy, he realised that he was bigger than he thought, and ran back towards Ireland, tearing the causeway up behind him. The remnants on the Scottish side lie around Fingal's Cave on the island of Staffa, and take the form of basalt columns. There are many stories about Fionn still remembered by the people of Antrim — his cleverness, his strength, and, in cases, his bad temper, as when he turned his mother into rock because she was nagging him for going too slowly as he was building the causeway.

However, there are also other, less light-hearted stories associated with this wild stretch of coast — of shipwrecks and deaths at sea, and the hard life of these hardy people. One of the great waves of Ireland, the wave of Tuaidhe was said to come in at Ballintoy, to the east of the causeway, and Ballycastle Harbour is notorious for its treacherous currents. If you make the walk along the cliffs eastwards towards Port Moon, you will pass Port na Spánaigh, where the Spanish Armada ship, the *Girona*, foundered in 1588. There were 1,300 people drowned in the wreck. The remains of the ship were discovered in 1967, when the gold and jewels found by divers were transferred to the Ulster Museum. The coastline is deeply indented and the little harbours are a litany of musical names – Port Coon, Port Moon, Portnaboe. The final point on the cliff walk, Dunseverick Castle, stands on the ancient site of Dún Sobhairce, one of the four royal roads which led from Tara. It was at Dún Sobhairce that King Rónán slew his son in jealousy and began the slaughter that would see the death of his friends and family. It is a fitting point to stop and reflect on an area that has changed so little since the first flows of lava headed northwards, and the fiery stone met icy water to become a landscape set apart.

FIONN'S VISITOR

Fionn often went to fight the giants in Scotland, and he made the Giant's Causeway as a convenient way of getting across without wetting his feet. However, there was a Scottish giant once, who decided to come across the causeway and fight with Fionn. Fionn's wife spotted him as the huge creature made his way over across the stones, and realised that he was twice the size of her husband. When he reached Fionn's house, the giant knocked on the door.

Bang, bang, bang.

Fionn's wife opened the door (we are not told which wife it was, but it seems likely that it could have been Gráinne, as she was obviously a woman of quick wits).

'Good day to you,' said the giant. 'I'm here to fight your husband.'

'Are you indeed?' asked Fionn's wife. 'Well, fair play to you. You had better come in and rest yourself, for he's away hunting. He'll be back soon.'

The giant came in and sat crouched by the fire, and the woman of the house offered him a drink and began to sing softly to the figure sleeping in the settle bed.

The giant took a closer look into the bed. There was a huge warrior there, with a bearded face and shoulders like an ox.

'Who is that?' He asked the woman of the house.

'That's the new baby,' said the woman. 'The ba – the last of fifteen. The rest are out hunting with their daddy. Isn't he a fine lad?'

The giant nodded and came forward to have a closer look. 'Indeed he is.'

The figure gave a little moan.

'Ah, the poor baba. Sure, isn't he teething?' said the woman. 'Would you mind putting some salve on his gums while I heat some milk for him?' She handed the giant a pot of white ointment.

The giant cautiously put his ointment-covered finger into the creature's mouth, then yelped and jumped away.

'He's after taking a big bite out of me,' he said. 'Didn't you say he was only getting his teeth?'

The woman sounded surprised.

'You must have hurt his poor gums. Well, he is teething. It's his wisdom teeth he's getting. Sure every baby of Fionn's is born with a full set of teeth apart from those last four.'

'And a big hairy face?' asked the giant. 'And legs like tree-trunks?'

The woman smiled indulgently.

'Indeed, that's the case. I'm telling you, I had a terrible time when this lad was born. Would you like me to tell you all about it? Three weeks in labour I was … but of course it was worth it – isn't he a grand little fella? But not one of them is a pick on their father.'

The giant took off out the door and ran all the way to Scotland, pulling the causeway up behind him as he went.

Fionn's wife laughed and said to the figure on the bed, who could no longer keep the grin off his face: 'Well, husband dear, you can get up now. I don't think that fella will be coming over looking to fight with you again.'

Emain Macha, Armagh

Emain Macha (the name means 'the twins of Macha') or Navan Fort, as it is also known, lies close to the town of Armagh in a countryside of rounded hills and hidden valleys, the south Armagh borderland. The great bowl-shaped mound is sited on a hill, surrounded by a circular rampart and ditch and with commanding views over the countryside. This is the place that was the main home of the Red Branch warriors, the army of Conchobhar Mac Neasa. Conchobhar was the king who was said to rule Ulster during the period when the great epic, the *Táin*, was set. He was the arch-enemy of Maeve and the sovereign lord of the great hero, Cú Chulainn. Emain Macha is an impressive structure and has a long history. The main remaining structure dates from around 100BC but the original settlement date was earlier, possibly as early as 700BC. It is one of the great royal sites of the pagan Celtic Iron Age – an honour shared with Tara, Cruachain and Dún Ailinne. Excavations on the mound began in 1963, and involved carefully removing the earthen mound and examining what lay beneath.

There seem to have been various phases of activity on the site. It was established that the inner structure was rebuilt nine times and the outer stockade six times during the period 700–100BC. It appears that, originally, five rings of huge oak posts were set up, which were then filled with thousands of limestone boulders to form a cairn 2.8 metres (9 feet) high. Then, the timber building was deliberately burnt and the remaining structure was covered with turf. This indicates that there was a ritual element in the construction, the meaning of which has been lost to us. The evidence seems to point to strong connections with the cult of sovereignty of the priest kings of the Iron Age who had sacred, as well as secular, duties. There are no historical sources on the founding of Emain Macha although it was certainly a palace, according to the descriptions in the stories. It is said that Conchobhar had three households at Emain Macha – the *Craobh Ruadh*, or Red Branch; the *Téte Brec*, or Place of the Shining Hoard, where the king kept his weapons and treasure; and the *Craobh Dearg* or Ruddy Branch, where he kept the severed heads of his enemies.

Emain Macha, as ritual centre as well as the home of the king, was a centre for the *aonach*, the seasonal meeting where buying and selling went on, games and horse races and feasts were held, and rituals were celebrated by the tribe.

There are actually two mounds on the site, both of which have been excavated. By the late Iron Age, the centre of one of these mounds seems to have held a huge central pole – perhaps of oak. The word 'branch' in the associated place names and the fact that nearby in Armagh there was a sacred oak grove seems to indicate that trees played an important role in the ritual here; the oak was sacred to the great

where the assembly was, and the red-haired woman turned to her husband and said, 'You have been unwise, my husband. It is not right that I should be stared at by this crowd, and I so near my time. What is it that the king wants?'

The king himself replied. 'Your husband has boasted that you can outrun my two best horses. We have set up a racecourse for you to do this.'

The woman went pale.

'Do not ask me to do this, noble king, for the children in my womb will come very soon. I beg your mercy – wait until after I have given birth and then I will run for you. Do not shame me in my hour of weakness.'

The king refused.

The woman looked at Crunnchu. 'Can you not save me from this, husband?' she asked.

But he only hung his head.

Then she looked around the great crowd of men. 'Someone among you plead for me,' she said. 'For has not a mother borne each of you?'

However, there was no mercy on any of the faces looking at her – only greedy anticipation of wagers laid and the thrill of the race. Perhaps in some there was even a desire to see the woman shamed and humiliated; but most of the men there, if they were thinking at all, thought only of possible loss or gain. Finally, the woman shouted, 'Shame on you all then, and shame on your children.'

The king said, 'Enough of this – start the race.' Then he asked, 'Woman, what is your name?'

The woman replied, 'My name is Macha and well you shall all remember it.'

The race began, and some turned their eyes away when they saw the woman, who seemed hardly able to stand, pull herself to the starting post. She took off her heavy robe and let down her long red hair, standing in her shift, her belly out before her like a plum ready to burst. At first, it seemed as if she could have no chance against the chariot drawn by the two swift horses, for she staggered forward for the first few yards. But as the race went on, something seemed to take her over, as if her anger had given her a strength beyond the lot of humans. By the halfway mark, she was running like the wind, and those who had betted on the king's greys were beginning to look downcast.

As she raced past the finish post, far ahead of the two sweating horses, the sky darkened and Macha gave a great cry and fell to the ground. There on the race track, before anyone could come to succour or shield her, she gave birth

Opposite:
Emain Macha,
County Armagh.

to two children – a boy and a girl.

All the men who heard the cry she gave were seized with a weakness, so that each one felt he had no more strength than that of a woman in childbirth. Macha drew herself up from the ground and stood before them. And now all that were there knew that she was no farmer's wife, but a goddess. She said to them, 'I have won the race, men of Ulster; and know that as punishment for your greed and your cruelty to a woman in pain, I put on you this curse. In your time of greatest need, the men of Ulster will be laid on their backs with a sickness which will have them crying in agony, weakened, at the mercy of their enemies. You will be like women at the time of their travail; you will know agony and helplessness; and there will be no one to help you. This sickness will remain on you for five days and four nights and it will continue to sicken your children until the ninth generation. And, as this is the place where my shame was seen, it will be called forever Emain Macha, or the place of the twins of Macha.'

'And as for you,' she said, turning to give her husband one last cold glance. 'You could have known riches and happiness such as no man has ever been granted. But instead you will live in sorrow and want, and misfortune brought on by your boasting tongue.'

Then she gathered up her children and walked away from the red blood that spattered the green grass and from the men who lay groaning in their seats, unable to move, powerless as new-born infants against the curse of Macha.

Time Chart

PERIOD	DATES IN IRELAND	ASSOCIATED FEATURES	ASSOCIATED SITES CONNECTED TO STORIES IN THIS BOOK	'CORRESPONDS' IN LEGENDARY TIME TO:	WORLD HISTORY CONTEXT
Palaeolithic Era	Pre-7500BC	None. No evidence of human habitation in Ireland.	None	The Mythological Cycle: stories of the Tuatha Dé Danann and the invasions of Ireland.	Traces of pottery from Japan, Brazil, the Sudan. Cave paintings in northern Spain and southern France.
Mesolithic Era (normally starts 12000BC but the second Ice Age in Ireland prevented habitation before 8000BC)	c.7500BC –3500BC	Middens, flint, shell and food remains. Earliest stone structures.	Possibly Carrowmore, Sligo.		Evidence of Neolithic culture/early farming in Near East, moving west and north.
Neolithic Era	c.3500BC –2000BC	Megalithic tombs: portal, passage, court and wedge tombs.	Carrowkeel, Newgrange, Knowth and Dowth, Mound of the Hostages at Tara, cairn on Knockainey, remains at Uisneach.		First pyramids in Egypt. Emergence of Minoan civilisation in Crete.
Bronze Age	c.2000BC –300BC	Standing stones, stone circles, beginnings of hill-forts.	Barrows at Knockainey, stone circles on Béara. Dún Aonghusa, as a hill-fort on a promontory, is thought to have been in its heyday during the Bronze Age.		Classical Greece.
Celtic Iron Age	c.300BC –500AD	Promontory forts, ringforts, hill-forts, cashels and cathairs.	The great ritual sites such as Emain Macha, Tara and Cruachain. Promontory forts at Howth, Caherconree, Béara, Dún Aonghusa and Tory. Grianán of Aileach.	Ulster Cycle Fianna Cycle (Early centuries AD)	Rise and fall of the Roman Empire, Great Wall of China.
Early Christian Era	c.500AD – first Viking invasions	Small churches, beehive huts, ogham stones. Ringforts still in use.	Ecclesiastical sites all over Ireland including those mentioned in stories at Inis Glora, Ardagh, St Mullins.	Cycles of the Kings.	'Dark Ages' in Europe.

Glossary of Main Characters Mentioned in the Text

AENGUS
Last king of the Fir Bolg; in legend, the builder of Dún Aonghusa on Inishmore. Not connected with Aonghus of the Tuatha Dé Danann.

AIDEEN
A form of Étaín.

AIFE, DAUGHTER OF DEALBHEATH
Princess, changed by malice into a crane and accidentally killed by Manannán Mac Lir.

AILBE
Daughter of Cormac Mac Airt.

AILBHE
Sister of Aobh and Aoife.

AILEACH
Scottish princess and wife of Friguan; the Grianán of Aileach was said to be built in her name .

AILILL ANGHUBHA
Brother of Eochaidh Aireamh, the high king who was the husband of Étaín.

AILILL MAC MÁTA
King of Connacht; husband of Maeve.

AILILL ÓLOM
King of Munster; rapist of Áine.

ÁINE
Goddess of the sun, brightness, fertility; tutelary goddess of Knockainey.

AOBH
Mother of the Children of Lir.

AODH
One of the children of Lir; changed into a swan by Aoife.

AOIBHEALL
Woman of the Sídh, associated with County Clare.

AOIFE
Daughter of Bodhbh; enchantress; second wife of Lir and stepmother to his children.

AONGHUS ÓG
One of the Tuatha Dé Danann, God of youth and love; Lord of Brú na Bóinne.

ART
High king; son of Conn; husband of Dealbhchaem.

BADBH
War-goddess; one of the three battle furies – often appeared as a crow.

BALOR NA SÚILE NIMHE (OF THE POISON EYE)
God of the Fir Bolg; killed by his grandson Lugh at the Second Battle of Moytura.

BANBA
One of the three sister goddesses of sovereignty of Ireland.

BARACH
Red Branch warrior; betrayer of the Sons of Usna.

BÉCUMA
Woman of the Sídh, sent into exile to Ireland; wife of Conn of the Hundred Battles.

BIRÓG
Woman of the Sídh who rescued Lugh from his grandfather.

BLÁI DEARG
See Sadhbh.

BLÁTHNAID
Daughter of Iuchar; wife of Cú Roí; lover of Cú Chulainn.

BÓCHNA
Mother of the seer Fintan; one of the first women to come to Ireland.

BODHBH DEARG
Tutelary god of Slievenamon; father of Aoife.

BÓINN
Goddess of the Boyne and of cattle; mother of Aonghus by the Daghdha.

BOLG
Deity associated with lightning; the Fir Bolg are his people. There are other interpretations of the word *Bolg*.

BRAN
Hound of Fionn; child of his sister when she took the form of a hound.

BRES
Half-Fomorian, half of the race of the Tuatha Dé Danann, Bres was elected their king after Nuadhu lost his arm but soon became a tyrant. He was eventually defeated by the troops of the Tuatha Dé Danann at the Second Battle of Moytura.

BRICRIU
Warrior, known as 'Poisoned Tongue', he caused dissension wherever he went.

BRIGHID, BRIGID
Goddess of smithwork, poetry and healing; later, the saint born in Louth and founder of the monastery at Kildare; celebrated at Imbolc on 1 February, the beginning of spring.

BUAN
One of the first people to come to Ireland, companion of Cessair.

CAER IOBHARMHÉITH
Woman of the Sídh; wife of Aonghus

CAILLEACH BHÉARRA
See Hag of Béara.

CAIRBRE LIFEACHAIR
King of Ireland, son of Cormac Mac Airt.

CAIRNEACH
Saint who cursed Muircheartach Mac Erca.

CAMÓG
One of the three Hags of Keshcorann.

CAOILTE MAC RÓNÁIN
One of the Fianna – its greatest runner.

CATHBAD
Druid and seer of the court of King Conchobhar Mac Nessa.

CEAT MAC MAGHACH
Renowned Connacht warrior sent by King Cairbre against the Fir Bolg.

CEITHLINN OF THE CROOKED TEETH
Wife of Balor and mother of Ethlinn.

CERNET
Mistress of Cormac Mac Airt.

CESSAIR
The first person to land in Ireland – she and all her people, except for Fintan, were killed in a great flood.

CIAN
Lover of Ethlinn, father of Lugh.

CLIACH
Famous harper who fell in love with one of the daughters of Bodhbh.

CLÍODHNA
Woman of the Sídh, lover of Aonghus Óg, associated with west Cork.

CNÚ DEARÓIL
Fionn's musician.

COLMAN
Seventh-century monk and saint.

COLMCILLE
Sixth-century Donegal saint and monk; founder of the great monastery at Iona.

CONAIRE MÓR
High King of Ireland; son of Mes Buachalla and a bird-spirit; grandson of Étaín.

CÓNAL
One the three great champions of the Red Branch warriors.

CONALL CEARNACH
Warrior sent by King Cairbre against the Fir Bolg.

CONALL, SON OF AENGUS
Son of the last king of the Fir Bolg, killed by Cú Chulainn.

CONÁN
Warrior of the Fianna and brother of Goll Mac Morna.

CONCHOBHAR MAC NEASA
King of Ulster during the period of the *Táin* and the Red Branch; killer of the Sons of Usna.

CONN
One of the Children of Lir, changed into a swan by Aoife.

CONN OF THE HUNDRED BATTLES
Conn Cét Chathach; high king; husband of Bécuma.

CONNLA
Son of Conn of the Thousand Battles, Connla was enticed away to the Land of Youth by a woman of the Sídh.

CORANN
Harper and poet of Tuatha Dé Danann.

CORMAC MAC AIRT
High king of Ireland; great law-giver; travelled to the realm of Manannán at Bealtaine, or May Eve.

COS CORACH
Musician associated with Slievenamon.

CRAOBH RUA
Red Branch warriors – soldiers of Conchobhar Mac Neasa, they were based at Emhain Macha.

CREDE
Woman of the Sídh and lover of Art, son of Conn.

CRIMTHAN
King who reputedly reigned for only one year (74AD) and is said to be buried on Howth Head.

CROMDES
A druid and magician of the Tuatha Dé Danann.

CRUNNCHU
Husband of Macha.

CÚ CHULAINN
Great hero of Ulster and of the Red Branch.

CÚ ROÍ
Great magician; killed by Cú Chulainn.

CUILLEANN
One of the three Hags of Keshcorann.

DA DEARGA
Host of the house in the Wicklow mountains where Conaire met his death.

DAGHDHA
The Great God; mated with Bóinn and the Morrigan; builder of Aileach; Keeper of the Cauldron of Plenty.

DÁIRE
Farmer of Cooley; owner of the Donn of Cooley.

DANU
Great goddess; mother of the Tuatha Dé Danann.

DEALBHCHAEM
Princess, rescued and married to Art.

DEALBHEATH
Legendary king who was the son of Ogma.

DEIRDRE
Lover of Naoise.

DIAN CÉCHT
Healer of the Tuatha Dé Danann who restored the wounded at the battle of Moytura.

DIARMUID UA DHUIBHNE
One of the Fianna; lover of Gráinne.

DONN
Lord of Death; places of residence included Knock Fierna, off Béara, the southwest coast of Kerry, and Doonbeg in Clare.

DONN OF COOLEY
The great Brown Bull; cause of the *Táin Bó Cuailnge*.

DUAIBHSEACH
Wife of Muircheartach Mac Erca.

ECHDAE
Sky god associated with horses; one of Áine's husbands.

EIBHLIU
Lover of Eochaidh Mac Maireadha, with whom she fled to the place where Lough Neagh later formed.

EICHE
Virgin saint, sister of St Mel and associated with Ardagh.

ÉIRE, ERIU
One of the three sovereign sister goddesses of the land of Ireland.

EITHNE
Wife of Conn of the Thousand Battles.

EITHNE, DAUGHTER OF CATHAOIR MÓR
Wife of Cormac Mac Airt.

ELCMAR
One of the Tuatha Dé Danann, the foster-father of Aonghus Óg.

EOCHAIDH
Horse god, husband of Áine.

EOCHAIDH ÁIREAMH
High king of Ireland; husband of the first Étaín.

EOCHAIDH MAC MAIREADHA

Lover of Eibhliu, with whom he fled to the place where Lough Neagh later formed.

EOGABEL

God and father of the goddess Áine, killed by the druid Fearcheas.

EOGHAN

Fifth-century king, baptised by St Patrick.

EOGHAN MAC DURTHACHT

Warrior of the Red Branch and slayer of Naoise.

EORANN

Wife of Suibhne.

ÉTAÍN, ÉADAOIN, AIDEEN

(1) Wife of Midhir, then through various transformations, wife of Eochaidh Aireamh; (2) Her daughter, daughter and wife of Eochaidh Aireamh; (3) Mes Buachalla, the cowherd's fosterling – daughter and granddaughter of Eochaidh.

ÉTAR

Father of Étaín in her mortal form and king of Echrad.

ETHAL ANBHUAIL

King of the Munster Sídh.

ETHLINN

Daughter of Balor and Ceithlenn; mother of Lugh.

FAND

Woman of the Sídh, she was the wife of Manannán and the lover of Cú Chulainn.

FAS

Milesian princess associated with the Glen Fas area of Kerry.

FEAR DORCHA

The Dark Man, the magician who enchanted Fionn's wife, Sadhbh.

FEARCHEAS

Leinster druid, he was the killer of Eogabel, the father of the goddess Áine.

FEDELM

Prophetess who foretold the slaughter of the *Táin Bó Cuailgne*.

FEIRCHEIRDNE

Cú Roí's harper.

FER FÍ

Brother of the goddess Áine.

FERDIA

Connacht champion; foster-brother of Cú Chulainn.

FERGUS MAC RÓICH

Ulster warrior, originally king of Ulster; went into exile in Connacht after Conchobhar tricked him into betraying Deirdre and the Sons of Usna; Maeve's lover.

FIACHRA

One of the Children of Lir.

FINIAN THE LEPER

Seventh-century saint, credited with founding Inisfallen Abbey in Killarney.

FINNBHEANNACH

The White-Horn – Ailill's great bull.

FINTAN, FIONNTAN MAC BÓCHNA

The oldest man – the seer who lived from the time of the first invasion of Ireland.

FINVARRA

In Connacht folklore – the king of the fairies who has his home at Knockma.

FIONN
Champion, hunter, hero; leader of the Fianna hunting troop.

FIONNABHAIR
Daughter of Maeve; promised to the Connacht champions as a reward for fighting Cú Chulainn.

FIONNUALA
One of the Children of Lir, changed into a swan by Aoife.

FIR BOLG
Descendants of the Nemedians, they were defeated by the Tuatha Dé Danann at the First Battle of Moytura but later returned to Ireland when they held fortresses on the western shoreline; they were finally defeated by King Cairbre.

FLIODHAS
Guardian of wild creatures, particularly deer; sometimes said to be the wife of Fergus Mac Róich and the mother of Lí Ban.

FÓDHLA
One of the three sister goddesses of sovereignty of Ireland.

FOMORIANS (FOMHÓIRE)
Race of malevolent beings who oppressed the Tuatha Dé Danann until eventually defeated by them at the Second Battle of Moytura.

FOTHADH CANAINNE
Mythical warrior and husband of the Hag of Béara.

FRIGUAN
Legendary builder of the Grianán of Aileach.

FUAMNACH
First wife of Midhir; enchantress who transformed Étaín.

GAIBHLEANN GABHA
Mythical smith said to live on the Béara peninsula.

GOIBHNIU
God of smithcraft – he forged magical weapons for the Tuatha Dé Danann at the second battle of Moytura.

GOLL MAC MORNA
One of the Fianna; killed by Fionn.

GRÁINNE
Daughter of Cormac Mac Airt; wife of Diarmuid and later of Fionn.

HAG OF BÉARA
In Irish, the *Cailleach Bhéarra*; appears in various forms throughout Ireland; often associated with harvest time and with creating physical features in the landscape.

HAWK OF ACHILL
Mythological bird to whom the seer Fintan told his story.

INCGEL
British sea-pirate whose warriors killed Conaire, son of Étaín.

IORNACH
One of the three Hags of Keshcorann.

IUCHAR
King of the Isle of Man; father of Bláthnaid.

LABHRAIDH
Druidic sorcerer, father of Fintan.

LAEG
Cú Chulainn's charioteer.

LAOGHAIRE
Son of Niall of the Nine Hostages and high king, converted to Christianity by St Patrick after many years of of opposition to the saint.

LEABHARCHAM
Female satirist and poet; nurse of Deirdre.

LÍ BAN
Princess transformed into a mermaid after the flooding of Lough Neagh.

LIR
One of the Tuatha Dé Danann, he lived at his *sídh* in Armagh; he was the father of children changed into swans by the enchantress Aoife.

LOINGSEACHÁN
Friend and helper of Suibhne.

LON MAC LÍOMTHA
Magical three-armed smith; lived in Keshcorann caves.

LUCHRA
Enchantress who, out of jealousy, turned Aife into a crane.

LUGH, LÁMHFHADA, LUGH OF THE LONG ARM
The many-skilled god, adept at all crafts and skills of battle; god of light and sun, celebrated at Lughnasa, the time of harvest; killer of his grandfather, Balor, at the Battle of Moytura, and later king over all the Tuatha Dé Danann.

MAC CÉCHT
One of the Tuatha Dé Danann; master-healer.

MAC ROTH
Messenger of Maeve of Connacht.

MACHA
Goddess of pastures, horses, fertility, kingship and, in one form, of battle; often known as Macha the Red.

MAEVE, MEADBH, MEDB
Queen of Connacht; main instigator of the *Táin Bó Cuailgne*.

MAIRIDH
King of Munster and father of Eochaidh; Eochaidh fled with his wife.

MANANNÁN MAC LIR
Deity of the oceans, and the magical otherworld, the Many-Coloured Land; in his human form, said to be buried in Lough Corrib.

MEL
Fifth-century saint and bishop, associated with Ardagh.

MES BUACHALLA
The third Étaín, mother of King Conaire.

MIDHIR
One of the Tuatha Dé Danann; lover of Étaín and dweller in Brí Léith.

MÍL
Leader of the last invasion of Ireland, when the Milesians defeated the Tuatha Dé Danann and sent them into the hollow hills.

MILESIANS, SONS OF MÍL
Last invaders of Ireland; the tribe who defeated the Tuatha Dé Danann.

MIS
Princess who went mad when her father was killed; was restored by the power of music; the Slieve Mish mountains in Kerry are called after her.

MOCHAOMHÓG
Hermit on Inis Glora who buried the Children of Lir.

MOLING
Saint and hermit; lover of nature and protector of Suibhne in his last days.

MONGAN
Son of Manannán Mac Lir and famous shape-shifter and magician.

MONGÁN
Moling's cowherd; killer of Suibhne.

MORGAN
Father of Dealbhchaem, killed by Art.

MORRIGAN
War goddess, one of the triple battle furies; said to come from the cave of Owneygat at Cruachan at Samhain, the feast of the dead at the beginning of November.

MUIRCHEARTACH MAC ERCA
High king of Ireland in the sixth century; loved by Sín who also killed him.

MUIRGIL
Wife of Moling's cowherd, Mongán.

NAOISE
Eldest of the Sons of Usna; lover of Deirdre; killed by Conchobhar.

NEMED, NEIMHEADH
Leader of the Nemedians; one of the husbands of Macha.

NEMEDIANS
The people of Nemed, the third tribe to invade Ireland; defeated by the Fomorion giants but the remnants of the tribe escaped and fled to the northern islands and to Greece.

NERA
Hero of the court of Maeve, who visited the Otherworld and married a woman of the Sídh.

NIAMH
Princess of the Otherworld; lover of Oisín.

NUADHU
God of the Tuatha Dé Danann; gave up kingship after he lost his arm at the First Battle of Moytura; known as Nuadhu of the Silver Arm.

OGMA
One of the Tuatha Dé Danann; credited with giving his name to ogham script, the most ancient form of writing in Ireland.

OISÍN
Son of Fionn and Sadhbh; lover of Niamh; returned to Ireland after 300 years in the Land of Youth and met St Patrick.

OSCAR
Son of Oisín; traditionally said to have been killed at the Battle of Gabhra, the Fianna's last and major defeat.

PARTHALON
Leader of the second invasion of Ireland; his people lived in Ireland until destroyed in a great plague.

PATRICK
Patron saint of Ireland, credited with introducing Christianity to the country in the fifth century AD.

RED BRANCH WARRIORS
See Craobh Rua.

RÓNÁN
Seventh-century king who slew his own son in a jealous rage.

ROS MAC DEADHA
Warrior sent by King Cairbre against the Fir Bolg.

SADHBH
Woman of the Sídh, wife of Fionn; mother of Oisín.

SCEOLAN
Fionn's hound.

SCOTA
Mythical queen of the Milesians.

SGANNLACH
Daughter of Fionn and wife of Goll Mac Morna.

SÍDH (PERSON)
Otherwordly, ever-young being with magical powers; mainly the later transformation of the Tuatha Dé Danann.

SÍDH (PLACE)
The mounds where the Sídh lived.

SIGE
King, father of Sín, killed by Muircheartach Mac Erca.

SÍN
Enchantress; lover and murderer of Muircheartach Mac Erca.

SUIBHNE
King of Dál Riada in Ulster; went mad at the Battle of Moira and spent the rest of his life in the trees until killed by a jealous cowherd.

TAILTIU
Foster-mother of Lugh, who instigated the Tailtiu games in her honour.

TORDRE
Retainer and spy of Conchobhar Mac Neasa.

TUATHA DÉ DANANN
Otherworld conquerors of Ireland; defeated the Fir Bolg and the Fomorians and ruled Ireland until they themselves were defeated by the Milesians; took refuge in the world of hollow mounds and in magical islands far out to sea, but often used their otherworldly powers to help or hinder mortals; later became known as the Sídh.

UAINIDHE
Mythological figure associated with Áine and commemorated on Knockainey Hill.

UILEANN RED EDGE
Mythical figure associated with Lough Corrib, the killer of Manannán Mac Lir.

USNA, SONS OF
The eldest of these three, Naoise, was the lover of Deirdre; the three brothers fled to Scotland with her until tricked into returning to Ireland where they were killed by Conchobar Mac Neasa.

Glossary of Archaeological Terms Used in the Text

Bronze Age *c.*2000BC–300BC
– the period when metal-working in bronze and gold was introduced to Ireland until the time of the introduction of iron.

Cairn
Large mound often covering a prehistoric burial structure.

Cashel (*caiseal*), cathair
Stone-built circular enclosures. These are the stone versions of the ringforts which were the dwelling-places of the farming population during the early Christian period, although some of them may have their origins in the Iron Age. These terms are often incorporated into place-names (*See* ringforts).

Celts
Generic term covering the tribes which had their origin in central Europe *c.*1200BC. The strongest surviving elements of their culture and language are on the western seaboard, including

Brittany, Scotland, Wales, Cornwall and, most particularly, Ireland.

Crannóg

A man-made island deliberately situated in the centre of a lake for the purposes of defence. The earliest examples date from the late Bronze Age and many continued in use up to the Middle Ages.

Cromlech

A portal tomb.

Dolmen

Term used to describe the remains of Megalithic tombs, consisting of a large flat stone laid on two uprights.

Dún

General term used to describe a dwelling in the ancient texts, usually with connotation of prestige and fortification.

Forts

Hill-forts:

Enormous circular enclosures, believed to have been used for the purposes of defence and, more especially, as tribal assembly places. There are about fifty of these in the country and they are usually placed on prominent sites in the landscape. It is now known that they had their origins in the late Bronze Age although they continued in use for a long time after that. Well-known examples are Dún Aonghusa and Dún Chonchobhair on the Aran Islands and Rathgall in County Wicklow.

Promontory Forts:

There are about 250 coastal promontory forts around Ireland, where a sea-girt promontory is defended on the land-side by banks of earth and stone. Inland promontory forts, which number fewer than a dozen, are in spectacular locations on the edge of mountain tops. A good example of the latter is Caherconree in County Kerry.

Grianán

Term used to describe a sun-palace.

Iron Age

*c.*500BC to *c.*500AD — the period when iron began to be used in Ireland.

Megalithic

General term used to describe prehistoric stone monuments.

Megalithic Tombs

Term used to describe prehistoric tombs built of massive stones. (Megalithic is from Greek *megas* – 'great, large' and *lithos* – 'stone'). Mostly built in the Neolithic period (New Stone Age) by the early farming population. Over 1,450 Megalithic tombs have been recorded in Ireland and they are classified into four types:

Court Tombs:

These have an open court leading to the burial area which consists of two or more chambers under a stone and earthen cairn. They have mostly a northern distribution. Creevykeel in County Sligo is one important site of this type of tomb.

Portal Dolmens:

The word dolmen, like cromlech, was formerly used for Megalithic tombs in general. The word comes from Breton *taol* (table), and *maen* (stone). The term is more often restricted to portal tombs today. There are 174 portal tombs in Ireland and they are spectacular monuments such as Poulnabrone in the Burren in County Clare. A large, flat capstone rests upon upright stones. These monuments are often known as *Leaba Dhiarmada agus Gráinne* in local lore as tradition has it that they were the resting places of the famous lovers during their flight from Fionn.

Passage Tombs:
There are 230 passage tombs in Ireland, each consisting of a narrow passage leading to a large chamber. They often have corbelled roofs under a cairn and carvings on the structural stones. The best and most famous collection of Megalithic art in Europe is found in the great tombs of the *Brú na Bóinne*, or Bend of the Boyne, complex in County Meath.

Wedge Tombs:
These are believed to be the latest type of Megalithic tomb. They consist of a rectangular chamber inside a cairn and are associated with Bronze Age activity. They are found mainly in the southwest of the country.

Mesolithic
Middle Stone Age – covering *c.*7500BC to *c.*3500BC. Pre-farming, hunter-gatherer stage of civilisation.

Neolithic
New Stone Age covering the period from the introduction of farming to the introduction of metal-working – *c.*3500BC to *c.*2000BC.

Ogham Stone
Upright stone carved with ogham script, usually the name and genealogy of an individual. The script dates from 300AD onwards.

Palaeolithic
Old Stone Age – the period directly after the Ice Age *c.*18000BC to *c.*7500BC. No evidence of life in Ireland.

Pillarstone
Upright stone, sometimes part of a stone circle.

Ring-barrow
General term for a circular tumulus.

Ringfort
A circular enclosure of earth or stone, the ringfort is the most frequently encountered field monument in Ireland. Ringforts number about 50,000 and are known by various names – cashel (*caiseal*) and cathair for the stone versions, *rath*, *lios* and *dún* in earthen form. They were the farmsteads, sometimes fortified, of the Irish population from the Iron Age onwards. Many of them were still occupied up to medieval times.

Map of Sites

Tory Island **28**

Giant's Causeway **11** **3** Ballycastle

13
Grianán of Aileach

Lough Neagh **22**

Emain Macha (Navan Fort)
10

5 Ben Bulben

16 Inis Glora

Keshcorann Caves
17

Cooley **7**

Ardee **2**

Rathcroghan **24** Ardagh Hill
1

23 Newgrange
and the
Boyne Valley

Tara **27**

20 Lough Corrib Hill of Uisneach

Howth Head **15**

9
Dún Aonghusa

Glencree **12**

8 Doonbeg

St Mullins
25

Knockainey **19**

Slievenamon
26

21
Lough Muskry

6 Caherconree
18 Killarney

4 Béara Peninsula

MAP KEY

*(See **Direction Key** for further information
on how to locate the sites)*

1. Ardagh Hill, Longford
2. Ardee, Louth
3. Ballycastle, Antrim
4. Béara Peninsula, Cork
5. Ben Bulben, Sligo
6. Caherconree, Kerry
7. Cooley, Louth
8. Doonbeg, Clare
9. Dún Aonghusa, Inishmore, Galway
10. Emain Macha (Navan Fort), Armagh
11. Giant's Causeway, Antrim
12. Glencree

13. Grianán of Aileach, Donegal
14. Hill of Uisneach, Westmeath
15. Howth Head, Dublin
16. Inis Glora, Mayo
17. Keshcorann Caves, Sligo
18. Killarney, Kerry
19. Knockainey, Limerick
20. Lough Corrib, Galway
21. Lough Muskry, Tipperary
22. Lough Neagh, Antrim
23. Newgrange, Meath
24. Rathcroghan, Roscommon
25. St Mullins, Carlow
26. Slievenamon, Tipperary
27. Tara, Meath
28. Tory Island, Donegal

Direction Key

A note on access

Up until quite recently, access through private land to sites of historic or scenic interest was not a problem in Ireland. This has now changed in some areas. For the sake of politeness, it is always better to request access if your route to a site leads you through private land.

Ardagh Hill, Longford

Situated just off the R393 between Mullingar and Longford. The hill is to the west of the village and it is possible to drive around it.

Ardee, Louth

Ardee is about 65 kilometres (40 miles) from Dublin on the N2 between Slane and Carrickmacross. The ford is to the left of the bridge leading into the town from the Slane side. There is parking to the left just over the bridge.

Ballycastle, Antrim

Ballycastle is situated on the extreme northeastern point of Ulster. Pan's Rocks are located on the western end of Ballycastle beach, just under Fair Head.

Béara Peninsula, Cork

The 'Ring of Béara' is well signposted from Glengarrif on the south and Kenmare on the north.

Ben Bulben, Sligo

The North Ben Bulben plateau can be reached from a starting point at Glenade Lough, on a branch road from the R280 between Kinlough and Manorhamilton. For up-to-date information on access, ask at the Tourist Office in Sligo town.

Caherconree, Kerry

Take the R561 west from Castlemaine and the right turn from Aughil's Bridge towards Camp. The route up the mountain is to your right.

Cooley, Louth

The peninsula is situated just to the north of Dundalk. Follow the signs from Dundalk after taking the N1 to leave the town. The Táin Trail is signposted at various points along the road which runs around the peninsula.

Doonbeg, Clare

Situated on the N67, about 10 kilometres (6 miles) north of Kilkee. Numerous small roads lead westwards into the dunes.

Dún Aonghusa, Inishmore, Galway

There are regular ferries to Inishmore from Rossaveal, west of Galway city, and there is also a flight service from the city by Aer Árainn. Dún Aonghusa is about a kilometre (half a mile) from the harbour on Inishmore.

Emain Macha (Navan Fort), Armagh

Take the A28 west from Armagh city; the fort is less than 2 kilometres (1.25 miles) away. The interpretative centre was closed during the summer of 2002.

Giant's Causeway, Antrim

Located between Bushmills and Dunseverick on the A2. Well-signposted.

Glencree

Take the minor road to the southwest of Enniskerry towards Lough Bray. It is possible to do a circuit of the glen and Knockree by car. Glencree can also be reached from the west, via the R115.

Grianán of Aileach, Donegal

West of Derry city on the N13 heading towards Letterkenny. It is signposted from the N13, and the access road to the Grianán is just beside the interpretative centre – a converted church.

Hill of Uisneach, Westmeath

From Mullingar, take the R390 towards Athlone. About 8 kilometres (5 miles) before Ballymore, it is signposted. The Catstone is signposted from the same road a little further on.

Howth Head, Dublin

Howth Head is just under 16 kilometres (10 miles) from Dublin city centre. Follow the R105 northwards along the coast. The Deerpark Hotel, site of Aideen's Tomb, is signposted from the road just before you reach Howth village, and the cliff walk to the promontory fort and the Baily Lighthouse is signposted from Howth Summit car park.

Inis Glora, Erris Peninsula, Mayo

You can travel to Belmullet by taking either the R313 from Bangor or the R314 from Ballycastle, both in the extreme north of Mayo. Inis Glora has no regular ferry service so ask locally to arrange travel to the islands. Geraghtys (097-85741) and Lavelles (097-85669) organise charters.

Keshcorann Caves, Sligo

Take the R295 from Boyle to Ballymote. There is an access road to the nearest point to the caves just after the village of Keash on the right-hand side. The route to the cave leads through private land.

Killarney, Kerry

The lakes are situated to the southwest of the town, well signposted on theN71.

Knockainey, Limerick

Take the R516 from Hospital to Bruff. The road to Knockainey is signposted to the right.

Lough Corrib, Galway

Annaghdoon is situated on the eastern shore of the lake off the N84. Cong is on the northern tip on the R346, and Clonbur is a little to the west.

Lough Muskry, Tipperary

The Glen of Aherlow is signposted to the south from Tipperary town. The village of Rossadrehid on the south side of the glen is the best starting point for the walk. The walk is signposted from the village and the return journey should take no more than three hours in total.

Lough Neagh, Antrim

Ardboe is situated just off the B73, on the west coast of the lough, not far east of Cookstown.

Newgrange and the Boyne Valley, Meath

The Brú na Bóinne complex lies between Slane and Drogheda. It is approximately 56 kilometres (35 miles) north of Dublin and is signposted from the N2. Rosnaree House is on the south bank of the Boyne on a minor road. Stackallen Bridge is on the Navan–Slane Road,

and Ardmulchan Church is signposted off the minor Navan–Slane Road which runs south of the river.

Rathcroghan, Roscommon

Situated between Tulsk and Frenchpark on the N5. Well signposted.

St Mullins, Carlow

Just off the R729 to the south of Glynn village between Borris and New Ross. Signposted.

Slievenamon, Tipperary

Kilcash is situated on the N76 between Kilkenny and Clonmel. Follow the signposts for the Slievenamon Drive.

Tara, Meath

Tara is signposted to the left of the N3 between Dublin and Navan. It is approximately 48 kilometres (30 miles) north of Dublin.

Tory Island, Donegal

A regular ferry service runs to Tory from Bunbeg and Magheroarty – the second is the much shorter route. Magheroarty is west of Gortahork on the R257. The ferry is very much influenced by weather conditions.

Bibliography

THE STORIES

Direct Translations

Dooley, Ann, and Harry Roe (translators), *Tales of the Elders of Ireland*, Oxford University Press, Oxford, 1999.

Gwynn, Edward, *The Metrical Dindshenchas*, Royal Irish Academy, Dublin, 1905.

MacAlister, RA Stewart (ed. and translator), *Lebor Gabála Érenn; The Book of the Taking of Ireland*, Pts 1–5, Irish Texts Society, Dublin, 1938.

Murphy, Gerard (ed. and translator), *Duanaire Finn*, Pts. 1–3, Irish Texts Society, Dublin, 1935.

O'Grady, Standish, *Silva Gadelica*, Williams and Norgate, London, 1892.

O'Keefe, JG (ed. and translator), *The Adventures of Suibhne Geilt*, Irish Texts Society, London, 1913.

Literary Translations, Re-tellings, and Studies

Arbois de Jubainville, Henri, *The Irish Mythological Cycle and Celtic Mythology*, Hodges Figgis, Dublin, 1903.

Bitel, Lisa M., *Land of Women; Tales of Sex and Gender*, Cornell University Press, Ithaca, NY, 1996.

Cross, Tom Peete, and Clark Harris Slover, *Ancient Irish Tales*, Barnes and Noble, New York, 1996.

Curran, Bob, *Complete Guide to Celtic Mythology*, Appletree Press, Belfast, 2000.

Dillon, Myles, *Irish Sagas*, Stationery Office, Dublin, 1959.

Dixon-Kennedy, Mike, *Celtic Myth and Legend – An A–Z of People and Places*, Blandford, London, 1996.

Gantz, Jeffrey, *Early Irish Myths and Sagas*, Penguin, London, 1981.

Green, Miranda, *A Dictionary of Celtic Myth and Legend*, Thames and Hudson, London, 1992.

Gregory, Augusta, *Lady Gregory's Complete Irish Mythology*, Smithmark, London, 2000.

Harpur, Patrick, *The Philosopher's Secret Fire – A History of the Imagination*, Penguin, London, 2002.

Heaney, Marie, *Over Nine Waves*, Faber and Faber, London, 1994.

Heaney, Seamus, *Sweeney Astray*, Faber and Faber, London, 1984.

Jackson, Kenneth, *A Celtic Miscellany*, Routledge and Kegan Paul, London, 1951.

Joyce, PW, *Old Celtic Romances*, David Nutt, London, 1879.

Kane, Sean, *Wisdom of the Mythtellers*, Broadview Press, Peterborough, Ontario, 1994.

Kinsella, Thomas, *The Táin*, Dolmen Press, Dublin, 1969.

Mac Cana, Prionsias, *Celtic Mythology*, Hamlyn, London, 1970.

Mallory, JP (ed.), *Aspects of the Táin*, December Publications, Belfast, 1992.

Meyer, Kuno, *The Death Tales of the Ulster Heroes*, Royal Irish Academy, Dublin, 1906.

Muller-Lisowski, Kate, 'Contributions to a Study of Irish Folklore: Traditions about Donn', *Béaloideas* 18, pp. 142–99.

Murphy, Gerald, *Saga and Myth in Ancient Ireland*, At the Sign of the Three Candles, Dublin, 1961.

Ó hÓgáin, Dáithí, *Myth, Legend and Romance*, Ryan Publishers, London, 1990.

Ó hÓgáin, Dáithí, *Fionn Mac Cumhaill*, Gill and Macmillan, Dublin, 1988.

Ó hÓgáin, Dáithí, *The Sacred Isle: Belief and Religion in Pre-Christian Ireland*, Collins Press, Cork, 1999.

O'Rahilly, Thomas, *Early Irish History and Mythology*, Dublin Institute for Advanced Studies, Dublin, 1946.

Rees, Alwyn and Brinley, *Celtic Heritage*, Thames and Hudson, London, 1991.

Rolleston, TW, *Myths and Legends of the Celtic Race*, George C. Harrap, London, 1911.

Sjoestedt, Marie Louise, *Gods and Heroes of the Celts* (trans. Myles Dillon), Turtle Island Foundation, Berkeley, 1982.

Smyth, Daragh, *A Guide to Irish Mythology*, Irish Academic Press, Dublin, 1988.

Stephens, James, *In the Land of Youth*, Macmillan, New York, 1924.

Stephens, James, *Irish Fairy Tales*, Gill and Macmillan, Dublin, 1995.

Wilde, Lady, *Ancient Legends of Ireland*, Poolbeg, Dublin, 2000.

THE SITES

Automobile Association, *Illustrated Road Book of Ireland*, Automobile Association, Dublin, 1966.

Bourke, Angela, *The Burning of Bridget Cleary*, Pimlico, London, 1999.

Brennan, JH, *A Guide to Megalithic Ireland*, Aquarian Press, London,1994.

Brenneman, Walter L., *Crossing the Circle at the Holy Wells of Ireland*, University Press of Virginia, Charlottesville, 1995.

Buckley, Victor, *The Archaeological Inventory of County Louth*, The Stationery Office, Dublin, 1986.

Cunningham, Noreen, and Pat McGinn, *The Gap of the North*, The O'Brien Press, Dublin, 2001.

Cuppage, Judith (ed.), *Archaeological Survey of the Dingle Peninsula*, Oidhreacht Chorca Dhuibhne, Ballyferriter, 1986.

Dames, Michael, *Ireland, a Sacred Journey*, Element Books, Shaftesbury, 2000.

Dames, Michael, *Mythic Ireland*, Thames and Hudson, London, 1992.

Devlin, Polly, *The Far Side of the Lough*, Gollancz, London, 1993.

Donnelly, Maureen, *The Nine Glens*, Donard Press, Bangor, 1977.

Durrell, Penelope, *Discover Dursey*, Ballinancarriga Books, Allihies, 1996.

Eogan, George, *Knowth and the Passage Tombs of Ireland*, Thames and Hudson, New York, 1986.

Evans, E. Estyn, *Prehistoric and Early Christian Ireland*, Batsford, London, 1966.

Flanagan, Laurence, *A Dictionary of Irish Archaeology*, Gill and Macmillan, Dublin, 1992.

Flanagan, Laurence, *Ancient Ireland; Life before the Celts*, Gill and Macmillan, Dublin, 1998.

Fox, Robin, *The Tory Islanders – a People on the Celtic Fringe*, Cambridge University Press, Cambridge, 1978.

Green, Miranda, *The Celtic World*, Routledge, London, 1995.

Hannigan, Ken, and William Nolan, *Wicklow, History and Society*, Geography Publications, Dublin, 1994.

Harbison, Peter, *Pre-Christian Ireland: from the First Settlers to the Early Celts*, Thames and Hudson, London, 1988.

Healy, Elizabeth, *Literary Tour of Ireland*, Wolfhound Press, Dublin, 1995.

Herity, Michael, *Rathcroghan and Carnfree – Celtic Royal Sites of Roscommon*, Na Clocha Breaca, Dublin, 1988.

Hickey, Elizabeth, 'The House of Cletty', *Ríocht na Midhe*, Vol. iii, No. 3, 1965, pp. 181–6.

Higgins, Jim, *Corrib County Archaeology*, Corrib Conservation Centre, Galway, 1991.

Kennedy, Gerald, *Irish Mythology, visiting the places*, Morrigan, Killala, 1993.

Kockel, Ulrich (ed.), *Landscape, Heritage and Identity*, Liverpool University Press, Liverpool, 1995.

Lacey, Brian, *The Archaeological Survey of Donegal*, Donegal County Council, Lifford, 1983.

Le Fanu, William, *Seventy Years of Irish Life*, Arnold, London, 1928.

Logan, Patrick, *The Holy Wells of Ireland*, Colin Smythe, Buckinghamshire, 1980.

McDonagh, Steve, *The Dingle Peninsula: History, Folklore, Archaeology*, Brandon, Dingle, 1993.

Mac Neill, Máire, *The Festival of Lughnasa*, Oxford University Press, Oxford, 1962.

Meehan, Cary, *A Traveller's Guide to Sacred Ireland*, Gothic Image, Glastonbury, 2002.

Morris, Henry, 'Where was Bruidhean Dá Derga?' *Journal of the Royal Society of Antiquaries of Ireland*, 1935, pp. 297–312.

Ó hÉithir, Breandán, *An Aran Reader*, Lilliput Press, Dublin 1991.

O'Doherty, John, *Aileach of the Kings*, Catholic Truth Society of Ireland, Dublin, 1908.

O'Donovan, John, *The Antiquities of County Clare*, Clasp Press, Ennis, 1997.

O'Flanagan, Michael, *Letters containing information relevant to the antiquities of Meath*, M. O'Flanagan, Bray, 1928.

O'Kelly, Michael J., *Early Ireland: an Introduction to Irish Pre-history*, Cambridge University Press, Cambridge, 1989.

O'Kelly, Michael, *Newgrange: Archaeology, Art and Legends*, Thames and Hudson, London, 1982.

Ó Ríordáin, Seán P., *Antiquities of the Irish Countryside*. Revised by Ruaidhrí de Valera, Routledge, London, 1979.

O'Sullivan, Muiris et al., *Archaeological Features at Risk*, The Heritage Council, Kilkenny, 2000.

O'Sullivan, Ted, *Bere Island*, Inisgragy Books, Cork, 1992.

Raftery, Barry, *Pagan Celtic Ireland: The Enigma of the Irish Iron Age*, Thames and Hudson, London, 1994.

Robinson, Tim, *Stones of Aran: Labyrinth,* Lilliput Press, Dublin, 1995.

Robinson, Tim, *Stones of Aran: Pilgrimage*, Lilliput Press, Dublin, 1986.

Slavin, Michael, *The Book of Tara*, Wolfhound Press, Dublin, 1996.

Smyth, Daragh, and Gerry Kennedy, *Places of Mythology in Ireland*, Morrigan, Killala, 1989.

Swan, Harry P., *Romantic Stories and Legends of Donegal*, WJ Barr, Letterkenny, 1969.

Taylor, Lawrence J., *Occasions of Faith: an Anthropology of Irish Catholics*, Lilliput Press, Dublin, 1995.

Watson, Philip, *The Giant's Causeway*, The O'Brien Press, Dublin, 2000.

Westropp, Thomas J., *Folklore of County Clare*, Clasp Press, Ennis, 2000.

Wilde, Sir William, *The Beauties of the Boyne and its tributary the Blackwater*, James McGlashan, Dublin, 1849.

Wilde, Sir William, *Lough Corrib, its Shores and Islands*, McGlashan and Gill, Dublin, 1872.